An Italian Grammar

SALZWASSER
VERLAG

Girolamo Volpe

An Italian Grammar

Reprint of the original, first published in 1863.

1st Edition 2022 | ISBN: 978-3-37500-794-2

Verlag (Publisher): Salzwasser Verlag GmbH, Zeilweg 44, 60439 Frankfurt, Deutschland
Vertretungsberechtigt (Authorized to represent): E. Roepke, Zeilweg 44, 60439 Frankfurt, Deutschland
Druck (Print): Books on Demand GmbH, In de Tarpen 42, 22848 Norderstedt, Deutschland

AN

ITALIAN GRAMMAR.

BY

GIROLAMO VOLPE

For the Use of Eton.

LONDON:

1863.

PREFACE.

This Grammar has been designed with the view of giving an impulse to the study of the Italian language, by developing the interest which is already more and more felt amongst English scholars and students, in the mónuments of Italian literature. In its plan, therefore, the work has reference, not merely to the current phrases of ordinary life, but to the growth and construction of the language, numerous examples of which have been extracted from the best authors. Thus, the book may be called a theoretico-practical Grammar, not only furnishing the correct syntax of the period, but also occasionally explaining the theory of the formation of the idioms, and imparting a true notion of their spirit. Heretofore, no work has appeared in which sufficient pains have been taken to supply the English student with a full knowledge of the language in its best authors, or the means of appreciating its power and beauty both in prose and verse. In the present instance, the Author has so arranged his materials, that, after a careful perusal, the student will have acquired a very considerable knowledge of the classical language of Italy. In order to carry out the design more effectually, he has not confined himself to laying down the bare rules, but examples have throughout been taken from the best authors.

The exercises consist of carefully executed English translations from the Italian prose writers. Annexed is a vocabulary, containing the original phrases precisely as they are found in the authors themselves, and following the same order of words. Every exercise illustrates some particular part of speech, which is brought prominently forward. After each exercise are appended some passages of verse, which offer the most convenient form of composition for committal to memory. In this manner the student is assisted in acquiring, step by step, a full knowledge of the grammatical laws.

Another specialty in this Grammar is, that the most obvious affinities of the Italian with the Latin language are noted in separate paragraphs, and printed in smaller type. This addition has been suggested by the observation that classical scholars acquire the Italian language with peculiar rapidity; and the Author's aim is, to afford an additional facility for such a class of students. He does not affect to discuss the affinities in question with any minuteness of philological research, but has limited his selection to those which are of practical utility in promoting a general knowledge of the modern tongue and its structure.

Particular attention has been paid to the nouns and verbs, since it has been found possible to point out many rules which will be found theoretically serviceable in displaying the most important affinities between the two tongues. Those, however, who are not acquainted with the Latin language, may pass over these paragraphs without any detriment to the completeness of the course.

During the progress of the task, several friends have been most liberal in affording their advice; and amongst them may be mentioned, J. R. Butlin, Esq., F.S.A.; F. T. Pratt, Esq., D.C.L.; and the Rev. Henry J. Hose, M.A.; whose kind and valuable assistance is acknowledged with gratitude. Even with this help, the Author feels that he cannot advance any pretension to the merit of having produced a Grammar free from error; he has simply done his best to render it as correct as possible, and wishes also to observe, that if the general plan of the work should be approved, such mistakes as are most likely to be found in the execution of any new method, may be easily removed on a future occasion.

37, *Weymouth Street,*

Portland Place.

CONTENTS.

CHAPTER I.—The Pronunciation.

		PAGE
	The Vowels	3
	The Consonants	5
	The Syllabication	9
	The Accent	11

CHAPTER II.—The Genders of Nouns.

Section 1.	General Remarks	28
„ 2.	Nouns which end in *o*	28
„ 3.	Nouns which end in *a*	32
„ 4.	Nouns which end in *e*	34
„ 5.	Other General Remarks	42
„ 6.	Endings of Genders in the Plural	43

CHAPTER III.—The Article.

Section 1.	The Article, as the external sign of Gender	44
„ 2.	Other uses of the Article	46
„ 3.	Special offices of the Article	54
„ 4.	The Articular Prepositions	56

CHAPTER IV.—The Plural Number.

Section 1.	The Plural Terminations	58
„ 2.	The Terminations in *co*, *go*, &c.	63
„ 3.	The Article as a sign of the Plural	68
	Exercises on the Plural	69

CHAPTER V.—The Cases of Nouns.

Section 1.	General Remarks	71
„ 2.	The Genitive Case	72
	Exercises on the Genitive	75
„ 3.	The Dative Case	77
„ 4.	The Ablative Case	77
	Exercises on the Dative and Ablative	78

PAGE

CHAPTER VI.—THE ADJECTIVE OF QUALITY 81
Exercises on the Adjective 86
General Exercises on the Nouns and Adjectives...... 88

CHAPTER VII.—THE AUGMENTATIVE & DIMINUTIVE FORMS.

SECTION 1. General Remarks.............................. 94
„ 2. The Latin Affinities noted 99
Exercises on the Augmentatives and Diminutives.... 107

CHAPTER VIII.—THE COMPARATIVES AND SUPERLATIVES.

SECTION 1. The Comparative 113
„ 2. The Comparative of Equality 120
„ 3. The Superlative 123
Exercises on the Comparatives and Superlatives 128

CHAPTER IX.—THE NUMERALS & INDEFINITE ADJECTIVES.

SECTION 1. The Numerals 130
„ 2. Indefinite Adjectives of Quantity 134
„ 3. Another Species of Indefinite Adjectives 137
Exercises on the Numeral & Indeterminate Adjectives 139
„ 4. The Indicative Adjectives 142
Exercises on the Indicative Adjectives.............. 147

CHAPTER X.—THE PERSONAL PRONOUNS.

SECTION 1. General Rules 150
„ 2. Special Rules 155
„ 3. The Reflexive Noun *se* 163
„ 4. The Pronominal Particles, *vi*, *ci*, *ne* 167
„ 5. The Possessive Adjective 169
„ 6. The Relative Pronoun.............................. 174
Exercises on Pronouns 177

CHAPTER XI.—THE REGULAR VERBS.

SECTION 1. The Verbal Forms 181
„ 2. Observations on *Essere* 183
„ 3. General Affinities of Latin and Italian Verbs........ 185
„ 4. Affinities of Latin and Italian Moods 187
„ 5. The Moods 189
„ 6. The Tenses 193
Exercises on the Regular Verbs...................... 196

CHAPTER XII.—The Irregular and Defective Verbs.

PAGE

Section 1. The Irregular Verbs 202
„ 2. The Defective Verbs 216
Exercises on the Irregular Verbs 217

CHAPTER XIII.—The Indeclinable Parts of Speech.

Section 1. The Prepositions 218
„ 2. The Adverbs 223
„ 3. The Conjunctions 223
„ 4. The Interjections 226
Exercises on the Prepositions, Adverbs, Conjunctions, and Interjections 228

ERRATA.

PAGE	LINE	
7	34	For "strong" read *hard.*
8	2	" "strong" read *hard.*
10	27	After "brilliancy" insert *What do I here on earth?*
21	12	For "the wall" read *to the wall.*
33	14	" "cronica" read *chronica.*
39	32	" "canon" read *cannon.*
40	9	" "dioceses" read *diocese.*
41	34	" "proper nouns" read *names.*
55	5	" "sona" read *sono.*
71	21	" "to whom" read *to which.*
74	14	" "that" read *their.*
76	12	After "forza" read *force.*
76	32	For "was" read *were.*
80	33	" "ran" read *run.*
113	33	" "substantive" read *adjective.*
139	27	" "after" read *since.*
141	28	" "managed" read *manage.*
153	31	" "thee" read *you.*

DIRECTIONS FOR THE EXERCISES.

The Student is requested to pay particular attention to these directions, before commencing the Exercises (p. 69.)

1. English words which are to be omitted in the Italian, are marked with an asterisk *.

2. Words which do not appear in the English sentence, but are required in the Italian, will be found either in the sentence itself, or in the Vocabulary in parentheses, as (the), &c. &c.

3. The words which have no mark must remain, whether they appear in the Vocabulary or not.

4. The phrases in most general use, after having been given several times in the Vocabulary, are gradually left out.

5. In the Vocabulary, the nouns are found in the singular form, and the adjectives in their masculine singular form; leaving to the student the task of making the necessary changes which the sentence requires.

6. The verbs, when regular, are given in English as well as in Italian, in the infinitive mood, and must then be arranged by the student; if irregular, the precise form required by the sentence is always given.

7. In the Vocabulary, the arrangement of the words is in accordance with the Italian original, regardless of the English construction.

8. When the English and Italian words are identical, the English does not precede the Italian in the Vocabulary, as for instance, if *nature* or *to detest* is to be translated, it is evident that in the Vocabulary, the Italian words *natura* and *detestare* are sufficient, without the incumbrance of the English word.

9. The obvious and direct meanings of words are also frequently omitted, because they are usually placed first in every Dictionary. For instance, if the English word *carriage* means *vehicle*, the Italian equivalent, *carrozza*, will not be found in the Vocabulary. If on the other hand it signifies the bearing or deportment of a person, the word *portamento* will be given.

10. When the phrase has any peculiarity in construction, it is given in its complete Italian form, which is always preceded by the English construction.

Names of Authors from whose Writings Examples have been taken:—

Alamanni.
Ariosto.
Boccaccio.
Buonarotti (Michel Angelo).
Bentivoglio.
Berni.
Bembo.
Bonfadio.
Bellincioni.
Cavalcanti (Cavalcante).
Corsini (Cardinal).
Chiabrera.
Caro.
Colonna (Vittoria).
Casa.
Dante.
Firenzuola.
Gozzi (Gasparo).
Guarini.
Il Malmantile (by Lippi).
Medici (Lorenzo).
Macchiavelli.
Petrarca.
Pegolotti (Alessandro).
Pandolfini.
Rucellai.
Sanazzaro.
Speroni (Sperone).
Tasso (Torquato).
Tasso (Bernardo).
Trissino.
Tassoni.
Villani (Giovanni).

ITALIAN GRAMMAR.

CHAPTER I.

On Italian Pronunciation.

In the Italian Language, the letters of the Alphabet are as follows:—*a, b, c, d, e, f, g, h, i, j, l, m, n, o, p, q, r, s, t, u, v, z.*

The letters k, w, x, y, are not used in Italian.

We will now make an analysis of the pronunciation of the vowels, and afterwards of the consonants, taking them one by one, in order to determine properly the sounds of syllabication.

The Vowels.

The sound of the Italian vowels is simple; but although simple, the most fastidious accuracy and harmony is necessary in pronunciation. The general rule is, that their sound should be from the throat, clear, and well developed, and without contraction or pouting of the lip.

These are the vowels in the Italian language, *a, e, i, o, u,* which are pronounced with five sounds, and no more.

The *a* is pronounced with a full sound, and with the lips well open. The tongue must be pressed against the under jaw, in a kind of concave arch, so that the articulation of this vowel may come directly from the root of the tongue, in a full utterance.

The pronunciation of *a*, approximates greatly to that of *a* in the English word *father*. There is no difference in its sound, whether it be at the beginning, or end, or in the middle of a word. It is simply pronounced less openly, and in a shorter time, when it precedes the accented syllable; on the contrary, the sound is prolonged, and becomes more open when the *a* itself is accented,—as in *accadère*, and *desideràre*; the *a*, though twice pronounced in the first word, does not take so much time as the *a* in *desideràre*, which has an open and prolonged sound. This difference is more clearly visible in the word *accalappiare*, to catch in nets. In *accalap*, the sound of the *a*, three times repeated, is neither full nor long, but the *a* in *piare* is on the contrary both. After the accent, the sound of *a* is less open and prolonged, than in syllables which come before the accent, as in *ajùta*, he succours. If the word terminates in *à*, with an accent (which is then expressed), the *a* has a short, strong, and loud sound, as in *carità*, charity; *fedeltà*, fidelity.

The *e* is a sound proceeding from a certain compression in the throat, and is formed more at the top of the throat, so as it were at its entrance. The angles of the mouth are much more acute, and the lips approach much more nearly, than when *a* is pronounced. The sound of *e* is not unlike the pronunciation of the English word *faith*. The *e* is nevertheless pronounced more or less openly; the open sound is that to which we have before alluded in the pronunciation of *faith*, the close sound is that of the English word *mellow*.

By constraining the vocal passages, beginning from the throat, and ending with the lips, and then making the interval between the tongue and the palate less, by raising the tongue towards it, speaking at the same time through the teeth, we obtain the sound *i*. This is not very unlike the English pronunciation of *ea*, as in *sea*, although it is always more slender and rapid in Italian, as in *visibile*, visible, *distintivo*, distinctive.

The form of *o* indicates the tendency to an opening, which the sound gives, when pronounced from the throat to the lips. It approximates to that of *a*, but is more full and round, and issues from different vocal organs. Like the vowel *e*, it may be either close or open; the open sound is like that in the English word *store*, the close sound is similar to that of *turret*, the pronunciation of which is something between the sound of *o* and *u*.

U is a vowel, which participates in a certain confused manner, in the sound of *o*. All the vocal organs are restrained and contracted, and the lips are slightly protruded in pronouncing *u*. The chief characteristic in the pronunciation of *u* is this, that while other vowels acquire their character from the throat and the root of the tongue, the lips giving merely a certain form, but not completing the sound, the vowel *u* is uttered by an exterior movement of the lips. The sound of *u* is similar to that of the English *oo* in *good*. When followed by another vowel, it is pronounced like the English *w*, as in *uomo*, a man, when *u* is pronounced like the *w* in *warm*, *wanted*.

The Consonants.

The consonants in the Italian language, are *b*, *c*, *d*, *f*, *g*, *h*, *j*, *l*, *m*, *n*, *p*, *q*, *r*, *s*, *t*, *v*, *z*.

The sounds of the various consonants, with these vowels, must now be determined. This will be done easily, if we follow the principle of always giving the above-mentioned sounds to the vowels, varied only by the properties of the different consonants.

Thus we say *ba*, *be*, *bi*, *bo*, *bu*, in which *b* takes its sound from the lips.

Also *ca*, *ci*, *ce*, *co*, *cu*.

C, with *a*, *o*, and *u*, has a hard sound, which comes from the root of the tongue in the throat, like the English sound with the same vowels, but without the least aspiration. With *e* and *i* it has a soft sound, as in *cilicio*, haircloth; *celeste*, celestial; *caccia*, the chase; in which cases the tongue effects its sound by pressing against the palate, as is done in the English *ch*. *C* may have also the hard sound with *e* and *i*, but then an *h* must be inserted. This is the only use of *h* in the Italian. Take as examples, *chiesto*, asked; *cherubino*, cherubim; *monache*, nuns; which are pronounced like *k* in English.

D and *t* are pronounced with a more decided dental sound than in English; although in English apparently they are pronounced with closed teeth, which is not the case in Italian. It is obtained by thrusting the extremity of the tongue with a sudden movement exactly between the teeth, and withdrawing it as suddenly; as in *disdetto*, denied; *adottare*, to adopt; *dado*, a die; *tetto*, the roof of a house.

F is pronounced as in English, but the lower lip is not so much pressed against the upper teeth.

G—*ga, ge, gi, go, gu*. With *a, o*, and *u* it is hard; but with *e* and *i* it is soft, and is pronounced like *j* in English, as in *joke, jar, adjourn*, but with more force, as *coraggio*, courage; *giro*, a circular motion; *gesto*, a gesture; *raggio*, a ray. The *h* in this case performs the same office as with *c*—rendering *g* hard before *e* and *i*, as *ghianda*, an acorn; *dialoghi*, dialogues; *droghe*, drugs.

H in Italian has no sound, excepting when it renders the *c* and *g* hard before *e* and *i*. *H*, at the beginning of words, has completely gone into disuse, and is only employed with four words, namely, *ho*, I have; *hai*, thou hast; *ha*, he has; *hanno*, they have; to distinguish them from *o*, or; *ai*, to the; *a*, to, *anno*, year. But with these, there is no aspirate.

J in Italian is pronounced like *i*, as in *gioja*, joy; but sometimes the sound is prolonged, as in *prodigj*, prodigies, *tempj*, temples.

L, m, n, p, are pronounced as in English. They are, however, pronounced somewhat more distinctly, according to the usual custom in the Italian language, as for example *immortale*, immortal, *infanzia*, infancy, *sapore*, taste, *non*, not.

When *l* with *i* follows *g*, the *l* is, as it were, dissolving, and the *g* is not pronounced, as in *figlio*, son, *consiglio*, counsel. There are, notwithstanding, some exceptions, as *negligente*, negligent, *Inglese*, English, in which *gl* is pronounced as in English, in the same words.

N following *g* gives to *g* a soft sound, which cannot easily be defined, and remains the same with all the vowels: as, *bisogno*, necessity, *indegno*, unworthy, *ognuno*, every one, &c. These words are pronounced as if an *n* came before the *g*, and an *i* followed it—that is to say, as if they were written thus, *bisongnio*, &c.

Q has always *u* after it, and is pronounced as in English, except that the lips open more quickly, and there is a fuller sound from the throat, as *questo*, this, *quattro*, four, *quota*, a share. The sound may be represented by the letters *kw*, as, *kwesto*, *kwattro*, &c.

R—*ra*, *re*, *ri*, *ro*, *ru*. *R* is pronounced with a strong and peculiar sound, like the *rolling* of a drum, which can with difficulty be described or defined. Its pronunciation is obtained by pressing the edges of the tongue all the way along against the teeth of the upper jaw; holding the tongue rigid, except the extremity, which being turned towards the roof of the mouth and left loose, trembles against the palate, struck as it were by the breath, which in a thin column rapidly issues from the throat. Thus the sound of the *r* is obtained, as *terra*, the earth, *guerra*, war, *intorno*, around. It is to be observed that the *r* is strongly pronounced when it is double or finishes a syllable, as *giorno*, day, *serra*, he shuts, *correre*, to run. At the beginning of a syllable it is pronounced more lightly, as *ridere*, to laugh, *tenere*, to hold, *intenerire*, to soften.

S is pronounced as in English, but with a less hissing sound. It has two distinct sounds; one of which we will call *the strong*, and the other *the soft*. The strong sound is used at the beginning of words, as in *sapere*, to know, *singolo*, each by itself, *signore*, sir. In these words the *s* is pronounced as in the English word *salt*. The *s* strong is also found in the middle of words, when it is doubled, as in *spesso*, thick, *addosso*, on the back; and also if preceding a consonant, as in *disdegno*, anger, *astro*, a star, *fischio*, whistling, in which kinds of words the letter *s* is always considered to begin a syllable, which is thus divided: *di-sdegno*, *a-stro*, *fi-schio*. The *s* soft, which should be pronounced as the English *z* in *zeal*, is used in the middle of words between two vowels, as in *sposa*, bride, *amoroso*, amorous, *caso*, chance.

T (*ta, te, ti, to, tu*). The same directions must here be followed, as given with *d*. The tongue should be pressed against the teeth with force, and suddenly withdrawn.

V—*va, ve, vi, vo, vu*—is pronounced as in English, only the inferior lip presses more slightly against the upper teeth, as it is said before of the letter *f*.

Z—*za, ze, zi, zo, zu*—has a peculiar hissing sound, sometimes like *ds* in English, sometimes like *ts*, but somewhat softer, as *zelo*, zeal; *dolcezza*, sweetness; *sapienza*, wisdom; *intenzione*, intention. We must now observe that *z*, if preceded by a consonant and followed by a vowel, or when it is doubled, has a sound which more nearly resembles *ts*, as *presenza*, presence; *scorza*, bark, or rind; *pazzo*, mad, where *z* is pronounced almost as *tsa* and *tso*, but with a soft hissing of the *s*. If *z* be between two vowels it is pronounced with sound more approaching to *ds*, as *lezione*, lesson; *avarizia*, avarice. If, lastly, it be in the beginning of a word, it takes a sound between the *ds* and *ts*, as *zelo*, zeal; *zuffa*, a riot; *zeffiro*, zephyr.

The combination of vowels with consonants is evident, and is discovered at once by pronunciation, as *ab, eb, ib, ob, ub, ac, ec, ap, op, or, ir*, &c.

The combination of consonants with the vowels which they precede is sufficiently clear. The syllable retains the sound of the vowel, united with that of its immediate consonant. Then the other consonant is compounded with it, not injuring the primitive syllable, but merely amplifying the elements which are modified by the vowel. Thus, if we have *re*, and wish *p* to precede it, the *re* remains and the composite sound *pre* is formed; if *s* is used, in like manner *sre* is formed. If *ba* is preceded by an *s*, *sba* is formed.

A syllable may consist of one vowel and two or more consonants; one or two consonants may precede, and one may follow, as in *sem*, *par*, *stan*, but their pronunciation is easily defined. *Ar* has its own fixed pronunciation; *pa* has the same, and without any material change the compound syllable *par* is formed; *an* has its own fixed sound, *ta* has the same, and thus *tan* is made. If *s* is prefixed, the syllable *stan*, which can be easily pronounced, is formed.

Of Syllabication.

Let us now consider the division of syllables. An exact knowledge of Italian pronunciation depends entirely on an exact knowledge of the division of syllables. The principle having been laid down, that all the letters must be pronounced distinctly, if a proper division of syllables be observed, a proper pronunciation will be obtained, which depends upon pronouncing all the letters distinctly and in conformity to exact syllabication.

The genius of exact syllabication we may thus define:—The consonant goes always with the following vowel, as in *ri-pe-te-re-te*, you will repeat. If there are two consonants in the middle of a word, these are divided one from the other, so that the one belongs to the first vowel, and the other to that which follows, as in *con-tra-di-cen-te*, contradicting.

S, however, is taken, together with the other consonant, as we have seen in the examples *di-sdegno*, *a-stro*.

G, when followed by *l* and *n*, is united with them in the same syllable, as *me-glio*, better; *o-gni*, each; *bi-so-gna*, it is necessary. If a mute is followed by a liquid, they are united as in *te-ne-bre,* darkness; *ce-le-bre,* celebre. But mutes united with liquids are usually found with another consonant, as *sem-pre,* always; *ras-sem-bra,* he resembles. Should the preceding consonant be *s*, it is taken with the following syllable, even if there are two other consonants following it, as *cò-strin-ge-re,* to force.

If the word begins with a vowel, the following consonant goes with the other vowel, as in *e-ser-ci-zio,* exercise. If a vowel comes between two consonants, and no other vowel follows, the two consonants are pronounced with the intermediate vowel, as in *con-fon-der* for *con-fon-de-re,* to confuse. Occasionally three consonants are found in the middle of a word. In this case the first consonant goes with the preceding vowel, and the others are always taken with that which follows, as in *in-tra-pren-de-re,* to undertake. United vowels are taken together as one syllable.

We will now give with these rules some lines of syllabication:—

Non ho io (di-cè-va ad al-ta vo-ce u-na lùc-cio-la) que-sto fo-co di den-tro che ri-splèn-de? O-ra che fo io quì in ter-ra? Per-chè non vo-lo sul-le sfe-re a ruo-ta-re que-sti miei no-bi-lìs-si-mi rag-gi dal le-vàn-te al po-nèn-te, e a for-mà-re u-na nuo-va stel-la fra le al-tre mie so-rèl-le del cie-lo?

Translation: Have I not (said a glow-worm, with a loud voice) from within myself this fire which shines so brilliantly? Why should I not fly above the spheres, that I might roll my most noble rays from east to west, and become a new star among my other heavenly sisters?

The Accent.

Italian words have only one syllable accented, and the voice is raised in pronouncing this syllable. Sometimes the accented vowel is prolonged in a certain *tonic* sound in the middle of a word. All the syllables which come before the accent are pronounced in the same tone and are kept on the same level. The voice is then raised, and occasionally prolonged where the accent falls. This having been pronounced, those which follow are pronounced in a low tone and quickly, without any oscillation of voice in the last vowel.

Let us take two long Italian words as an example of these rules, as *am-ma-lia-trì-ce*, an enchantress; *ab-bon-de-vol-mèn-te*, abundantly. The accent usually falls on the penultimate syllable—that is to say, the last but one. Sometimes it falls on the last syllable, often on the antepenultimate, and now and then on the syllable before the antepenultimate.

When the accent falls on the last syllable, it is always represented by the sign ̀ being placed over the last vowel. In that case the vowel takes a loud and rapid sound, finishing the word abruptly with a sudden stop, as *pre-ci-pi-tò*, he precipitated, e-i-i-*ò*; *fe-rì*, he struck, e-*ì*; *a-ma-bi-li-tà*, amiability, a-a-i-i-*à*. It is clear, therefore, that the accent can always be distinguished in reading, when it falls on the last syllable.

The accent falls on the penultimate in all dissyllables, in which the accent does not fall on the last syllable.

A great many polysyllables have the accent on the penultima, some have it on the last syllable, and it is not unfrequently found on the antepenultimate. The accents, however, not being written down, excepting those which are over the last syllable, it is difficult to know in what cases the antepenultimate is accented.

We could give besides some further rules, but these would suppose a considerable knowledge of the Grammar, and would therefore be out of place. Practice, and the voice of the instructor, will do much. Thus, for example, it may be said, that the third persons plural of verbs, in every tense but the future, have the two last syllables short. The accent, therefore, must necessarily fall on the antepenultima, except in the third person plural of the future, which ends in *nn,* as *crederanno,* they shall believe; and in a few other cases, as for instance, that of the third person plural of the present, which has its three last syllables short, when the penultima of the first person is short, as from *Io desìdero,* I desire, comes *eglino desìderano,* they desire. To discuss this matter further would be at present inappropriate. We therefore conclude by saying, that the vocal accentuation of polysyllables must be learnt chiefly by use, and rules can only be of occasional service.

We may however remark, that those who are acquainted with Latin, will find it of great use in discovering the place where the accent falls, as the original Latin quantity is very rarely changed in Italian. Thus *fàcile* comes from *facilis,* *crèdere* from *credere* in both languages, and *apostolo,* from the Latin *apostolus.*

The chief rule in pronouncing Italian, is to utter clearly all the letters, vowels as well as consonants, attending also to the rules of syllabication, which have been already dwelt upon. A few slight deviations from this rule must be noted.

In the first place we see that *c,* with *e* and *i,* is pronounced *ce* and *ci,* which is precisely the English *ch.* Now, according to the rules for the combination of letters, if *ce* and *ci* have *s* before them, they ought to have the sound of the English *ch* mixed with that of *s.* It is not so, however; *c,* when joined to *s,* has another sound, which is not double. It generates, as it were, a new letter, pronounced like the English *sh,* or perhaps a little more marked. Thus *scena,* a scene, is not pronounced in the way that the English pronounce s-ch, as if it were *s-chena,* but like the English *sh,* as if it were *shena.*

In like manner will the word *scioperato*, an idle fellow, be pronounced *sh-ioperato*, and so all along.

If an *h* be placed after the *c*, and before the *e* or the *i*, the rule is enforced, that the *c* should be pronounced like *k*. It will thence be pronounced, if preceded by *s*, as *sk*. Thus *schioppo*, a musket, will be pronounced like *sk-ioppo*, *scheda*, a schedule, like *sk-eda*.

Another deviation from the general rule is, that the vowel *i*, when followed by another vowel, is frequently compounded with the other vowel in such a manner, that one vowel sound results from the two being united. This seems particularly when *cc* or *gg* precede *i*, as in *caccia*, the chase; *raggio*, a ray; *serpeggiare*, to wind about; *aggiustare*, to adjust; and more especially if the second vowel is accented, as it is seen in *serpeggiàre*, and also at the end of the word, as *serpeggiò*, he crept round; *rincacciò*, he repulsed; *quaggiù*, here below. The two vowels, however, compose a simple sound, even if there is only one *c*, or one *g*, but not so decidedly, as *ciondolare*, to dangle; *adagio*, adage; *cacio*, cheese; but if they are monosyllables, the sound becomes again decisive, as in *ciò*, that; *già*, already.

A few observations should now be made on the pronunciation of *e* and *o*, in order to explain when these vowels should be open, and when close, the other vowels not having these alternations.

However much we may reflect on this subject, we shall find it impossible to determine when *e* and *o* should be pronounced in a close or open manner. Much has been written, but it always remains undecided, as far as rules are concerned, especially with regard to the pronunciation of *o*, although it is of great importance to be correct in this matter, for the sake of euphonic requirements.

We can, however, give some general directions, leaving the master to form the pronunciation of the pupil in every special case, as rules, which should be reliable and of general application, cannot be given. The teacher is, however, recommended not to let an *e* or an *o* pass without being well pronounced, so that through him the pupil may become accustomed to read correctly.

E is close in all infinitives ending in *erc*, and in the derivations of tenses, from the first *e* in *ere*, as in the imperfect, the future, &c. Thus, from *vedére*, to see, we have *vedéva*, I was seeing; *vedésse*, that he might see; *vedréte*, you will see.

Some forms of common grammatical words, have the e acute, as *questo*, this; *quéllo*, that; *dél*, *dégli*, of the; *egli*, he, *ella*, she; *désso*, himself.

E is acute in words derived from the Latin, in which the original *i* is changed into *e* in Italian, as *léttera*, a letter.

The *e* is acute in words which end in *è*, as *perchè*, why; *affinchè*, in order to; *poichè*, since; and also when words end in *è*, as *potè*, he was able; *mercé*, recompense.

The open *e* occurs frequently, and under many circumstances, but no rule can be given in this case. We give, nevertheless, some examples of the open *e*, as *ècco*, behold; *apèrto*, open; *vècchio*, an old man; *assèdio*, a siege; *tèdio*, weariness; *èbbe*, he had; *corrègge*, he corrects; *lègge*, law.

But although the *e* is often close, and often open, it is not so subject to strict euphonic restriction, nor it is always considered a grave error, to give one sound instead of the other; and so much so, that in many cases the *e* is pronounced open in one part of Italy, and close in another.

Much more precise is the Italian language, in the pronunciation of the vowel *o*; the distinction between the open and the close sound, constituting one of the most principal euphonic elements of that tongue.

The rules, however, for the right pronunciation of *o*, are those which vary most of all in their application.

The following directions for the right pronunciation of *o* are the safest and most important, although they bear no proportion whatever to those cases which cannot be brought under any general rule.

At the end of words which end with an accent, the *o* is always open, as, *canterò*, I will sing; *vedrò,* I will see; *amò,* he loved; *Nicolò*, Nicholas.

O is open in words derived from the Latin, which have changed the Latin *au* into the Italian *o,* as *poco,* few; *oro,* gold; *alloro,* the laurel; *tesoro,* a treasure; *godo,* I enjoy, from *paucus, aurum, laurus, thesaurus, gaudeo.*

O is open in Italian words in which the *o* is preceded by *u,* as *cuore,* the heart; *figliuolo,* a son; *uovo,* an egg; *tuono,* thunder; in which words the *u* can be left out, especially in poetry.

O is also open in monosyllables which end in *o,* as *fo,* I do; *sto,* I stand; *do,* I give; *ciò,* this.

O is close in words derived from the Latin, in which the Latin *u* is turned into *o,* as in *volto,* the face; *stolto,* foolish; *volgo,* the common people; *molto,* much; *dolce,* sweet; *abbondo,* I abound. Most other dissyllables, which have an *o* in both syllables, or an *o* in the first syllable, which is not derived from the Latin *u,* have the *o* open, as *tosto,* directly; *sonno,* sleep; *rosa,* a rose; *folle,* mad; *molle,* soft, or weak; *occhio,* eye; *morso,* a bite.

O is close in the syllables after the accented one, as *intèrno,* internal; *apòstolo,* an apostle; *rimòrso,* remorse; *àvolo,* grandfather.

O is close in substantives which come from the Latin, in *io, ionis,* as *ragione,* reason; *affezione,* affection; *tensione,* tension.

These are the rules of most general application, which make the *e* and the *o* open or close. The *e* is not, however, so difficult to an Englishman, as he is naturally inclined to make it open or close in the proper place,—while, even in Italian, as we said, it is not always decided whether *e* should be pronounced in one way or the other.

It is otherwise with *o*. The English have no natural inclination to pronounce it rightly, but on the contrary are very often inclined to make the open *o*, close, and *vice versâ*. *O* is also more definitely pronounced, being never ambiguous, and of the greatest importance in accentuation—nay, we have observed that the *tonic* sound of Italian verse depends much on the pronunciation of *o*. Thus we necessarily think it of the greatest importance to secure its right pronunciation for the English student. For this purpose we shall make a general rule, that every open *o* shall be printed, all through this Grammar, in a different type than the word to which it belongs.

Here we will conclude our short treatise on the pronunciation of the Italian language, by saying that we have not thought it necessary to make any particular mention of diphthongs, since all the letters (vowels as well as consonants) are always fully pronounced. It would, therefore, be useless to treat of diphthongs; and so much for the pronunciation.

Here follows a Fable in the Italian language, as a preliminary exercise for reading. It will have an English interlinear translation, in order to prepare the student for a slight practical knowledge of the language, while he at the same time makes progress in the study of the Grammar. This we more readily do, as we do not think it advisable to give exercises to translate, for some pages. The reason for this determination, we will mention in the proper place.

Exercise for Italian Reading.

LE PERE.

THE PEARS.

Narrano le antiche cronache, ch' egli fu già in Portogallo
Relate the ancient chronicles, that there (it) was once in Portugal
un uomo dabbene, il quale avea un suo unico figliuolo da lui
a man good who had a his only son by him
caramente amato, e vedendo ch' egli era di animo semplice e
dearly loved, and seeing that he was of mind simple and
inclinato al ben fare, stavagli sempre con gli occhi addosso,
inclined to well doing, (he) was to him always with the eyes upon
temendo che non gli fosse guasto da' corrotti costumi di
fearing that not to him should be spoiled by corrupt customs of
molti altri. Di che spesso gli tenea lunghi ragionamenti,
many others. Of that often with him he held long discourses,
e gli diceva che si guardasse molto bene dalle male
and to him said that himself (he) should guard very well from the bad
compagnie; e gli facea in quella tenerella età comprendere
companies; and to him made in that tender age understand
chi facea male, e perchè facea male. Il fanciullo udìa le
who did ill, and why (he) did ill. The boy heard the
paterne ammonizioni, ma pure una volta gli disse: di che
paternal admonitions, but yet one time to him he said: of what
volete voi temere? Io son certo che non mi si appiccherà
wish you to fear? I am certain that not to me itself will fasten

mai addosso vizio veruno, e spero che avverrà il con-
ever upon vice any, and I hope that (it) will happen the con-
trario, ch' essi ad esempio di me diverranno virtuosi. Il
trary, that they at example of me will become virtuous. The
buon padre conoscendo che le parole non faceano quel frutto
good father knowing that the words not made that advantage
ch' egli avrebbe voluto, pensò di ricorrere all' arte;
which he would have wished, thought to have recourse to (the) art,
ed empiuta una cestellina delle più belle e più vistose
and (having) filled a little basket of the most fine and most comely
pere che si trovassero, gliene fece un presente. Ma
pears which one might find, to him of them (he) made a present. But
riconosciuto a certi piccioli segnali che alcune poche di
(having) recognised by certain slight tokens that some few of
esse erano vicine a guastarsi, quelle mescolò con le buone.
them were near to be spoilt, those (he) mixed with the good.
Il fanciullo si rallegrò, e come si fa in quell' età, volendo
The boy himself rejoiced, and as is done in that age, wishing
egli vedere quante e quali fossero le sue ricchezze,
he to see how many and of what sort they were his riches,
mentre che le novera e mira, esclama: oh padre!
while that them (he) enumerates and views, exclaims: oh father!
che avete voi fatto? A che avete voi mescolate queste
what have you done? Why have you mixed these
che hanno magagna, con le sane? Non pensar, figliuol mio,
which have blemish with the sound? Not think, son mine,
a ciò, risposegli il padre; queste pere sono di tal natura,
to this, replied to him the father; these pears are of such nature,
che le sane appiccano la salute loro alle triste. Voi
that the sound communicate (the) healthiness their to the bad. You
vedrete, ripigliò il fanciullo, che sarà fra pochi giorni il
will see, replied the boy, that it will be in a few days the
contrario. Sì, sarà, non sarà, il padre lo prega che
contrary. Yes, it will be, not it will be, the father him begs that
le lasci per vederne la sperienza. Il figliuolo,
them (he) should leave to see of it the proof. The son,
benchè a dispetto, se ne contenta. La cestellina si
although in despite, himself with it contents. The little basket is

chiude in una cassa, il padre prende le chiavi. Il putto gli
shut in a chest, the father takes the keys. The lad to him
era di tempo in tempo intorno, perchè riaprisse; il
was from time to time about, in order that (he) should re-open; the
padre indugiava. Finalmente gli disse: questo è il
father delayed. Finally to him (he) said: this is the
dì; ecco le chiavi. Appena potea il fanciullo attendere,
day; here (are) the keys. Scarcely could the boy wait
che la si voltasse nella toppa. Ma appena fu la cestellina
that it should be turned in the ward. But hardly was the little basket
aperta, che non vede più pere, le quali erano tutte coperte
open, that not he sees more pears, which were all covered
di muffa e guaste. Oh! nol diss' io, grida egli, che
by mustiness and spoilt. Oh! not it have said I, cries he that
così sarebbe stato? Non è forse avvenuto quello ch'
thus it would have happened? Not is perhaps happened that which
io dissi? Padre mio, voi l' avete voluto. Non è questa cosa
I said? Father mine, you it have wished. Not is this a thing
che ti debba dare tanto dolore, rispose il padre baciandolo
which to thee ought to give so much pain, replied the father kissing him
affettuosamente. Ma tu ti lagni ch' io non abbia
affectionately. But thou thyself complainest that I not have
voluto credere a te delle pere. E tu qual fede
wished to believe in thee concerning the pears. And thou what faith
prestavi a me, quand' io ti dicea che la compagnia de'
didst grant to me, when I to thee said that the company of the
tristi guasta i buoni? Credi tu ch' io non possa compen-
bad spoils the good? Believest thou that I not can compen-
sarti di queste poche pere che hai perdute? Ma io non
sate thee for these few pears which thou hast lost? But I not
so chi potesse compensar me, quando tu mi fossi
do know who could compensate me, if thou to me shouldst be
guasto e contaminato.
spoilt, and contaminated.

GASPARO GOZZI.

General Directions for the Student.

The paragraphs which are distinguished by *figures* form in themselves a *complete* course of Grammar for the pupils who do not understand Latin.

The other paragraphs in *smaller type* and distinguished by *letters*, united as they are with the former, form together with them another *complete* Grammar for the use of students who are acquainted with Latin.

In these paragraphs in small print the affinities between the Italian and Latin languages are developed; by this means facilitating greatly the study of Italian to English classical students or scholars.

In the first pages we give not only the table of nouns, but also of regular verbs, simple tenses, and the auxiliary verbs *essere*, to be, and *avere*, to have. This we do in order to habituate the student at once to the general forms of existence in nouns, and to the conditions of existence in verbs, which taken together form the substance of discourse. We also have the design to accustom the student to make good use of the exercises, and shall effect this by giving only the infinitives of the regular verbs, leaving to him the task of conjugating them according to the type given at the beginning. The irregular verbs in the exercises will be given in their full form according to their position in the sentence in which they are found.

The Exercises will not begin until some progress has been made in the study of the Grammar, in order that they may be better understood, and the labour of the student well bestowed. In the selection of exercises, we have taken care to give extracts from Italian authors, translated into English for this purpose, and have also endeavoured, as far as possible, that they should be so chosen that the particular part of speech which they are designed to illustrate should always predominate. Thus, for example, in some, nouns will predominate; in others, pronouns; in others again, verbs regular or irregular, and so on.

Finally, in order to give the exercises at once a peculiar zest and a double bearing, they will frequently be followed by select passages of Italian poetry, translated into English prose. Each of these extracts will chiefly relate to the same part of the Grammar, with the exercise itself. In this manner the student, knowing the literal English meaning, will easily read, understand, and commit them to memory.

These directions should be carefully perused and thought over before commencing the study of this Italian Grammar.

Model of the Declensions of Nouns.

MASCULINE NOUNS.

	Singular.		Plural.
Nom.	*Il muro*, the wall.	Nom.	*I muri*, the walls.
Gen.	*Del muro*, of the wall.	Gen.	*Dei muri*, of the walls.
Dat.	*Al muro*, the wall.	Dat.	*Ai muri*, to the walls.
Ac.	*Il muro*, the wall.	Ac.	*I muri*, the walls.
Abl.	*Dal muro*, from the wall.	Abl.	*Dai muri*, from the walls.
	Nel muro, in the wall.		*Nei muri*, in the walls.
	Col muro, with the wall.		*Coi muri*, with the walls.
	Pel muro, for the wall.		*Pei muri*, for the walls.
	Sul muro, upon the wall.		*Sui muri*, upon the walls.

Nom.	*Lo scritto*, the writing.	Nom.	*Gli scritti*, the writings.
Gen.	*Dello scritto*, of the writing.	Gen.	*Degli scritti*, of the writings.
Dat.	*Allo scritto*, to the writing.	Dat.	*Agli scritti*, to the writings.
Ac.	*Lo scritto*, the writing.	Ac.	*Gli scritti*, the writings.
Abl.	*Dallo scritto*, from the writing.	Abl.	*Dagli scritti*, from the writings.
	Nello scritto, in the writing.		*Negli scritti*, in the writings.
	Collo scritto, with the writing.		*Cogli scritti*, with the writings.
	Per lo scritto, for the writing.		*Per gli scritti*, for the writings.
	Sullo scritto, upon the writing.		*Sugli scritti*, upon the writings.

Nom.	*L' errore*, the error.	Nom.	*Gli errori*, the errors.
Gen.	*Dell' errore*, of the error.	Gen.	*Degli errori*, of the errors.
Dat.	*All' errore*, to the error.	Dat.	*Agli errori*, to the errors.
Ac.	*L' errore*, the error.	Ac.	*Gli errori*, the errors.
Abl.	*Dall' errore*, from the error.	Abl.	*Dagli errori*, from the errors.
	Nell' errore, in the error.		*Negli errori*, in the errors.
	Coll' errore, with the error.		*Cogli errori*, with the errors
	Per l' errore, for the error.		*Per gli errori*, for the errors.
	Sull' errore, upon the error.		*Sugli errori*, upon the errors.

FEMININE NOUNS.

	Singular.		Plural.
Nom.	*La penna*, the pen.	Nom.	*Le penne*, the pens.
Gen.	*Della penna*, of the pen.	Gen.	*Delle penne*, of the pens.
Dat.	*Alla penna*, to the pen.	Dat.	*Alle penne*, to the pens.
Ac.	*La penna*, the pen.	Ac.	*Le penne*, the pens.
Abl.	*Dalla penna*, from the pen.	Abl.	*Dalle penne*, from the pens
	Nella penna, in the pen.		*Nelle penne*, in the pens.
	Colla penna, with the pen.		*Colle penne*, with the pens.
	Per la penna, for the pen.		*Per le penne*, for the pens.
	Sulla penna, upon the pen.		*Sulle penne*, upon the pens.

Nom.	*L' ape*, the bee.	Nom.	*Le api*, the bees.
Gen.	*Dell' ape*, of the bee.	Gen.	*Delle api*, of the bees.
Dat.	*All' ape*, to the bee.	Dat.	*Alle api*, to the bees.
Ac.	*L' ape*, the bee.	Ac.	*Le api*, the bees.
Abl.	*Dall' ape*, from the bee.	Abl.	*Dalle api*, from the bees.
	Nell' ape, in the bee.		*Nelle api*, in the bees.
	Coll' ape, with the bee.		*Colle api*, with the bees.
	Per l' ape, for the bee.		*Per le api*, for the bees.
	Sull' ape, upon the bee.		*Sulle api*, upon the bees.

Model of the Simple Tenses of the regular Conjugations of the Verbs.

cant-àre (to sing). crèd-ere (to believe). nutr-ìre (to nourish).

PRESENT TENSE.

	I sing.	I believe.	I nourish.
S.	cànt-o,	crèd-o,	nùtr-o.
	cànt-i,	crèd-i,	nùtr-i.
	cànt-a,	crèd-e,	nùtr-e.
P.	cant-iàmo,	cred-iàmo,	nutr-iàmo.
	cant-àte,	cred-ète,	nutr-ìte.
	cànt-ano,	crèd-ono,	nùtr-ono.

IMPERFECT.

	I was singing, *or* I sang.	I was believing, *or* I believed.	I was nourishing, *or* I nourished.
S.	cant-àva,	cred-èva,	nutr-ìva.
	cant-àvi,	cred-èvi,	nutr-ìvi.
	cant-àva,	cred-èva,	nutr-ìva.
P.	cant-avàmo,	cred-evàmo,	nutr-ivàmo.
	cant-avàte,	cred-ovàte,	nutr-ivàte.
	cant-àvano,	cred-èvano,	nutr-ìvano.

PRETERITE.

	I sang, *or* I did sing.	I believed, *or* I did believe.	I nourished, *or* I did nourish.
S.	cant-ài,	cred-èi *or* ètti,	nutr-ii.
	cant-àsti,	cred-èsti,	nutr-ìsti.
	cant-ò,	cred-è *or* ètte,	nutr-ì.
P.	cant-àmmo,	cred-èmmo,	nutr-ìmmo.
	cant-àste,	cred-èste,	nutr-ìste.
	cant-àrono,	cred-èrono *or* èttero,	nutr-ìrono.

FUTURE.

	I shall *or* will sing.	I shall *or* will believe.	I shall *or* will nourish.
S.	cant-erò,	cred-erò,	nutr-irò.
	cant-erài,	cred-erài,	nutr-irài.
	cant-erà,	cred-erà,	nutr-irà.
P.	cant-erèmo,	cred-erèmo,	nutr-irèmo.
	cant-erète,	cred-erète,	nutr-irète.
	cant-erànno,	cred-erànno,	nutr-irànno.

CONDITIONAL.

	I should *or* would sing.	I should *or* would believe.	I should *or* would nourish.
S.	cant-erèi,	cred-erèi,	nutr-irèi.
	cant-erèsti,	cred-erèsti,	nutr-irèsti.
	cant-erèbbe,	cred-erèbbe,	nutr-irèbbe.
P.	cant-erèmmo,	cred-erèmmo,	nutr-irèmmo.
	cant-erèste,	cred-erèste,	nutr-irèste.
	cant-erèbbero,	cred-erèbbero,	nutr-irèbbero.

IMPERATIVE.

	sing (thou).	believe (thou).	nourish (thou).
S.	cànt-a,	crèd-i,	nùtr-i.
	cànt-i,	crèd-a,	nùtr-a.
P.	cant-iàmo,	cred-iàmo,	nutr-iàmo.
	cant-àte,	cred-ète,	nutr-ìte.
	cànt-ino,	crèd-ano,	nùtr-ano.

SUBJUNCTIVE MOOD.

PRESENT TENSE.

	that I sing *or* may sing.	that I believe *or* may believe.	that I nourish *or* may nourish.
S.	che io cànt-i,	che io crèd-a,	che io nùtr-a.
	che tu cànt-i,	che tu crèd-a,	che tu nùtr-a.
	ch' egli cànt-i,	ch' egli crèd-a,	ch' egli nùtr-a.
P.	che cant-iàmo,	che cred-iàmo,	che nutr-iàmo.
	che-cant-iàte,	che cred-iàte,	che nutr-iàte.
	che cànt-ino,	che crèd-ano,	che nùtr-ano.

IMPERFECT.

	I might sing.	I might believe.	I might nourish.
S.	che io cant-àssi,	che io cred-èssi,	che io nutr-ìssi.
	che tu cant-àssi,	che tu cred-èssi,	che tu nutr-ìssi.
	ch' egli cant-àsse,	ch' egli cred-èsse,	ch' egli nutr-ìsse.
P.	che cant-àssimo,	che cred-èssimo,	che nutr-ìssimo.
	che cant-àste,	che cred-èste,	che nutr-ìste.
	che cant-àssero,	che cred-èssero,	che nutr-ìssero.

INFINITIVE MOOD.

PRESENT TENSE.

to sing.	to believe.	to nourish.
cant-àre,	crèd-ere,	nutr-ìre.

PARTICIPLE PRESENT.

singing.	believing.	nourishing.
cant-ànte,	cred-ènte,	nutr-ènte.

GERUND.

singing.	believing.	nourishing.
cant-àndo,	cred-èndo,	nutr-èndo.

PARTICIPLE PAST.

sung.	believed.	nourished.
cant-àto,	cred-ùto,	nutr-ìto.

Auxiliary Verbs.

The Auxiliary Verbs are *avère*, to have; *èssere*, to be.

Pre. Ind.	*Ho*, I have, etc.	Pre. Ind.	*Sòno*, I am.
	hài.		*sèi*.
	ha.		*è*.
	abbiàmo.		*siàmo*.
	avète.		*siète*.
	hànno.		*sòno*.
Imper.	*avèva*, I had.	Imper.	*èra*, I was.
	avèvi.		*èri*.
	avèva.		*èra*.
	avevàmo.		*eravàmo*.
	avevàte.		*eravàte*.
	avèvano.		*èrano*.
Pret.	*èbbi*, I had.	Pret.	*fùi*, I was.
	avèsti.		*fòsti*.
	èbbe.		*fu*.
	avèmmo.		*fùmmo*.
	avèste.		*fòste*.
	èbbero.		*fùrono*.
Future.	*avrò*, I shall have.	Future.	*sarò*, I shall be.
	avrài.		*sarài*.
	avrà.		*sarà*.
	avrèmo.		*sarèmo*.
	avrète.		*sarète*.
	avrànno.		*sarànno*.
Condit.	*avrèi*, I should have.	Condit.	*sarèi*, I should be.
	avrèsti.		*sarèsti*.
	avrèbbe.		*sarèbbe*.
	avrèmmo.		*sarèmmo*.
	avrèste.		*sarèste*.
	avrèbbero.		*sarèbbero*.

Impera.	*àbbi*, have (thou).	Impera.	*sìi*, be (thou).
	àbbia.		*sìa.*
	abbiàmo.		*siàmo.*
	abbiàte.		*siàte.*
	àbbiano.		*sìano.*
Sub. Pr.	*àbbia*, I may have.	Sub. Pr.	*sìa*, I may be.
	àbbia.		*sìa.*
	àbbia.		*sìa.*
	abbiàmo.		*siàmo.*
	abbiàte.		*siàte.*
	àbbiano.		*sìano.*
Imperf.	*avèssi*, I might have.	Imperf.	*fòssi*, I might be.
	avèssi.		*fòssi.*
	avèsse.		*fòsse.*
	avèssimo.		*fòssimo.*
	avèste.		*fòste.*
	avèssero.		*fòssero.*
Inf.	*avère*, to have.	Inf.	*èssere*, to be.
Ger.	*avèndo.*	Ger.	*essèndo*, being.
Part. Pas.	*avùto*, had.	Part. Pas.	*stato*, been.

All compound tenses are formed analogously to the English. Only *essere* is, in its compound tenses, conjugated by itself.

Example.

ho avùto,	I have had.	sono *stàto*,	*I have* been.
hanno avùto,	they have had.	sono *stàti*,	*they have* been.
avremo avùto,	we shall have had.	saremo *stàti*,	*we shall have* been.
avendo avùto,	having had.	essendo *stàto*,	*having* been.

Avère is used for the compound tenses of active verbs, as *ho imparàto*, I have learnt.

Essere is used with passive verbs, as *io sòno lodàto*, I am praised; *sòno stàto lodàto*, I have been praised.

ITALIAN GRAMMAR.

CHAPTER II.—Section I.

1. In the Italian language, the noun is subject to the following practical modifications, in its general grammatical conditions of gender, number, and case.

Of Gender.

2. The gender of nouns in Italian, is masculine or feminine. The neuter gender is entirely wanting.

3. The gender can in a great measure be determined from the termination of substantives.

4. Nouns which end in *o* are *masculine,* and the exceptions are very rare.

5. Nouns ending in *a* are *feminine,* but the exceptions are more numerous.

6. Those ending in *e,* may be masculine or feminine, and are numerous; but very few nouns end in *i,* and these are often masculine, but some are feminine. Those ending in *ù* (which always have the accent) are still fewer, and most of them are feminine. We will now give the particular rules, with corresponding examples.

Section II.

Nouns which end in o.

7. All nouns ending in *o* are masculine, with a very few exceptions.

(*a*) The categories of nouns ending in *o,* may be fixed as two. The category of nouns, of Latin derivation, and the category of those which are not of Latin derivation.

(*b*) Substantives of Latin derivation, are those which represent the most usual ideas amongst men, since naturally during the transformation of the Latin tongue into the vulgar Italian, the most necessary words did not fall into disuse, but were preserved in their primitive essence, with slight changes in form.

(*c*) All nouns of the Latin second declension, having the nominative mostly in *us*, but sometimes in *er*, and in the neuter gender in *um*, which have been preserved in the Italian language, have entered with the termination *o* and are in gender masculine.

8. Some examples of these are the following:—as *animo*, spirit; *occhio*, eye; *panno*, cloth; *rivo*, stream; *titolo*, title; *vento*, wind; *alabastro*, alabaster; *àrbitro*, arbitrator; *fabbro*, smith; *ministro*, minister; *libro*, book; *collo*, neck; *esiglio*, exile; *giudicio*, judgment; *braccio*, arm; *esempio*, example; *vestigio*, trace; *naufragio*, shipwreck; *pericolo*, danger.

(*d*) Also nouns of the fourth declension, by analogy of the termination in *us*, have been changed into a masculine termination in *o*.

EXAMPLES.

Atto, act; *canto*, song; *conato*, effort; *consesso*, a meeting; *consolato*, consulship; *corso*, a race; *esercito*, an army; *flusso*, a flowing; *gemito*, a groan; *gusto*, taste; *latrato*, barking; *magistrato*, magistrate; *muggito*, a lowing. *Tribù*, from *tribus*, ending in *ù* feminine, is an exception.

(*e*) The rule that the Latin *us*, should be changed into *o* masculine, is so general in its nature, that those nouns which finish in *us* feminine in Latin, become masculine in Italian, as *myrtus*, *laurus*, *populus* (the tree), *ficus*, and some other feminine trees; are *mirto, alloro, pioppo, fico*, masculines in Italian.

9. The fruit of a tree is with us feminine, and has either the feminine termination in *a*, or the common in *e*. The tree is masculine, with a termination either masculine in *o*, or common in *e*.

(*f*) In this case the *a* Latin neuter plural of the fruit ending in *a*, is turned in Italian into *a*, feminine singular. Therefore, *cera-*

sum and *cerasus*, in which the fruit is neuter, but the tree is feminine, make in Italian *ciliegia*, (fem.) the fruit, and *ciliegio*, (masc.) the tree; *corniola*, (fem.) is the fruit, and *corniolo*, (masc.) the tree; *pera*, (fem.) is the fruit, and *pero*, (masc.) the tree; and among words ending in *e*, *il noce*, is the tree, and *la noce*, the fruit.

EXAMPLES.

L'ombra del noce è nociva.

The shade of the nut-tree is injurious.

Le pesche sono fredde ed umide.

The peaches are cool and juicy.

Il pesco è un arbore piccolo.

The peach-tree is a small tree.

I ciliegi sono di diverse specie.

Cherry-trees are of different kinds.

Egli mangia le ciliegie a ceste.

He eats cherries by the basketful.

La campagna era ripiena di ulivi, di màndorli, di ciliegi, di peschi e di molti altri alberi fruttiferi.

The country was full of olive-trees, almond-trees, cherry-trees, peach-trees, and many other fruit trees.

La contrada è abbondevole di castagni.

The country is full of chestnut-trees.

Le castagne calde in Italia piacciono molto.

Hot chestnuts are very popular in Italy.

10. *Fico, pomo, cedro, arancio,* are used for the tree as well as the fruit.

11. The noun *mano* is feminine, although it has its termination in *o*, as

E toccollo colla mano dritta, e dissegli.

And he touched him with the right hand, and said to him.

E tornarono a casa colle mani vuote.

And they returned home with their hands empty.

Eco is masculine, when it does not include the idea of mythological personification, as

Quei luoghi mandavano un eco (masc.) più volte ripetuto.

Those places were sending forth an echo many times repeated.

Nelle valli Eco trista (fem.) risuonava.

In the vallies plaintive Echo was resounding.

12. The proper names of women ending in *o*, which are of Greek derivation, are also feminine, because the essential law which makes them feminine is stronger than the exigency of a simple grammatical form, which is purely accidental. *Atropo, Aletto, Ero, Saffo, Calisto, Erato*, are therefore feminine.

13. A few names of cities end in *o*, and are feminine, as *Corinto, Efeso, Lepanto, Taranto, Otranto.*

(*g*) These and other nouns retain the feminine gender, because they are the names of cities. They are frequently derived from Latin forms in *us* and *um*, as *Corinto* from *Corinthus*, *Taranto* from *Tarentum*, and others.

(*h*) *Uomo*, man, *corpo*, body, *tempo*, time, *lato*, side, *uopo*, need, are perhaps the only nouns in common use, which have the termination in *o*, and are not derived from the second or fourth declension.

14. Some other nouns which end in *o* are feminine; but these are used only in poetry, and never in prose. Take these as examples:—*Imago*, image; *Cartago*, Carthage; *testudo*, tortoise; and a few others.

Latitudo, latitude; *longitudo*, longitude; *similitudo*, similitude, are also feminine.

(*i*) These nouns are not derived from the second, but from the third declension.

15. Nouns which end in *o*, and are not of Latin derivation, are all masculine. Nouns of this kind preserve the stamp of the primitive language, which is different from any that is spoken, and are for the most part *onomatopœic*, (similar in sound and meaning); others are taken from the new modes of war adopted by nations, or have been introduced into the language with the new progress of science.

Here are given some of these taken at hap-hazard:—

Scudiscio, whip or scourge; *scroscio*, the noise of violently falling water; *ràngolo*, secret inward anxiety; *cicisbeò*, one who is busy in courting women; *ciondolo,* a pendant; *guinzaglio,* a slip for a greyhound; *garbuglio,* garboil; *bordo,* a border, or the sides of a ship; *ronzio,* hum or buzz; *rivellino,* a ravelin.

Section III.

Nouns which end in *a*.

16. Nouns which end in *a* are feminine.

(*j*) Those which are derived from the first Latin declension retain the Latin form together with the Latin gender.

EXAMPLES.

Ala, wing; *amica,* sweetheart; *antenna,* sailyard; *argilla,* clay; *bestia,* beast; *cantilena,* song; *capra,* goat; *catena,* chain; *cena,* supper; *cella,* cellar; *esca,* food; *finestra,* window; *gemma,* gem; *ira,* anger; *gallina,* hen; *lacuna,* puddle; *gleba,* clod; *lima,* file; *lingua,* tongue; *luna,* moon.

(*l*) In the Latin language the majority of nouns ending in *a* are feminine. There are, however, some words ending in *a*, and derived from the first declension, which are masculine both in Italian and Latin. These we will place under the following rule:—

17. When nouns are designed (whether they be of Greek derivation or the contrary) to signify an office only exercised by men, in spite of the termination in *a*, they are masculine, as *Papa,* Pope; *patriarca,* patriarch; *monarca,* monarch; *duca,* duke; *poeta,* poet; *moralista,* moralist; *oculista,* oculist; *legista,* lawyer.

(*m*) Nouns ending in *ista* evince a Latin derivation, but are found far more frequently in the Italian language.

18. Finally, the proper names of men ending in *a* are masculine, as *Andrea, Anassagora, Pittagora.*

(*n*) We may here notice some etymological deviations. *Cometa* is feminine, although in Latin it is masculine. The Latin words *Boa* and *bova* are feminine, but the Italian *boa* is masculine. We have also the Latin noun, *boja,* or *bojæ, arum,* fem. (a collar round the neck), from which most likely the Italian *boja*, masc., the executioner.

(*p*) There may be also a few nouns, which are feminine when ending in *a*, but nevertheless have another Latin form; as *Arma* is in Italian feminine, and ends in *a* and also in *e*; in Latin it is of the neuter gender and second declension, and possesses no singular.

EXAMPLES.

Sono provveduti di arme leggere, e non di gravi.

They are provided with light arms, and not with heavy ones.

Prese le sue arme con se, e partì.

He took his arms and departed.

Armi can always be put in the place of *arme*: it then comes from *arme* in the singular.

(*q*) Likewise, the Italian *cronaca* (fem.) comes from *cronica, cronicorum*, Latin neuter. Here are the following examples:—

Matteo Villani scrisse la Cronaca del Mondo.

Matteo Villani wrote the Chronicles of the World.

Si trova nelle Cronache di quei tempi.

It is found in the Chronicles of those times.

In Italian there is tho word *ragna*, which comes from *araneum*; and *ragno*, which comes from *aranea*.

EXAMPLES.

Le mosche cadono nella ragna.

The flies fall into the cobweb.

I ragni tendono i lacci per prendere insetti.

Spiders stretch out snares to catch insects.

19. There are nouns also which end in *à* with an accent and are feminine, as *carità*, charity; *bontà*, goodness; *libertà*, freedom; *pietà*, piety; &c.

(*r*) Such nouns are derived from the third Latin declension, and are formed from the nominative by omitting the *s*, and consequently have their termination in *à*, upon which the accent is required.

(*s*) Here it must be noted that these etymological deviations of nouns of Latin derivation ending in *a*, which have been placed under general rules, are so rare in proportion to those of genuine derivation, that they cannot be considered as weakening the general rule. Great part, indeed, of such deviations as we have shown, and shall shortly prove at greater length, are for the most part caused through the want of a neuter gender in the Italian language, which naturally originates some anomalous deviations from the general rules of affinity between the two languages. But even these deviations themselves confirm the general rules.

20. There are also other nouns ending in *a*, which are masculine, viz:—

Assioma, axiom; *diadema*, diadem; *poema*, poem; *sistema*, system; *tema*, theme; *epigramma*, epigram; *dramma*, drama, and some others.

(*t*) These are all neuter Latin nouns of the third declension, with nominatives in *a* of pure Greek derivation.

EXAMPLES.

Gli assi*o*mi sono verità di per se evidenti.
Axioms are self-evident truths.

Il clima temperato è bu*o*no per gli animali e le piante.
A temperate climate is good for animals and plants.

Il diadema era pieno di gemme e pietre preziose.
The diadem was full of gems and precious stones.

Un poema didascalico non ha che poca inspirazione.
A didactic poem has but little inspiration.

Il sistema Aristotelico e già antiquato e fuori d' uso.
The system of Aristotle is now antiquated and out of use.

This will be found sufficient with regard to nouns ending in *a*.

SECTION IV.

Nouns which end in e.

21. A great number of nouns end in *e;* of these one portion is masculine, and the other feminine; so that we *shall do well to consider the termination in e* common.

(*u*) The general criterion may be assumed that such nouns are derived from the third Latin declension—and some, but very few, from the fifth—being derived as to their termination from the singular ablative of both declensions.

(*v*) According to the general rules, which we have before given, nouns are feminine in Italian if they are feminine in Latin, and masculines and neuters in Latin are masculine in Italian.

Take these as examples:—*Amore,* love; *ardore,* ardour; *favore,* favour; *orrore,* horror; *esortazione,* exhortation; *vocazione,* vocation; *altare,* altar; *nèttare,* nectar; *animale,* animal; *ape,* bee; *nube,* cloud; *vate,* poet; *febbre,* fever; *verme,* a worm; *dragone,* dragoon; *falcone,* hawk; *scorpione,* scorpion; *pace,* peace; *auspice,* diviner; *radice,* root; *neve,* snow; *dente,* tooth; *nutrice,* nurse; *pece,* pitch; *tridente,* trident; *mente,* mind; *amaritudine,* bitterness; *beatitudine,* bliss; *faraggine,* medley; *prurigine,* itching; *vèrgine,* virgin; *voragine,* whirlpool; *erede,* heir; *piede,* foot; *ariete,* ram; *ospite,* guest.

22. There are some nouns ending in *ore* which sometimes belong especially to man, but are often changed when applied to women, into *ice,* as *monitore,* monitor; *monitrice,* (fem.); *motore,* mover; *motrice,* (fem.); *amatore,* lover; *amatrice,* (fem.).

EXAMPLES.

Fortuna de' beni recatrice e rapitrice.—*Bem.*

Fortune is the producer and destroyer of wealth.

E di questo consiglio fu autrice una ch' ebbe nome Polissa.

And of this advice, one who had the name of Polissa was the proposer.

Era in quei tempi Minuccio tenuto finissimo cantatore e sonatore.

In those times Minuccio was considered the finest singer and musician.

23. Others, again, when they do not end in *ore* in the masculine, have often the feminine in *essa,* as *abate,* abbot—*abatessa,* abbess; *papa,* pope—*papessa,* popess; *leone,* lion—*leonessa,* lioness; *profeta,* prophet—*profetessa,* prophetess; and some others.

(*z*) We have just said that nouns derived from the third Latin declension usually terminate in *e,* being formed from the ablative singular. There are, however, some exceptions, for which we will endeavour to lay down rules.

(*aa*) Nouns derived from the Greek are to be excepted when they end in the nominative in *a*. These are formed from the Latin nominative, end in *a*, and are masculine, from the Latin neuter.

These nouns are named among the masculine exceptions terminating in *a*. (V. *t*., Section iii.)

(*bb*) We must also except some of those nouns which in Latin end in *o* in the nominative, and in *inis* in the genitive, and in Italian poetry may either be derived from the nominative and have their ending in *o*, or on the contrary be used in their form of regular derivation from the Latin ablative, according to the exigencies of the verse. These, however, are few.

EXAMPLE.

L' un *margo* e l' altro del bel fiume adorno
Di vaghezza e d' odori olezza e ride.—*Tas.*

Both margins of the beautiful adorned river are smiling with beauty and redolent with sweets.

These nouns have been already named among the exceptional nouns in *o*. (V. § 14 & *i*., Sec. ii.)

(*cc*) Nouns of the third declension, ending in *as*, *atis*, and *us*, *utis*, are also to be excepted. These are formed from the nominative, and in Italian change *as* into *à* and *us* into *ù*, remaining in the same gender.

Take as examples:—*Età*, age; *bontà*, goodness; *città*, town; *novità*, novelty; *gravità*, gravity; *voracità*, voracity; *virtù*, virtue.

These nouns ending in *a* are named in the Sec. iii. § 19, and *r*; and those in *ù* are alluded to in the Sec. i. § 6.

(*dd*) Nevertheless, both in prose and poetry, these nouns often assume the termination of the Latin ablative in *te*, which by a caprice of language can at pleasure be changed into *de*: as *etate* and *etade*; *bontate* or *bontade*; *pravitate* or *pravitade*.

EXAMPLES.

Per sua bontà e piacevolezza è amato assai.

On account of his kindness and agreeableness he is very much loved.

"All' alta impresa caritade sprona."—*Petr.*

To the great undertaking charity urges.

" Fecemi la divina potestate."—*Dante.*

The Divine Power made me.

" Con povertà volesti anzi virtude,
Che gran ricchezza posseder con vizio."—*Dante.*

Thou desirest to possess virtue with poverty, instead of great riches with vice.

" Fondata in casta ed umil povertade."—*Petr.*

Founded upon chaste and humble poverty.

(*ee*) There are also some Latin neuters ending in ***en***, ***inis***, which take their termination from the nominative, letting the ***n*** drop, as ***fiume***, ***germe***, ***nome***, ***certame***, ***reggime***.

EXAMPLES.

Vennero ad un fiume e quivi abbeverarono le loro bestie—*B.*

They came to a river, and there they watered their beasts.

" Vidi gente alla riva d' un gran fiume."—*Dan.*

I saw people at the bank of a great river.

" Che svelto ha di virtute il chiaro germe."—*Petr.*

Which has plucked off the noble bud of virtue.

L' uno ebbe nome Spinelloccio, l' altro ebbe nome Zeppa.
—*Bocc.*

The one had the name Spinellocio, and the other had the name Zeppa.

(*ff*) Not a few nouns are to be excepted which are changed into a form, apparently derived from the first declension, as ***caritas***, ***largitas***, ***paucitas***, ***duritas***, ***feritas***, ***spissitas***, &c., which make ***chiarezza*** or ***chiarore***, ***larghezza***, ***pochezza***, ***durezza***, ***fierezza*** or ***ferocia***, and ***spessezza*** or ***spessore***. The reason of this is, that there is a tendency (unless harshness of sound would occur) to change nouns of the other categories into the termination in *a*, as if they were of the category of the first declension.

EXAMPLES.

La chiarezza del Sole vince ogni altro lume.

The slpendour of the Sun overpowers all other light.

La prodigalità si può distinguere dalla larghezza in più modi.

Prodigality may be distinguished from liberality in many ways.

La pochezza dei buoni non può scusare la malvagità de' molti.

The scarcity of good people cannot excuse the wickedness of the many.

(*gg*) This tendency to deviation is more conspicuous in nouns derived from the fifth Latin declension, so that the scarcity of these nouns in Latin becomes an almost total deficiency in Italian. This happens through the circumstance that not many of these few nouns were accepted in our tongue—and even these few changed the termination *ie* (with which Italian ears have little sympathy) into *a*. This is found specially in Italian nouns, which end in Latin in *ties, tiei*, which then change the *t* into *z* or *zz*, and the *ies* into *a*. Thus from *amarities* is made *amarezza;* from *avarities, avarizia;* from *mollities, mollezza*; from *crassities, crassezza;* from *durities, durezza;* as, from *luxuries, lussuria;* from *materies, materia*. There is not, however, an absolute want of the termination *ie* in nouns of pure derivation from the Latin fifth declension—as, for example, *barbarie, canizie, carie, congerie, pernicie speoie.*

EXAMPLES.

Queste frutta hanno perduta gran parte della loro amarezza.

These fruits have lost a great part of their bitterness.

Ogni vizio invecchia colla persona, ma sola l' avarizia sempre ringiovanisce e rinfresca.

Every vice grows old with the person, but avarice alone always becomes young and revives.

Colui si mostra così negligente, come se la pigrizia gli fosse sorella.

He shows himself as negligent as if Idleness had been his sister.

Il pianto significa mollezza d' animo.

Weeping is a proof of effeminacy of mind.

(*hh*) Some nouns in *e* are of the common gender, as *calle*, path; *fune*, rope; *giovane*, youth; *fronte*, forehead; *fine*, end; *carcere*, prison; *dimane*, morrow; and few others.

EXAMPLES.

"E' riducemi a ca' per questo calle."—*Dante.*

It brings me back home by this way.

"Giva soletta per le calle amena."

She was going quite alone through that agreeable road.

Un amore a lieto fin pervenuto in una novelletta intendo raccontarvi.—*Bocc.*

I intend to relate to you, in a short tale, a love story brought to a happy end.

"Dolce alla fine, e nel principio acerba."—*Petr.*

Sweets in the end, and in the beginning bitter.

This kind of nouns is, for the most part of the common gender, also in Latin.

(*ii*) The only remaining difficulty is to determine the gender of nouns ending in *e*, which are not of Latin derivation. However much we may consider this matter, we shall not discover any definite rule; use alone will give the requisite knowledge. We may observe that they are not numerous, inasmuch as many nouns of this class end in *o* or in *a*, and are consequently of the corresponding gender.

(*jj*) We however should perhaps not be far wrong in laying down the principle, that many of these words were introduced through new social or political conditions, or through the introduction of new expressions, brought into use by new discoveries, or scientific progress, or modern methods of conducting war. Allowing this, the French language, which is so generally known, would be of great use—supposing the principle to be assumed, that those nouns which in Italian have their termination in *e*, follow the same gender as that which the same words possess in French. A great number of these words besides belong to the male sex especially, and are therefore masculine. We will mention a few of these nouns, taken as they come. *Cannone*, canon; *babbione*, baboon, or a sot; *poltrone*, an idle fellow; *candelliere*, candle-stick; *barile*, caske; *bastione*, bastion; *arcione*, arzon, or saddle bow; *cotone*, cotton.

(*ll*) Many such nouns, moreover, which have relation to sciences, which are either new or in a state of progress, are of Greek derivation, since the Greek language holds sway always in a new scientific nomenclature. In such a case, those of Greek origin would not be refused as an addition to the Latin tongue, which, although a dead language, has in itself so much of the Greek element. And thus nouns of this description, may be subjected to the general rules, as if they were of pure Latin derivation.

24. To finish the treatise of the terminations of nouns, and their genders, we will observe that there are but few nouns ending in *i*. Some of these are *diocesi*, dioceses; *metropoli*, metropolis; *tesi*, thesis; *sintassi*, syntaxis; *crisi*, crisis, &c.

(*mm*) They are of Greek derivation, introduced into the Latin language, in the third declension, with an exceptional nominative termination in *is*, and are feminine in gender.

EXAMPLES.

Gl' Indiani posseggono quindici regni e ciascuno ha la sua metropoli.

The Indians possess fifteen kingdoms, and each has its own metropolis.

L' eclissi del sole è spaventosa ai popoli barbari.

An eclipse of the sun is a cause of dread to barbarous people.

25. *Dì*, for day, is a monosyllable in *i* with an accent, and is masculine. The days of the week have the termination *dì*, and are masculine, as *Lunedì*, Monday; *Martedì*, Tuesday; &c. *Sabbato* and *Domenica* are exceptions.

E' invalsa la superstizione di considerare il Venerdì giorno nefasto.

The superstition of considering Friday an unlucky day prevailed.

26. Several names of men ending in *i* are naturally masculine, as *Giovanni*, John; *Luigi*, Louis. Also some nouns of number, as, *dieci*, *undici*, &c., &c., and *venti*.

EXAMPLE.

Il *dieci* è numero pari, l' *undici* ìmpari: il *dodici* è numero di grand' uso nel traffico, il *tredici* è numero malauguroso.

Ten is an even number, eleven an odd one; twelve is a number of great use in commerce; thirteen is a number of ill-omen.

27. In family nouns, the termination in *i* is very common,

and may almost be said to be an Italian characteristic. These may be considered to have their origin in the plural of a primitive individual noun—as, for instance, *Brunello* might have been used collectively in the form of *Brunelli; Alamanni* might have been in its primitive state *Alamanno; Villani,* from *Villano,* countryman, &c.

28. Nouns ending in *i*, which are of foreign derivation, are masculine, as *il Chilì, il Mississipì, il Tamigi,* the Thames, &c.

29. There are also nouns which have a double nominative termination. Some of these we will mention: *corriero* or *corriere,* courier; *cavaliero* or *cavaliere,* knight; *pensiero* or *pensiere,* thought; *scolaro* or *scolare,* student.

EXAMPLES.

Dardano fu il primo cavaliere che cavalcasse cavallo con sella e freno.—*Gio. Vil.*

Dardanus was the first horseman who rode a horse with saddle and bridle.

Il più cortese cavaliero che mai cignesse spada.

The most courteous cavalier that ever girded on a sword.

Il pensiero (*or*, il pensiere), a modo di denaro, può esser falso, cioè reo, ma colorito di bene.—*Caval.*

The thought, like money, may be false, that is evil, but coloured with good.

30. Some other nouns also have a double termination in *a* and *e*. But these usually adopt afterwards one alone of the terminations, and the other becomes antiquated, as *ala* or *ale,* wing; *arma* or *arme,* arm; *canzona* or *canzone,* song; *dota* or *dote,* dowry; *froda* or *frode,* fraud; *fronda* or *fronde,* leaf: which now, by established use, select these terminations, *ala, arma, canzone, dote, frode, fronda*—although, in some cases, the antiquated form can still be used.

31. The very few substantives ending in *u*, or rather *ù*, are fem., as *gioventù,* youth; *schiavitù,* slavery; *servitù,* servitude; *tribù,* tribe; *virtù,* virtue. Some few others, which are proper nouns of places, as *Cefalù, Corfù, Perù,* are masculine. Besides these, the revered name of the Saviour is *Gesù.*

SECTION V.

A few General Remarks on Gender.

32. Animals, in the first place, should have either one termination or the other, according to their gender. Thus, animals whose names end in *o* in the masculine, should in the feminine gender change *o* into *a*; and those ending in *e* should retain the termination of the common gender, their sex being made manifest by the context or other circumstances.

33. But a great number of animals have one gender only, as far as regards their grammatical form. If masculine, they remain always masculine; if feminine they continue so.

These are those species, to the genders of which men pay no attention, as being not domestic animals. Domestic animals have two genders with different grammatical forms. The others one gender only.

Domestic animals :—*Cane*, dog—*cagna*, female dog; *bue*, ox—*vacca*, cow; *gatto*, cat—*gatta*, female cat; *cavallo*, horse —*cavalla*, mare.

Animals which are not domestic :—*Volpe*, fox; *leopardo*, leopard; *scoiàttolo*, squirrel; *porco-spino*, porcupine.

EXAMPLES.

"E di fuor trasse,
La lingua come bue che 'l naso lecchi."—*Dante.*

And put his tongue out as an ox which licks his nose.

Le vacche dee l' uomo scegliere, molto alte, lunghe, e di grandissimo corpo.

A man ought to choose his cows very tall, long, and of very great bodies.

Ci cacciano in cucina a dir delle favole colla gatta.—*Bocc.*

They drive us into the kitchen to tell stories to the cat.

Far la gatta morta.—*Prov.*

To play the part of the dead cat.

Amici come cani e gatti.—*Prov.*

Friends, like dogs and cats.

La volpe andando per un bosco, sì trovò un mulo.—*Nov.*

The fox going through a wood found there a mule.

La volpe lascia il pelo, ma non il vizio.—*Prov.*

A fox changes his hair, but not his vicious disposition.

34. Fishes, whose sex is usually not taken into account, have one gender only. Even *la balena,* the whale, does not change its gender.

EXAMPLES.

Più stringi l' anguilla e più fugge di mano.—*Prov.*

The more you press an eel, the more it slips from your hand.

Stordito boccheggia come un barbio.

He, like a fool, gasps as a barbel.

V' era una balena che non mi dà il core contar la sua grandezza.—*Berni.*

There was a whale so large, that I am afraid to tell you what was its size.

35. *Il leone,* the lion; *il lupo,* the wolf; *l' orso,* the bear; and some others, have two genders, although not domestic animals, possessing a classical, or poetical, or typical, or figurative signification, or being found in apologues of ancient writers.

36. Some animals, which are not domestic, have without reference to their sex, two genders with one single termination, viz., the common one in *e,* as *lepre,* hare: *serpe,* serpent; *tigre,* tiger.

EXAMPLES.

Il cane dà la caccia alla lepre.

The dog gives chase to the hare.

Il lepre è così chiamato, perchè corre con celeri piedi.

Lepre is so called because it runs with swift feet.

Section VI.

Endings of Genders in the Plural.

37. Regarding the general forms of the plural, not as to number, but as to gender, *o* masculine, and *e* common in the

singular number, are changed into *i* in the plural, as *ministri*, ministers; *libri*, books; *poeti*, poets; *amori*, loves; *altari*, altars; *nubi*, clouds; *madri*, mothers.

38. The termination *a*, when feminine, changes into *e* in the plural, as *donne*, women; *antenne*, sail yards; *catene*, chains; *lacune*, puddles, &c.; from *donna*, *antenna*, *catena*, *lacuna*, in the singular.

39. But the masculines which end in *a* in the singular, have the plural in *i*, as from *papa*, pope; *patriarca*, patriarch; *profeta*, prophet; *moralista*, moralist; *poema*, poem; *sistema*, system; are formed in the plural, *papi*, *patriarchi*, *profeti*, *moralisti*, *poemi*, *sistemi*. These are the general rules of the plural forms, of the masculine or feminine gender. In another place, we shall speak of the forms of the plural, as a number.

CHAPTER III.—Section I.

Of the Article, as the external sign of Gender.

1. The Italians at first made use of the article *lo*, before all masculine nouns. But writers and speakers at length found *il* was more homogeneous and pleasing to the ear, with a great quantity of nouns, and in most cases adopted *il*, in place of *lo*. Thus the sound of *il padre*, the father; *il sasso*, the stone; *il cane*, the dog; *il bosco*, the wood; *il muro*, the wall; *il campo*, the field; *il libro*, the book; *il tempo*, the time; *il fuoco*, the fire; *il capo*, the head, pleasing them better than that of *lo padre*, *lo sasso*, *lo cane*, *lo bosco*, &c., by little and little they changed the original *lo* into *il*, which has now become the general article of the Italian language.

2. But on the other hand they found, that by the same rule of euphony, the sound of *il* was unadapted to some words, as *specchio*, mirror; *stipite*, the side post of a door; *scolare*,

scholar; *Spagnuolo,* Spaniard; inasmuch as the pronunciation was more difficult with *il,* than with *lo.* They retained, therefore, with masculines of this kind, the original article *lo,* and continued to say *lo specchio, lo scolare, lo Spagnuolo, lo scherzo,* the joke; *lo scettro,* the sceptre; *lo scrigno,* the cash; *lo scritto,* the writing; *lo strepito,* the noise.

3. Observing therefore, that this euphonic exigency occurs in those masculine nouns, which begin with *s,* and one consonant, which is *s* called *s impura,* it has thence arisen, that by a rule, which has no exceptions, the article *lo* should be retained in all those masculine nouns which begin with *s,* followed by another consonant.

4. We say a rule without exception, solely with reference to grammar. It is not the case in an æsthetic sense, as sometimes in poetry, the article *il* is substituted for *lo,* even with nouns beginning with *s,* and another consonant. Examples of this are not entirely wanting even in prose.

5. The same thing occurs with the few masculine nouns, which begin with *z,* but the rule is here of more capricious application. Thus we say, *lo zio,* the uncle; *lo zecchino,* the sequin; *lo zelo,* zeal; but nevertheless, in nouns beginning with *z,* the article *il* is often used in place of *lo.* Thus, *il zelo, il zio, il zucchero,* the sugar, are very frequently used.

EXAMPLES.

Io sono pur nato per essere il zimbello della fortuna.

I am indeed born to be the sport of fortune.

Come i piacevoli modi eccitano benevolenza, i zotici e rozzi procacciano odio.

As agreeable manners excite good-will, so those that are rough and rude produce hatred and contempt.

Il contadino vide il serpe venire a lui moltiplicando i zùfóli.

The countryman saw the serpent coming towards him, multiplying his hissings.

Non si sentiva uno zitto.

There was not heard a whisper.

6. While making these changes of the article, they did not wish to abandon the practice of placing the article *lo* before nouns beginning with a vowel, as they conceived, that in such cases, it produced a more pleasing and homogeneous sound than *il*. Lest however, the sound of the two vowels united, should cause any difficulty, the *o* of the article is left out, and an apostrophe is inserted, as *l' amore*, love; *l' aspetto*, the aspect; *l' incontro*, the meeting. But this, for the sake of variety of sounds, and elegance of language, does not hinder the writer from occasionally expressing the entire article.

7. The article *la* was adopted only by feminine nouns, as *la donna*, the woman; *la lupa*, the she wolf; *la casa*, the house; *la pagina*, the page; *la sorella*, the sister; *la figlia*, the daughter; *la morte*, death.

8. This article, from the same reason, which has been given with regard to *lo*, admits the apostrophe also, in place of the vowel *a*, before nouns beginning with a vowel, as *l' anima*, the soul; *l' amica*, the female friend; *l' energìa*, energy; *l' inventrice*, the inventrix; *l' eleganza*, elegance.

It now becomes necessary to speak of the other uses of the article, which bear special reference to the Italian language.

Section II.

On the other uses of the Article.

9. The principal office of the definite article, is to determine individuality among general nouns, which have no distinctive appellation.

This office is almost the only one which belongs to the the article in the English language.

10. There are cases, in which the individualising of the universal noun, by means of the definite article, is not necessary, in order to develop the intrinsic meaning of the sentence.

Through the love of brevity, the article is then omitted. Thus the expressions, *andare in chiesa,* to go to church; *mettere il danaro in borsa,* to put the money in the purse; *il grano fu riposto in granajo,* the corn was put in the granary; are preferable, although the article can be properly used.

Casa, home, for the same reason, and also to indicate an exclusiveness of possession inherent in the idea itself, is without the article. Thus we say, *Vado a casa,* I go home; *Sto in casa tutto il giorno,* I stay at home all the day; *Le faccende di casa,* the household affairs; and other similar expressions which exclude the article.

11. The article is used in Italian when it is intended to designate all collective individualities of one species and one kind, referring themselves in a conspicuous manner to the entire species and kind, separately from others in the great categories of existences—as for example, *L' uomo è il dominatore della terra,* man is the lord of the earth; *L' animale costituisce un regno della natura fisica,* the animal race constitutes a kingdom of physical nature. In the same manner, we say *dare il veleno,* to administer poison; *seminare il grano,* to sow the corn; *segar le biade,* to cut the corn.

This makes it necessary to observe the difference between Italian and English, in which these words usually do not require the article.

12. The abstract nouns, by reason of a certain moral determination of existence are used with the article. Thus we say, *la speranza,* hope; *la collera,* anger; *la dolcezza,* sweetness; *l' amore,* love; *l' odio,* hatred; *il sospetto,* suspicion.

EXAMPLES.

"E tratto dalla collera avventosse,
Col pugno chiuso al Re di Sericana."—*Arios.*

And impelled by anger, he rushed with a clenched fist on the King of Sericana.

"Cominciò egli allor sì dolcemente,
Che la dolcezza ancor dentro mi suona."—*Dan.*

He commenced then (to sing) so sweetly, that the sweetness still sounds within me.

La gloria è ombra della virtù, e sèguitala ancor mal suo grado.

Glory is the shadow of virtue, and follows it even in spite of itself.

13. Proper names, indicating an absolute individuality, do not require the article. But there are some nouns which signify an individuality, which is hypothetical—that is to say, which does not exclude from the human mind the possibility of imagining multiplicity; although by nature they are eminently individual, and possess a superior and exclusive physical importance. These make use of the article, as if they wished by force of the article to render themselves more conspicuous. Thus we say, *la terra,* the earth; *il sole,* the sun; *la luna,* the moon.

EXAMPLES.

Il sole vivifica tutte le cose ed a tutte dâ bellezza e forma.

The sun quickens all things, and gives them beauty and form.

E poco appresso levatasi la luna, e 'l tempo essendo chiarissimo, egli vegghiava.—*Bocc.*

And the moon rising soon after, and the weather been very clear, he kept awake.

Oscurissimo di nuvoli era il cielo.—*Bocc.*

The sky was very dark with clouds.

14. Things which are not in their nature singular, as are *la terra, il sole,* &c., but yet have in certain circumstances a singular sense, through a kind of exclusive energy which they possess, receive the article, as *il capo,* the head; *la mano,* the hand; *il collo,* the neck; *il petto,* the breast.

EXAMPLES.

Tentò più volte col capo e colle spalle se alzar potesse il coperchio.—*Bocc.*

He tried many times with his head and shoulders, if he could succeed in raising the lid.

"Le bionde treccie sopra il collo sciolte."—*Petr.*

Her fair tresses falling down her neck.

The names of human dignities which express a certain individuality hypothetical but not necessary; or if determined, determined solely by relations of place and time, are used with the article: as for example, *il Papa, il Re, l' Imperatore, il Podestà.*

16. The names of celebrated authors, and especially those of past times, with those of the most eminent moderns, on account of their acknowledged excellence, are used with the article. Thus we say, *il Boccaccio, il Petrarca, l' Ariosto, il Tasso, l' Alfieri;* and also *il Monti, il Manzoni, il Foscolo,* with regard to authors of our own time, or a little before. The same thing occurs with the most famous artists, as *il Buonarotti, il Tiziano, il Tintoretto*—although we do not say *il Raffaello,* but simply *Raffaello*; and also *il Rossini, il Verdi, il Mercatante,* as great musical composers.

As the article is not used in Latin, it is never placed before the names of Latin classic authors.

17. Foreign classical writers have or have not the article, according to taste. Thus we say, *Milton* or *il Milton; Schiller* or *lo Schiller; Shakspeare* or *lo Shakspeare.* But in mentioning French authors, the article is not admitted: we do not say *il Rousseau, il Voltaire.* When the author is mentioned with his full name—of family and individual—the article is omitted: as, for example, we say *Ugo Foscolo, Torquato Tasso, Alessandro Manzoni.*

EXAMPLES.

Il Boccaccio diede maravigliosa abbondanza alla lingua Italiana.

Boccaccio gave surprising copiousness to the Italian language.

Il Petrarca scrisse versi d' amore con molto decoro e nobiltà, seguendo, la scuola Platonica.

Petrarch wrote love verses with great propriety and dignity, following the Platonic school.

L' Alfieri è un arditissimo tragico.

Alfieri is a most daring tragedian.

Il Foscolo non iscrisse molto, ma scrisse potentemente.

Foscolo did not write much, but he wrote most powerfully.

18. Names of families are used frequently with the article, when they are applied to one individual who is not present, and by way of qualification, as *Il Frangipani è un uomo onesto,* Frangipani is an honest man; *Il Francesconi è ammalato,* Francesconi is ill; *Il Pucci gli scrisse una lunga lettera,* Pucci wrote him a long letter.

Unless these are expressed in the way of qualification, they do not bear the article, as *Egli scrisse a Pucci,* He wrote to Pucci; *Incontrai questa mattina Francesconi,* I met Francesconi this morning.

19. Again, if the appellative of respect—*Signor*—is added to the family name, the article precedes this appellative. Thus we say, *Il Signor Fracassi; Il Signor Ruffini.* Here it is to be observed that, with the family name, it is usual to say *Signor,* not *Signore.* We also say, when addressing any one personally, *Signore,* and not *Signor* in the vocative case.

20. When the family name is applied to a lady, either with or without the term *Signora,* the article always precedes, as *la Fossombroni,* or *la Signora Fossombroni, la Franceschi,* or *la Signora Franceschi, la Baretti,* or *la Signora Baretti.*

21. The christian names of ladies, are used with the article, in familiar style, when ladies are mentioned, with whom we may have ties of relationship or friendship. Thus, by *la Catterina, la Giovannina, la Francesca,* we understand our Catterina, our Giovannina, our Francesca, who may be either sister, or cousin, or friend. If we wish to indicate a woman of humble class, as a servant, or dependant, the article is required. With the exception of these cases, it is necessary to place the addition *Signora,* between the article and the name, as *la Signora Catterina, Giovannina, &c.*

22. *Monsignore, Madama, sua Eccellenza, sua Altezza,* &c.,

are used without the article, as well as *Messere* and *Madonna*, which are now obsolete. But *la Madonna*, when used for the Virgin Mary, requires the article.

23. Nouns of appellation, when applied to men, are used without the article, because they indicate an absolute individuality. But if an adjective is added, they require the article, because this adjective renders them to a certain extent universal nouns, as we say, *il bello Adone*, the beautiful Adonis; *il vecchio Carlo*, the old Charles, or rather old Charles; *il buon Francesco*, the good Francis.

24. An individual, who is known only by a nickname, is mentioned with the article, the individuality being both absolutely, and then by implication, pointed out by the adjective. Thus, supposing that any one had a strange aspect, long hair, and other peculiarities, which acquired for him the name of *Stregone*, sorcerer, we should say—

Oggi pranzò da me lo Stregone.

To day the *Stregone* dined with me.

Also, if any one were distinguished in a certain province, we will say, for violence and oppression, and thus acquired the name of *brigante*, brigand; he might then be called solely by that name, but with the addition of the article, and thus one would say—

Il primo che incontrai stamane fu il Brigante.

The first person whom I met this morning was *il Brigante* (the brigand).

25. All territorial designations, whether of continents, or empires, or kingdoms, or provinces, are used in preference with the article, as *l' Europa*, Europe; *la Francia*, France; *la Prussia*, Prussia; *la Venezia*, Venetia. Where, however, a province or a district is mentioned, the noun itself is changed into an adjective, the substantive *territory* being understood. Thus we say, the enemy has invaded *il Bolognese, il Vicentino, l' Agordino*,—that is to say, the Bolognese territory, &c.

26. The names of countries are either masculine or feminine,

according to their termination. If they end in *a*, they are feminine, as *la Francia*, France; *l' Inghilterra*, England; *la Spagna*, Spain. Those which end in other vowels, are masculine, as *il Portogallo, il Perù, il Chilì*, as well as those countries, which either do not end in a vowel, or if they have one, retain nevertheless a foreign termination, as *l' Annover, il Canadà*, Canada; *lo Slewig*, Sleswick; *il Mecklebburgh*, Mecklenburgh, &c. With the preposition *in*, the article is permitted, but not required, as for instance, *In Inghilterra vi sarà quest' anno molta abbondanza di raccolto*, In England this year, the harvest will be very abundant; *In Francia manca il danaro*, In France is scarcity of money. In these cases we might also say, *Nell' Inghilterra, nella Francia.*

27. Cities and villages, which indicate complete individuality, are used without the article. For reasons which we have before mentioned, if an adjective is added, they require the article. Thus we say, *la bella Parigi*, beautiful Paris; *l' antica Roma*, ancient Rome; *la vasta ed imponente Londra*, vast and imposing London. There are a few exceptions which do not deserve notice. Use will afterwards point them out.

28. The names of islands are expressed with the article. Most of them end in *a*, and therefore have the feminine article. Those which have a termination, which is not Italian, are masculine, as *il Ceylan, il Madagascar*. Very few, however, are to be found, which are conspicuous, and retain at the same time a not Italian termination.

If they are little known, they are defined by adding their name of appellation, as *l' Isola di Man*, the Isle of Man. Groups of islands are put in the plural, with the feminine article *le*. Thus, *le Molucche*, the Molucca islands; *le Azzorre*, the Azores; the plural appellative, *isole* (islands), being understood.

29. The greater part of the islands of the Mediterranean are used without the article. The reason for this may possi-

bly be, either that they retain their old Latin names, or even if they do not retain them, the Italians, through their immediate proximity, never ceased to make mention of them, and consequently retained the primitive Latin usage, which rejects the article. Thus we say, *Cipro, Candia, Malta, Corfù, Zante.* But we say, *la Sardegna,* Sardinia, (the island); *la Sicilia,* Sicily; because there are historical and topographical reasons for considering them provinces.

30. The names of rivers are used with the article, and are either masculine or feminine, according to their termination, as *il Tagliamento, il Ticino, la Senna,* the Seine; *la Vistola,* the Vistula; *il Reno,* the Rhine. Those which end in *e,* are masculine, as *il Tevere,* the Tiber; but by an occasional caprice, some have two genders, as *il Piave,* or *la Piave,* and *il Brenta,* or *la Brenta.* Those which have a foreign termination, are masculine, as *l' Oder, il Dnieper, il Don.*

31. Before the names of seas and gulfs, is placed the general denomination of *mare,* or *golfo,* with the definite article, followed by a genitive denoting place, which sometimes may be changed into an adjective, as *mare di Toscana,* or *il mare Tirenno,* the Tuscan sea, a name anciently given to part of the Mediterranean; *il golfo di Venezia,* gulf of Venice; or, *il golfo Adriatico,* the Adriatic. *Il mare Mediterraneo,* the Mediterranean sea, has no genitive; neither has *Oceano,* ocean; for we say always *l' Oceano Antartico,* or *Artico, l' Oceano Atlantico.* In these cases, the appellatives, *mare* or *oceano,* can always be left out.

32. Mountains are used with the generic appellative, and require the article, as *il monte Bianco, il monte della Luna,* but sometimes the word *monte,* mountain, is not expressed, as *il Chimboraco, lo Spluga.* Chains of mountains are sometimes expressed in the masculine plural, with the article, as *i Pirenei,* the Pyrenees; *i Carpazi,* the Carpathian mountains; *gli Apennini,* the Apennines. Sometimes they are feminine, as *le Alpi,* the Alps; *le Cordelliere,* the Cordilleras; *le Ande,* the Andes.

33. Lakes have the generic appellative, in the masculine, with a genitive of the place, from which they derive their name, as *il lago di Ginevra,* the lake of Geneva; *il lago di Como,* the lake of Como; *il lago di Costanza,* the lake of Constance.

34. The other geographical denominations of hills, promontories, capes, bays, straits, isthmuses, &c., have always their generic appellative, with the corresponding article, (*baja,* bay, has it therefore in the feminine,) joined to the name of the place from which they take their name.

35. These rules we have thought right to give, for the better known geographical names. There are, however, ever so many variations, in the less known denominations of places, or geographical peculiarities, and there are also not few arbitrary exceptions in foreign geography. In fact, with regard to the first case, why should we call one particular mountain *il Serva,* and not *la Serva,* although it has its termination in *a*? Why is *Arno,* the river Arno, used without the article? *Il Tevere,* the river Tiber, is more famous, and of Latin derivation, but it is used with the article. Then, as to foreign names, why should we say *il Volga,* the Volga, in the masculine, when other rivers, ending in *a,* are feminine, as *la Vistola?* But these investigations are too minute, and we will therefore here conclude our remarks on geographical denominations.

Section III.

The special offices of the Article.

36. The article is repeated with nouns, which are of different gender or number, and on the contrary, is prefixed to the first alone, when the nouns are of the same gender and number, as for example: *il palazzo della Signoria, gli uffici publici, e le abitazioni private furono invase e saccheggiate dal feroce nemico;* the palace of the government, the public offices, and private

habitations were invaded, and were sacked by the ferocious enemy. But in an emphatic sense, or when used in oratory, the article may properly be repeated, even when the nouns are of the same gender and number, as for example, *la fede, la speranza, la carità, sona le ancelle di salvezza nel credente;* faith, hope, and charity, are the handmaids of salvation to the believer.

37. The infinitive mood is used sometimes as a substantive, according to the Latin usage, but with more force, on account of the masculine article, which is often prefixed to the infinitive itself. Thus we say, *il parlare è dote distintiva dell' uomo,* the power of speaking is the distinctive gift of man. This might also be expressed by this sentence, *la favella è dote distintiva dell' uomo,* speech is a distinctive gift of man—there, the verbal idea contained in the verb substantive, *il parlare,* ceases, and in its place remains the concrete idea expressed by the substantive, *la favella.* The following sentence gives a clear example of this rule:—

Del naso sono tre gli ufficj: il respirare, l' odorare, e 'l fare per quelle cavernette la purgazione del cèrebro.—*Firenz.*

The nose has three offices: breathing, smelling, and the purging of the brain by means of those little caverns.

38. It is also a peculiarity of the Italian language to give the significations of substantives to the adverbs, as *come, quando, perchè, dove,* by prefixing the masculine article: thus we say, *il come, il quando, il dove, il perchè,* in place of the corresponding substantive, *il modo, il tempo, il luogo, la cagione.*

EXAMPLES.

Del come non ti caglia, ma il perchè ti dirò.—*Bocc.*

Do not think about the manner how, but the reason why, I will tell you.

Ed egli pregava Dio che gli rivelasse il perchè.

And he prayed God that he would reveal to him the reason why.

"E 'l dove, e 'l quando tutto gli narrai."—*Dante.*

And the place where, and the time when, I told all to him.

39. In sentences like the following, the article is left out:

Non come uomini, ma come bestie morieno.—*Bocc.*

They died not like men, but beasts.

Con fanti e cavalli discese in Italia, e ne la devastò.

With infantry and cavalry he descended into Italy, and devastated it.

Vi ho recato danaro.

I have brought you ready money.

Amo più belle parole che busse.

I love fair words better than blows.

In these examples, it is evident that there is no particular or decisive definition of a thing: the noun is merely mentioned in a general comprehensive way.

40. The article, as the external sign of gender, is subject to the following changes in the plural:—

The article *il* is changed into *i*, and *lo* into *gli*, in the plural. The feminine article *la* makes *le* in the plural. These articles take the apostrophe in the singular; but preserve, notwithstanding, the entire form in the plural, unless the noun begins with the same vowel as that which is at the end of the article. Thus *l' erudito*, *l' occhio*, *l' anima*, have in the plural *gli eruditi*, *gli occhi*, *le anime*. On the other hand, *l' innocente*, *l' eleganza* have in the plural *gl' innocenti*, *l' eleganze*. But of this we will speak farther when we have to treat of the plural forms.

Section IV.

On (the Articular Prepositions, or) the Prepositions connected with the Article.

If we had regard solely to logical order, these prepositions should be noticed in the chapter which treats of the formation of cases. In this place, however, we deviate from the strict rules of logical order, in the hope that we may facilitate the study of the forms, and render the student more fit to write exercises, by now making mention of the article, when assimilated with the prepositions *di, a, da, in, con, per, su,* as a simple grammatical form.

42. When the definite article follows these prepositions (we shall hereafter treat of the occasion and the use), it assimilates itself with them in the following manner:—For *di il* is put *del;* for *di lo, dello;* for *di la, della;* for *di i, dei;* for *di gli, degli;* for *di le, delle;* and for *di l'* and *di gl', dell'* and *degl'*, the abbreviations for *dello, della, degli, delle*—each of these words making but one word.

43. The prepositions *a* and *da* are followed by the article, according to the same law of assimilation; and are thus formed, *al, dal; allo, dallo; alla, dalla; ai, dai; agli, dagli; all', dall'; agl', dagl'*, when there is an apostrophe.

44. It has been found both easy and convenient to assimilate the article with prepositions, *in, con, su,* in order to avoid too great an abundance of monosyllables, which would accord but little with the genius of our language. Thus we write *nel, nello, nella, nei, negli, nelle,* and *nell'* and *negl'*, where there is an apostrophe, in place of *in il, in lo, in la, in i, in gli, in le,* and also *in l', in gl'*.

According to the same law, the article is assimilated with the preposition *con:* as, for instance, *col, collo, colla, coi, cogli, colle, coll', cogl'*. The same thing happens with regard to *su,* as *sul, sullo, sulla, sui, sugli, sulle, sull'*.

Grammarians say that *per* is treated in the same way, and make *pel, pello, pella, pei, pegli, pelle, pell', pegl'*. But although many examples of these forms with *per* are found, and especially in classical authors, still this inelegant form may reasonably be rejected; and we may adopt the rule that we should say *per la, per gli, per le, per l',* and *per gl',* only retaining the expression *pei,* instead of *per i.*

The dislike to allowing any composition with *per* is so great, that it is contended that *per il* should be avoided, and that *per lo* should be used instead of *per il.* We may, however, remark that *pel* can be used much more properly than *pella* and *pelle,* and that to use *per lo,* when the article is *il,* savours of affectation.

CHAPTER IV.—SECTION I.

The Plural Number and its Terminations.

The general theory for the formation of the plural number is as follows:—

1. The general termination of the plural is in *i,* as *i padri,* the fathers; *le madri,* the mothers; *i decreti,* the decrees; *i libri,* the books; *gli amori,* loves; *i fenili,* hay-lofts; *le nubi,* the clouds.

2. Nouns feminine, which in the singular number end in *a,* in the plural end in *e,* as *le donne,* the ladies; *le antenne,* poles or sailyards; *le catene,* chains; *le lingue,* tongues; &c. On the other hand, nouns masculine, which end in *a,* have the ending of the plural in *i,* as *i Papi,* Popes; *i patriarchi,* patriarchs; *i profeti,* prophets; *i moralisti,* moralists; *i diademi,* diadems; *i poemi,* poems.

(*a*) The plural terminations of nouns in Italian are derived from those in Latin. The consonant endings are rejected, because there are no complete words in Italian which end in a consonant. It is possible, however, that this curtailmeut may be accidental, as we shall see afterwards.

(*b*) Hence it happens that the Italians have adopted only the plural terminations *e* and *i*—that is to say, those of the first and second declensions in nouns, having rejected the diphthong *æ* from the first declension, and reduced it into *e.* The consonant terminations are fused into *e* or *i,* according to their genders or derivations, with the exception of slight deviations, always retaining, however, the vowel ending, as we shall perceive, in this and the following section.

3. Nouns which end with an accented vowel have their

plural invariable—the singular termination always remaining:—as *le città*, cities; *le età*, ages; *le volontà*, wills; *le virtù*, virtues. (*V.* Ch. ii., Sec. iv., § *cc.*)

EXAMPLES.

"Le città son nemiche, amici i boschi
A' miei pensier."—*Petr.*

Cities are hostile, but woods are friendly to my thoughts.

La persona che si confessa, non solamente dee dire i peccati, ma eziando le male volontà.—*Passavanti.*

Who confesses ought to say not only his sins, but even his wicked wishes.

4. Nouns which end with the accent, and do not vary in the plural, may have, nevertheless, their plural in *i*, in poetic or grave style, if the singular has acquired the termination in *te* or *de:* as *le cittadi* or *cittadi*, cities; *le virtuti* or *virtudi*, virtues. (*V.* Ch. ii., Sec. iv., § *dd.*) This occurs, however, seldom, as abstract nouns have little regard for the plural, which is indeed almost superfluous to them.

EXAMPLES.

"Io nol dissi giammai, nè dir porria
Per *oro*, per cittadi, *o* per castella."—*Petr.*

I have not said it, nor could I say it for gold, for cities, or for castles.

5. The few monosyllabic nouns which we have in Italian are indeclinable: as, *re*, king; *piè*, foot; *grù*, a crane; which make in the plural, *i re*, *i piè*, *le grù*, *&c.*

"Chi dal mal far si guarda,
Dei Re non ha paura."—*Fra Jacopo da Todi.*

He who takes care not to do evil, has no fear of kings.

"Ed ei tenea de' piè ghermito il nerbo."—*Dante.*

And he held fast the ancles with his clutches.

6. These also retain, but only in elevated style, their entire and regular form; and these have the plural in *i*, as *i Regi*, *i piedi*, from *il Rege*, *il piede.*

(*c*) This is in accordance with their Latin derivation. *Dì*, day, however, has no other plural, having *i dì*, although in the singular may be used with elegance *die*, for *dì*, as,

"Voi vigilate nell' eterno die."—*Dante.*

"Ye are the watchers in th' eternal day."

7. Some nouns, which in the singular masculine end in *o*, in the plural become feminine in *a*, or have both terminations and genders, masculine in *i*, feminine in *a*. Those, which make the plural solely in *a* feminine, are few, and may be here mentioned: *le centinaja*, from *centinajo*, a hundred; *miliaja*, from *miliajo*; *le paja*, from *pajo*, a pair; *le uova*, from *uovo*, egg; *le risa*, from *riso*, laughter; and a few others. *Mille*, a thousand, has the plural *mila*.

EXAMPLES.

Egli tenne questo corso per più paja d' anni.

He kept on in this manner for many couples of years.

Non vedete voi, mio padre, ch' egli ha un par d' occhi, ch' e' pare spiritato?—*Fir.*

Do you not see, father, that he has such a pair of eyes, that he appears a possessed person?

Alla fante fece portare i due capponi lessi e molte uova fresche.—*Bocc.*

He gave order that two boiled capons, and many new eggs, should be brought by the maid servant.

8. Nouns which have their singular termination in *o*, and have the plural in *i* masculine, or *a* feminine, are more numerous.

(*d*) The reason for that is analogous to that given in the Ch. ii. Sec. ii. *f.*, and Sec. iii. *s.*, where it is shown that from neuter plurals, you may in some cases form singular feminines. In this case, many nouns chiefly of the second declension and the neuter gender, are subjected to the general rule, of changing the neuter singular into *o* masculine. Their plural ends in *a*, and they did not choose to change the *a* into *i*, as ought strictly to have been done, they preferred retaining the *a* neuter of the Latin plural, which becomes feminine for the want of the neuter in in Italian; but are not excluded from the advantage of preserving the masculine gender in the plural, as if it were formed in the ordinary manner. This method, however, cannot be adopted with so much elegance or propriety.

9. Some of these nouns are as follows:—*il braccio*, the arm —plural, *i bracci*, or *le braccia*, the arms; *il castello*, the castle—plural, *i castelli*, and *le castella*, castles; *il fondamento*, the foundation—plural, *i fondamenti*, and *le fondamenta*; *il labbro*, the lip—*i labbri*, or *le labbra*, lips; also *anello*, a ring; *braccio*, an arm; *calcagno*, the heel; *ciglio*, the eye: *corno*, the horn; *dito*, the finger; *frutto*, fruit; *fusa*, a spindle; *gesto*, a gesture; *ginocchio*, a knee; *grido*, a cry; *labbro*, the lip; and some others.

"Lo collo poi colle braccia mi cinse."—*Dan.*

Then he threw his arms around my neck.

"Tre volte il cavalier la donna cinse
Colle robuste braccia."—*Tasso.*

Three times the cavalier encircled the lady with his robust arms.

Tutti gli altri mari, bracci di mare, golfi escono dall' oceano.

All the other seas, arms of the sea, gulfs, issue from the ocean.

"E' bella cosa
Starsi nel letto e far castelli in aria."

It is a fine thing to remain in bed, and build castles in the air.

Siccome ancora si può vedere per le fondamenta delle dette mura.—*Bocc.*

As yet may be seen by the foundations of the said walls.

Con quelle labbra, che parean due rubinetti, sorridendo, rispose.

With a slight smile she replied, her lips appearing like two rubies.

Mentre la mia misera vita sosterrà questi membri.—*Bocc.*

Whilst my unhappy life will support these limbs.

(*e*) If we choose to enter into the significative spirit of these words, we shall find that the majority of them convey an idea of extension, diffusion, relaxation, accumulation, &c., which does not agree with the compact, prompt, and vigorous idea, which we connect with the masculine gender, and not being able to remain as neuters, they have changed themselves in the plural number, into the feminine. We have enlarged on this subject, since such nouns, although they are not numerous, constitute a noble part of our language.

10. It is natural that some variation of meaning should be met with in these two plural forms, of the same word. To hunt them out would be a pleasing task, but out of place, at the commencement of the study of a language.

(*f*) We will therefore only notice the most remarkable instance of such a difference. *Membro* forms both *membri* and *membra*; but we must observe that *membra*, in its neuter primitive sense, is used to indicate the principal parts of the body, which could not be called *membri* with so much propriety. But when it is intended to express in a figurative sense, individuals, composing a moral body, an association, or the personality of a legal assembly, the persons who are component parts of such bodies, are called *membri*, as *i membri del parlamento, del consiglio, della società*, members of parliament, of council, of society. And this is natural, since members signifying on this occasion masculine persons, lose their primitive characteristic of the neuter gender in *a*, and turn it into the characteristic *i*, which denotes the masculine gender. This example confirms our assertion, that nouns terminating in *a* plural, although feminine in form, may properly be considered neuters.

11. It is only to be remembered, that when there is no difference of meaning, both forms may be used, but the plural in *a* is more elegant. But when a masculine idea is expressed, by the termination in *i*, this cannot be changed into the other form in *a*, as in the above example.

12. Some nouns have no singular, on account of their signification being naturally frequentative or plural. Thus, the word *le nozze*, nuptials, is not used in the singular. The same is the case with *esequie*, funerals; *spezie*, spices, because they have the frequentative sense.

Le molle, fire-tongs; *le fòrbici* or *cesoje*, scissors; on account of their material construction being double, have no singular.

13. There are also other nouns which have no plural, as *il miele*, honey; *la prole*, offspring; *la progenie*, progeny; *la*

stirpe, family; and a few others—the singular including the idea of individual multiplicity.

14. Other variations in the singular and plural terminations of nouns might be noted; but it would be a departure from the simplicity of a grammar to describe all the gradations and differences which may be met. It is sufficient to notice those which are most generally found.

Section II.

The Plural Terminations continued.

15. One of the greatest difficulties which must be encountered in the Italian language, is to fix a rule for the plural of nouns which have their singular termination in *co* and *go*. This problem has not been resolved by grammarians in a satisfactory manner. So vague and uncertain are the rules, that Buommattei, a famous grammarian, and a subtle speculator on the nature of our language, comes to this conclusion:—"I do not believe," says he, "that this distinction can be learned except by practice, because I, after much thought and study, have not been able to discover any rule. I, therefore, am of opinion that no rule will apply, and that in this case it is necessary to obey use solely." We will, however, endeavour to give some directions of our own, and these require a kind of short digression.

16. Let us, then, set out with the principle, that nouns which in the singular number end in *co* and *ca, go* and *ga*, have the *c* and the *g* hard. The regular formation of the plural would be, to change the masculine terminations *a* and *o* into *i*, and *a* feminine into *e*. But in this case *ci* and *ce*, *gi* and *ge*, would have a soft sound.

17. It often happens, however, that it would be contrary to the spirit of the Italian language to allow *c* and *g* to lose the hard sound in the plural. The reasons for this, it is not

necessary to discover, even if it were possible to do so, which we greatly doubt. The Italians have provided for this euphonic exigency by inserting an *h* between the *c* and the *g* and the *e* plural; and by this means these letters retain the hard sound. This is the only use which is made of the letter *h*.

All nouns feminine which end in *ca* and *ga*, insert in the plural the *h* between the *c* or *g* and the *e*, as *monaca*, a nun—*monache*, nuns; *ricca*, rich—*ricche*; *cuoca*, a cook—*cuoche*; *fatìca*, fatigue—*fatìche*; *bottega*, a shop—*botteghe*; *strega*, a sorceress, *streghe*; *piega*, a fold—*pieghe*; and others.

The real difficulty is, to determine which of the nouns masculine terminating in *co* and *go*, should insert the *h*, and which not.

18. In the first place, we may say that nouns masculine, ending in *ca*, always insert the *h* between the *c* and the *i*, as *monarca*, a monarch—*monarchi*; *patriarca*, a patriarch—*patriarchi*; and others. We will also add that, as far as we know, no nouns masculine end in *ga*.

19. Nouns which end in *co* and *go* have the syllable before *co* and *go* either long or short.

If the syllable is long, we are justified in laying down the general rule, that they take the *h* in the plural, in order that the *c* and *g* may remain hard. Dissyllables in *co* and *go* have their accent on the first syllable, which is consequently long. These will insert the *h* in the plural;—in fact, we find that *Greco*, a Greek; and *porco*, a pig, are the sole exceptions, making in the plural *Greci* and *porci*. *Mago*, a magician, has *magi* in the plural, but only when the three magi are mentioned; otherwise, the plural is *maghi*.

20. Polysyllables having the accent on the penultimate, which is therefore long, insert the *h* in the plural. The only positive exception which we find, is *amico*, a friend, which makes *amici*.

21. With regard to those which have the penultimate

short, we shall not be far wrong if we consider that, as a general rule, those which end in *co* have the plural without *h*. Those which end in *go* are used with the *h*—with these exceptions: *teologo*, a theologian—*teologi*; with its kindred words, as *filologo*, a philologer; &c. *Aspàrago*, asparagus, makes *asparagi*, in the plural.

22. A difficulty now remains, concerning a certain class of nouns, ending in *co*, which is not numerous. These have the penultimate short, but nevertheless, some have the plural invariably with the *h*. The number of these, however, is few, and we can easily point them out, as *abaco*, a counting-board; *manico*, a handle; *càrico*, a load; *dimentico*, forgetful; *fondaco*, a warehouse; *rammàrico*, a complaint; *stitico*, morose; *traffico*, traffic. We are not certain that there are any others.

23. Some nouns, however, ending in *co* and *go*, have a short syllable before *co* and *go*, and yet have the power, though not necessarily, of inserting the *h*. There is one noun also, *mendico*, a beggar; which, although it is long in the penultimate, does not insert the *h*. As far as these few nouns are concerned, the student must content himself with the knowledge, that these nouns are few in number, and may adopt or reject the *h* at pleasure. It would not be, therefore, necessary to pay much attention to them: they are, however, here inserted:—*mendico*, a beggar; *mònaco*, a monk; *chirurgo*, a surgeon; *pràtico*, expert; *domestico*, a domestic; *reciproco*, reciprocal; *salvàtico*, wild; *stomaco*, stomach; *apologo*, an apologue; *astrologo*, an astrologer; *anàlogo*, analogous; *diàlogo*, a dialogue.

24. Thus, without reckoning these promiscuous nouns, the exceptions to our general rule amount only to about thirteen, singled out in the §§ 19, 20, and 22, besides the few words ending in *logo*. We have, therefore, good reason for preferring our theory, to the indecisive and involved explanations which have hitherto been given.

25. One objection, however, may be made to our theory. How, it may be said, can a foreigner possibly know which of the nouns ending in *co,* has the penultimate short? To this, our reply is, that they *are not* those nouns which have a consonant before *co,* for these have the penultimate long.

26. As to those with vowels, there is no certain rule, and the student must be satisfied with knowing them by practice. But it will be sufficient to observe, for the benefit of those who are acquainted with Latin, that most nouns which have a short vowel before the termination *co,* are of Latin derivation, and retain the Latin quantity. Thus, at a glance, they will be recognised by the student. Of this we will give a few examples: *armonico,* melodious; *idèntico,* identical; *barbàrico,* barbarian; *bèllico,* warlike; *benèfico,* beneficient; *didascàlico,* didactic; *itàlico,* italic; *logico,* logical; *profètico,* prophetical. What English student of Latin, does not know that these have the vowel before *co* short? Other nouns, which are not of Latin derivation, have the penultimate short by analogy, as, *bisbètico,* whimsical; *frenètico,* delirious; *zotico,* rustic.

27. Not a few Italian nouns end in *io.* According to the general rule, the *o* should be changed into *i.* This, however, as the letter *i* would be twice repeated, would not be approved by the Italians. But, on the other hand, to have the plural ending in one *i,* does not always give satisfaction, although that sometimes occurs, and instead the *j,* which is considered equivalent to *ii,* is used. The grammarians give indecisive rules, as to when either course should be adopted. We will confine ourselves to saying that, if double *cc* and *gg,* as well as *g* followed by *l,* and *sc* should precede *io,* then a rapid sound is given to *io,* the result as it were, of one new vowel composed of the two; so to make the plural, it will be enough to change *cio, gio, glio,* and *scio,* into *ci, gi, gli,* and *sci,* as *laccio,* a snare; *impaccio,* an obstacle; *omaggio,* homage; *ostaggio,* a hostage; *ammiraglio,* an admiral; *fascio,* a bundle; *figlio,* a son; *foglio,* a leaf of a book; make in the plural,

lacci, impacci, omaggi, ostaggi, fasci, figli, fogli, etc. *Bacio,* a kiss; *malvagio,* wicked; make *baci, malvagi,* because old authors used to write *bascio, malvaggio.*

28. When other consonants precede the *i,* or when there is only one *c* or *g,* there is then a sufficient reason, as the *i* is longer in the singular, for making it prolonged in the plural, as in *temerario,* rash; *studio,* study; *precipizio,* a precipice; *beneficio,* a kindness; *tempio,* a temple; *principio,* a beginning; *prestigio,* an illusion; *ufficio,* a duty, &c.; in which words, and others, you would not do wrong in using the *j.*

29. According to modern orthography, however, *i* is often used, where it was usual to write *j*; but although this is frequently done, the custom is not yet universal. We shall adhere the more willingly to the *j,* for this reason: that if *i* is used as a substitute for *j,* a greater force than is usual would be given to *i,* as a substitute for the prolonged pronunciation of *j,* which is equal to two *ii.*

30. In spite of this modern innovation, there are words which cannot dispense with the *j* in the plural: as *principio,* a beginning; *beneficio,* a kindness; *tempio,* a temple; which if they are not written with a *j,* might be confounded with *prìncipi, benèfici, tempi,* which are the plurals of *prìncipe,* a prince; *benèfico,* beneficient; *tempo,* time.

31. Nouns feminine, which end in *cia* and *gia,* have the plural in *ce* and *ge,* because the *i,* on account of its rapidity, and its homogeneous sound, does not appear in the pronunciation. Thus, *Guancia,* cheek; *lancia,* lance; *greggia,* sheepfold; *freccia,* arrow; make *guance, lance, gregge, frecce.* These nouns, however, might retain the *i,* without causing any difference in pronunciation.

32. When other consonants precede the *i,* the feminine nouns, which have their singular in *a,* follow the genera rule, and change the *a* into *e.* In these cases, *i* has a more relaxed sound in the singular, and for this reason, is retained in the plural; as *coppia,* a couple—in the plural makes *coppie;*

nebbia, a fog—*nebbie*; *bestemmia,* blasphemy—*bestemmie*; *spoglia,* spoil—*spoglie*; *balia,* nurse—*balie*; *furia,* fury—*furie,* etc.

33. Nouns in *io* and *ia,* which have the accent on the *i,* follow the general rule in the plural, and change the *o* and *a* into *i* and *e,* retaining the accented preceding *i.* Thus, from *stropiccìo,* a clawing up and down; *calpestìo,* a trampling noise; *restìo,* restive; *teologìa,* theology; *farmacìa,* pharmacy; are formed *stropiccìi, calpestìi, teologìe, farmacìe.*

34. Nouns which end in *jo* in the singular, necessarily cast out the *o* in the plural, as it would otherwise be changed into *i,* and the strange plural form of *ji* would be the result. This would be equivalent to *iii,* which would be allowable neither in orthography or pronunciation. Thus, from *lavatojo,* a laundry; *bujo,* darkness; *mugnajo,* a miller; *librajo,* a bookseller; are made *lavatoj, buj, mugnaj, libraj,* which by orthographical caprice may be written *lavatoi, bui, mugnai;* but not *librai.*

35. Nouns, which in the singular end in *i,* suffer no change in the plural—and this naturally, as *i* is the characteristic of the plural. Thus, *diocesi,* a diocese; *analisi,* an analysis; *dì,* day; make in the plural *le diocesi, le analisi, i dì.*

36. Some nouns change the plural without observing the ordinary rule: as *bue,* an ox; *moglie,* a wife; *uomo,* a man; make in the plural *buoi* (and also *bovi,* from *bove*), *mogli, uomini. Dio,* God, from a sentiment of reverence, is quite changed in the plural *Dei,* in order to show that the Deity himself has nothing in common with the *Dei bugiardi,* false gods; which word assumes, for the same reason, the article *gli,* instead of *i:* as *gli Dei bugiardi,* the false gods. The possessive pronouns, *mio,* mine; *tuo,* thine; *suo,* his; have *miei, tuoi, suoi,* in the plural.

Section III.

The Article as a sign of the Plural.

37. We have already given the simple theory of the article,

as an external sign of the plural, which is not subject to exceptions. It will, therefore, suffice if we refer the reader to Chapter III., which treats of the article. We will only say that *li* is sometimes used instead of *i* by ancient authors, and even by some of the moderns; but this form is now not merely antiquated but objectionable; although, in other expressions, the antiquated form is considered elegant.

38. We, also, here repeat, as being an important principle, that the articles, which have the apostrophe in the singular, exclude it in the plural—although some contrary instances, even in good authors, are not wanting. So *l'opinione*, opinion, makes *le opinioni; l' occhio*, the eye—*gli occhi; l' erudito*, the learned man—*gli eruditi*. If, however, the noun begins with the same vowel as that which ends the article, in that case the apostrophe is required, as *l' innocente*, the innocent man—*gl' innocenti; l' eleganza,—l' eleganze*. The article may also have the apostrophe in the masculine plural, as an exceptional abbreviation. Thus, for *dei, degli, ai, agli, dai, dagli*, may be used *de', a'*, and *da'*.

Now that the office of the article is sufficiently determined, we will begin to treat of the cases and their signs.

Here we think it, however, most convenient to begin our series of Exercises, which was postponed for the purpose of enabling the student to derive the greatest possible advantage from them, as was suggested in the "Directions," p. 20.

Observation.

The Vocabulary of the Exercises is always so arranged as to contain in the translation of the student, the original Italian, as it is found in the various authors.

Exercises on the Plural.

1. As in the spring, meadows, plains, woods, banks, valleys, mountains, rivers, lakes, everything which one sees is agreeable: the earth smiles; the sea smiles; the air smiles; heaven smiles. Every part, every thing is full of light, of songs, of scents, of sweetness,

of genial warmth. Thus, in youth, whatever one says, whatever one does, whatever one beholds, everything is pleasing, everything is acceptable; every state, every soul is full of festivity, of pastime, of jokes, of cheerful pursuits, of adventures, of joy, of repose, of peace.—*Bembo.*

As, *siccome;* spring, *primavera;* meadow, *prato;* plain, *campo;* wood, *selva;* bank, *piaggia;* valley, *monte;* river, *fiume;* lake, *lago;* everything, *ogni cosa;* which one sees, *che si vede;* agreeable, *vaga;* to smile, *ridere;* earth, *terra;* sea, *mare;* air, *aria;* heaven, *cielo;* *parte;* thing, *cosa;* is full, *è piena;* light, *lume;* song, *canto;* scent, *odore;* sweetness, *dolcezza;* genial warmth, *tiepidezza.* Thus, *così;* youth, *giovinezza;* whatever one says, *ciò che si dice;* one does, *si fa;* one beholds, *si mira;* everything, *tutto;* pleasing, *piacevole;* acceptable, *caro;* state, *stato;* soul, *anima;* full, *ripiena;* festivity, *festa;* pastime, *solazzo;* joke, *giuoco;* joy, *allegrezza;* cheerful pursuit, *piacimento;* adventure, *ventura;* *gioja, riposo, pace.*

2. Fables have been published by poets, in order that in the persons of others we might see shadowed our own customs, and the image of our life painted.—*Cic.*

Fable, *favola;* published, *messo fuori;* *poeta;* in order that, *acciocchè;* in the; of others, *altrui;* *persona;* to see, *vedere;* shadowed, *adombrato;* our own, *i nostri;* *costume;* painted, *dipinto;* *immagine;* of our, *della nostra;* life, *vita.*

3. The parts of riches are money, jewels, precious vessels, and other furniture and ornaments of the house; to possess much land, and that fertile, cattle, many servants in number, greatness, and excellent beauty, and many other things from which to derive profit.

Part, *parte;* (the) riches, *ricchezza;* money, *danaro;* jewel, *gioja;* vessel, *vaso;* *prezioso;* other, *altro;* furniture, *masserizia;* *ornamento;* house, *casa;* *possedere;* much, *assai;* land, *terreno;* that*, *fertile;* cattle, *bestiami;* *servo;* (*in* translate) *per;* *numero;* greatness, *grandezza;* *bellezza;* *eccellente;* other thing many, *altre cose molte;* to derive (from them), *da trarne;* profit, *frutto.*

4. The ladies laughed to such an extent, that one might have drawn all their teeth.—*Bocc.*

The ladies, &c... that one, *faceano le donne sì gran risa che;* all, *tutto;* their*; (the); tooth, *dente*, one..drawn, *si sarebbero loro potuti levare.*

5. Smoke, flames, sparks, blaze, and clouds and volumes of pitch, ascended from it to heaven.

Smoke, *fummo;* flame, *fiamma;* spark, *favilla;* blaze, *vampa;* cloud, *nube;* *volume;* pitch, *pece;* ascended (translate, from it went), *n' andavano;* heaven, *cielo.*

Exercises in Reading.

Ecco altre isole insieme, altre pendici
Scopriano al fin, men erte ed elevate,
Ed eran queste l' isole Felici;
Così le nominò la prisca etate;
A cui tanto stimava i cieli amici,
Che credea volontarie e non arate
Qui partorir le terre; e 'n più graditi.
Frutti, non culte, germogliar le viti.

Qui non fallaci mai fiorir gli olivi,
E 'l mel dicea stillar dall'elci cave,
E scender giù da lor montagne i rivi
Con acque dolci, e mormorio soave;
E zefiri e rugiade i raggi estivi
Temprarvi sì, che nullo ardor v' è grave:
E quì gli Elisi campi, e le famose
Stanze delle beate anime pose.

Tasso, Ger. Lib. Ca. xv.

Translation.—Lo! at last they discovered other islands and cliffs together, less perpendicular and less elevated. These were the Fortunate Islands, as the primitive age named them; and to whom the heavens appeared so favorable, that they thought that the earth would offer its fruits spontaneously, without the labour of the plough, and the vines, without being cultivated, would present their most acceptable gifts.

Here (they would say) the olive trees flourished, never failing to give their fruit; and the honey would drop out of the hollow ilexes; and the streams would descend down from the mountains with their sweet waters and grateful murmurs; and that the zephyrs and the dew would temper the summer heats, so as to prevent their being oppressive: and here they imagined were the Elysian Fields and the famous habitations of the happy souls.

CHAPTER V.—Section I.

The Cases of Nouns.

1. It would be unseasonable, as well as immethodical, to involve those who study a language, in a labyrinth of words dependent on prepositions. Besides uselessly arresting the

progress of the student, by troubling him thus early with arbitrary and idiomatic expressions, it would be impossible to unravel the meaning of these peculiarities, when the pupil only possesses an elementary knowledge of the language.

For this reason, we shall only occupy ourselves for the present with the prepositions, *di*, *a*, *da*, in their most obvious and regular meaning.

2. *Di* marks the genitive case, *a* the dative, and *da* the ablative.

Section II.

The Genitive Case.

3. The chief duty of the preposition *di*, of, both in this and other languages having *segnacasi*, is to indicate the genitive case, which is a certain modification of the substantive.

The modification made by the genitive case, is either intrinsic or extrinsic, that it is to say, it either affects the substance of the noun, or its accidents.

4. The intrinsic genitive determines the matter, or some substantial quality of the first substantive. The preposition is used without the article, for since the office of the article is to define the substantive, it cannot well be used, if one substantive constitutes an integral part of the existence of another substantive.

5. Thus, we say, *la colonna d' oro*, the column of gold; *il serto di rose*, the garland of roses; *il cucchiajo d' argento*, spoon of silver, or silver spoon; and in a figurative sense, *il cuore di marmo*, the heart of marble; *natura di ferro*, a nature of iron, or an iron nature; *amore di padre*, love of a father; *coraggio di soldato*, courage of a soldier. In these examples, *d' oro* and *d' argento*, point out the matter, and *di padre*, *di soldato*, indicate a general quality. The sense of genitives, with a simple preposition, is always general and indeterminate.

6. These intrinsic modifications of the genitive are all

qualificative, and an adjective could always be used in their place, at least in a logical sense, if not with good taste, as *colonna marmorea*, a marble column; *amore paterno*, paternal love; *ira celeste*, celestial anger; *fiori primaverili*, spring flowers.

7. If the genitive causes an extrinsic modification of the substantive, it is not essential, but accidental; the two substantives being two things, the one distinct from the other. This kind of genitive, therefore, has a definite signification. When we say, *l' amore del padre*, the love of the father; the ideas of *amore* and *padre*, are not inseparably connected, since one could be, in our mind, separated from the other without injury. For instance, if *il padre*, the father, is subtracted, the idea of *amore* still remains in other fathers. *La casa del prelato* shows this still more clearly, as we of course know that the idea of *casa*, a house, might exist without the substantive *prelato*, prelate.

In this kind of genitive the dominant idea is that of possession. The more this idea is developed, the more absolute is the character of the genitive case. In this manner does the genitive produce the idea of possession.

8. In Italian, the genitive of possession is always determined by the genitive which follows the thing possessed. The possessive pronouns must, however, be excepted, since they are contractions of the genitives of pronouns, as we shall see when we come to speak of possessive adjectives.

9. A general rule may therefore be deduced, that *di*, the sign of the genitive, when used without the article, indicates an intrinsic relation. When on the other hand the article is added, it signifies an extrinsic relation. The article defines and individualises the substantive, while, where the intrinsic relation exists, the substantive in the genitive is indeterminate.

We have dwelt at greater length on the use of *di*, with the genitive case, because the Italian grammarians have involved themselves in long and useless discussions on this subject.

Passing over others, we will make mention of Buommattei, as the most distinguished among them. This author treats of this subject at great length, but does not decide the question in a satisfactory manner, although he condemns the erroneous doctrines of Bembo. This last-mentioned writer, who is still renowned, involved himself in many false doctrines with regard to the proper reasons for omitting or adopting the article with *di*. It may, therefore, easily be seen that this important part of the Italian Grammar has always remained undecided; and for this reason we have no hesitation in bringing forward our own theory, not pretending to see further than those great masters, but being convinced that the language, in that respect, is now more defined than it was at that time.

10. Another office of the genitive case, is to signify the indefinite adjective *qualche* or *alcuno*, which is understood if the noun is in the genitive, and answers to the English word *some*. This usage agrees perfectly with that of the French language. We say, for example, *Io aveva del denaro nella borsa che mi fu rubata,* I had money in my purse, of which I was robbed; which is the same thing as saying, *Io aveva qualche danaro nella borsa.* In English, as we have before remarked, *del* is translated by *some.* Also, *Io gli dò ogni mattina delle frutta,* I give him fruit every morning; which is equivalent to *alcune frutta.* In fact, if another indeterminate adjective is placed, the genitive is omitted, as *molto danaro,* much money; *poche frutta,* little fruit.

11. In the same manner, it occasionally seems that nouns, which properly speaking, are of the nominative or accusative case, are found in the genitive, through an apparent irregularity in the language. This occurs also in French, and in English, resolves itself into the word *some. Del danaro fu gittato per lui senza prò,* money was thrown away by him without profit; instead of *qualche danaro fu gittato per lui senza prò. Vi sono degli uomini che speculano troppo e*

perdono molto, there are some men who speculate too largely, and lose much. In this sentence, *degli uomini* is in the nominative case, being substituted for *alcuni,* as if the sentence were *sono alcuni uomini.* In French, the expression, *des hommes* would be used, in English, as before, the word *some. Comprammo delle pera eccellenti (delle* for *alcune)*; we bought *some* excellent pears, will suffice as an instance of the accusative in the same circumstances as the nominative.

(*a*) In Latin, the expressions, ***sunt homines***, or ***sunt aliqui ex hominibus***, or ***inter homines***, might be used. In the same manner, we might say, ***sunt aliqui hominum***, and also, but more elegantly, ***sunt quidam homines***.

12. We may also say, properly, *mi diede di bei fiorini d' oro,* he gave me some beautiful golden flowers; for *mi diede alcuni, e non pochi, fiorini d'oro.*

These are the most general offices of the genitive case. Of genitives of other kinds, which are rather words or phrases than real genitives, especially if they come after the verbs, we will speak in the proper place.

Exercises on the Genitive.

1. In their intercourse these men presented a beautiful image of honesty and friendship, not feigned, not flattering, not the slave of fortune, but free, sincere, and true.

In their, *nella loro*; intercourse, *consuetudine*; these, *cotui*; man, *uomo*; to present, *presentare*; beautiful, *bello*; *imagine*; *onestà*; friendship, *amicizia*; feigned, *infinto*; flattering, *lusinghiero*; slave, *ischiavo*; *fortuna*; but, *ma*; free, *libero*; *sincero*; true, *verace*.

2. This world is like a stage; whoever looks upon it from without sees nothing but the miracles and splendours of gems of gold, and of lights, of greatness and of skill, and symmetry; but whoever looks upon it from within, does not find there anything else but distress, confusion, rubbish and props.—*Guar. Lett.*

This world, *questo mondo*; like, *come*; stage, *scena*; whoever, *chi*; upon it, *la*; to look, *mirare*; from (of), *di*; without, *fuori*; not, *non*; to see, *vedere*; there, *quivi*; anything else than, *altro*; but, *che*; miracles, *mara-*

viglia; *splendore*; *gemma*; gold, *oro*; light, *lume*; greatness, *grandezza*; skill, *artificio*; *simmetria*; within, *di dentro*; not there, *non vi*; to find, *trovare*; distress, *angustia*; confusion, *sconcerto*; rubbish, *rottame*; prop, *puntello*.

3. Pallas, with his arrogance exceeding the condition of a freedman, became to him fastidious.

Pallante; with his, *colla sua*; *arroganza*; to exceed, *passare*; *condizione*; freedman, *Liberto*; to him, *gli*; became, *era venuto*; *a fastidio*.

4. The loss of happiness causes one to know the force of affection, inasmuch as neither does prosperity show the friend, nor adversity conceal the enemy.

Loss, *perdita*; happiness, *felicità*; causes, *fa*; to know, *conoscere*; *forza*; affection, *dilezione*; inasmuch as, *imperciocchè*; neither, *nè*; *prosperità*; does show, *mostra*; friend, *amico*; nor, *nè*; *avversità*; (does) conceal, *nasconde*; enemy, *nemico*.

5. Your letters, for the importance of the sentences, the choice of the words, and the variety of figures, can deservedly delight everyone; and not only being imbued throughout with grace, and love, but also plainly displaying the candour of mind, depth of learning, and refinement of the manners of him who writes them, have been to me more agreeable than any one could imagine.

Your, *la vostra*; letter, *lettera*; importance, *gravità*; *sentenza*; choice, *elezione*; word, *parola*; *varietà*; *figura*; can, *possono*; deservedly, *meritamente*; *dilettare*; everyone, *ognuno*; only, *solo*: being, *per essere*; imbued throughout, *tutte piene*; with (of) *di*; *grazia*; love, *amore*; but, *ma*; also, *anco*; plainly, *apertemente*; displaying, *per portare in fronte*; *candidezza*; mind, *animo*; depth, *profondità*; learning, *dottrina*; refinement, *gentilezza*; manner, *costume*; of him who them, *di chi le*; to write, *scrivere*; to me, *mi*; more than anyone could imagine, *sopra quello che si possa pensare*; agreeable, *gioconde*.

THE CALENDAR.

6. On a table was marked all the days of the year, and the various movements of the seasons, and the inequality of night and day, together with the observations of the hours, not a little necessary for the living, and the not false prognostics of the seasons, and when the sun with his motion foretels fine weather, and when rain, and when winds, and when hail, and what days of the month are fortunate, and what unfavourable to the work of mortals.

Calendar, *Lunario.*

On a (in the one), *nell' una; tavola;* marked, *notato;* all, *tutto;* day, *dì;* year, *anno; vario; movimento; stagione; inegualità;* night, *notte;* day, *giorno;* together, *insieme; osservazione;* hour, *ora;* a *; little, *poco; necessaria;* living, *vivente; falso; pronostico;* season, *temperie;* when, *quando;* sun, *sole;* with his, *col suo; movimento;* to foretell, *denunziare;* fine weather, *serenità;* rain, *pioggia;* wind, *vento;* hail, *grundine;* what, *quali;* moon, *luna; fortunato;* unfavorable, *infelice;* work, *opera; mortale.*

Section II.

The Dative Case.

13. The dative case indicates direction, and some other relations of a similar kind existing between one noun and the other, which cannot be conceived, without a certain transition or passage from one substantive to the other. This includes a verbal idea, and the dative is in fact necessarily dependant on a verb, not on a noun, or rather on a noun in a condition of transition. The preposition *a* constitutes the dative, either with the article or without it, subject to no other condition than that applied generally to articles, according to the directions given on the uses of the articles, in Chapter III.

(*b*) In Italian, the dative is more comprehensive than in Latin, since the construction of verbs of motion, with the preposition *ad*, and the accusative, is by the Italians turned into the dative.

14. Thus, for example, *Giacomo parla a Giovanni,* indicates the relation of direction from *Giacomo* to *Giovanni,* in the transition from the state of silence, to that of speaking to *Giacomo. Io dò al mio servo cinque scudi al mese,* I give to my servant five scudi a month. *Al mio servo* indicates a relation between me and the servant, with the transition from a state of tranquillity, to giving five scudi a month.

Section III.

The Ablative Case.

15. The ablative case is a sign either of origin or of removal between two substantives. If of origin, it includes

the idea of continuation; if of removal, it suggests the notion of separation. But the idea of origin or removal, includes the idea of a transition of state, in one substantive, which proceeds from the other. Now this cannot take place without the aid of a verb, hence the ablative case is defined by the verb, and indicated by the preposition *da.*

16. Take this sentence, *da Rea Silvia nacque Romolo e Remo,* from Rhea Sylvia were born Romulus and Remus. The substantive from which the effect of the birth of Romulus and Remus took place, is Rhea Sylvia, and the condition of transition expressed by the verb *nacque,* is effected by Romulus and Remus, who are the agents. Also, *Paolo partì da Roma nel mese di Febbrajo,* Paul departed from Rome in the month of February. Rome is the quiescent substantive in the ablative, and Paul is the subject of the verb, which expresses the transition of removal between Paul and Rome.

17. Another kind of ablative case comes into use when the verb is changed from the active to the passive voice. Under these circumstances, the agent is put in the ablative, with the preposition *da.* For instance, *il padre ama il figlio,* the father loves his son; is changed into *il figlio è amato dal padre.* In this case, the word padre, from being the subject, becomes the ablative case; the condition of being loved, being assigned of course to the son, who is the quiescent substantive.

This ablative, however, is not of so explicit a nature, that in similar expressions it should in all languages require the ablative case. It is used indeed in Latin, as well as in Italian, but neither in French, which for this purpose employs the preposition *par,* nor in English, in which the word *by* is used.

Exercises on the Dative and Ablative.

1. The mastiff runs in haste at the stone which the traveller has thrown at him, and bites it both with passion and rage.

Mastino; to run, *correre;* in haste, *in fretta;* at (to) stone, *ciottolo;* which, *che* ; traveller, *viandante* ; at (to) him, *gli* ; has thrown, *abbia gettato contro* ; it, *lo* ; to bite, *mordere* ; both, *.; passion, *stizza* ; *rabbia.*

2. No condition could equal mine.

No condition, *nessuno stato* ; could, *potrebbe* ; equal, *agguagliarsi* ; to (the) mine, *mio.*

3. It is sufficient that in preserving faith to my lover, I should be firmer than any rock.

It is sufficient, *basta* ; that, *che* ; in (the); preserving, *serbar* ; *fede* ; to (the); my, *mio* ; lover, *amante* ; I should be, *io mi sia* ; firmer, *più salda* ; than, *di* (of); any, *ogni* ; rock, *scoglio.*

4. You know not how at any time to do good works, but in order to please (to) the people and to be praised by them.

You, *voi* ; not ; to know, *sapere* ; to do, *far* ; at any time, *mai* ; *buono* ; work, *opera* ; but in order, *se non per* ; to please, *compiacere* ; *popolo* ; to be of it, *esserne* ; to praise, *lodare.*

5. From pride arises display, ostentation, pomp. From it arises* disdain for one's* inferiors, persecution of one's* equals, envy of one's* superiors. From it is born* the avenging one's-self furiously of all insults; from it covetousness in acquiring; from it avarice in keeping hold of anything*; from it impatience in toleration; from it readiness to give offence.

From (the) pride, *superbia* ; to arise, *nascere* ; (the) display, *fasto* ; *ostentazione* ; *pompa* ; from it, *da lei* ; (the) disdain, *dispregiare* (inf.) ; (the) inferior, *minore* ; (the) *perseguitare* (inf.); (the) *uguale* ; (the) *invidiare* (inf.); (the) superior, *maggiore* ; the avenging; *ricattarsi* ; furiously, *rabbiosamente* ; of all, *di tutto* ; insult, *villania* ; (the) covetousness, *ingordigia* ; in (the), *acquistare* (inf.); *avarizia* ; in (the) keeping hold, *ritenere* ; *impazienza* ; in (the) *tollerare* (inf.) ; from it readiness, *facilità* : to (in the) give offence, *nell' offendere.*

6. O that Capodimonte is indeed a beautiful thing! So much so is it, that for that somewhat small palace, with that bit of a peninsula bathed by that lake, smiled upon by those pretty islands, adorned by those gardens, and surrounded by those shades, I would give as many Tempes and as many Parnassus as ever were.

Oh, that! *oh, quel!* indeed, *pur* ; *bello* ; thing, *cosa!* So much so is it, *tant' è*. For that, *per quel* ; palace, *palazzotto* ; that, *quel* (fem.); bit, *poco* ; of a * ; *penisola* ; to bath, *bagnare* ; lake, *lago* ; to smile upon, *vagheggiare* ; pretty island, *isoletta* ; *ornato* ; *giardino* ; surrounded, *cinto* ; shade, *ombra* ; I would give, *io darei* ; as many, *quanto* ; *Tempe, Parnaso* ; were, *furon* ; ever, *mai.*

7. **Death does not permit itself to be moved to pity by beauty, by fortitude, by nobility, by youth, and with the same scythe cuts down the green and the dry.—*Bocc.***

Death, *morte;* does . . . itself, *non si lascia;* to be moved, *muovere; pietà;* (the) *bellezza;* (the) *fortezza;* (the) *nobiltà;* youth, (the) *giovanezza;* same scythe, *stessa falce;* to cut down, *segare;* green, *verde;* dry, *secco.*

8. **The beautiful lady, whom he loved so much, has lately departed from his* heart.**

Bello; donna; che; to love, *amare;* so much, *cotanto;* lately, *da ultimo;* (to him), *gli;* has (is), *è; partire;* from (the); heart, *cuore.*

9. **From his youth up to the present time, he was inflamed beyond measure with the* highest and most* noble love.—*Bocc.***

From (the); his, *sua;* youth, *giovanezza;* up to, *infino a; questo tempo;* beyond measure, *oltre modo;* he was; inflamed, *acceso;* with (by) highest, *altissimo; nobile;* love, *amore.*

10. **Andreuccio came from Perugia to Naples to buy horses.—*Gio. Vill.***

Came, *venne;* to (for); buy, *comperare;* horse, *cavallo.*

11. **And not without great fatigue I shall endeavour to extract from books, chronicles, and authors, the exploits and deeds of the Florentines.**

Without, *senza;* great, *grande; fatica;* (myself), *mi;* to endeavour, *provare;* to extract, *ritrarre;* book, *libro; cronaca; autore;* exploits, *gesto;* deed, *fatto; Fiorentino.*

Sentences of Poetry.

1. **"Montano, io mi dormiva in quelle grotte,**
E' n sulla mezzanotte,
Questi can mi destâr bajando al lupo;
Ond' io gridando, 'al lupo, al lupo, al lupo!
Pastor correte al lupo,' più non dormii."—*Sanaz.*

Oh, Montano, I was sleeping in those grottos, and at midnight these dogs woke me up, baying at the wolf; whereupon I crying out "wolf, wolf, wolf! shepherds ran after the wolf," slept no more.

2. **"E stilla il mel dagli elci, e dagli ulivi."**

And the honey drops from the ilex, and from the olives.

3. **"Pien d' un vago pensier, che mi disvia**
Da tutti gli altri."—*Petr.*

Full of a fanciful thought, which diverts me from all others.

4. "Come il gelo alle piante, ai fior l' arsura,
La grandine alle spiche, ai semi il verme,
Le reti ai cervi, ed agli augelli il visco,
Così nocivo all' uom fu sempre amore."

Guar. Pas. Fid.

As the frost to the plants, the heat to the flowers, the hail to the ears of corn, the worm to the seeds, the nets to the stags, the lime to the birds, so injurious to man has love always been.

CHAPTER VI.

The Adjective of Quality.

1. Italian adjectives may be divided into three classes, according to the different offices which they discharge, with respect to the nouns to which they belong.

2. If they modify the noun in quality, they are called qualificative; if they determine the quantity of the noun they may be called numeral; and if they modify the quantity in an indeterminate manner, they may be called indefinite, and pass through all gradations from totality to nullity. Adjectives of this class may also modify the noun through collocation, and in that case may be called indicative, and include always the idea of identity in their signification.

Each species of adjective is subject to its own rules.

3. The largest class is the qualificative, which includes all modifications of the substantive, that are accidental in their nature. We say accidental, because with regard to the necessary qualifications, called attributes, the substantive comprehends them in itself, without their being externally added; and if occasionally they are added, such adjectives are merely used figuratively or emphatically, and are employed most frequently in poetry, in order to render more vivid the idea conveyed by the word itself, as, *candido avorio*, white ivory;

la fiorita primavera, flowery spring; *l' ardente sole*, the burning sun.

4. Qualificative adjectives are formed after the same laws which regulate substantives. The only difference is that they are not subject to exceptions, but are invariably regular.

(*a*) If they are derived from the Latin, and have their termination in *o* in the masculine, they always make the feminine in *a*. If they are derived from adjectives having the form of nouns of the third declension, they adopt the common termination in *e*.

5. Adjectives have their form determined by their termination, and in the masculine always end in *o* or *e*. Thence, the application of the rules concerning the terminations of gender and number is exactly the same as that of nouns.

6. The English student must be carefully warned always to refer the adjective to the noun to which it belongs, and to give it the same gender and number. This is the more necessary, as English adjectives are in these respects immutable.

(*b*) Those who are acquainted with Latin are already accustomed to make the adjective agree with its substantive in gender and number.

7. Adjectives of quality, which are joined to two substantives in the singular, assume the plural number, although the singular may be used. If the substantives are of different genders, they adopt the masculine, as being the more worthy.

8. In the Italian language, the adjective may be placed either before or after the substantive. In English, on the contrary, it is placed before the substantive; in French, generally after it.

9. The adjective is generally used after the substantive, when the design of the adjective is to modify the form or condition of the substantive, which is thereby absolutely defined: as, for instance, *Le diedero per marito un uomo malvagio*, They have given her a wicked man for a husband.

Malvagio has in this sentence a distinct and decisive influence over the noun to which it belongs; and the most rustic speaker would, by a kind of natural instinct, place it after *uomo.* The words *che era,* who was, might be supposed to be understood. Take again this phrase: *Cavallo restio non fa buon servigio nè sotto il carretto nè sotto la carrozza,* A restive horse is of no use either for a cart or a carriage. *Restio* comes after *cavallo,* because it indicates a positive condition of *cavallo,* the horse—namely, that it does not perform any kind of service well. It could not be placed in any other position without weakening its decided signification, which includes the affirmation *ch' è restio,* that it is restive. Thus we write, *Il nemico corse il territorio Romano, e ne lo devastò tutto,* the enemy overran the Roman territory, and devastated it all. In this sentence, *Romano* comes after the noun, for the same reason.

10. The grammarians make use of other distinctions; but this appears to us the surest means of deciding in what cases the adjective should be placed after the noun. The same rule will explain these phrases, *dormire a ciel scoperto,* to sleep under the open sky; *tira un vento umido,* a moist breeze is rising; *scrivere a posta corrente,* to write by the next post.

11. When the adjective has merely an elegant or emphatic sense, and there is no direct necessity to couple it with the substantive, in order to give it a decisive sense, it may be placed before the substantive; as, for example:

> "Sonar per gli alti spaziosi tetti
> S' odono grida, e femminil lamenti:
> L' afflitte donne, percotendo i petti,
> Corron per casa pallide e dolenti,
> E abbraccian gli usci, e geniali letti,
> Che tosto hanno a lasciar a strane genti."—*Ariosto.*

Throughout the spacious houses were heard cries and lamentations of lofty females. The afflicted women beat their breasts, and pale and mournful run through their houses, and embrace the doors and the genial beds, which they have so soon to leave to strangers.

In these cases it would not be wrong to place the adjective after the noun; but to do so would be inelegant, and offensive to good taste.

12. As in Latin, and in other languages to a greater or less extent, the adjective is frequently used alone, without the substantive, in cases where the word *uomo*, man, may be understood: as, for instance, in these sentences:

Il giusto non permette che i mali esterni ed accidentali gli turbino l' animo.

The just man does not allow external and accidental evils to disturb his mind.

Praticate i buoni e fuggite i cattivi, se volete essere buoni voi stessi, e tenervi lontani da ogni malvagità.

Consult the good and avoid the wicked, if you wish to be good and to keep yourselves free from all wickedness.

Così per li gran savj si confessa
Che la Fenice muore, e poi rinasce.

Thus, by great sages it is avowed that the phœnix dies, and then is born again.

13. Since the adjectives *bello*, beautiful; *grande*, great; *buono*, good, occur often in daily life, it is desirable to note a peculiar abbreviation which they suffer when they are placed before the substantive. Under these circumstances *bel, gran, buon* are written, if the noun is masculine and would require the article *il* before it, as *bel giorno*, a fine day; *gran libro*, a great book; *buon re*, a good king. On the other hand, *bello, grande, buono*, are used if the natural article of the noun is *lo*, as *bello scritto*, a beautiful writing; *grande stato*, great rank; *buono scolare*, a good scholar. In the plural, *bei* or *begli* is used according to the same rule; but *buoni* is used in both cases. The feminine of *bello* makes *bell'*, if the noun commences with a vowel, as if the article *l'* were used; as *bell' anima*, beautiful soul: the same occurs with *bello* (mas.), if the following substantive begins with a vowel, as *bell' anello*, a beautiful ring. Both *grande* and *grandi* may be written *gran*, but the full form is preferable in the abovementioned cases.

Quello, that, is always subject to the same rule in this circumstance of its collocation, as *bello:* and, for the sake of analogy, *augello*, *uguale*, *anello*, *animale*, if not ending the sentence, are subject to the same rules as *bello* and *grande*. So we say, *augel canoro*, *animal grazioso*, *augello splendido*, *animale stupido*, *ugual parte*, *ugual riserbo*, *uguale scritto*, *uguali aspetti*, &c.

We may finally remark, that if adjectives of this kind follow the noun, they are then used without any abbreviation whatever.

EXAMPLES.

"Chè i be' vostr' occhi, donna, mi legaro."—*Petr.*

For your beautiful eyes, O lady, have taken me captive!

"Da duo' begli occhi, che legato m' hanno."—*Petr.*

From two beauteous eyes, which have taken me captive.

"Gittansi di quel lido ad una ad una
Per cenni come augel per suo richiamo."—*Inf.* 3.

At signals they throw themselves forward from that bank one by one, as birds do, by means of their decoying bird.

"Come gli augei che vernan verso il Nilo,
Alcuna volta di lor fanno schiera."—*Dante.*

As birds which go to winter at the Nile, sometimes they assemble in a large company.

Some adjectives govern the genitive, dative, or the ablative case; as, *abbondante di*, abounding in; *scarso di*, deficient in; *incapace di*, incapable of; *accetto a*, acceptable to; *disutile a*, useless for; *pronto a*, ready for; *alieno da*, averse from; *esule da*, banished from; *sicuro da*, secure from. On close observation, however, it will be found that all such adjectives are in reality dependent on the verb *essere*, understood, which gives a verbal sense to the adjective.

Adjectives of this kind must, therefore, be considered as verbal expressions, and subject to the government of the verb. On this account we will speak of them in our treatise on the Verbs, in which we intend to show that their influence over the genitive is merely apparent; and that the dative and ablative cases, when used with them, are of the same nature as when they are governed by verbs.

Exercises on the Adjectives.

1. Small teeth—but not too small—square, equal, in regular order, separated, white, and above all like ivory—and set off by the gums, which rather appear like a border of crimson than of red velvet, and connected together, and well set in them.—*Fir.*

Tooth, *dente;* small, *piccolo;* but, *ma;* not too small, *non minuto;* square, *quadro; eguale;* in* (with); regular, *bello; ordine; separato;* white, *candido; avorio;* like, *simile;* above all, *sopra tutto;* from (the) gums, *gengiva;* which, *che;* appear, *pajono;* like . . . crimson, *orlo di cremisino;* than, *che;* velvet, *velluto;* red, *rosso;* connected . . . them, *ornato, legato, rincalzato.*

2. The maker of an organ has not made all the pipes equal amongst themselves; but this one thin, that thick—that one sweet, that mute—that shrill, and that loud—that capable of receiving much wind, and that very small. He has in that proceeded with the* greatest skill, because exactly from such inequality results that harmony which would not be found amongst pipes of one note.

Maker, *fabbro; organo;* made, *fatto;* all, *tutto;* pipe, *canna;* amongst themselves, *fra di loro; eguale;* this one, *qual;* thin, *sottile;* that, *qual;* thick, *grosso;* that one, *qual;* sweet, *dolce;* that, *qual; muta;* that shrill, *stridula;* and that loud, *tonante;* that *capace;* of* (to) receiving, *ricevere;* much, *molto;* wind, *fiato;* that, *quale;* very small, *pochissimo;* He, *egli;* that, *ciò;* to proceed, *procedere;* with the greatest skill, *arte somma;* because, *perchè;* exactly, *appunto;* such, *tale; inegualità; risultare;* that, *quello; armonia;* which, *che;* would . . . found, *non si troverebbe;* amongst, *tra;* of one note, *unisono.*

3. It is desirable that* the mouth should be rather inclined to* being* small than great; and that the lips should not be very thin, nor yet excessively thick, but of such a kind that their vermilion may appear clearly* above the fleshwhich surrounds them.

It is desirable, *si desidera;* mouth, *bocca;* should . . . inclined, *piuttosto pendere;* (in the) small, *piccolo;* than, *che; grande;* and . . . be, *e non sieno;* lip, *labbro;* very thin, *molto, sottili;* nor yet, *nè anche;* excessively, *soverchio;* thick, *grosso;* but . . . that, *ma in guisa che;* (the) *vermiglio;* their, *loro;* may appear, *apparisca;* above, *sopra;* *lo incarnato;* them, *le;* to surround, *circondare.*

4. And her hair was curled, long, golden, and falling upon her* white and delicate shoulders.

(The) her hair, *suo capello* (pl.); curled, *crespo;* *lungo;* golden (of gold), *oro;* upon, *sopra;* (the) white, *candido;* *delicato;* shoulder, *omero;* to fall, *ricadere* (par. pre.).

Exercises in Reading.

1. " Deh mira (egli cantò) spuntar la rosa
Dal verde suo modesta e verginella;
Che mezzo aperta ancora e mezzo ascosa,
Quanto si mostra men, tanto è più bella:
Ecco poi nudo il sen, già baldanzosa,
Dispiega: ecco poi langue, e non par quella,
Quella non par che desiata avanti
Fu da mille donzelle, e mille amanti."

Tasso, Ger. Lib.

Lo! observe (he sang) the rose budding, modest, and like a virgin, from its green bed; which still half open and half shut, the less it shews itself, is so much the more beautiful. Behold, then, gay with its naked bosom it expands, and lo! then it fades, and does not appear that, which was before so much desired by a thousand damsels and a thousand lovers.

2. " Quasi ascosi avea gli occhi nella testa,
La faccia macra, e come un osso asciutta;
La chioma rabbuffata, orrida e mesta,
La barba folta, spaventosa e brutta.—*Arios.* Or. Fu.

He had the eyes, as it were, sunk in the head, the face meagre, and dry like a bone, the hair in disorder, horrid and tangled, the beard thick, frightful and wild.

We will now proceed to give a series of Exercises, which will include nouns in all their cases, and also adjectives which have relation to quality. In these Exercises, all the rules which have hitherto been laid down, will be brought into practice, and the examples given will be taken from the best authors.

General Exercises on the Nouns and Adjectives.

1. Aristotle says, magnanimity is the knowing how* to bear well prosperity and misfortune, and honor and ignominy; it is the not being astonished with the delights of a numerous* body* of clients, of power, of victories, and also having (inf.) greatness and superiority of mind.

Says, *dice;* (the) *magnanimità;* is, *si è;* the knowing, *sapere;* bear, *portar bene;* (the) prosperity, *felicità;* (the) misfortune, *disgrazia;* (the) *onore;* (the) *ignominia;* the not being astonished, *il non maravigliarsi;* delights, . . . victories; *delizia;* (of the) *clientela,* (of the) *podestà,* (of the) *vittoria;* also, *anzi;* greatness, *altezza;* *superiorità;* mind, *animo.*

2. Charity, as the sun of all heaven, is the beauty, and ornament, and clearness, and light of every other virtue.—*Bocc.*

Carità; as, *come;* sun, *sole;* all, *tutto;* (the) heaven, *cielo;* beauty . . light, *bellezza;* *ornamento;* *chiarezza;* *lume;* every, *ciascuno;* other, *altro;* *virtù.*

3. When either a comet or any* other new light has appeared in the air, most people having* turned to heaven, look to that quarter where that miraculous light shines.

When, *quando;* either, o; *cometa;* or o; *altro;* new, *nuovo;* light, *luce;* has appeared, *è apparita;* *aria;* most people, *il più della genti;* turned, *rivolto;* heaven, *cielo;* to look, *mirare;* to that quarter, *colà;* where, *dove;* that, *quel;* *maraviglioso;* light, *lume;* to shine, *risplendere.*

4. Cicero, in the "Brutus," said, that the beauty of the Greek style commenced with the Athenians, in the times of Thucydides and Pericles, inasmuch as before those two they wrote without ornaments. The first, however, who introduced in Rome style and elegant language were Marcus Cornelius Cethegus, and Cato the Censor, and then followed so many others. Our language still increases, and has not yet finished its course, as the Latin and Greek have done; nevertheless, to the present time, one may say that we have our Ciceros, our Demosthenes; since, Boccaccio, Casa, Passavanti, Bembo, Sperone, and some others, in our language, are not less elegant than what Cicero and Demosthenes were in Greek and Latin.—*Tassoni.*

Cicerone; *Bruto;* said, *disse;* that, *che;* *bellezza;* *stile;* *Greco;* to commence, *cominciare;* with the (from the); *Ateniese;* in the (to the); time, *tempo; Tucidide; Pericle;* inasmuch as, *imperrocchè;* before . . . wrote, *innanzi a questi due si scriveva;* without, *senza; ornamento;* first, *primo;* however, *poi;* who, *che; introdussero; Roma;* language, *favella elegante; Marco Cornelio Cetego; Catone Censorino;* then, *indi;* to follow, *seguire;* so many others, *tant' altri.* (The) *lingua;* our, *nostra;* still, *tuttavia;* to increase, *crescere;* to finish, *finire;* yet, *ancora;* (the) its, *suo; corso;* as, *come;* done, *fatto;* (the) *Latino; Greco* (f.); nevertheless, *nondimeno;* (it) *egli;* one, *si;* can, *può;* to . . . time, *finora;* say, *dire;* (the) our, *nostro; Cicerone* (pl.); *Demostene* (pl); since, *poichè;* less, *meno;* some, *alcuno;* other, *altro;* in our, *nella nostro; favella;* than that, *di quello che;* were (may be); in (the), &c.

5. To embrace the knees was, in ancient times, a* sign of reverence which was particularly made use of in supplication, as may be seen in Livy, Plutarch, and in Dionysius, where Valeria and the Roman matrons are represented prostrate as suppliants to Marcius Coriolanus. Thus, also*, in the "Odyssey," we have that Ulysses in no other manner offers his prayers to Arete, the* wife of Alcinous; and in the first and eighth book of the "Iliad," the same act is performed in heaven by Thetis to Jupiter.

To embrace, *abbracciar;* knees, *ginocchio;* in ancient times, *anticamente;* a * *segno; reverenza;* which, *che;* particularly, *singolarmente;* made use of, *usavasi; supplica;* as, *siccome;* may be seen, *può vedersi; Livio; Plutarco; Dionisio;* where, *ove;* are (were) represented, *rappresentavasi; matrona, Romana, prostrata; supplichevole; Marcio Coriolano;* thus, *così; Odissea;* that, *che; Ulisse;* no (not), *non;* other, *altro; maniera;* to offer, *offrire;* (the) his, *le sue; preghiera;* wife, *moglie; Alcinoo;* first, *primo;* eighth, *ottavo; Iliade;* the same, *stesso; atto;* is (comes), *viene;* performed, *prestato;* heaven, *cielo; Teti; Giove.*

6. This fresh flower, frail in its glory, which is called by us beauty, and so greatly ensnares minds with its allurements, O my sweet love! is like a blooming rose which, with the dawning light of day, expands smilingly its fragrant petals; but, lo! in a short time, it loses the beautiful purple of its head, it loses its fragrance and its elegant form, and at the close of day also falls cast down and useless.

This . . . flower, *questo giovanile fiore;* frail, *caduco;* its, *suo gloria;* which, *il quale;* by (among) us, *infra di noi;* is called, *si addomanda · beltà;* so greatly, *cotanto;* to ensnare, *invescare;* (the) mind, *animo;* with (the), *co';*

its, *suoi; allettamento;* o; o; sweet, *dolce;* love, *ben;* my (mine) *mio;* like, *simigliante;* blooming, *vermiglio;* . *rosa;* which, *che;* light, *luce;* day, *giorno;* dawning, *nascente;* to expand, *spiegare;* smilingly (smiling), *ridente;* (the); fragrant, *odorato;* its, *suo;* petals, *cespo;* but, *ma; ecco;* in . . . time, *in breve tratto;* to lose, *perdere; bello; porpora;* of (the); its, *suo;* head, *capo;* (the), *fragranza;* elegant form, *vaghezza;* its, *suo;* at the, *al;* close, *cader;* to fall, *cadere;* also, *ancor;* it, *essa;* cast down, *afflitto;* useless, *disutile.*

7. Good girls ought not to have either eyes, or ears, or tongues and this tale is told. There* had been prepared on the table the head of a kid. Then the father, joking with his daughter, took from the head the eyes, the ears, and the tongue; and having* drawn them to his own plate, said: "Good girls ought to have neither eyes, nor ears, nor a tongue:" then seizing his daughter suddenly, and drawing the brains on her plate, he added, "but the* brains, yes!"

Good, *buono;* girl, *fanciulla;* ought . . . have, *non hanno da avere;* either (neither), *nè;* eye, *occhio;* or (nor), *nè;* ear, *orecchio;* tongue, *lingua;* is told (one tells), *si narra;* this, *questo;* tale, *novella; preparare;* table, *mensa;* head, *testa;* of a (of the); kid, *capretto;* then, *allora;* father, *padre;* joking, *scherzando;* with (the) daughter, *figlia;* took, *prese;* from the (of it) head, *di essa testa;* drawn, *tratto;* to his own plate, *sul suo tondo;* said, *disse,* &c.; then, *quindi;* to seize, *pigliare* (ger.); suddenly, *subito;* brains, *cervello;* (he), *egli;* added; *soggiunse;* but, *ma;* yes, *sì.*

8. Gracefulness is nothing else than a silent law, given and impressed by Nature on you ladies, in motion, in* carriage, in the so adapting the whole person, as well as the separate members, with grace, modesty, and elegance; with measure, taste, and in such a manner that no one movement, no one action should be without rule, without manner, without measure or design.—*Firenzuola.*

Gracefulness, *leggiadria;* is . . . than, *non è altro; che;* silent, *tacito;* law, *legge;* given, *dato;* impressed, *promulgato;* by (the), *natura;* on (to) you, *voi;* woman, *donna;* in (the) motion, *muovere;* carriage, *portare;* in . . . adapting, *adoperare così;* whole, *tutto;* (the) *persona;* together, *insieme;* as well as, *come; membro;* separate, *particolare; grazia; modestia;* elegance, *gentilezza; misura;* taste, *garbo;* and . . . manner, *in guisa;* that no one, *che nessun; movimento; azione;* should be, *sia;* without, *senza regola; modo; misura; disegno.*

9. It is a* manifest thing that* human beauty is a frail flower.—*Bocc.*

Manifesto; thing, *cosa;* is; (the) *umano; bellezza; fiore;* frail, *caduco.*

3. At the foot of a holm-oak a goatherd was sitting, who playing delighted the herds.

At the, *a;* foot, *piè;* holmoak, *elce;* to be seated, *sedere;* goatherd, *caprajo;* who, *che;* to play, *suonare; dilettare;* herds, *mandra.*

10. They are to be detested who take advantage of the work of ministers, as they would make use of lemons. While they have any* juice and fragrance they hold them in estimation as well in the chamber on the* ebony tables, as on the sideboards in cups of silver. Then removed to the tables of the great, their rinds serve as an ornament for noble banquets, and their juice is welcome in the same manner as every spice which the remotest isles of the Moluccas and Ceylon transmit to us. The juice, then, having* been* squeezed out with all the* strength of the* fist, no one regards that fruit which was delicately handled by hands ornamented with jewels. Rejected by the appetite almost like a disgusting thing, it is thrown with the vilest sweepings into the dust-hole.—*Card. Corsini.*

They are, *sono;* to be, *da; detestarsi;* (those) *coloro;* who, *che;* to take advantage, *si approffitare;* works, *opera; ministro;* as, *come;* they . . . use, *si usa; limoncelli.* While, *fino a che;* they, *questi;* juice, *sugo; fraganza;* they . . . estimation, *si tengono in pregio;* as well, *sì; camera;* tables, *tavolino;* (of) *ebano;* as, *come;* sideboards, *credenza;* cup, *bacino;* silver, *argento;* then, *indi;* to remove, *transportare; tavola;* of the great, (lordly), *signorile;* to serve, *servire;* (the) their *loro;* rinds, *scorza;* as an (for), *per; ornamento;* for (of) *nobile;* banquet, *imbandigione;* (the) their; welcome, *gradito;* in the . . . as, *quanto;* every, *ogni;* spice, *condimento;* to us, *a noi;* to transmit, *tramandare* (subj.); island, *isola; rimotissima; Molucche;* Ceylon, *Zeilan.* To squeeze out, *premere;* then, *poi;* juice, *liquore;* with the (to) all, *tutto;* strength, *forza;* fist, *pugno;* no one, *niuno;* then (more), *più; riguardare;* that, *quel;* fruit, *pomo;* which, *che;* delicately, *gentilmente;* to handle, *trattare;* hand, *mano;* to ornament, &c., *ingiojellare;* rejected . . . thing, *e quasi abbominevole rifiuto dell' appetito;* it is thrown, *si getta;* sweepings, *spazzatura; più vile;* into the; dusthole, *mondezzari.*

Reading of Poetry.

1. " Giace l' alta Cartago; appena i segni
Dell' alte sue rüine il lido serba:
Mu*o*iono le città, mu*o*iono i regni;
C*o*pre i fastí e le pompe arena ed erba:
E l' u*o*m d' esser mortal par che si sdegni.
*O*h n*o*stra mente cupida e superba!"

Tasso, Ger. Lib., Can. xv., 20.

Lofty Carthage is fallen, and scarcely does the shore preserve signs of her famous ruins. Cities perish, kingdoms perish, the sand and grass cover the parade and pomps of them : and it appears that man disdains to be mortal. O our covetous and proud mind!

2. " Sì, e n*o*, nel capo mi tenzona."—*Dante.*

Yes, and no, dispute in my head.

3. " E veggio il meglio, ed al peggior m' appiglio."—*Petr.*

I see what is best, and I follow what is worst.

4. " Lei nel partir, lei nel tornar del sole,
Chiama con voce stanca, e prega, e plora."—*Tasso.*

At the setting and at the return of the sun, he calls upon her with an exhausted voice, and prays, and weeps.

5. La verginella è simile alla rosa,
Che 'n bel giardin sulla nativa spina,
Mentre sola e sicura si riposa,
Nè' gregge nè' pastor se le avvicina;
L' aura soave, e l' alba rugiadosa,
L' acqua e la terra al suo favor s' inchina:
Giovani vaghi, e d*o*nne innamorate
Amano averne e seno e tempie ornate.

Arios. Orl. Fur.

The virgin is like the rose, which, when in a beautiful garden on its native thorns, all alone it reposes in security, neither flocks nor shepherds approach it. The sweet air and the dewy dawn, the water and the earth, pay homage to it. Youths in love and enamoured ladies delight to have their bosoms and temples adorned with them.

6. O Primavera, gioventù dell' anno,
Bella madre de' fiori,
D' erbe novelle e di novelli amori.—*Guarini.*

Oh, Spring! youth of the year, beautiful mother of flowers, of tender herbs, and of fresh loves.

7. Vaghe ninfe del Po, ninfe sorelle,
E voi di boschi, e voi, d' onde marine,
E voi de' fonti, e dell' alpestri cime.—*Tasso.*

Ye elegant nymphs of the Po, ye sister nymphs, and ye of the woods, and ye of the waves of the sea, and ye of the fountains, and of the wild mountain tops.

Il Cavallo.

8. Grande il Cavallo, e di misura adorna
Esser tutto devria quadrato e lungo:
Levato il collo, e dove al petto aggiunge,
Ricco e formoso, e s' assottiglie in alto;
Sia breve il capo, s' assimiglie al serpe;
Corte l' acute orecchie, e largo e piano
Sia l' occhio, e lieto, e non intorno cavo;
Grandi, e gonfiate le fumose nari;
Sia squarciata la bocca, e raro il crino;
Doppio, eguale, spianato, e dritto il dorso;
L' ampia groppa spaziosa; il petto aperto:
Ben carnoso le coscie, e stretto il ventre;
Sian nervose le gambe, asciutte e grosse;
Alta l' unghia, sonante, cava, e dura;
Corto il tallon, che non si pieghi a terra;
Sia rotondo il ginocchio, e sia la coda
Larga crespa setosa, e giunta all' anche.

Alam. Colt.

The Horse.

The horse should be large and well proportioned, square built and long, the neck raised, and where it joins the chest, full and graceful, and diminishing above; the head should be small, and like that of a serpent; short the ears and pointed; the eye should be full and gentle, and bright, and not hollow within; large and distended the panting nostrils, the mouth should be wide, the mane fine, the back broad and even, flat and straight, the haunches large, the chest open, the thighs well covered with flesh, the stomach flat; the legs should be sinewy, wiry and large, the hoof high and sonorous, hollow and hard; the heel short, so that it should not touch the earth; the knee should be round, and the tail full and crisp, hairy, and well set on the haunches.

CHAPTER VII.—Section I.

The Augmentative and Diminutive Forms.

1. If anyone were to ask what adjectives were most generally used in every condition of life or phase of progress, either individual or national, we should not hesitate to mention at once the words *grande*, great; *piccolo*, little. Should it be enquired again what adjectives occupied in this respect the second rank, we should answer *bello*, beautiful, and *brutto*, ugly; and after these, *buono*, good, and *cattivo*, bad. And in so doing we should be quite right, as what is more interesting to the human race, and employed in a broader sense, either physical or moral, than extension, form, or excellence? Are not things of the humblest, as well as of the most elevated nature, usually especially subject to the conditions of greatness or littleness, or beauty or ugliness, or goodness or badness, qualities which are applicable in all kinds of cases, to all sorts of persons or things, and at all times?

2. Since it is acknowledged that adjectives are modifications of substantives, we may easily imagine that there are substantives which assume a new form when a new attribute is applied to them. If this occurred very often, we should have an enormous increase of nouns, with a proportionate diminution of adjectives. The study of any language would thus be impossible, as it would be necssary that the whole of human life should be devoted to its acquirement. Adjectives, therefore, prevent the necessity for employing an inordinate number of substantives.

3. If, however, general fixed forms can be given to nouns in place of adjectives, so often repeated, as *grande, piccolo, buono, cattivo, bello,* and *brutto*, it would certainly be very advantageous to employ them, in order to avoid the annoyingly frequent repetition of these adjectives. By adopting

this course, the language would most certainly acquire fresh spirit and vigour.

4. Every language has a tendency to supersede some of these generic adjectives by adopting, in place of them, some variation of the noun. But although this is the case with all languages, the Italian tongue alone has full possession of the advantage of being able to dispense with them, by a method sufficiently regular in itself and consistent with energy and propriety of style. This is effected by adding certain syllables to nouns, which thus acquire a new signification, borrowed from the adjectives which are suppressed, or rather expelled, by means of these intrusive syllables.

5. We purpose to give a full account of the theoretical formation of these augmentatives and diminutives, which, as we have before remarked, are the exclusive possession of the Italian language—that is to say, in their full abundance, usefulness, and regularity. This will be followed by copious exercises, in order that a foreigner may be able fully to enter into their spirit. The grammarians have, up to the present time (we know not for what reason), treated this subject very superficially.

6. When a man wishes to give a more than ordinary idea of greatness or extension to a substantive, he makes use of the termination *one*: as will be seen in the following sentences:—

Quell' avarone ha paura ch' io nol richiegga di qualche cosa.

That great miser is afraid that I should ask something of him.

Ho procacciato un cappellone grande alla Spagnuola, e stivaloni grossi da cavalcare.

I have procured a very large Spanish hat and very large riding boots.

7. After this change, the gender is usually masculine even in cases where it was originally feminine; for this reason, that the application of the augment is presumed to diminish grace; but, on the other hand, to increase vigour—grace

being usually indicated by the feminine gender, and vigour by the masculine: as in these examples :—

"Cospetto, che tu sei un bel donnone.—*Berni.*"

By Jove! what a fine large woman thou art!

Colui avea un vocione che spaventava tutti i fanciulli che l' udivano.

That man had a rough voice, which frightened all the children that heard him.

It is not, however, unusual for feminine nouns to retain their gender; but this is considered to be done with less propriety. Under these circumstances, their termination is changed into *ona:* as, for example,

Codeste dottoresse hanno certe parolone in bocca da far basire, chiunque le intende.

These doctresses are wont to utter certain big words, to the amazement of whoever listens to them.

8. The adjective occasionally assumes the augmented termination in *one,* by way of inelegant exaggeration. This, however, only occurs in a low style of composition. In these cases, when the adjective is applied to feminine substantives, it assumes the feminine termination *ona*: as appears in this sentence—

Colui è un riccone, ma è uno spilorcio esoso, e la moglie sua non è meno avarona di lui, ed è di più una insopportabile brontolona.

That man is very rich, but he is a hateful miser, and his wife is not less covetous than himself. She is, moreover, an unbearable grumbler.

9. Should this augment be intended to convey the idea of ugliness, or any bad quality, the terminations *accio* and *accia* are used—the noun, of course, preserving its original gender.

EXAMPLES.

Il detto ribaldone con quella sua vociaccia ch' ei suonava per quel suo nasaccio, disse.—*Bem., Lett.*

The before-mentioned great rascal, with that loud and harsh voice of his, which sounded through that big nose of his, said.

Egli avea fatto un poema che poteva simigliarsi veramente ad un gran campo ripieno di molte erbaccie.

He had made a poem, which might in truth be likened to a great field full of many weeds.

Colui è un tale omaccio che non sa dir parola senza provocare chi l' ascolta.

He is such a disagreeable man that he cannot say a word without provoking every one who listens to him.

10. When it is wished to give an idea of littleness or grace, or when we desire to diminish the intensity or force of an adjective (which cannot be done without conveying an idea either of grace and elegancy, or of pettiness and insufficiency,) the termination *ino* and *etto* are used, frequently in nouns, and more rarely in adjectives.

EXAMPLES.

" L' arco ripiglia il fanciullin di Venere,
Che di ferir non è mai stanco e sazio."—*Sanaz.*

The little child of Venus, who is never wearied, and satisfied with striking, again takes up his bow.

" E ben mille
Zampilletti spruzzar l' erba di stille."—*Tasso.*

A thousand little streamlets sprinkled the grass with drops.

11. Some substantives and adjectives end in *otto* and *otta*, *occio* and *occia*. These participate equally in the nature of the augmentative and diminutive: indicating not so much an absolute increase in greatness, as a kind of mean point between the great and little, but inclining rather to the great. Words ending in *otto* and *otta* often include the idea of a more than slight degree of vigour, and even greatness, and beauty; the idea of grace, however, being excluded, as in these words, *giovanotto*, a youngster; *contadinotto*, a lusty young countryman. They sometimes incline to the diminutive idea: as *signorotto*, *acquilotto*, a young eagle; *leprotto*, a young hare; and these have to a certain extent a depreciating meaning.

EXAMPLES.

Non veggo a buono spazio comparir per di quì fuor della porta nessuno, se non che due giovanotti cittadini.

I do not see out of doors for a good distance any one coming this way, except two youngsters of the city.

Deh, guata là, come l' è belloccia oggi questa Tonia.—*Fir.*

Oh, look there! how charmingly blooming is to-day that Tonia of ours.

12. *Uccio, uccia, uzzo, uzza,* convey an idea of depreciation, as *tisicuzzo,* a poor man with a consumptive air; *omuccio,* an insignificant man; *capelluccio,* a common little hat; *casuccia,* a poor little house. This idea, however, is not in all these cases intended to be given by the diminutive signification; or, at any rate, it is moderated, especially if these terminations are employed with proper names of persons; in which case they have something endearing rather than otherwise: as, *Andreuccio, Mariannuccia.*

EXAMPLES.

Una donnuccia, che non ha persona in casa, e si guadagna la vita a filare.

A poor humble little woman, who has no one in the house and gains her bread by spinning.

Una boccuccia piccolina, le cui labbra chiudono due rubinetti.—*Bocc.*

A pretty little mouth, the lips of which enclose two little rubies.

"E ben ver che una donna sì divina
Non istà bene in bocca ad un par mio,
Che sono un poetuzzo da dozzina."—*Casa.*

It is very true that a woman so divine is not fitted for the lips of one like me, who am a very poor poet to be bought by the dozen.

Un certo bel giovane, nel cui bel volto appena appariva alcun segnuzzo di pelo.—*Firen.*

A certain fine young man, on whose handsome countenance scarcely appeared any slightest traces of a beard.

13. If the diminutive forms, when regarded as terms of endearment, are used for the purpose of conveying the idea of littleness, with some exclusion of grace, they often end in

ello and *ella*, which, however, may have the same signification as *etto* and *etta*.

EXAMPLES.

"Con quel furore, e con quella tempesta,
Ch' escono i cani incontro al poverello."—*Dante.*

With that fury and that rage with which dogs rush out against the poor little beggar.

Feminella che torcendo il fuso si guadagnava il pane.

A poor humble woman who, by turning the spindle, miserably gained her bread.

"Levata era a filar la vecchierella,
Discinta e scalza, e desto avea il carbone."—*Petr.*

The little old woman had risen to spin, ungirt and barefooted, and had lighted the coal.

"Vedi l' erbetta, i fiori, e gli arboscelli,
Che quella terra sol da se produce."—*Dante.*

Behold the slender grass, the flowers, and the little shrubs, which that land produces of itself.

Section II.

Other Remarks upon the Augmentatives & Diminutives.

14. Having previously observed that some diminutive forms are used in a favorable sense, and others in a contrary manner, we now desire to give some rules, which may assist the student in discovering in which way they are used. After some reflection we find that the difference of meaning originates in the nature of the objects themselves. Some nouns have in their own nature a certain force and grandeur, and therefore cannot assume the diminutive form without a certain loss of dignity, as *ometto, omino, omuccio, saccentuzzo, medicuccio, poetuzzo,* &c. These are terms of depreciation, as they imply a certain degree of diminution of their original excellence, which consists in moral and intellectual force. On the other hand, there are nouns which in their very nature convey an idea of littleness or grace. These are used by

way of endearment: as, from *donna*, a lady, are derived *donnina, donnetta* (which last word is also used in a depreciating manner); from *ragazza*, a girl, *ragazzina* and *ragazzetta*, &c. This rule we consider to be of general application, although we do not assert that it is invariably correct.

15. Words ending in *astro*, convey an idea of depreciation; but not to so great an extent as those ending in *accio* and *accia*. They are used chiefly in a moral sense; as, *medicastro, poetastro.*

EXAMPLE.

Mi noja meno il raglio d' un somaro, che i versacci d' un poetastro.

The braying of a donkey annoys me less than the bad verses of a wretched poet.

16. *Aglia* is used as a term of depreciation, and is applied in a comprehensive sense to bodies of men: as, *soldataglia*, a troop of bad soldiers; *ragazzaglia*, a crowd of urchins; *sbirraglia*, number of hirelings; *marmaglia*, the mob.

EXAMPLE.

Quel brigante accogliea rubatori e soldataglia, e con essi correa il paese d' intorno e ne lo devastava.

That brigand received robbers and the refuse of soldiers, and with them overran the surrounding country, and laid it waste.

Ame conveys the same meaning, but with less intensity, as *gentame*, rabble; and is used occasionally in an impersonal sense, as *carcame*, a carcase; *ossame*, a heap of bones.

17. There are also other expressions of a still more special nature, which are applied to individuals on account of some personal peculiarity, or to the members of different professions, or are used in sundry other ways. Of these there are countless variations, which represent in a lively manner the idea intended to be given. Although we do not mean to descend to minute particularity, we shall, notwithstanding, devote some further space to a subject which is in itself so important,

and also so essentially necessary for the acquirement of a proper knowledge of the Italian language.

18. No rule, however, can always be applied to these various terminations, of which each possesses its own shade of meaning. From *giallo*, yellow, we have *giallone*, *gialliccio*, *gialluccio*, *giallastro*, *giallògnolo*; from *nero*, dark, *nericcio*, *nerastro*; from *bianco*, white, *bianchiccio*, *biancastro*; from *rosso*, red, *rossigno*, *rossiccio*, *rossastro*, *rossetto*. These appear to be formed with a certain degree of regularity; but what can we say for the following words?—From *buco*, a cavity, are formed *bugigatto* and *bugigattolo*; from *triste*, *tristanzuolo*; and from *bello*, *bellone*, *bellino*, *belloccio*, *belluccio*. In like manner, from the adverb *bene*, well, are formed *benone*, *benino*; and from *poco*, little, *pochetto*, *pochino*, *pocolino*, *pochettino*, and so on. We will now give a few explanations, in order to show the great variety of these words. *Giallone* gives the idea of a diseased and unhealthy complexion, and is applied especially to women: as, for example, *Ella è giallona come un arancio*, she is as yellow as an orange. How can we find for this word any precise equivalent?

Gialliccio is a colour of a rather undefined nature, and indicates rather a tendency than any definite tint. The same thing occurs with *rossiccio*, *bianchiccio*, *nericcio*, the meaning of which can be rendered to some extent by the English termination *ish*—as, yellowish, whitish, reddish. There comes, however, *giallognolo*, which is a kind of diminutive of *gialliccio*; and what English word will convey a faint modification of the term yellowish? How, too, shall we translate *giallastro*, which denotes a diffusion of the colour *giallo*, yellow; less intense, perhaps, but still more unpleasing, as is expressed in this sentence:—*L' itterizia dà un color giallastro alla pelle, che funesta l' animo del riguardante.* The jaundice imparts to the skin a livid yellow, which horrifies the spirit of any one who beholds it. Or how again shall we express in English the words *nerastro*, *biancastro*, and *rossastro*, all of which are augmentatives of depreciation, and denote, by means of the termination *astro*, an indefinite yet heightened shade of colour, which is very displeasing to the eye. *Buco*, a hole, makes *bugigatto*, a lurking-place—something more inconvenient than an ordinary hole; and *bugigattolo*, the second diminutive, is applied to the most miserable hovels. *Triste* again, which often signifies badness, is also used in the sense unsightly, with regard to a person of melancholy appearance. But how shall we interpret *tristanzuol*, the diminutive of *triste*, which denotes anyone of a sickly aspect? as, for instance, in Boccaccio, who in one of his novels compassionately describes a wretched and sickly-looking newly-married old man, by using these words, *tristanzuol tisicuzzo*. We might continue for a long time our description of the different augmentative and diminutive terminations; but in so doing, we should far exceed the limits we have allotted to our present Grammar. In the Exercises will be found everything which is needful on this subject.

(*a*) As we formerly announced that it was our design in this work, to subject to definite rules the affinities between the Latin and Italian languages, the English student may perhaps be surprised that we have not attempted to draw any comparison between Latin and Italian nouns of this description.

This has been done, however, designedly. There is usually a kind of general resemblance between the Latin and Italian forms, but with regard to the diminutives this is not the case. The spirit of the Latin diminutives is of such a different character, and the resemblances are so subtle, that to trace them out would be rather the work of philology than of Grammar. We will, however, endeavour to draw a parallel to some extent between Latin and Italian augmentative and diminutive nouns.

(*b*) The Romans possessed no augmentative, the form *one* having no equivalent in Latin. This termination has, it is true, in Latin, to a certain extent, the power of giving an idea of increased magnitude. Thus, *capito, onis*, one who has a large head; *fronto, onis*, one with a broad forehead; and *pedo, pedonis*, one who has a broad foot; bear a strong resemblance to the Italian augmentative, although they cannot be considered precisely the same; and they are so few and unusual, that it is not worth while to notice them, as the source of our augmentatives.

It is, however, very probable that the Italian *one* has for its original type, the Latin form of nouns in *o*, *onis*, which, when applied to men, conveys naturally in most cases a sense of depreciation, although this bad meaning is only in a few cases given by the Italian *one*. Take as examples, *combibo, onis*, a pot companion; *balatro, onis*, a pitiful fellow, a babbler; *calcitro, onis*, a kicker; *ganeo, onis*, a debauchee; *helluo, onis*, a gormandizer; and other nouns, which in the ablative case end in *one*.

(*c*) This Latin termination, used both in an inelegant and disgusting sense, suggested the Italian termination *one*, which retained the idea of magnitude, but discarded that of contempt. The Latin termination in *o, onis*, is chiefly used in a depreciatory sense, as is proved by many words, and among others by the term *mango, onis*, not preserved in Italian, which is defined to mean one who trims and paints things, horses, and even boys and girls, pampering them to set them off, and sell them the dearer. This word has given rise to the verb, odious if applicable to human beings, *mangonizo*.

(*d*) The Italian does not preserve the bad sense of the termination *one*, for this reason, viz.: that on account of the flexibility of its form, and facility of its articulation, it was easy to invent an *onomatopœic* sound, which should convey the idea desired; and this was accordingly done, by adopting the termination *accio*.

(*e*) We have in Latin no example of any approximation to the termination *accio*, unless we take the word *homuncio, onis*, a little man, as an instance. This word resembles clearly the Italian *omaccio* and *omaccione*, which seem to have been derived from the Latin in two different ways, the first word being taken from the Latin nominative, and the second from the Latin ablative. The same thing happens with the Italian words, *ladro, ladrone*, which are equivalent to the Latin *latro*, a robber; and are derived respectively from its nominative and ablative case.

(*f*) *Uccio* is an onomatopœic sound, which finds no parallel in Latin, unless we consider that *capitium, ii*, a covering for the head, which in Italian is changed into *cappuccio*, may be an instance. We do not, however, consider that a solitary example of this kind, which is also somewhat irregular in form, can be sufficient to establish a rule; for even *armenticius*, belonging to the herd, has a slight resemblance to *bianchiccio*, whitish; *arsiccio*, rather dry; and notwithstanding, the one word has decidedly nothing in common with the others.

(*g*) We have no doubt that these forms are indigenous; and that, in the Tuscan dialect especially, they may be considered to be the remains of the old Etruscan language. It is also, we consider, quite certain, that the termination *ino*, when used in an endearing sense, is Etruscan, and by no means Latin, for in the latter tongue the termination *inus* expresses only a relation of kind, as, *anserinus*, of the goose kind; *leoninus*, leonine, or of the lion kind.

(*h*) In the Etruscan tables, in fact, we find among the few words which have come down to us, enveloped in mystery, that in the mortuary epitaphs of young girls, the termination *ina* is used, and there can be no doubt, as Lanzi observes, that it is used as a form of termination, which is expressive of endearment from parents towards young daughters. This discovery induces us to push our hypothesis still further, and to assert that *ino, ina*, is probably an Etruscan diminutive, which has come to us through the Tuscan dialect, and has finally become an appurtenance of the Italian language. No class of nouns, moreover, seems to be more subject to every kind of modification, whether augmentative or diminutive, endearing or abusive, than the proper names of women. This is a peculiarity of the Tuscan dialect, which has been imparted to the rest of Italy. *Catterina*, Catherine, is perhaps naturally a diminutive, but to how many alterations of every kind has this name been subject? We have *Catterina, Cattarinetta, Cattarinella, Cattarinuccia*, and also *Cattarinona, Cattarinaccia*. From *Elisabetta*, Elizabeth, we have *Betta, Bettina, Bettinuccia, Bettinella, Bettinona, Bettinaccia*, and so on. If the names of women, which have in themselves a tendency in every language to endearing modifications, are subject to such numerous changes in Italian, (and it can at the same time be proved that the termination *ina* has a positively Etruscan derivation), may we not infer that many of these verbal modifications are in reality of the remotest Etruscan origin?

(*i*) In conclusion, we may observe that many of the special and secondary Italian diminutives are derived from the Latin, and are in fact almost identical. Thus *ello* is a Latin diminutive: a the Latin *asellus*, a little ass, is in Italian, *asinello;* the Latin *fenestella*, a little window, is in Italian, *fenestrella*. This termination is often turned into *etta*, as *fabella*, a fable, *favoletta;* *lamella*, a little thin plate of metal, *laminetta*; also from *ulus*, *ula*, a termination not used in Italian, we have *herbula*, a little herb, *erbetta; casula*, a little cottage, *casetta; flammula*, a little flame, *fiammella; frigidulus*, somewhat cold, *freschetto; latrunculus*, a robber, *ladroncello; paginula*, a small page, *paginetta*. A termination derived from *ulus* is occasionally preserved in Italian, as *pellicula*, a little skin, *pulviscolo*, in Latin, *pulvisculus*, small dust; *minuscolo*, *majuscolo*, from the Latin *minusculus*, *majusculus*.

(*l*) *Olus* (fem. *ola*) is not retained as a diminutive, but is adopted as a common form: for example, *figliuolo*, *figliuola*, have the same meaning as *figlio*, a son; *figlia*, a daughter; and *figliuoletto*, *figliuoletta* are the proper diminutives—or rather *caro figliuolo*, *cara figliuola*. The same thing occurs with *capriola*, which does not mean the same as the Latin *capreola*, but *caprea* and *capreola* would be *capretta*.

18. We may also note a peculiarity of the Italian language, which tends to make it more elegant. The names of the smallest and most beautiful birds have naturally a diminutive termination: as, *cardellino*, a goldfinch; *fringuello*, a chaffinch; *usignuolo* or *rosignuolo*, a nightingale, (in Latin *luscinia* and *lusciniola*,) which is also written *usignuoletto*. Here we give an example:—

> "Mal può durare il rosignuolo in gabbia,
> Più vi sta il cardellino e più il fanello,
> La rondine in un dì vi muor di rabbia."—*Arios. Sat.*

With difficulty can the nightingale live in a cage; the goldfinch remains there more easily, and still more the linnet; the swallow in one day would die there of rage.

19. From the natural genius of the augmentatives and diminutives, it is sufficiently clear that most of them are applied to the human race, and in the second place to domestic animals, and then to things which have certain relations with man. They are also commonly used with adjectives, which denote moral qualities which especially belong to mankind: *carina*, little dear; *graziosetta*, a little graceful thing; *dispettosetta*, a little rather peevish thing.

(*m*) In Italian these expressions are more useful than in Latin, as well as more numerous, since the Latin diminutives are more indefinite and arbitrary.

20. These terminations give great additional spirit to comic and satiric writings. The words which are naturally most subject to these modifications are *uomo*, man, and *donna*, woman; and these may be said to convey an idea of moral judgment, coupled with a simple physical signification.

From *uomo* we have *omenone, omaccio, omuccio, ometto, omino, omicino, omiciatto, omiciattolo*, and also perhaps *omuncolo*.

From *donna, donnòne, donnona, donnaccia, donnina, donnuccia, donnetta, donnettina*.

21. The diminutives in *otto* and *uccio* have the same restriction as *one*, and are never used in any works which are written in a grave style; but at times, in burlesque poetry, as well as in light or humorous prose. In serious poetry and grave prose, *etto* and *etta* are used: at times, but not so often, *ello* and *ella*; and *uzzo* and *uzza* are very rarely found, and instead of the augmentatives, the corresponding adjectives, when required, are resorted to and joined to the substantive.

22. Some adverbs of qualification are liable to all these modifications: as, from *bene*, well, *benone, benino*; from *poco*, little, *pochino, pochetto, pochettino*.

23. We shall finally conclude our theory of the Augmentatives and Diminutives with the following rules:—

It sometimes happens that augmentatives may be doubled: as, *omaccione, omenone,* in order to give a greater degree of energy, either in a good or a bad sense, to the noun: as from *uomo, omone, omenone,* which last term means a man who is fit for anything, as he is big in body and has large brains. *Omaccione,* from *omaccio,* on the contrary, means a downright insufferable, brutal, huge man.

In the same manner, the diminutives are doubled in a pleasing sense: as, *fiorellino* (from *fiore, fioretto*), a very small and pretty flower; *cosettina,* a very small and indifferent thing, to be understood in a good sense, as if it were modestly qualified by the person who presents it.

EXAMPLES.

La prego di accettare questa cosettina.

I entreat you to accept this small present.

Ho una cosettina da dirvi.

I have a very little thing to tell you.

We have pursued our favourite subject so far, that we have almost transgressed the limits of this Grammar. We, however, did not desire to shorten this chapter, for two reasons: firstly, on account of the importance of the subject (which will be even more clearly displayed in the following exercises); and secondly, because grammarians have devoted very little attention to the matter.

Exercises on the Augmentatives and Diminutives.

1. And he was seen before all the others, without arms, on a very large horse.

To see, *vedere;* before (to), *avanti a;* all, *tutto;* other, *altro;* *arma;* *grosso;* horse, *cavallo* (*one* aug.)

2. Their poetry was full of compound and long words, called by the Latins "*sesquipedalia*" (a foot and a half long), and by us, by chance, big words.

(The) their, *loro;* *poesia;* full, *pieno;* word, *parola;* *composto;* *lungo;*

to call, *chiamare*; *Latino*; *sesquipedali*; us, *noi*; at hazard, *per avventura*; word, *parola* (aug. *one*).

3. I made him jump like a young stag.

Him, *lo*; made, *faceva*; jump, *saltare*; like, *come*; stag, *cervo* (ending in *iatto* for young).

4. That quack carried the sentence of death every time that he entered into the chamber of the sick, and signed it in his prescriptions.

That, *quel*; quack, *medico* (pej. *astro*); to carry, *portare*; *sentenza*; death, *morte*; every, *ogni*; time, *volta*; that, *che*; to enter into, *entrare in*; *camera*; sick, *ammalato*; to sign, *firmare*; in (the) his, *suo*; prescription, *ricetta*.

5. We are little less than altogether a great handful of insipid great blockheads.

Little less, *poco meno*; than, *che*; altogether, *tuttiquanti*; great (fine), *bello*; handful, *mano*; insipid, *sciocco*; blockhead, *ignorante* (*one*).

6. These miserable wretches were plunged to the* throat in a deep bog, from which they could not extricate themselves by all the force they could exert.

Were plunged, *si profondarono*; these . . . wretches, *que' misero*; throat, *gola*; bog, *pantàno*, (for deep, make the word *pantàno* end in *accio*); from . . . not, *da cui non veniva lor fatto*; by . . . exert, *per isforzi che facessero*; extricate themselves, *cavarsi*.

7. The steersman of the ship, taking it easy at the stern, does a work by far more important than all that well-nerved rabble.

Steersman, *Governatore*; ship, *nave*; taking it easy, *adagiarsi*; at the stern, *poppa*; does, *fa*; work, *opera*; by far, *di gran lunga*; more, *più*; important, *fruttuosa*; than, *di*; well nerved, *nerboruto*; rabble, *ciurmaglia*.

8. It will be necessary that she confess this thing, in spite of her most stubborn will.

It . . . necessary, *bisognerà*; to confess (pres. subj.) *confessare*; in spite . . . will, *a suo marcio dispetto* (ending in *accio*).

9. Begone! get into the house, chatterbox, and take care not to talk with any one.

Begone, *orsù*; get . . . house, *vàttene in casa*; chatterbox, *cicalaccia*; take . . . talk, *e fa che non favelli*; any one, *persona*.

10. The inhabitants of marshy places eat little; they* are an* ill-favoured, ill-conditioned people, and of a* bad disposition.

Abitante; marshy, *palustre*; place, *sito*; to eat, *mangiare*; *poco*; ill-favored, *brutto*; people, *gente* (for ill-conditioned, *ame*, the pej. of *gente*); bad, *mala*; disposition, *natura*.

11. And above about a hundred steps, there is a receptacle where bones are placed.

And above, *e più su*; about a, *da*; hundred, *cento*; step, *passo*; there, *vi*; receptacle, *ripostiglio*; where, *dove*; are placed, *si pone*; (the) bones; *osso* (end in *ame*).

12. The drunkard becomes a very bloated, despicable man, of rough manners and a disgusting countenance.

Drunkard, *bevitore*; to become, *diventare*; a very . . . man, *uomo* (make *omaccione*); rough, *rozzo*; *maniera*; countenance, *aspetto*; *disgustoso*.

13. He is such a disagreeable man, that he cannot say a word withont provoking (inf.) him that listens to him.

He, *colui*; a; such, *tale*; man, *uomo* (end it in *accio*); that . . . without, *che non sa dir parola senza*; to provoke, *provocare*; him that, *chi*; to him, *lo*; to listen, *ascoltare*.

14. Not only the insignificant fellows, but also those who pretend to learning, are liable to make many mistakes.

Not only, *non solo*; *uomo* (make *omiciattolo*); also, *anco*; those . . . learning, *barbassori*; liable, *soggetto*; *a far*; mistake, *sciocchezza*; many, *assai*.

15. However, he had in himself, although he was avaricious, some faint sparks of gentility.

However, *pure*; in himself, *in se*; although, *quantunque*; *avaro*; he was, *fosse*; some, *alcuna*; *favilla*, spark (for faint, give the end in *uzza*); *gentilezza*.

16. Within that cloth were gracefully depicted some tiny animals after the Greek custom.

Within, *dentro*; (to) that, *quel*; cloth, *drappo*; some, *alcuno*; animal, *animale* (end in *uzzo*); after, *secondo*; *costume*; *Greco*; gracefully, *vagamente*; *dipinto*; (there) *v'*; were, (had) *avea*.

17. A mouth with a graceful outline of a pretty rosy tint.

Graceful, *grazioso*; outline, *rilievo*; of a . . . tint, *vermiglia* (dim. *uzza*).

18. A streamlet which flowed down over rocks of hard stone.

Stream, *fiume* (*dim. icello*); which, *il quale*; flowed, *andava in giro*; over (for) rock, *balza*; stone, *pietra*; hard, *viva*.

19. She, to ensnare him, sometimes looked at him, uttering at* times* low touching sighs.

She, *ella;* to (for) ensnare him, *per uccellarlo;* sometimes, *alcuna volta;* him, *lo;* to look, *guardare;* (some), *alcun;* sighs, *sospiro,* (dim. *ettò*); to utter, *gettare* (ger).

20. A poor humble woman washed her pots and pans with sand and with salt water, and made them* beautiful.

Poor, *povera;* woman, *femmina* (dim. *etta*); her, *suoi;* pots and pans, *stovigli;* with (the) sand, *rena;* water salt, *acqua salsa;* to wash, *lavare;* made, *faceva;* *bello.*

21. The trees, envious and old, oppress with their shade the young shrubs growing underneath, nor allow them to flourish.

Tree, *albero;* *invidioso;* old, *vecchio;* *opprimere;* with (the) their, *colla loro;* shade, *uggia;* shrub, *arbusto,* (dim. *arbuscello*); underneath, *sotto;* to grow, *nascere* (par. pre.); nor, *nè;* to allow, *permettere;* them, *loro;* to* (the) flourish, *fiorire.*

22. He who was not at all at a loss for words, with some of his old woman's tales, made her remain altogether satisfied.

At all, *mica;* at . . . words, *povero di parole;* some tales, *con certe sue filastroccole* (dim. of *filastrocca*); her, *la;* made, *fece;* *rimanere;* altogether, *tutto;* *soddisfatto.*

23. Every slight heat of a* little fever carries away with it youth and beauty.

Every, *ogni;* heat, *caldo* (dim. *icciuolo*); *piccolo;* *febbre;* to carry, *portar via;* with it, *seco;* (the) youth, *giovanezza;* beauty, *bellezza.*

24. Who become sweetly pretty, and charmingly pleasing to a* wonder.

Who, *la quale;* to become, *riuscire;* pretty, *bella,* (dim. *ina*); *piacevole,* (dim. *ina*); wonder, *maraviglia.*

25. Go and endeavour to drag on life, so wretchedly consumptive and squalid you appear to me.

Go, *andate;* and endeavour . . life, *provatevi a vivere;* so *così;* consumptive, *tisico* (dim. *uzzo;* squalid, *tristanzuol* (dim. of *triste*); to me, *mi;* to appear, *parere,*

26. The poison of a viper is nothing else but a certain yellowish fluid.

Poison, *veleno;* of a viper, *viperino;* nothing (not); is; else, *altro;* but *che;* *certo;* fluid, *liquore;* yellow, *giallo* (dim. *ògnolo*).

27. Dried earth has a whitish colour, approaching to ashes.

(The) earth, *terra;* dried, *secca;* has; *color;* white, *bianco* (*chiccio*, dim.); approaching, *traente;* to ashes, (to the) *uni cenerognolo.*

28. Who was in truth a pleasing and fresh thorough country-woman, swarthy and strong built.

La quale; in (the) truth, *vero;* was; *piacevole; fresca;* countrywoman, *foresozza* (dim. of *forese*); *bruna*, (aug. *azza*); strong built, *ben tarchiata.*

29. Let me go and see and hide myself in some lurking hole above in the* house.

Let me, *lasciami;* go, *andare;* (to) see, *a vedere;* and (of) to hide myself, *nascondermi;* lurking hole, *bugigatto*, (dim. disp. *bugigattolo*); above, *su;* in house, *in casa.*

30. Many people occupy themselves in petty things, wholly idle and of no importance.

Many, *molti;* to occupy themselves, *si trattengono;* thing, *cosa* (dim. *etta;* dim. *ettina*); wholly (of great) *grande;* idleness, *ozio;* and of no, *di niun;* importance, *pregio.*

31. The Creator has not left the smallest flower of the* grass, nor any leaf of tree without harmony.

Creatore; not has; to leave, *lasciare;* the smallest flower, (no one very small flower,) *niuno;* flower, *fiore* (dim. of dim. *fiorellino*); grass, *erba;* nor any, *niuna;* leaf, *foglia;* without, *senza;* (the) harmony, *concordia.*

Reading of Poetry.

1. "Certi nostri assai pinzoccheroni,
   Che fan del collo il campanil di Pisa."

Bellinci. Son.

Certain of our fanatics in numbers, who make a tower of Pisa of their necks.

2. "E che si, ch' io mi cavo
   Una delle pianelle,
   E che tal te ne stampo in sul mostaccio
   La forma e la misura,
   Che tu non la dimentichi mai più."—*Buonar.*

O indeed I feel disposed to take off one of my slippers, and so to stamp the forms and measure of it on your ugly phiz, that you should never forget it.

3. "L' erbetta verde e i fior di color mille."—*Petrar.*

The green tender herb, and the flowers of a thousand colors.

4. "Non è figlia del Sol la Musa mia,
Nè ha cetra d' *o*ro e d' èbano contesta;
E' rozza villanella, e si trastulla,
Cantando a aria, conforme le frulla."—*Ricciar.*

My muse is no daughter of the sun, nor has she harp formed of gold and ebony. She is a rough country girl, and amuses herself singing by ear, as the whim seizes her.

5. "Il più bello fiorellino
Se' tra fiori, o mammoletta,
Che non brami ir fastosetta,
Tra le pompe del giardino.

Tu col capo a terra chino,
G*o*di star sola soletta,
Ove fresca è più l' erbetta,
Ove folto è più lo spino.

Ma se avvien che alfin t' ad*o*cchi,
Nice altera, e te divella,
Perchè in seno a lei trab*o*cchi;

Dì tu a Nice vanarella,
Dille allor, che il sen le tocchi:
Me somiglia, e sarai bella."—*Ales. Pegol.*

Thou, O little violet, art the most beautiful floweret amongst flowers, who dost not wish to go forth as a conceited little thing amongst the pomp of the garden.

Thou, with thy head bent to the earth, delightest to stand alone—quite alone, where the tender herb is fresher,—where the thorn is thicker; but if it should happen that at last the proud Nice should cast her eyes on thee, and pluck thee, in order that she may place thee in her breast, say then to the little coquet Nice, say to her, when thou touchest her breast: "Resemble me, and thou wilt be beautiful."

6. "E mentre che leggea sopra il quaderno,
Gli apparve un spiritel lungo una spanna,
Sull' *o*rlo della pentola a sedere:
P*o*i crebbe in forma spaventosa e fiera,
E disse, 'che comanda il mio signore?'"—*Triss.*

And whilst he was reading his magic book, there appeared to him a little imp, long as a span, sitting on the edge of the pot. It then grew into a fearful and fierce form, and said, "What does my lord command?"

7. "Un verde praticel pien di bei fiori."

A green pretty little meadow full of beautiful flowers.

8. "E quale il cicognin, che leva l' ala,
Per voglia di volare, e non s' attenta
D' abbandonar lo nido, e giù la cala."—*Dante.*

And as the young stork, which raises the wing from the wish to fly, and does not dare to leave the nest, and lets it fall.

9. "Lento non più che volator smeriglio,
Che su drappel di allodolette scende."—*Chiab.*

Not more slow than the flying hawk, descending on a flight of little larks.

10. "Tacendo divenimmo là 've spiccia
Fuor della selva un picciol fiumicello."—*Dante.*

In silence we came to the spot, where there gushes forth out of the wood a pleasing streamlet.

CHAPTER VIII.

The Comparatives and Superlatives.

Section I.—The Comparatives.

1. The words which are most peculiarly subject to comparison are adjectives which constitute the accidental conditions of substantives. Verbs may be also considered liable to it—the general verb of existence, *essere*, to be, being excepted, as it conveys no idea of gradation, but only one of simple existence. Adverbs also, which indicate the accidents of verbs, are subject to comparison, inasmuch as they mark the qualifications of verbs, and more properly of the substantives to which the verbs belong. From this origin may be deduced the degrees of comparison.

2. These variations may express conditions of *more* or *less*, or simply equality; and in Italian are not expressed, as in Latin, by modifying the form of the substantive, but by prefixing

the adverbs *più*, more, and *meno*, less. Take as an example: *Pietro è più saggio di Paolo*, Peter is wiser than Paul.

It continually happens that two substantives possess the same accidental quality, but one in a greater or less degree than the other. These may be properly termed the comparatives: for we find, with regard to them, that one substantive is *more* beautiful, *more* dear, *more* great, *more* happy than another; or *less* beautiful, *less* dear, &c., than the other. This is the most simple form of comparison, when the same accidental quality is applied to two substantives.

3. It may also occur that a substantive possesses two or more qualities, between which a comparison may be made—the elements which admit it having in themselves a special or general analogy. Thence arises the comparison of qualities which have relation to one and the same substantive: as, *Pietro è più prudente che dotto*, Peter is more prudent than learned.

4. Sometimes the action of two different substantives is manifested by a kind of analogy, to a greater or less extent in one than the other; and the expression of this difference constitutes another comparison, which we may call verbal. It is either directly displayed in the verb itself, or manifests itself by means of the adverb, as, *Pietro scrive più speditamente di Giovanni*, Peter writes more expeditiously than John. The verbal accident is here the adverb *speditamente*. As to the former case, in this sentence, *Pietro parla meno di Giovanni*, Peter speaks less than John, the verbal comparison of speaking is instituted between Peter and John; and we may say that this expression can be considered to be an adjectival comparative, since *parla* may be resolved into *è parlante*, and then the form would be changed as follows, *Pietro è più parlante di Giovanni*.

5. A single substantive may demonstrate greater or less energy; and that is expressed by the verb, either by itself or with the help of an adverb, in certain actions which may be

referred to it. In such actions certain peculiar analogies are subject to comparison, in order to establish a greater or less degree of efficacy in a substantive: as, *Paolo parla più che non opera*, Paul speaks more than he works. In this case *il parlare*, speaking, and *l' operare*, working, have themselves the analogies of being more or less active; by which the one verb possesses greater efficacy in this respect than the other. In the example, *Paolo parla più giudiciosamente che non opera*, Paul speaks more judiciously than he works, the comparison falls on the adverb.

6. These are the possible cases of comparison. Every shade of comparison can be reduced to one of these forms, whatever may be the construction of the sentence, which in Italian is very varied, as will at once be evident to those who investigate this subject. We are enabled, therefore, to lay down the following rules:—

Comparison takes place between the qualities of substantives, whether expressed by adjectives, verbs, or adverbs, and may be reduced to two categories.

1stly. Comparison, by means of an adjective or adverb applied to two or more substantives.

2dly. Comparison, by means of two adjectives or adverbs applied to a single substantive.

We make mention of adverbs rather than verbs, because all verbs include in themselves the qualifications of substantives.

Having made these preliminary remarks, we will now endeavour to lay down rules in a more definite manner than is usual for the Italian forms of comparison, which appear arbitrary, and in some measure unlike those used in French and English. The English *than* and the French *que* are used with comparatives; and according to analogy, the Italian *che* ought to be used in the same manner. In place of *che*, however, *di*, or *di* with the article, is used, so that the substantive requires only the *segnacaso* or the article with it, according to the rules of the article previously given.

This rule might, however, be sufficiently clear if the same solution of the comparative were always adhered to; but in certain cases *che* is substituted for *di.* Rules are given by the grammarians, which though embarrassingly numerous, are by no means exact. We will endeavour to explain this matter on a plan of our own.

7. The comparative has a *di* as the link in simple comparative forms—that is to say, when one quality is applied to two substantives, in a greater or less degree.

EXAMPLES.

Egli non è donna al mondo che sia più caritatevole di lei.

There is not a woman in the world that is more charitable than she.

"Più felice di te non vede il sole."—*San.*

The sun does not behold any one more happy than thou art.

Chi sostiem giuste cause parla più eloquentemente di chi ne sostien d' ingiuste.

He who supports just causes speaks more eloquently than he who supports unjust ones.

Giovanni agisce più degnamente di Paolo.

John acts more worthily than Paul.

8. *Che* is used when the comparative form is less direct—that is to say, when there is but one substantive only, and the comparison is made between qualities relating to it.

EXAMPLES.

"Non conversiamo sempre cogli amici,
In questa più oscura che serena
Vita mortal, tutta d' invidia piena."—*Ario.*

We do not converse always with friends in this mortal life, which is more cloudy than serene, and altogether full of envy.

Il cavaliere si credeva di entrar in un bel castello, quando vidde ch' era una bicocca, più per rifugio di capre che per ricetto di soldati.

The knight thought that he was entering into a beautiful castle; when he saw that it was a ruinous place, more fit for a place of refuge for goats than for the reception of soldiers.

Through a certain caprice of the language it at times occurs that *che* is often used with the words *di quello* prefixed. This mode of expressing the comparative is less usual, but is quite proper and elegant. In this case the last example would be written thus: *più per rifugio di capre di quello che fosse* (or *non fosse*) *per ricetto di soldati.*

The *non* is merely a pleonasm, which is frequently used in cases of comparison.

9. The conclusion at which we may arrive is this, that *di* is used with the more simple and direct comparative forms. When, on the other hand, the meaning is more complicated, the sentence more involved, and the attributes more numerous, *che* is employed. If we have the two simple forms, and the comparison is not made directly with the second substantive, but some other words—as, for instance, a verb or even a sentence—intervene, and the second noun is thereby much separated from the first; in such cases the second substantive on which the comparison falls is severed from the first, and recourse must be had to the assistance of *che,* as will be seen in this example:

Meglio riescono le ópere fatte con energia e presto—abbenchè molti sostengono con grande pertinacia il contrario a dispetto della sperienza di tuttogiorno—che non siano le ópere stentate, e non tirate innanzi con fervore.

Works that are done with energy and quickly succeed better, although many maintain the contrary with great pertinacity, in spite of everyday experience, than those which are delayed over, and not carried out with zeal.

This sentence would be in its simple form:—

Le ópere fatte con energia e presto riescono meglio delle stentate e non tirate innanzi con fervore.

This solution would be inadmissible in the former involved sentence in which *che* is used instead of *di.* These examples of involved construction in the simple comparatives are, however, of rare occurrence.

10. Examples, moreover, may easily be found in authors, —and in considerable number, especially when the intention is to fix the mind particularly and with more than usual force on the comparison;—in which, if even the second noun comes directly after the first, and the comparative form be eminently simple, *che* is used; although it is by no means wrong, but rather a proof of grammatical correctness, to use the *di*. On the other hand, when *che* is required, its place can under no circumstances be supplied by *di*.

EXAMPLES.

"E dopo il pasto ha più fame che pria."—*Dante.*

And after the repast he is more hungry than before.

Il legame dell' amicizia stringe molto più fortemente di quel della parentela; conciossiachè gli amici noi liscegliamo, ed i parenti ci sono dati dalla fortuna.

(In this sentence we can say with greater vigour, *che quel della fortuna.*)

The bond of friendship binds much more strongly than that of parentage, since we ourselves choose our friends, and our parents are given us by fortune.

11. It would now appear that, with such numerous and arbitrary exceptions the rule, that the genitive case should be used in making a comparison, can scarcely be considered to be of great importance. Under these circumstances, therefore, it might be thought that we should consider it an exceptional rule.

This, however, we are by no means disposed to admit; but considering that cases of simple comparison, without the introduction of other words, or any involved construction, are of far the most frequent occurrence, we do not hesitate lay it down as a primary rule, that *di* is used in place of *che* in determining the comparative degrees of *more* and *less*.

12. In § 2 we asserted that the comparative form is not incorporated with the adjective or adverb, as in the Latin language, and very frequently in English, but is expressed by placing *più*, more, *meno*, less, before the adjective or the adverb.

There are, notwithstanding, adjectives of comparison which have their own proper form, and dispense with the assistance of *più* and *meno:* as, for example, from *buono* we have *migliore;* from *cattivo, peggiore;* from *grande, maggiore;* from *piccolo, minore.* The reason of this is easily explained: for *buono, cattivo, grande,* and *piccolo* are the adjectives that are most extensively used in human life, and were ever in the mouths of men, even when the Roman Empire had fallen into decay, and civilisation was lapsing into barbarism.

In speaking the new language men were neither able nor willing to dispense with these forms, which therefore descended from father to son, without any one having the idea of making a change by adopting the forms of the other comparatives. Thus in Italian those forms, which were of frequent occurrence, retained their Latin shape.

EXAMPLES.

"E l' aspettar del mal è mal peggiore,
Forse, che non parrebbe il mal presente."—*Tasso.*

And the expectation of evil is perchance a worse evil than would appear the actual evil.

Meglio quei guerrieri amavano di morire in battaglia che viver in servaggio.—*Gio. Vil.*

Those warriors had rather die in battle than live in slavery.

"E veggio il meglio ed al peggior m' appiglio."

I see the better, and pursue the worse.

13. All that has been said concerning the adverb *più* may be considered to refer to the adverb *meno.* The only difference is, that the meaning is reversed.

EXAMPLE.

Se il giovanetto fu lieto assai, la letizia della fanciulla non fu minore di quella di lui.—*Bocc.*

If the youth was very joyful, the joy of the girl was not less than his.

Section II.

The Comparative of Equality.

14. We will now consider another form of comparison, namely, that of equality.

The same elements existing which are subject to the comparison of *more* or *less*, there is naturally the same capacity in words to admit the relation of equality, as well as that of excess or defect. We possess, therefore, the comparative of equality.

15. This is expressed by the words *così . . . come, sì . . . come, tanto . . . quanto, altrettanto . . . quanto, quanto più . . . quanto più;* and, leaving out the antecedent altogether, by the simple *come* or *quanto.*

16. To determine properly the force of all these forms would partake too much of the character of metaphysical research, and would have no satisfactory result. It is sufficient to observe, that one of these relations has a qualificative value; the other a quantitative. With *più* and *meno* there is no need to enter into this question; for in applying these forms, there is no practical difficulty to overcome.

17. But with the comparatives of equality a decided distinction is made according as they are applied to express quantity or quality, in the adverbial correlative forms. If an equality in qualification is intended, *così* or *sì* is used, as in this example:—

Ho inteso sempre dire che la troppa diligenza e così mala, come la trascuraggine.

I have always heard say that too much diligence is as bad a thing as carelessness.

In this case *così* unites the qualification *mala cosa,* applied to diligence, with *mala cosa* understood after *come,* and applied to carelessness in a purely qualificative sense. *Conosco quel che tu dì così bene come te,* I know what you say as well as you do, is another example of this kind.

18. To express, however, the comparative of equality respecting quantity, we make use of the form *tanto . . . quanto.* This form is always indeterminate, not fixing the precise limits of quantity. Thus we say, *Il tempo è un bene di cui tanto ne ha il povero quanto il ricco,* Time is a possession of which the poor man has as much as the rich. It can be easily seen that in this case there is no form expressing a concrete and determinate quantity.

19. We may also observe that the comparative form, which expresses qualificative equality, may adopt the quantitative form; but the reverse is not the case. Thus we may say: *L' uomo povero ed onesto è così degno di rispetto come il ricco ed onesto uomo,* The poor and honest man is as worthy of respect as the honest rich man.

20. In this case, *tanto* and *quanto* may be substituted for *così* and *come,* and then they are used in a qualificative sense. But if I were to say, *Non ho speso tanto tempo a persuadere tutto il popolo, quanto ne ho speso a persuader lui solo,* I have not spent as much time in persuading all the people, as I have spent in persuading him alone; *tanto* and *quanto* would be used in a quantitative sense, and their place could not be supplied by *così* and *come.*

21. We may here also observe, that in the comparative form of qualificative equality, this form itself may be simplified by leaving out *così* and *tanto,* and using only *come* and *quanto.* In a former example, which we have given, we have said, although in slightly different words, that *La troppa diligenza è mala cosa come* (or *quanto*) *la trascuraggine.* But if *tanto* and *quanto* are exponents of quantity, the entire form must be used without any sort of contraction.

22. There is another kind of comparative which denotes equality, and which may be said to be mixed up with excess or defect. This, of course, would be a mathematical contradiction, and we are therefore induced to treat the form of equality as a pleonasm, and allow the idea of excess or defect to predominate. Of this peculiar construction, we now give an example:—

Il peccatore tanto più corre abbandonatamente, quanto più aperte le vie trova.

The more the sinner finds his course open, the more unrestrainedly he rushes on.

It is certain that in this sentence, *tanto* and *quanto* are pleonasms, the sense being complete without them. We may assert, however, that *tanto* and *quanto* serve to denote the *proportional* quantity of excess or defect, as if we were to say, *il più che la via è aperta, e più in adeguata proporzione egli corre abbandonatamente.*

23. The form *altrettanto* . . . *quanto* is rarely used, but is subject to the same conditions as *tanto* . . . *quanto,* and it expresses relations of quality as well as of quantity.

This is the best definition which we have been able to give of the theory of the comparative form, which at first seems sufficiently simple, but is in reality involved and full of difficulty. This becomes evident, when we consider under how many different circumstances the comparative may be used. We find on one occasion the comparative form, as used with regard to words and sentences in a particular sense; on another occasion, it will be of a full and absolute nature, embracing generality. It may have relation directly to qualities or to actions or to many other things, and in all these circumstances the comparatives are subject to gradations of superiority, inferiority, or equality. A variety of forms may be added in Italian, which is, in this respect perhaps, more copious than in any other. In these forms an *ellipsis* is often used, and the mind is left to fill up the comparison, which is only implied in the sentence. It will be found, that we are not mistaken when we say, that this is one of the greatest difficulties in the Italian language, for those who wish to subject every portion of the language to a strict theoretical examination of principles. The grammarians have usually evaded this difficulty, by treating this subject in a very superficial manner. We have endeavoured to give some rules, but confess that we have found our task sufficiently arduous. What we have not been able to effect, we hope will be completed by future linguists who may be pleased to treat this complicated subject.

The superlative now remains to be noticed by us, but this, which is a plainer and more easy matter, we will reserve to the next Section.

Section III.

The Superlative.

24. It frequently happens, that the qualification ascribed to the substantive is of so heightened a nature, that it does not admit any comparison whatever with others. Under these circumstances, the superlative degree is used. This does not absolutely exclude the idea of comparison, but in this case the comparison would be indefinite, and rather exercised on the genus or species than the individual, although the individual is signified by the substantive, from which the comparison proceeds.

We will take as an illustration this sentence of Seneca, *Agli uomini ricchissimi e felicissimi fa noja ogni cosa*, which in English may be given thus: To the richest and most fortunate men, everything causes *ennui*. Here we have two superlatives, *ricchissimi* and *felicissimi*. From these the idea of comparison is not excluded, but it is vague and generic, inasmuch as it is referred not to the individual, but to the species. *Ricchissimi*, for instance, signifies those who are superior in their riches and felicity to other men, but does neither indicate how many, nor of what class. It is simply understood that they are superior not only to the individual, but also to the species and genus, although the superiority is not so absolute as to render an exception impossible.

25. We have also a superlative of a more concrete nature, in which the comparison is from a substantive, and falls upon a class or species, but in a peremptory manner, which is as if it were impatient of comparison. This, however, does not exclude the idea of a dependent substantive, on which the force of comparison should be exercised, but this comparison must always be distinguished from the idea of full superiority in the first substantive, that enjoys the qualification in excess.

26. We must here observe, that we do not intend to assert that these superlatives indicate a condition of complete excellence, in the æsthetic sense of the word. Here we do not make mention of excellence, but of superiority, which may exist even in a thing by nature bad—as, for instance, *Quell' uomo è perfidissimo,* that man is most perfidious. In this sentence, *perfidissimo,* indicates a superiority in genus and species, that is to say, among the human race, without pointing out any individual. But superiority in this case is taken in a bad sense, like the "bad eminence" of Milton.

27. To continue our second distinction, pointed out in the § 25, this species of superlatives, which admits the support of a concrete idea, and claims excellency over a given specified class, may be termed the comparative superlative (or the superlative of comparison), as those of the first class are absolute superlatives. Thus we find in Petrarch this sentence:—

"Foco che m' arde alla più algente bruma."

A fire which burns me in the coldest winter.

There is something of a more concrete nature in the expression, *la più algente bruma,* than if were to say, *il foco cocen-*

tissimo, the hottest fire. He means also to imply, that if the coldest part of the winter season were picked out, even at that time the fire would burn with equal fierceness. If we had used the other form, *fuoco cocentissimo*, which is more absolute, decisive, and generic, and in appearance more ample and efficacious, the energy of the moral notion which Petrarch wished to convey of his unquenchable love would have been considerably weakened.

28. We explain the distinction between these two kinds of superlatives, in order to put in a clear light the two different forms which they adopt. The superlative absolute has its form in *issimo* and *issima*, which are added to the termination of the noun. The other, which is the comparative superlative (the grammarians call it the superlative of relation), makes use of the simple comparative form *più* with the definite article before it: as we see in this example, *alla più algente bruma*. The article determines the point of excellence in a given class of substantives, and shows how much this individual exceeds every other of the said class. This species of superlatives, when the second substantive is expressed, uses with it *di*, the sign of the genitive case.

(*a*) It is evident that the Romans gave to the Italians the superlative in *issimus, a, um*. The masculine in *us* and the neuter in *um* are in Italian changed into *o*, according to the general rule, and it assumes *a* in the feminine.

(*b*) Also the few Latin adjectives which have their termination in *errimus*, the superlatives of words ending in *er*, follow in Italian the same rule. The Italians, however, have not adopted the termination in *illimus*, but have changed it into *issimo*: as, from *facillimus*, *facilissimo*. Thus, we may subject this class of superlatives to the following general rule :—

29. The very small class of adjectives which terminate in *bre* and *gro* make the superlative absolute in *errimo*.

30. We may say concerning the exceptional superlatives, *ottimo*, best; *pessimo*, worst; *massimo*, greatest; *minimo*,

least, the same which we have said of the comparatives. We must observe, however, that this kind of superlative admits the regular forms more readily than those which are exceptional, and that these last, in special cases, have something affected and unusual. Thus, we do not say: *Egli è un uomo minimo,* he is a very little man; but instead of *minimo* use the word *piccolissimo.* But, on the other hand, we might say, *Io sono il minimo fra voi tutti,* I am the least among you all; because this expression bears a moral sense. *Egli si appigliò a pessimo partito,* he adhered to the worst course, is a graver form of words than *ad un partito cattivissimo. Massimo* is not often used, and all the more rarely, that it is usually applied to the Divinity.

31. It is clear that as adverbs are subject to the comparative degree, they may also adopt a superlative form. We will also remark that the form *mente* is given to them after they have been made superlative, *mente* being added to the *feminine* form. Thus, from *piacevole,* pleasing, is formed *piacevolissimo*; and from this again, the adverbs *piacevolmente* and *piacevolissimamente.* There are others of this kind, but they are not very numerous.

32. Superlatives, having in themselves an enlarged signification, are liable to be paraphrased, or expressed in an exaggerated form, or even to have the superlative sign to a certain extent doubled. Of this peculiarity we will give some examples, in order that it may be better understood.

EXAMPLES.

Un sasso altissimo fuor di misura, e repente sì ch' egli era impossibile salirvi sopra.—*Fir.*

A rock, high beyond all measure, and also so precipitous, that it was impossible to ascend it.

In altissimo fuor di misura, the duplicate superlative occurs with a sort of vague exaggeration.

Colombe candidissime più che neve.—*Bembo.*

Doves whiter than snow.

This is another kind of exaggeration, as it is by no means usual to put the superlative in the place of the positive. The regular form would be, *candide più che neve.*

Egli aveva una moglie che era delle più pessime e più malvagie femmine che nascessero mai sotto la cappa del cielo.

He had a wife who was one of the worst and most wicked women that were ever born under the canopy of heaven.

The superlative preceded by *più* is a rare though energetic expression. *Più pessime,* in this example, conveys the idea better than if we substituted *delle più cattive.*

Another way of expressing energy is by repeating the adjective and the verb. This is very forcible, but should be used with caution, for fear of giving a childish turn to a sentence.

Fiocaggine, che a mio credere vuol essere ostinata molto molto, e bisogna lasciarla guarir alla natura, vera medicatrice de' mali.

Ostinata molto molto is put for *ostinatissima.*

It is necessary to leave to nature, the true healer of diseases, the cure of general debility, which to my thinking threatens to become more and more obstinate.

We will make mention also of a few other expressions, as *essere dolente a morte,* to be grieved even to death, for *dolentissimo ; felice che nulla più* (that is, without any comparison), for *felicissimo ; translucido,* for *lucidissimo.* The latter phrase we may illustrate in this manner, *Si specchiavano nel translucido laghetto che non era da aura leggerissima turbato,* they gazed upon that most lucid lake, which was not disturbed even by the very slightest breeze.

These, and many other phrases, will induce us to recognize the rich variety of the Italian language. This we may, in some measure, refer to the tendency to exaggeration, which distinguishes the children of the South. But these exaggerations with us, for the most part, do not become turgid, but are restrained within the limits of good taste.

Exercises on the Comparatives and Superlatives.

1. I do not think that a* man more just and more worthy of honor than Scipio Africanus could be found amongst the heathen. —*Bocc.*

To think, *credere;* worthy, *degno* (translate, of honor worthy); was ever born, *nascere* (imp. subj.); amongst, *infra;* heathen, *Gentile.*

2. The world believes that, by doing (the) things at one's ease, one does them better; but one might say that works that* are* labored over, and not executed at once with spirit, succeed worse than those which* are* done with a resolute determination.—*Caro, lett.*

To do, *fare* (gerun.); at one's ease, *adagio;* one . . . better, *si facciano;* but . . . say, *ma si potrebbe dire;* laboured, *stentato;* and not . . . spirit, *e non tirate innanzi con fervore;* to succeed, *riescire;* determination, *spirito.*

3. So* great a flood is repaired more easily by letting it take its course, than by checking it.—*Caro, lett.*

(To a) great; flood, *piena;* one, *si; riparare;* by . . . course, *a darle il suo corso;* by (to) . . . it, *farle ritegno.*

4. The girl, not accustomed to voices uttered in this manner, fearful of something* worse, began to tremble like the unsteady reed moved by soft breezes.—*Bocc.*

To accustom, *usare;* to (of); voices . . . manner, *così fatte voci;* fearful, *timido;* unsteady, *mobile;* reed, *giunco;* moved, *mosso;* by (the) soft, *soave; aura.*

5. The sheep and the goats, which were more desirous of feeding than of repose, began to go clambering over difficult and broken places.—*Sanazz.*

Sheep, *pecora;* (she)* goat; *capra;* which more of; to feed (themselves), *pascersi;* than to (of); repose (turn of reposing); were desirous, *eran vaghe;* began . . . climb, *cominciarono ad andarsi arrampicando;* (for) places, *luogo;* difficult, *arduo;* broken, *dirupato;* (of the); wild, *selvatico; monte.*

6. Some minds, the less easily they* learn matters* of doctrine, with the greater difficulty they allow them to escape out of the mind.—*Speron.*

Alcuno; mind, *ingegno;* the less, *quanto meno; apprendere;* matters of doctrine (the), *dottrina;* with the greater, *tanto più;* difficulty, *difficilmente* (adv.); allow . . . escape, *le si lasciano uscir di mente.*

7. The sea has not so many grains of sand, nor the heavens (sin.) so many stars, as things doubtful and full of danger may every day happen to the living.—*Bocc.*

The sea . . . sand, *non ha il mare tante arene ;* nor, *nè ;* doubtful, *dubbioso ;* may, *possono ;* every day, *tutto dì ; addivenire ; vivente.*

8. It is necessary that the sorrowful soul should show itself to grieve,* when it is wounded by grave thoughts, as the body, when it* is pierced by troublesome wounds.—*Firenz.*

That . . . to grieve, *che così mostri dolersi l' anima addolorata ;* when, *ove ;* by grave thoughts; is wounded, *punto ;* by troublesome, *molesto ;* wound, *piaga ;* pierced, *trafitto.*

9. There is nothing which so much attracts and allures, as the sympathy from which it arises, that the good love (subj.) the good. —*Cic.*

There is nothing, *niente v' ha ;* so much attracts, *attragga ; allettare* (subj.); sympathy, *somiglianza ; dalla quale ;* it arises, *viene.*

10. A young man, very comely and well behaved, placed in the girl the greatest love.—*Bocc.*

Very, *assai ;* comely, *leggiadro ;* well behaved, *dabbene ;* placed, *pose ;* in the (to the); girl, *fanciulla.*

11. Although the cold was very severe, and the roads very muddy, and much snow had fallen, that man made no halt in any place, and pursued his journey.

Although, *quantunque ;* was (subj.); severe, *aspro ; via ;* muddy, *fangoso ;* had (might have); fallen, *caduto ;* made no halt, *non fe' sosta ; proseguirì ; cammino.*

12. A little meadow, full of the freshest and most minute grass, and depicted with many kinds of the most elegant flowers.—*Bembo.*

Prabello ; of . . . grass, (plu.) *erba ;* full, *pieno ;* and; with (of); kind, *maniera ;* elegant, *vago ; dipinto.*

13. We both of us sat down on the margin of a fresh and most limpid fountain, which, just as if it* had been of the purest crystal, shewed the secrets of its* translucent bed.—*Sanazz.*

We . . . sat down, *noi ci ponemmo amendue a sedere ;* on (to); *màrgine ;* just as, *non altrimenti ;* (that) *che ; cristal lo ;* been had, (subj.); of (the); *translucido ;* bed, *fondo ;* to show, *manifestare.*

14. Most acceptable, in truth, to me have been your sweetest letters.

Acceptable, *grato ; veramente ;* sweet, *soave.*

15. There are some* fastidious (2) persons (1), whose friendship is as* easily rent asunder as the finest veil.—*Casa, Gal.*

There are, *vi sono; fastidioso;* (the) friendship, *amicizia;* whose, *delle quali;* easily, *leggermente;* as, *a guisa;* of the (of a); fine, *sottile;* is rent asunder, *si squarcia.*

16. Endeavour (thou) to be in favour with the honest and most worthy citizens.—*Pandolf.*

Endeavour (thou), *procura;* (of) to be; favour, *grazia;* worthy, *integro; cittadino.*

17. He was the worst man, perhaps, that ever was born.—*Bocc.*

That perhaps, *che forse;* ever, *mai;* to be born, *nascere;* (sub. imperf.)

18. Of the highest praise and commendation those fathers are indeed worthy, who, with the* greatest prudence, endeavour to bring their sons up well, to refine their manners, and to give them the best instruction.—*Scamozzio.*

Praise, *lode;* are; indeed, *veramente;* worthy, *degno;* those, *que';* greatest, *ogni;* to endeavour, *cercare;* to bring . . . up, *di bene allevare i figliuoli;* to refine their manners, *costumarli*;* them, *loro; documenti.*

CHAPTER IX.

The Numerals and Indefinite Adjectives.

Section I.—Numerals.

Adjectives of quantity naturally follow adjectives of quality, and we will now, in the first place, treat of adjectives of number.

The cardinal numerals may be used as substantives as well as adjectives, and are:—1, *uno;* 2, *due;* 3, *tre:* 4, *quàttro;* 5, *cinque;* 6, *sèi;* 7, *sètte;* 8, *òtto;* 9, *nòve;* 10, *dièci;* 11, *ùndici;* 12, *dòdici;* 13, *trèdici;* 14, *quattòrdici;* 15, *quìndici;* 16, *sèdici;* 17, *diciasètte;* 18, *diciòtto;* 19. *diciannòve;* 20, *vènti;* 21, *vent' ùno:* 22, *venti dùe, &c.;* 30, *trènta;* 31, *trent' ùno,* &c.; 40, *quarànta;* 50, *cinquànta;* 60, *sessànta;* 70, *settànta;* 80, *ottànta;* 90, *novànta;* 100, *cènto;* 200, *duecènto;* 300, *trecènto;* 400, *quattrocènto, &c.,*

1000, *mille;* 2000, *due mila,* &c.; 1,000,000, *un milione* or *miglione.*

The ordinal numerals are:—*Primo, secondo, terzo, quarto, quinto, sesto, sèttimo, ottàvo, nono, dècimo, undècimo* or *decimo primo, duodècimo* or *dècimo secondo, tredicèsimo* or *dècimo terzo, dècimo quàrto, dècimo quinto, décimo sesto, dècimo sèttimo, dècimo ottàvo, dècimo nono, vèntesimo, ventèsimo primo, &c., trentèsimo, quarantèsimo, cinquantèsimo, sessantèsimo, settantèsimo, ottantèsimo, novantèsimo, centèsimo, mìllesimo;* first, second, third, &c. *Last* is rendered by *ultimo, ultima.*

1. *Uno* is declinable in the singular, and varies according to the gender of the noun to which it is prefixed. We were unwilling to term it an indefinite article, because it always serves either as a number indicating unity, or as an indicative adjective. In the first case it may be illustrated by this sentence:—

Un uomo venne oggi a casa mia per portarmi un messaggio.

A man came to-day to my house, and brought a message.

Of the secondary meaning we may take this sentence as an example:—

Egli avvenne che un uomo, che era da tutti tenuto onesto, fu imprigionato come ladro.

It happened that a man, who was considered honest by every one, was imprisoned as a robber.

Here *un uomo* is used for *un certo uomo,* and *certo* is without doubt an indicative adjective.

2. All the numerals are indeclinable, except *uno,* one, and *mille,* a thousand. *Uno* makes *un, uno,* and *una,* according as the noun requires the definite article *il, lo,* or *la. Mille* is used when it is intended to express one thousand; when there are more, we use the variation *mila,* following by analogy the Latin *mille, millia.*

3. Numerals are increased by addition. Thus, when we once arrive at *cento,* a hundred, we repeat *cento* with each

succeeding number, until we reach *duecento,* two hundred. From *duecento,* two hundred, we proceed to *trecento,* three hundred, and so on. In like manner, *mille* is repeated with regular progressive additions until we come to *due mila;* and so with the rest.

4. The substantives following, *ventuno, trentuno, quarantuno,* are put in the singular and agree with *uno,* not with *venti.* Thus *ventuno, trentuno* suffer the changes to which *uno* would be liable if used alone. Thus, we use *ventun, ventuno,* or *ventuna,* according to the form of the noun to which it belongs: as, *datemi ventun soldo, ventuno scudo, ventuna lira sterlina,* give me twenty-one pence,—crowns,—pounds.

5. *A due a due, a tre a tre,* are phrases expressive of *due dopo due,* two after two, *tre dopo tre,* three after three, in order of sequence. But *a quattro a quattro* is not used in this sense, because it is a phrase which usually has this meaning, *on four feet.* Thus, *a quattro a quattro* is to walk on four feet, or on all-fours.

6. The hours are defined in the following manner. The sentence begins with *sono,* which is equivalent to, *they are;* then follows the article *le* (plural), and finally the number: as, for example, *Sono le cinque,* it is five o'clock. *Le* is the feminine article (plu.) of the word *ore,* hours understood. The article may be omitted; but it is in that case necessary to introduce the word *ore* after the number, as *sono cinque ore.* In the phrase, *è un ora,* one o'clock, it is evident that *è* must be used instead of *sono.*

7. The fractions of *ora* are expressed by means of addition. Thence we say, *è un ora ed un' quarto,* it is a quarter-past one; *sono le due e venti minuti,* it is twenty minutes past two; *sono le tre e tre quarti,* it is a quarter to four. If only a few minutes are wanting to the completion of the hour, we make use of the following expressions: *Vi vogliono,* or *vi mancano, otto, dieci,* or *dòdici* (eight, ten, or twelve) *minuti alle quattro, alle cinque,* &c.

8. The Italian collective numerals end in *ina* and *ajo*, as *decina*, ten; *centinajo*, a hundred; *miliajo*, a thousand; and so on. These numerals are substantives, like the English words *a dozen* (Ital. *una dozzina*), and *a score (una ventina)*, and have plurals in *ine* and *aja*. Thus we say, *una decina, una ventina, una trentina, un centinajò, due decine, due centinaja, un migliajo, due miliaja*, &c.

9. Dates are written in this manner:—

Il 12 Agosto, 1862;
Li 12 Agosto, 1862; or simply,
12 Agosto, 1862.

The last method is the more modern, especially in manuscripts and in letters. For the first day of the month we write, *il primo*, or the numeral *I*, and not *l' uno Dicembre.*

10. The ordinals *primo, secondo, terzo*, &c. suffer modifications in gender, number, and case, because they do not indicate the number of a substantive, but modify it as adjectives of quality; and in strictness signify an accident of the substantive itself. The quantity is in the distribution, not in the object itself, and they may therefore be considered extrinsic; while, on the other hand, *uno, due*, &c., have an intrinsic meaning, qualifying substantially the noun in its quantitative condition.

11. In the case of the six ordinals following *decimo* it is better to use the second form, and to say *decimo primo, decimo secondo, decimo terzo*, instead of *undecimo, duodecimo, tredecesimo*. This is done to produce an easier sound. Likewise the Latin termination is not commonly used in the ordinals of *venti*, twenty, &c., and we say commonly, *ventesimo, trentesimo, quarantesimo*, These forms are, however, allowable, and in certain cases even preferable, as in the following instances:—

All' undicesimo, dodicesimo, &c., libro della Storia d' Italia del Guicciardini.

In the eleventh, twelfth, &c., book of Guicciardini's History of Italy.

E la dodicesima volta che vi ripeto la stessa cosa.

It is the twelfth time that I have repeated to you the same thing.

12. The historical succession of sovereigns of the same name is indicated, as in English, by affixing to the proper name the Roman form of the cardinal number which expresses the order of succession; and this cardinal uumber is read off as an ordinal without any definite article preceding it. Thus Charles I., Henry VIII. (which in English are read off Charles the First, Henry the Eighth, and more rarely Charles First, Henry Eighth) are in Italian written *Carlo I., Enrico VIII.*, and reads off *Carlo Primo, Enrico Ottavo.* In the cases where the Italian has two forms—a single and a double one—for the ordinal (as in the ordinals from "eleventh" to "sixteenth" inclusive), the latter or double form is always employed in such phrases as the above. Thus *Luigi XI., Gregorio XVI.*, are read off, *Luigi Decimo Primo* (not *undicesimo*), *Gregorio Decimo Sesto* (not *sedicesimo*).

SECTION II.

Indefinite Adjectives of Quantity.

13. Adjectives modifying a noun in a quantitative and indefinite sense pass through many gradations from totality to nullity, when used to indicate an accident of a substantive. We shall speak of these at some length as we find their theory very confused in Italian Grammars, especially in those which are intended for the use of foreigners.

14. It is evident that when used to signify the two extremes of totality and nullity, they can scarcely be called indefinite, as *tutto*, for instance, which embraces all genera and all species, and *nessuno*, none, which excludes from its subject all genera and species. They cannot, however, be considered entirely definite, as they do not indicate the individual genus and species.

15. The indefinite adjectives are: *Alcuno*, some; *qualche*, some; *qualunque*, or *qualsisia*, *qualsivoglia*, *&c.*, whosoever, or whatever; *ciascuno*, each; *ciascheduno*, every one; *qualcuno*, some; *parecchi*, some; *ogni*, every one; *nessuno*, *veruno*, not any one; *certo*, certain; *molto*, much; *poco*, little; *tutto*, the whole; *nulla*, none; and a few others.

16. *Qualche* indicates an indefinite number of a restricted nature, like the English *some*. *Mi diede qualche danaro*, means this, He gave me some, but a limited quantity of money. It is always used with the singular number. *Parecchi*, which is used in the plural alone, increases the signification of quantity to a greater extent, as in this sentence: *Parecchi uomini mi hanno parlato di questo*, a pretty good number of men have spoken to me of it.

17. *Ogni* embraces all the specialities of case and circumstance, and fixes attention on the individual genus, without determining the number. *Tutto* embraces the individuality of the genus or species collectively, as *Tutti combatterono volontariamente*, all fought willingly, that is to say, all, as many as were there, fought willingly.

18. *Tutto* is used with the article, but is not preceded by it; for in that case it would lose its indeterminate character, which would be impossible. The article, however, may precede the noun, because the noun in some measure takes a definite character from the genus or species to which it belongs. Thus, in the sentence, *Tutti i campi sono desolati dalla siccità*, all the fields are laid waste through want of rain; *i campi*, the fields, are definite in the sense of *quei tali campi, di tal e tal paese*, those particular fields, of such and such territory, and are therefore so far particularised. *Tutte le fanciulle oneste sono rispettate*, all honest girls are respected. In this case, the *fanciulle*, girls, are rendered definite by the adjective *oneste*, by which the kind of girls is specified. *Tutto* is frequently used with numerals, and then acquires the signification of a special numerical totality, and

is used in these kind of phrases, *Tutti e due, tutti e tre, etc., fecero il loro debito inverso di lui*, Both, all the three, &c., did their duty towards him.

To omit the article after *tutto*, is usually a peculiarity of the graver style. This is especially done in verse, through a love of poetical elevation, which often delights in forsaking common modes of speech.

19. It often happens, that after having announced totality, in a defined manner and under individual considerations with *ogni*, it is desired to announce the absence of any exception whatever, for the sake of energy. For this purpose, a comprehensive and indeterminate adjective must be used, and this is the adjective *qualunque*, whoever or whatever, which is occasionally resolved, as it were, into the following verbal expressions: *qualsivoglia* and *qualsisia*, or *qualsivogliano* and *qualsisieno*, which are either singular or plural according to the number of the substantive.

EXAMPLES.

Ogni uomo qualsiasi è odioso al misantropo.

Every man is odious to the misanthrope.

(This is the same as if *qualunque* were used.)

Per profitti qualsiensi (*or* qualsivogliano) non m' indurrò mai a far cosa indegna di uomo bennato ed onesto.

I will never be persuaded, in order to obtain any advantage whatever, to do anything unworthy of a well-born and honourable man.

Qualsiasi il danno (*or* qualunque danno) che me ne venga ho gia preso il mio partito.

Whatever loss may ensue, I have taken my own course.

(This is the same as saying *ogni danno, qualsiasi, che me ne venga, io ho già preso il mio partito.*)

It is evident, that in these phrases, the adjective of *collective* totality is here excluded, and that the adjective of *individual* totality is put in its place, in order that attention may be drawn to the idea of individuality.

20. These indeterminate adjectives, which have a relation

to quantity, may be considered also to be applied to the substantive *uomo.* Most of them might be supplemented by the word *uno,* which in English may be rendered by *body,* or *one, uno* being applied to the noun *uomo,* man.

In this manner are used *ognuno, taluno, nissuno* or *niuno, ciascuno* and *chiascheduno,* or *cadauno,* to use; the latter, however, savours of affectation. *Chiunque,* in spite of its pronominal form, belongs also to this category, seeing that it indicates *any man whatever,* without any exception of condition.

21. *Uno,* when added to these radical adjectives, may be applied to a *thing,* as well as to a *person,* but in this case it is not used alone, the substantive being understood, but the substantive is always expressed.

EXAMPLES.

Non mi diede alcun danaro.
He gave me no money.

Nessuna cosa mi è tanto gradita.
Nothing is so gratifying to me.

Nessuna parola può rimuovermi del mio proposito.
Nothing that can be said, will move me from my purpose.

The substantives of negative totality, equivalent to the Latin *nihil,* are *niente* and *nulla.*

Section III.

Another species of Indefinite Adjectives.

22. *Tanto,* so much; *quanto,* how much; *molto,* much; *poco,* little; *troppo,* too much; *altrettanto,* as much as; may in Italian be classed among indefinite adjectives of quantity, inasmuch as they are connected in the manner of adjectives with the noun, the signification of which they modify. This we should specially bear in mind, as in French this class of words is used adverbially, with a partitive genitive after them. We must also remember, that they are of the same character as the adjectives, which we have before

mentioned. In fact, every one must see that they express an indeterminate gradation in the same manner as *alcuno, ogni, parecchi, tutti.*

Molti uomini, expresses an intermediate quantity between *parecchi uomini,* and *tutti gli uomini; pochi danari,* is a kind of middle point between *alcuni danari,* and *nessuno danaro; Troppe parole,* signifies something beyond *molte,* with the idea of excess; but still under the same quantitative condition.

23. *Tanto, quanto, altro,* are more difficult to define, although they belong to the same category of adjectives. These, whether isolated or dependent one on the other, include the idea of indeterminate quantity, which modifies the substantive. The following sentences are examples:— *Quante belle cose si vedono a Parigi!* How many fine things are seen at Paris! Does not this sentence convey the same meaning as, *Come molte belle cose si vedono a Parigi? A che valgono tanti discorsi,* of what use are so many words? Does not this allude to *troppi discorsi che si fanno,* the too many speeches which are made? *Tanto* and *quanto* are also sometimes mutually dependent, as *Vi erano nel teatro tante persone quante sie se potevano contenere,* there were in the theatre as many persons as could be held. In this sentence, *tante* is the indefinite number of the persons contained in the theatre, and includes the adverb *così,* as. *Quante* completes the meaning of *tante,* and includes in itself the force of the conjunction *come,* as, which is the correlative of *così,* and is strictly only the repetition of *molte,* with a clearly defined relation to *così,* which narrows to a certain extent the signification of *molte,* being proportional to the capacity of the theatre. In this dependence of *quanto* upon *tanto,* the idea of indefinite quantity is comprised. Finally, in this sentence:—*Quanti danari mi darete, tanti* or *altrettanti ve ne restituirò,* As much money as you will give me, so much shall I return to you. This, of course, means—Whether you give me much or little money, I shall give it back.

24. *Cotanto* has the same signification, but is considered to be a more energetic form than *tanto.*

(*a*) *Tanto* and *quanto* partake but seldom of the Latin signification of *tantus, quantus,* which includes necessarily the idea of greatness. But if *tanto* and *quanto* in most cases have lost their primitive Latin signification of greatness, it is not so with regard to the quantitative meaning, which they still retain.

EXAMPLE.

Quanti denari egli ha tanti ne spende.
As much money as he has, so much he spends of it.

Exercises on the Numeral and Indeterminate Adjectives.

1. The hour for seeing him again appears to me a thousand years.

Appears to me, *fàmmisi;* the hour; for (of) seeing him, *rivederlo;* a thousand years.

2. The second attack* of* fever are wont when* they* seize the weak patients, who have relapsed, to have a more injurious effect upon them than the first.

More the second fevers; are wont, *sogliono;* to seize, *sopravvenire*,(gerund); to have . . . effect, *offendere;* the weak . . . relapsed, *ricaduti infermi;* than the; first, *premiero.*

3. One must consider that as the Dawn, as she* has three states, and three distinct colours, so she* has three names: white, vermilion, and orange.

One must, *s' ha da; considerare;* Dawn, *aurora; bianca; vermiglia;* orange colour, *rancia.*

4. After your (2) departure (1), I have lost four teeth more, and what* with decayed and broken ones, I find I* have* now only two in all.

Partita; your, *vostra;* I have lost, *ho scapitato di;* (of) more, *più;* with decayed, *fra morto;* broken, *ferito;* I of them, *me ne;* to find, *trovare;* in all, *in tutto;* two only (adj.)

5. You are one of those wiseacres, who are always looking for (the) five feet to a sheep.

You are; one . . . wiseacres, *un cert' uomo;* who . . . looking, *che cercate sempre;* to a (the); sheep, *montone.*

6. And if your Lordship should there see anything else which does not please you, I pray you to let me be acquainted with it, because I shall always hold it a favour to be corrected by one like you, and by heaven, by any one else but Castelvetro.

And if; your Lordship, *Vostra Signoria;* there; to see, *vedere,* (imp. subj.); anything else, *altro;* to you, *le;* to please. *soddisfare* (imp. subj.); to let . . . with it, *di farmene avvertito;* because; I . . . a favour, *mi terrò sempre a favore;* (of) to be; like you, *suo pari;* by (the), *pel;* by . . . else, *da ogni altro;* but, *che.*

7. Too much severity produces hatred, and too much indulgence disobedience, and it happens to men as to the chords of the musical (2) instruments (1), which if any one tightens too much, they break, and if any one relaxes them too much, they sound without obtaining from* them* harmony or concord.

(The) too much; *austerità; generare;* indulgence, *remissione; inobbedienza;* and to (of the) men; happens, *interviene;* to (of); which . . . too much, *che chi le tira troppo;* they break, *si rompono;* if any one, *chi;* them; *rilasciare;* without . . . concord; to sound, *risuonare.*

8. Greek fables are the* source* of instruction to men, inasmuch as some of them under allegories contain representatives* of* the work of nature; others are a comfort under human calamity (pl.); others chase from our minds disturbances and terrors; and others extinguish in us incorrect opinions; and others have* been* invented, to be* of* some other most important use to* us*.

(The) Greek; to men; of; *documento;* inasmuch as, *imperocchè; contenere;* work (pl.) *opera;* of (the); a (of); *conforto;* under; (to the); to chase, *scacciare;* from (the) our; mind, *animo; perturbazione;* others in us; *estinguere;* incorrect, *le menrette; inventare,* (are); some, *qualche;* use, *utilità.*

9. Nature in every age, in every country, in every custom, is always one and* the* same thing.

Nature; country, *provincia;* custom, *abito; sempremai;* is; one; thing; same.

Readings in Poetry.

1. Questo mondo è, come il proverbio dice,
Una gabbia di matti: ognuno è matto,
Ognuno ha la sua sorte di pazzia:
Chi pecca in una e chi in un altra cosa:

Infin siam tutti pazzi; e chi si tiene
Il più savio è il più matto:
Ognun si crede
D' aver più ingegno e cognizion degli altri,
Ognun vede i difetti del compagno,
Nè vede i suoi, nè se stesso conosce.—*Bentivoglio.*

This world is, as the proverb says, a cage of madmen; every one is mad, every one has his own kind of folly; one sins in one thing, and one in another,—in short, we are all fools, and he who holds himself the most wise is most mad. Every one fancies himself to possess more genius and knowledge than others. Every one sees the defects of his companion, but sees not his own and knows not himself.

2. Come nell' alto mar legno talora,
Che da due venti, sia percosso e vinto,
Ch' ora uno innanzi l' ha mandato ed ora
Un altro al primo termine respinto,
E l' han girato da poppa e da prora.—*Arios.*

As on the deep sea a ship sometimes, which is struck and overcome by two winds, so that now one has carried it forward, and now the other has driven it back to its first position, and they have turned it "forward and off."

Blind Beggars.

3. La strada i più si fanno col bastone:
Altri la guida segue d' un suo cane;
Che canta a piè d' un usdio un' orazione,
E fa scorci di bocca e voci strane,
Chi suona il ribecchin, chi 'l colascione:
Così tutti si van buscando il pane.—*Malman.*

The most of them managed with a stick to find their way. Some of them follow the guidance of their dog; one sings at the bottom of a gate a prayer, and makes grimaces with his mouth, and strange sounds; one plays the rebeck, one the guitar; thus all go begging their bread.

The Ants.

4. Qual va, qual vien, qual sola, e quale in schiera,
E qual grave di peso e qual leggera.

Some go, others come, some alone, and others in companies, and some laden with burden, and others light.

5. Come le pecorelle escon dal chiuso
   Ad una, a due, a tre, e l' altre stanno,
   Timidette atterrando l' occhio e' l muso,
E ciò che fa la prima, e l' altre fanno,
   Adossandosi a lei, s' ella s' arresta,
   Semplici e quete, e lo 'mperchè non sanno.—*Dante.*

As the young sheep come out of the fold by one, two, and three, and the others remain, half afraid, bending to the ground their eye and mouth; and that which the first does, so also do the others, falling upon her if she stops, simple and quiet, and know not the reason why.

6. N' usciron d' improvviso altri con pali,
   E con forche, e con bronchi aguzzi al fuoco;
   Altri con mazze noderose e gravi,
   E tutti con quell' armi, che a ciascuno,
   Fecer l' ira e la fretta.—*Virg. Enei.*

They issued forth from thence unexpectedly, some with sticks and with pitchforks, and with stakes pointed in the fire; some with clubs knotty and heavy; and all with such arms as anger and haste had supplied to each.

Section IV.

The Indicative Adjectives.

26. We have already given a distinct definition of the indeterminate adjective of quantity, and will now proceed to consider those which are neither qualificative nor quantitative, and are usually placed under the category of pronouns. It will however be seen, that in reality they are not pronouns, but belong to a distinct class of adjectives, which has a distinct office of its own.

27. These adjectives are, *questo,* this; *quello,* that; *codesto,* that near you; *costui, colui,* this one, that one; *costei, colei,* the feminines of *costui, colui; altro,* another; *altrui,* of others; *tale,* of such kind; *quale,* the same as; and some others.

28. These adjectives include in themselves the ideas of individuality and collocation. On account of this they are called indicative adjectives, as they define the condition of

the substantive by position and identity; and are, by means of these, distinguished from every other individuality. They never use the definite article, but are naturally considered to include it in themselves.

29. *Questo* indicates that the substantive to which it is united is an object of a certain nature, which is near the person who speaks.

Quello indicates a certain object placed in a certain place, at some distance from the speaker, and from the person whom he addresses. Take the following examples:—

Questo garzoncello s' incomincia a domesticar con quella gente strana ed ardita.

That gentle lad begins to domesticate himself with that strange and daring people.

Vedi il padre di questo, e vedi l' avo.

Behold the father of this man, and behold the grandfather.

Queste parole amaramente punsero l' animo del re.

These words bitterly pierced the mind of the king.

30. In Italian we have a third indicative adjective, *cotesto*, which defines the object itself and its position, which is considered to be near the person who is addressed.

(*b*) *Questo, codesto,* and *quello,* derive from the Latin *hic, iste,* and *ille.*

31. It must also be observed that adverbs, which may be considered indeclinable adjectives of the verb, have their similar varieties of meaning; indicating—1stly, a place distant from the person addressed, *là or lì*, there; 2dly, a place near the speaker, *quà* or *quì*, here; and 3dly, a place near the person addressed, *costà* or *costì*, there.

The following passages will define their respective meanings:—

Innanzi che codesto ladroncello che v' è costà dallato vada altrove, decidetevi un tratto cosa dovete farne di lui.

Before that little thief who is beside you goes away, decide at once what you ought to do with him.

"E tu che se' costì, anima viva,
Partiti da cotesti che son morti."—*Dante.*

And do thou, who art there (in that very place) O living soul! depart from those (who are near you) that are dead.

32. When speaking of men, *quegli* and *questi* are used mostly in the singular number, but not *codesti;* for a lady, *questa, quella, codesta.*

EXAMPLE.

Quegli rispose, io son caduto in una fossa.

He answered, I have fallen into a ditch.

33. *Costui, costei, colui, colei,* belong exclusively to men and women, and are not subject to the changes of meaning, which are given to *questi, quegli, codesto,* but have a certain special meaning of their own, which we will presently define.

The first remark which we will make is—that all these words are in appearance pronouns, for they stand alone, and express a substantive, which is understood. They are, however, by no means substitutes for the nouns. On the contrary, if the noun were expressed, they would still be used, since they must rather be considered accidents of the noun, which have the word *uomo* understood, as with *costei, colei, &c., donna* is understood; and the force of our argument will be at once felt, if we make use of the longer epithets, *quest' uomo, questa donna, quell' uomo, quella donna.*

It is evident that the *i* in these adjectives, is a characteristic vowel, indicating *uomo* or *donna,* &c.

34. *Questo* and *quello,* placed in opposition in one sentence, have the force of *the latter* and *the former* in English, or *hic* and *ille* in Latin. We will give this sentence, as an example:—

Io spesso mi avvenni con persone di maniere più tosto ruvide e dure, e con altre tutte amabilità e dolcezza, e tirai la conclusione che spesso quelle vi potranno forse fare del bene e servigj importanti, e quasi mai del male, e queste vi potranno facilmente ingannare ed insidiarvi. Non intendo peraltro dir che fra queste e quelle non vi sia il giusto mezzo di una franca amabilità.

I have often met with persons of rather rough and harsh manners, and again with others who are all amiability and sweetness, and have drawn this conclusion, that the former may often do you good, and render you important services, and will scarcely ever injure you, while the latter may often deceive and plot against you. By this, of course, we do not intend to imply that a just mean of frank amiability between the latter and the former does not exist.

35. *Costui* and *colui, costei* and *colei,* have sometimes the signification of scorn and contempt.

EXAMPLES.

Non vi lasciate inviluppare dalle lisciate parole di costui, le quali sotto un falso velame di bontà, ricoprono un veleno manifesto.

Do not let yourself be ensnared by the blandishing words of that fellow, which, under a false veil of goodness, disguise a manifest venom.

Che uomo è costui il quale nè vecchiezza, nè infermità, nè paura di morte dalla sua malvagità l'hanno potuto ritrarre.

What man is this fellow whom neither old age, nor infirmity, nor fear of death, have been able to withdraw from his wickedness?

36. Sentences may be found, in which *costui* and *colui* have only the simple signification of *questi* and *quegli,* but this occurs more frequently in books than in conversation, as in the following sentence:—

Ella che si era avveduta del guatar di costui, per uccellarlo, alcuna volta guatava lui, alcun sospiretto gettando.

She who had noticed his peeping at her, in order to ensnare him, looked at him occasionally, breathing out at times a sigh.

37. These adjectives have also a certain faculty of adding sublimity or exaltation to the signification. With *costui* this, however, is not the case, and rarely with *colui,* but frequently with *costei* and *colei,* which are used by the poets, when the mind being agitated, exalts the person who causes the agitation. Sometimes this is used by those who exalt the

gifts of beauty, as Petrarch does, and it will be seen in the following examples:—

"Costei per fermo nacque in Paradiso."—*Pet.*

This gracious lady was for certain born in Paradise.

"Colei che sola a me par donna."—*Pet.*

The one who alone to me appears an exalted woman.

38. *Altri*, which we have included in the class of adjectives of indeterminate quantity, has also in certain cases the meaning of an indicative adjective, when used as a correlative of *questo*, and other indicative adjectives, as in these examples: *Questi è pronto ad ubbidirmi, l'altro è protervo ai miei comandi*, this one is ready to obey me, but the other is disobedient to my commands. *Questo libro è buono, l'altro è cattivo*, this book is good, but the other is bad. In this case *altro* is used with the article, for without the article it could not be used to signify any particular substantive.

39. *Altrui* is a genitive derived from *altri*, as for instance: *Invidia è tristezza dentro nata nell' animo d' alcuno per la felicità altrui* (or *d' altri*), Envy is a kind of melancholy engendered in the mind of any one by the prosperity of others. If *altrui* be used with the definite article, it indicates the *property of others*, as: *Chi toglie l' altrui, o che sia per violenza o per frode, è un ladro*, He who takes the property of others, whether by violence or by fraud, is a robber.

40. *Tale* and *cotale* are likewise indicative adjectives, and denote the condition of unchanged individuality, enforcing as it were the idea of it. *Tali parole non mi garbano*, Such words do not please me. Words of this determinate character, and which are by no means changed, do not please me. *Cotali uomini sempre mi furono nemici*, Such men were always enemies to me—that is to say, A certain class of men who are, as they are, were enemies to me.

41. *Quale* has an approximative signification to *tale*, but with a certain diversity in confirming the hypothetical tendency and condition. *Quali sieno le vostre ragioni, non*

mai mi persuaderete, Whatever your reasons may be, you will never persuade me. *Le vostre ragioni,* Your reasons are so and so; and if they were thus, as they are (which qualifies the immutability), they do not satisfy me.

42. *Tale* is a correlative of *quale,* and is only the expression of *quello* in a kind of immutable manner. *Quale è il padre tale è il figlio* is equivalent to *Quello che è il padre, il medisimo,* or *così è il figlio.*

43. The possessive adjective we will not discuss at present, as they are simply pronouns placed in the genitive of possession under an adjective form. We shall, therefore, proceed in the first place to the pronouns.

Although we may have omitted something in the theory of adjectives which are not qualificative, we believe we have treated them with sufficient fulness, and have ensured their right use in the Italian language being thoroughly understood.

Exercises on the Indicative Adjectives.

1. This man* in his first age was addicted to the habit of passing off little stories—nay, even lies!

This; was (himself), *erasi;* addicted, *dato;* habit, *arte;* to pass off (to sell), *vendere;* story, *parola* (dim. *etta*); nay, *anzi;* lie, *menzogna.*

2. For* a* long time the Church was in tribulation on* account* of* (for) heresy, and on this account had many wars (sing.)

Long, *gran;* was the Church; *eresia;* on this account, *per questo; molto;* war, *guerra;* had (perf.).

3. It is better to love a robber than he who is daily telling* lies.

Maggiormente è da amare; robber, *ladro;* he who, *quello che;* is, *sta;* daily, *cotidianamente;* (in); lie, *bugia* (plu.).

4. At times some people* fatigue themselves in clearing the field of others, whilst their own is quite full of thorns and nettles.

Talora; affaticarsi; in (to); to clear, *purgare;* (the) of others, *gli altrui; campo;* whilst, *mentre che;* (the) their; own, *medesimo;* quite full, *tutto;* thorns, *pruni.*

5. Consider, whether it* appear just to you, that a man should insolently enter into the vineyards (sing.) and (into the) fields of other people, and gather there the harvest and vintage.

Consider; if; to you, *vi;* appear, *paja;* *insolentemente;* a man; should enter, *entri;* field, *campo;* of others; there; (should) gather the harvest, *faccia le ricolte;* and the vintage, *vendemmia* (plu.).

6. I know well that these words of mine will produce little fruit, and that nothing is more thrown away than blame upon him who neither is capable of what* is* right, nor fears the punishment of wicked (2) deeds (1).

I know; of mine, *mia;* *parola;* will produce, *hanno a far;* nothing, *nessuna cosa;* throw away, *gettare;* (the) blame, *riprensione;* upon (in); him, *colui;* *capace;* of (the) right, *giusto;* nor, *nè;* *castigo.*

7. If we wish to appropriate friendship to our own advantage, and not to the advantage of him whom we* may love (ind.), this will not be (fut.) friendship, but rather traffic.

We wish, *vogliamo;* to appropriate, *riferir;* to the; advantage, *uso;* our own, *nostro;* advantage, *comodo;* him, *colui;* whom, *che;* *amare;* *traffico.*

8. He cuts off from friendship honesty and its dignity, who practises (2) it (1), that he may derive advantage from it.

Colui; to cut off, *togliere;* (translate) the honesty to the friendship; its, *la sua;* *dignitade;* that he may derive from it, *per averne utile.*

Sentences on Poetry.

1. Che dolce più, che più giocondo stato
Saria di quel d' un amoroso core?
Se non fosse l' uom sempre stimolato,
Da quel sospetto rio, da quel timore,
Da quel martir, da quella frenesia,
Da quella rabbia, detta gelosia.—*Arios.*

What could be sweeter, what a more delightful state than that of a loving heart, if it were not that man is always excited by that guilty suspicion, by that fear, by that torture, by that frenzy, by that madness, called jealousy?

2. Quanto giova il mirar pender da un' erta,
Le capre e pascer questo *o* quel virgulto!—*Sanaz.*

How delightful it is to see the goats hanging on a precipice, and plucking here and there the shrubs!

3. Io parlo per ver dire,
Non per odio d' altrui *o* per disprezzo.—*Pet.*

I speak to tell the truth, not from hatred of others, or from contempt of them.

CHAPTER X.

The Personal Pronouns.

Declensions of Personal Pronouns.

FIRST PERSON.

SINGULAR.				PLURAL.			
Nom.	I,	*io.*		*Nom.*	We,	*noi.*	
Gen.	Of me,	*di me.*		*Gen.*	Of us,	*di noi.*	
Dat.	To me,	*a me.*	*mi.*	*Dat.*	To us,	*a noi.*	*ci* or *ne.*
Acc.	Me,	*me.*	*mi.*	*Acc.*	Us,	*noi.*	*ci* or *ne.*
Ab.	From, *or* by me,	*da me.*		*Ab.*	From, *or* by us,	*da noi.*	

SECOND PERSON.

SINGULAR.				PLURAL.			
Nom.	Thou,	*tu.*		*Nom.*	You,	*voi.*	
Gen.	Of thee,	*di te.*		*Gen.*	Of you,	*di voi.*	
Dat.	To thee,	*a te.*	*ti.*	*Dat.*	To you,	*a voi.*	*vi.*
Acc.	Thee,	*te.*	*ti.*	*Acc.*	You,	*voi.*	*vi.*
Voc.	O thou,	*o tu.*		*Voc.*	O you,	*o voi.*	
Ab.	From, *or* by thee,	*da te.*		*Ab.*	From, *or* by you,	*da voi.*	

THIRD PERSON *Masc.*

SINGULAR.				PLURAL.			
Nom.	He, *or* it,	*egli* or *esso, ei, e'.*		*Nom.*	They,	*eglino* or *egli, ei, essi, e'.*	
Gen.	Of him,	*di lui.*		*Gen.*	Of them,	*di loro.*	
Dat.	To him,	*a lui.*	*gli*	*Dat.*	To them,	*a loro.*	
Acc.	Him,	*lui.*	*lo* or *il.*	*Acc.*	Them,	*loro.*	*li* or *gli.*
Ab.	From, *or* by him,	*da lui.*		*Ab.*	From, *or* by them,	*da loro*	

THIRD PERSON *Fem.*

SINGULAR.			PLURAL.		
Nom. She *or* it,	*ella* or *essa.*		*Nom.* They,	*elleno* or *esse.*	
Gen. Of her,	*di lei.*		*Gen.* Of them,	*di loro.*	
Dat. To her,	*a lei.*	*le.*	*Dat.* To them,	*a loro.*	
Acc. Her,	*lei.*	*la.*	*Acc.* Them,	*loro.*	*le.*
Ab. From, *or* by her,	*da lei.*		*Ab.* From, *or* by them,	*da loro*	

Section I.

Rules on the Personal Pronouns.

1. *Io* and *tu, noi* and *voi,* are the nominative forms of pronouns of the first and second person; *egli, ei, e', eglino, egli, ei, e',* in the masculine, and *ella* and *elleno* in the feminine, are forms of the third person. The singular nominatives are quite distinct from the other cases, which have the form *me, te, lui, lei.* This does not happen, however, with the form of the oblique plural cases, which have *noi, voi,* as in the nominative. Those, however, which are of the third person, have *loro* in the masculine, as well as in the feminine.

2. The genitive is formed with the *segnacaso* (case-sign) before the forms of the oblique cases, as *di me, di te, di lui, di loro.* A true genitive, however, with a genitive form, does not exist in the personal pronouns, for in that case it takes the form of the possessive, as we shall see when we come to treat on that subject. The personal pronoun has, under other circumstances, a genitive form, which is apparent but not true, as for example, after the verb as,—*egli parla a lungo di lui nella sua lettera,* he speaks at length concerning him in his letter; that is to say, *intorno a lui,* about him.

3. The dative case is expressed by *a,* and the ablative by *da.* They are subject to the rules of cases, as well as nouns, but without the article as is natural, because they are by them-

selves individually defined, and, in fact, stand chiefly in the place of proper nouns. The accusative, like the noun, is governed by the transitive verb, but there is another accusative with the pronoun *se*, by means of which the agent in a verb exercises a transitive signification on itself, and becomes also the patient. This we will discuss at greater length, when we speak of the pronoun *se*. The vocative case is wanting in the first and third person, since their nature does not allow of a vocative. In the second person, it is the same as the nominative, as—*O tu, il più giusto degli uomini*, O thou, the justest of all men; *O voi, che udite i lamenti d' un infelice*, O ye, who hear the lamentations of an unfortunate.

4. The forms of the genitive and ablative cases appear well defined and simple, but those of the dative and ablative are two-fold. They are as follows:—*a me*, or *mi*; *a noi*, or *ci*, *a*, *te*, or *ti*; and so on with the other datives and accusatives. These will form the subject of our consideration.

In these pronouns we see that all the dative and accusative cases have two forms. The one is complete and the other contracted. We will now endeavour to state, under what circumstances the one and the other are respectively used.

The contracted form is most generally used, although there are cases in which the entire form is employed. Of these we will speak hereafter, as being rare and exceptional. It is now our task to observe the rules and the manner of using the contracted form of each pronoun, taken by itself. We will first of all take the pronoun *io*, and then the application of the same rule will be easy, with regard to other datives and accusatives.

5. The dative of *io* is *a me* or *mi*. We must now determine when *mi* should be used instead of *a me*.

The general rule is to use *mi* in common discourse, and under all ordinary circumstances of life and thought. It goes with the verb, for we know that the dative, as well as the accusative, is a dependency of the verb. This contracted dative, which by our hypothesis is *mi,* and which may be also *ti, ci, gli, vi,* is expressed after the verb.

6. Every dative and accusative case is used before the verb in a contracted form, throughout the whole indicative and subjunctive mood, as *io ti scrivo,* I write to you; *egli mi vedeva,* he saw me; *voi mi parlate,* you speak to me; *che dessi mi veggano,* that they may see me. With the compound tenses it goes before the auxiliary verbs. Thus it will be said, *egli mi aveva parlato,* he had spoken to me; *noi gli avevamo scritto,* we had written to him; *voi mi avrete ammonito.* Take as example the following stanza of Ariosto.

"Uno il saluta, un altro se gl' inchina;
Altri la mano, altri gli bacia il piede,
Ognun quanto più può se gli avvicina,
E beato si tien chi presso il vede,
E più chi 'l tocca, chè toccar divina,
E sopra natural cosa si crede.
Lo pregan tutti, e vanno al ciel le grida,
Che sia lor Re, lor capitan, lor guida."—*Arios.*

One salutes him, another bows to him; others kiss his hand, others his feet. Every one approaches to him as much as he can; and, whoever sees him near, considers himself happy, and more so he who touches him, because he thinks that he touches some divine and supernatural thing. All entreat him, and their cries ascend to heaven, to be their King, their captain, their guide.

7. This contracted form of the dative and accusative is used after the verb, with the infinitive mood, the simple and compound gerund, and the second person singular, and the first and second persons plural of the imperative—but not with the third persons singular and plural. It also follows the present participle and the past also, if the auxiliary gerund is silent. We must then say, *Egli venne a vedermi* instead of *a mi vedere.* It will be seen, from the form *vedermi,* that the *e* final is taken from the infinitive, in order to assimilate the contracted form of the pronoun. Following the same rule, it is also united to the gerund, as in this phrase, *Vedendolo*

si consolò tutto, Seeing him he was entirely consoled; and to the imperative, as *Sgridami, che hai ragione*, Rebuke me, for you are right.

EXAMPLES.

Vedetelo, che bravo ragazzo.
See him, what a good boy he is.

Mi scriva sovente, ed ío gli risponderò ogni volta.
Let him write often, and I will reply to him every time.

Mi obbediscano, e si chiameranno contenti.
Let them obey me, and they will be (themselves) satisfied.

" Par che la sua viltà rimproverarsi
Senta nelle altrui glorie, e se ne rode."—*Tasso.*

It appears that he felt his cowardice reproved in the glory of others, and vexes itself at it.

Prepariamoci a morire col viver bene, e da Cristiani.
Let us prepare ourselves for dying by living well and as Christians.

Il sonno sottilmente sottentrava negli occhi non avvedentisi.
Sleep gradually stole into the eyes not perceiving it.

8. If the contracted pronouns are two, one is always in the dative case, and the other in the accusative, and follow the same rule in their position with the verb; but the *i* of the pronoun which precedes the other is changed into *e*. Thus *egli me lo disse* must be used instead of *egli mi lo disse*, he said it to me. In this sentence *Non dimenticate di ricordarmelo*, Do not forget to remind me of it, *me lo* is used instead of *mi lo*, and when joined to the infinitive, gerund, or imperative, becomes one word.

EXAMPLES.

Parti (for ti pare) ch' io abbia paura a dirtelo?
Does it seem to thee that I am afraid to tell it you?

E' debbe portar quella veste al sarto, per farsela rassettare al suo dosso.
He must take that garment to the tailor, to get it fitted to his back.

9. If *gli*, to him, precedes another pronoun, in place

of changing the *i* into *e*, as is done by the other pronouns, it is left entire, and an *e* is introduced between *gli* and the other pronouns. We say, for instance, *glielo, gliela, gliele, gliene,* not *glilo, glila, glile, gline.*

EXAMPLES.

Piena di stizza glielo tolse di mano.

Full of rage she snatched it from his hand.

Monna Tessa corse coll' unghie nel viso a Calandrino, e tutto glielo graffiò.—*Bocc.*

Monna Tessa rushed with her nails at the face of Calandrino, and she scratched it (to him) all over.

10. In the table of pronouns it will be seen, that the masculine contracted form of *egli* is *gli* for the dative singular, and the *feminine* is *le.* But if a personal pronoun in the accusative comes after *le,* it is changed into *gli,* although it (*gli*) is a masculine form. This expedient is adopted for the sake of euphony; since, to say *lelo, lela, lele, lene* would sound harsh, and therefore the forms *glielo, gliela, gliele, gliene,* are adopted instead, as in this sentence:—*Glielo dissi cento volte, ma ella non volle ascoltarmi,* I told it to her a hundred times, but she would not heed me.

11. It happens occasionally that two sentences are placed one in opposition to the other, and in that case two dative cases of personal pronouns are sometimes placed in opposition to each other, either by way of comparison or antithesis. In that case the contracted form is abandoned, and the entire form is substituted. This happens even when there are not the two opposite sentences before mentioned, but when only one sentence occurs. This sentence must, however, have something which gives it peculiar energy in expression or construction. Take the following example:—

Egli mira lei ed ella lui, ed in quel mirarsi d' ambidue l' occhio loro visibilmente s' infiammava d' ira, e parea che mettesse lampi, forieri della prossima tempesta.

He looks at her and she at him, and in this looking at one another the eyes of both of them were inflamed with anger, and it appeared that they flashed lightning, the forerunner of the approaching tempest.

"Gridò Erotimo allor, 'l' arte maestra
Te non risana, o la mortal mia destra.'"—*Tasso.*

Erotimo cried out then, 'the master art of healing did not thee, or my mortal right hand.'

Section II.

The Special Rules.

12. Having given the most general and difficult rules which affect the personal pronouns, we will now proceed to notice some of their properties, which are of a more special nature.

The nominative case is not usually expressed, as it is sufficiently indicated by the termination of the verb. The first person of the present is rarely found with the pronoun, except to give a certain degree of simplicity or force, as in this sentence, *Io sono ben sfortunata,* I am unfortunate indeed, *Io* is used in order to make the expression more forcible. Take as another instance, *Io ben m' avvidi io, che ei mi voleva ingannare, ma pure io non rimasi di confidarmi a lui, sperando che ciò non fosse.* This *io* is also repeated after the verb, and gives an air of simplicity to the phrase, but is more commonly used by uneducated persons and children. The following sentence will be an instance of it:—

Io non so a che io non mi tengo, che io non ti ficco le mani negli occhi e traggogliti.—*Bocc.*

I know not how I can restrain myself, from thrusting my hands into your eyes and pulling them out.

13. The characteristics of the plural being so decided in their nature, the pronoun may be all the more safely left out. Thus, *eglino* and *elleno* are rare, the general form of the verb sufficing for the expression of the third person plural. *Egli* is often written instead of *eglino,* and sometimes even *ei* and *e'.*

14. It is important to know that poetry loves to express

the personal pronouns, in order to give the sentence unusual energy and dignity. It does not, therefore, easily allow the omission of pronouns, a practice which in common discourse has become almost universal. The pronoun, when used in the nominative case, and still more in the vocative, with the verb, gives great additional energy, as,

"Tu piangi, Soliman, tu, che distrutto
Mirasti il regno tuo col ciglio asciutto!"—*Tass.*

Thou weepest, O Soliman, thou that hast seen with dry eyes thy kingdom destroyed.

15. In those tenses where the person endings resemble each other, it is desirable that the personal pronoun should be expressed under all circumstances, when there is any danger of ambiguity, as for example, in this phrase, *Amava Gianotto moltissimo*, it is not known whether *io amava*, or *egli amava*, or *ella amava*, is meant. It will then be proper to introduce the pronoun. If the context of the sentence explains the ambiguity, it is better to omit the pronoun, as *Mi fiderò di voi tuttavia, ma vi credeva più onesto*, I will still trust in you, but I thought you more honest. Here there is no occasion to say *io vi credeva*, since there is no ambiguity whatever. Again, if we find this sentence, *Se credessi di riescire, vorrei avvertirnelo*, If I thought I should succeed, I should wish to tell him of it, the verb *credessi* does not require *io*, although the first and second persons of the imperfect subjunctive are alike, for this reason, that *vorrei* is known to be the first person, and therefore *credessi* must be the same.

16. Pronouns are frequently found after the verb in other occasions, besides those of the infinitive, etc., as we have mentioned in § 7, although they may at the same time be placed before them. This rule requires a little further explanation.

There are verbal expressions which submit easily to this kind of assimilation. This happens especially in the imperfect and preterite, and most often in their third person singular.

EXAMPLES.

Ella vergognavasi di rammaricarsene con alcuno, sì perchè n' era stata fatta avveduta innanzi, sì per le beffe che ne avrebbe avuto.

She was ashamed to complain about it to any one, both because she had been warned of it before, and on account of the jests which she would have suffered about it.

Trovossi egli a Parigi in povero stato.—*Bocc.*

He was at Paris in a poor condition.

Presemi per la cappa, e tiratomi appiè, tante mi diè, che tutto mi ruppe.—*Bocc.*

He seized me by the hood, and threw me down at his feet, and gave me so many blows, that he quite demolished me.

17. If the verb ends with an accent, as is commonly the case with many of the third persons in the preterite, and always in the first person of the future, and if the personal pronoun in the dative and accusative case is assimilated with the verb, the new compound word doubles the consonant with which the pronoun begins. The same thing happens with every verb of a monosyllabic form, as often as it is united to a pronoun, either in obedience to a rule, or voluntarily. We write, *Dammi il libro che jeri leggevi*, Give me the book which you were reading yesterday; where, instead of *dami*, we say *dammi*. *Dillo a lei prima che altri lo sappiano*, Say it to her before others know it. *Dillo* is a compound of *di* and *lo*. *Stanco della vita cittadinesca dassi alla vita ritirata campestre*, Wearied with a town life, he betakes himself to a retired country life. In this sentence, *dassi* is put for *egli si dà*; and we give also the following classical examples on this rule:—

"Ogni pelo arricciossi,
E scolorossi al Saraceno il viso;
La voce ch' era per uscir fermossi."—*Arios.*

Every hair stood on end, and the countenance of the Saracen lost its color; the voice, which was on the point of being uttered, was stopped.

"Le agghiacciò il sangue, e impallidille il viso."
—*Arios.*

He caused her blood to freeze, and her face to turn pale.

"Per erto calle a vera fama vassi."

By steep paths one mounts to true glory.

"Vi pianterò quì, e lascierovvi in asso."

I shall fix you here, and leave you quite alone.

18. It is found that assimilations with the third person are more natural than those with the first person, and the former, therefore, occur more frequently in authors; but examples are not wanting of their being added to the first person, in various tenses, and even in the preterite of the first conjugation.

"Vantomi in lui scoprir gli ultimi sensi,
E i secreti pensier trargli dal petto."—*Tasso.*

I boast myself of discovering his deepest feelings, and of extracting his secret thoughts from his breast.

"Piòvonmi amare lagrime dal viso."—*Petrar.*

Bitter tears rain down from my face.

19. The third person plural has also pronouns sometimes joined to it, as *risolveransi* for *si risolveranno*; *domandavansi l' un l' altro*, for *si domandavano.*

20. The accent on the verb is retained, notwithstanding the addition of the personal pronouns. In such a case, it may occasionally happen that in these compound words, three short syllables may occasionally follow, as, *Dìtemelo presto, che non ho tempo da perdere,* say it to me immediately; for I have no time to lose. *Dite* is the original verb, and as the accent is preserved in its original position, *dìtelo, dìtemelo,* will be said.

Loro and *a loro,* being dissyllables, have no contracted form. They are used as they stand, but there is a slight indication of a contracted form in the power which is given of inserting or omitting *a*, the sign of the dative, at pleasure.

21. *Gli* is used by authors with elegance in the place of *li*, in the accusative plural masculine. *Li*, however, cannot be

used elegantly for *gli*, to him, although it is often found even in the best authors.

The accusative masculine singular has *il* as often as *lo;* these are indeed used indifferently. But *lo* must be used in place of *il*, when the verb commences with *s*, joined to another consonant. We write *lo sgridai*, and not *il sgridai*, although it can scarcely be considered an error to write *il sgridai.*

EXAMPLES.

Egli, per vaghezza di così ampia eredità che da loro ne li verrebbe, gli avvelenò.

He, coveting such a large inheritance, that from them would come to him, he poisoned them:

Where *gli*, them, is for *li*, and *li*, to him, is for *gli*.

I beni medesimi di questo mondo sono la nostra infelicità; perchè non avendogli, non si gode, e avendogli, bisogna necessariamente lasciargli *o* perdergli, poichè *o* noi ce ne andiamo prima di loro, *o* dessi, che sono pur fragili come noi, se ne vanno innanzi.—*Peranda, lett.*

The very goods of this world are our misery; because not having them, we do not enjoy them, and having them, we must necessarily leave them or lose them, since either we shall go away before them, or they, since they are also fragile as we are, will go away before us.

22. *Me lo, te lo, ve lo, se lo* may also be united when they precede the verb and make *melo, telo, velo,* &c. They may also be abbreviated; and in that case appear under the forms *mel, tel, vel.* If *non* is added to *il* or *lo, nol* may be used. *Glien* may also be used for *gliene*, as *egli glien parlò.* He spoke to him of it.

" L' onore è di tal costume,
Che s' è perduto, nol racquisti mai."—*Rucel.*

Honor is of such a nature, that if it be lost it can never be acquired again.

23. In the Italian language there is a familiar custom, which has extended itself throughout society, of making use of the third person feminine singular when addressing an

individual in polite conversation. The singular feminine is used when there is only one person; the plural when more are addressed. This is also the case in speaking to a gentleman, and then the past participle is made masculine. In writing letters the same form is used, the principle being the same both in writing and speaking.

EXAMPLE.

Abbiamo determinato per obbedienza e per ossequio di legger l' opera insieme, e le prometto che se mai, il che pure è impossibile, ci fossimo per iscorgere qualche piccolo neo, tanto il Signor Carlo, che io, gliel avviseremo.—*Redi, lett.*

We have determined, in obedience to and compliance with your wishes, to read the work together; and I promise you that if ever, which is almost impossible, we should discover any speck of a fault, Signor Carlo, as well as myself, will apprise you of it.

24. If *voi* is used, the sound is rather unpleasing; it is also considered an inelegant and foreign form. *Voi* is used when addressing persons of inferior condition, as a servant; but even with dependents, if the relation is confidential, the *voi* is omitted and the *tu* given. Among gentlemen, however, who are on terms of friendship, but scarcely of intimacy, use is made of *voi*, when conversing among themselves. In family life, and with near relatives, *tu* is used in conversation. Vulgar people say *voi* to their father or mother. Those who are of higher station say *ella*. The custom has been introduced, and especially among daughters, of saying *tu* to their father and mother, but the innovation is perhaps not to be praised,—at least it has not been adopted generally.

25. In choice compositions it is considered elegant to place the pronoun before the gerund and the infinitive mood. It is moreover a fixed rule, that the pronoun should be placed before a negative imperative, which must be preceded by *non*, not. For instance we say—*non mi date parole come il solito vostro, ma datemi danari*, Do not give me words according to your custom, but give me money. The third persons of the

imperative do not take the pronoun at the end because strictly speaking such an imperative is in fact scarcely to be considered an imperative at all. *Che mi oda bene prima di andare,* Let him hear me well before he goes, is the same as —*voglio che mi oda bene,* &c., I wish that he should hear me well, &c. and also in Virgil we have,

"Ma la terra m' ingoi, e' l ciel mi fulmini,
E nell' abisso mi trabocchi in prima,
Ch' io ti violi mai, pudico amore."—*Ene. lib.* 4.

But may the earth swallow me up, and may heaven thunder on me, and may I be overwhelmed in the abyss, before I ever violate thee, O chaste love!

26. It is usual to join *me, te, se,* with *con,* and to use these forms *meco, teco, seco*; *nosco* and *vosco* may occasionally be found, but to use them cannot be considered elegant.

EXAMPLE.

Però non entrate meco nè in preconj nè in prologhi; quando volete di me cosa ch' io possa, basta un cenno.—*Caro. lett.*

However do not enter into any apologies or preambles with me; when you wish anything from me that I can do, a hint is sufficient.

Seco medesimo is used, and is occasionally found in the following curious, though not inelegant, form: *con sol me medesimo meco,* all alone.

27. The interjection *ecco,* used to indicate the presence of an object, takes the pronoun at the end, and puts it in the accusative case, as *èccomi,* behold me, or here I am, *èccoti, èccolo.* In French the pronoun precedes, as *me voilà, te voilà,* &c. The English must always take particular care not to use the verb *essere* with *ecco,* although the equivalent form in their language would be, Here I am, &c.

28. *Medesimo* and *stesso* are used as a species of pronominal complement, since they are never found alone, but are always followed by a pronoun, as *Io medesimo,* or *io stesso,* both of which answer to the English *I myself: di te medesimo* or *stesso; a voi medesimi* or *stessi; a lei medesima* or *stessa; a*

loro medesime or *stesse.* It will be observed that *medesimo* and *stesso* agree with the pronoun in gender and number, as if they were adjectives. They may, in fact, be considered adjectives which signify the accidents of a substantive or pronoun.

EXAMPLES.

"D' ogni conforto ignudo, e a me medesmo
Nojoso e grave."—*Bembo.*

Deprived of every comfort, and to myself wearisome and a burden.

Sono tutto ritirato in me stesso, e il pensare è il viver mio.—*Bonfad. lett.*

I am altogether withdrawn into myself, and to think is my life.

"Che sol se stessa e null' altra somiglia."—*Petr.*

Which resembles herself alone, and none other.

"Temerò me medesmo, e da me stesso
Sempre fuggendo, avrò me stesso appresso."—*Tas.*

I shall fear myself, and always flying from myself, shall ever be near myself.

Thus, *quella donna medesima* (or *stessa*) *che viddi jeri, venne da me anche oggi,* That same lady whom I saw yesterday, came to my house to-day. *Medesima* indicates identity in a forcible manner, and is an expression which denotes energy, and therefore partakes of the nature of an adjective, since its design is to fix in the mind that the lady is the same and no other than the one I saw yesterday. In Italian it possesses more energy, than its English equivalent *self* or *selves,* as in the former language it has a more decided expression than in the latter.

29. We have also *esso* and *desso,* which appear to have the same signification. This, however, is not the case, for *esso* is simply the pronoun *egli,* and is applied more frequently to things than persons.

Desso, on the contrary, is a generic pronoun, which is used to indicate both persons and things, and distinguishes their identity in a clearer manner. When at the commencement of a sentence, it gives great energy; and it is used more generally by authors than all the other forms put together.

Section III.

The Reflexive Noun "se."

30. Among the words which are least subject to grammatical definitions we must certainly place the personal noun *se.* Does it belong to the category of nouns? no; for having no nominative case it cannot well in itself bear the meaning of a substantive. It cannot be called the oblique case of *egli,* because *egli* has *lui.* It has, besides, no pronominal condition similar to *egli.* *Se* is, therefore, a mere pronominal form, as complement of the verb, and its peculiar duty is to limit the action of the verb to the agent himself, without allowing it to proceed beyond him—that is to say, to render the action of the verb entirely subjective. Thus, if I say, *Egli si crede felice,* he thinks himself happy, it is the same thing as saying, *crede se felice.* This *se* cannot be considered a pronoun, but has a pronominal form and fixes the action of *credere* on the agent himself, without allowing any expansion.

31. The word *se,* which denotes the verbal action confined to the operator, acquires for itself force by the addition of the qualificative word *stesso,* which in English is represented by *self.* In Italian the expression is more forcible, from the fact of its being sometimes inserted and sometimes omitted. In English, on the contrary, it is used always with the personal pronoun, when it is employed in performing the peculiar office of *se,* which, as we have said before, is to limit the action of the verb to the agent.

32. If we consider fully the office of *se,* we shall find that it is substituted for other substantives, which would complete

the action of the verb either by means of a direct regimen through the accusative, or an indirect complement through the other cases. *Se* performs the same office with the verb, but with the condition that the action of the verb is restrained to the subject in the nominative,—which, at the same time, in the manner we have stated, becomes, as it were, a kind of dependent.

33. Thus, to render this theory more plain, by means of an example, we will give a sentence, where the verb has the dependent in the dative case, and this dependent dative is represented by *a se.*

We will take, in this instance, the sentence :—*E 'l santo uomo era sì abituato al servizio di Dio, che il mondo nullamente poteva a se trarlo,* And the holy man was so habituated to the service of God, that the world could by no means draw him to itself. The complement of the verb *trarre* is the dative expressed by *a se,* by means of which the action is completed in the operator itself, which is *the world.* In another sentence—*Il popolo si vestì a festa per andare incontro al re,* The people clothed themselves in their festival garments, in order to meet the king; *si* is the accusative case, denoting that the action of clothing is finished in the subject itself, and does not depart from it. In this phrase, when *se* takes the place of the substantives in various cases, as a necessary complement of the verb, it is always rendered in English, by *himself, to himself, themselves, herself,* or *to themselves, to herself, oneself.*

34. The same may be said with regard to the other examples which follow, with other verbal dependencies.

EXAMPLE.

Il duca queste cose sentendo, a difesa di se tutte sue forze apparecchiò.

The duke hearing these things, had prepared all his forces for his own defence, or to defend *himself.*

We see that *di se* is the genitive *di* after *a difesa*, which does not proceed beyond the agent, that is to say, the duke, who prepares himself for his own defence. The prepositions *sopra, appresso, verso, infra, con*, are used in the same manner.

EXAMPLES.

Egli tirò sopra di se la cortina.
He drew the curtain over himself.

Ciascuna per se parea ben degna di poema ed istoria.
Each by herself appeared well worthy of song and history.

In all these cases *se* might acquire additional force, by joining to it *stesso* and *medesimo*, or *stessa* and *medesima*.

35. Here an uncertainty arises, whether *se* is in all cases expressed by an English equivalent, or whether in this respect there is some diversity between the two languages.

If the verb has a direct complement, or an indirect one, which requires either the accusative case or other cases after it; and *se* is substituted for the external noun dependent on the verb, the verbal dependency being expressed by the agent himself, the corresponding pronoun is always used in English. This is exemplified in the former sentence, *Il popolo si vestì, o vestì se stesso a festa.* If the verb *vestire* were transitive, in the sense of *vestire un fanciullo*, to clothe a child, it would be changed by means of *si* into a reflected condition, and at the same time would remain transitive; the sole difference being, that the action does not pass on, but is reflected on the agent, who becomes also the patient. In such a case the English *himself* would be a necessary addition.

If the verb has the dative case after it, the same thing may be said. The reflected pronoun *a se*, being a substitute for an external noun in the dative case, must have the reflected pronoun also in English. As for instance in the first example, *il mondo non poteva trarlo a se*, the natural construction of *trarlo* is with the dative case. Thus we say, *trarlo alla casa*, or *a casa*, to take him home; *trarlo alla perdiziom*, to draw him to perdition. Under these circumstances, also, the equivalent of *se* is retained in English.

36. But there is another species of verbs called *neuter passive*, which do not possess any transitive force, that is to say, they are not able to cause the action to pass from one substantive to another. The action in these verbs is therefore restrained to the agent, and cannot bear a transitive sense, either direct or indirect. This effect of reaction is expressed in Italian by the particles, *mi, ti, si, ci, vi*, which render these verbs reflected. In English, this complement of neutral action is usually wanting, and the verb remains in its simple neuter form. Otherwise they translate it by some other phrase, and not with *himself*, &c.

Some of these verbs are, *ammalarsi*, to become ill; *affligersi*, to grieve; *riposarsi*, to repose; *accorgersi*, to perceive; *attristarsi*, to become sorrowful; *beffarsi*, to scoff. Verbs of this kind are often expressed in English by the passive voice, as *contentarsi*, to be contented.

EXAMPLES.

Frederico Imperatore si ammalò forte.

The Emperor Frederick became very ill.

Riposatosi un tratto, egli riprese la via con maggior alacrità.

Having taken some rest, he resumed his journey with greater alacrity.

Egli si levò dritto, e gittando fiamme dagli occhi, disse.

He rose straight up, and flashing fire from his eyes, said:

Più mesi passarono, avanti che di ciò niuna persona s' accorgesse.

Several (or many) months passed before any person observed this.

We may here observe that, in our treatise on the personal pronouns, and also in other parts of this Grammar, we have devoted some attention to the theory of the verb. We shall, therefore, be able to spare the student as well as ourselves the trouble of referring to it again, when we have to speak of the verbs. This is the only method which can reasonably be adopted, as the student is already advanced considerably in the knowledge of the verbs, seeing that we have from the beginning never missed any opportunity that has arisen of giving information concerning them.

37. It sometimes occurs that the verb has *se* after it, with no other design than to confirm the internal moral condition of the substantive, without any other dependency whatever. Under these circumstances, use is made of the affixed cases, *mi, ti, ci, si.* These are introduced in order to increase energy, but may frequently be left out in Italian. In English, affixes of this kind are never used.

EXAMPLES.

Io mi credo che le suore sono tutte a dormire.
I believe that the sisters (nuns) are all asleep.
(Here *mi* is a pleonasm.)
Dal palagio s' uscì, e fuggissi a casa mia.
He went out of the palace, and fled to my house.
(Here the *si* before *uscì* and after *fuggì* is a pleonasm.)
Che tu con noi ti rimanga per questa sera, m' è caro.
It is pleasing to me that you should remain for this evening with us.
(Here *ti* is a pleonasm.)
Io mi sono il più infelice dei mortali.
I am the most unfortunate of mortals.
(*Mi* is in this sentence a pleonasm.)

Section IV.

The Pronominal Particles "vi, ci, ne."

38. The pronominal particle *vi,* which takes very commonly the form *ci,* is used often to signify *intorno,* about; *per,* for; *in,* in; *sopra a questa o quella cosa,* upon this or that thing; *in ciò,* in this; *sopra ciò,* about this; *sopra quello,* about that; and to use more general terms, is used in English for of, to, at, in, for, and upon it or them.

In French, *y*, which is not referred to any person, may be considered to be its precise equivalent. In this sentence, *E' una bella occupazione per lui; egli vi aspirava da lungo tempo,* It is a good occupation for him; he aspired to it long since. The French form would be thus: *Il y aspirait,* &c.

EXAMPLES.

Egli vi ha lavorato intorno molto tempo, ma non vi troverà il suo conto.

He has laboured for a long time about this matter, but he will not find advantage from it.

In French, *il n'y trouvera pas son avantage.*

Quando la cosa è già decisa, sia in bene, sia in male, non c' è più da pensarvi.

When the thing is already decided, whether for good or evil, there is no thinking more about it.

In French, *On n'y doit plus penser.*

Per quanto belle cose vi dicano, non vi ponete pensiero, *or* non vi credete.

Whatever fine things they may say, do not believe in them.

In French, *n'y pensez pas, n'y croyez pas.*

39. *Vi,* which more familiarly is turned into *ci,* has often the force of an adverb, and signifies in that place, *colà,* there, thither, within, and in French is rendered by *y.*

EXAMPLES.

L' ho rintracciato per mare e per terra (everywhere), e non ve l' ho trovato.

I have sought him by land and sea, and have not found him there.

(In French, *Je ne l'y ai trouvé pas.*)

Quando credete voi andarvi (andarci) in quel luogo *or* colà.

When do you think you shall go to that place or thither?

(In French, *d'y aller.*)

40. *Vi* is necessarily changed into *ci,* when there is another *vi* derived from the pronoun *voi,* as *Jeri ho veduto un bel giardino; io vi ci condurrò,* I saw yesterday a beautiful

garden. I shall take you there. *Vi ci* is here used instead of *vi vi.*

41. *Ne* resembles the above mentioned *vi,* but has a more decided character, and corresponds perfectly with the French *en.* It is referred to persons as well as things, and signifies for, with, about, of, to him her, it, them, as well as some of.

EXAMPLES.

Quella donna vi è molto cara, poichè *ne* parlate sempre.

That lady is very dear to you, for you are always speaking of her.

(In French, *vous en parlez toujours.*)

Di mille scudi che aveva, non gliene sono rimasti che pochissimi.

Of the thousand scudi (crowns) which he had, a very few of them only have remained to him.

(*Ne,* means of them.—French, *en sont restés.*)

Questo affare è ben intricato, e non si sa come se ne caveranno, *ne* for *da questo.*

This affair is very intricate, and I do not know how they will get out of it.

(In French, *en tireront.*)

We will also give some other phrases, as *Io ne sono sorpreso di ciò,* I am surprised at it—J'en suis surpris; *Che ne dite?* What do you say about it?—Qu' en dites vous? In this case, *ne* is equal to *intorno a ciò,* about it. *Ne volete voi,* is equivalent to *di questa cosa,* of this thing, do you wish for it? —En voulez vous? *Datemene un poco,* Give me a little of it; *ne* is here the same as *di ciò,* of it. *Se volete* del danaro, ve *ne* darò, If you wish for money I will give some to you. *Ne* is here equivalent to *qualche poco di quello,* a little of it—Je vous en donnerai.

Section V.

The Possessive Adjectives.

42. The possessive adjectives are *mio,* mine; *tuo,* thine; *suo,* his; *nostro,* ours; *vostro,* yours; which make in the

plural *miei, tuoi, suoi,* in an irregular manner. *Nostri* and *vostri* are the plural of *nostro* and *vostro;* and *loro* is a possessive, which has the same meaning as the English *their.*

43. Every possessive adjective is equivalent to the genitive of a personal pronoun, and is in fact a real genitive. All the other genitive cases of these pronouns are merely apparent; they are dependent on the verb, and not true genitives, since the only true genitive depends on the noun. Thus the personal pronoun has no true genitive expressed, inasmuch as its true genitive is only to be found in the possessive adjective.

44. And so the possessive, being virtually a pronoun, in a grammatical sense is properly called an adjective. This is proved by the fact of its agreeing with the noun, in gender, number, and case. *Mio, tuo, suo,* &c., have the form of the first class of adjectives, and may be considered *grammatically* as adjectives, though *substantially* as pronouns.

45. In the first and second person, the possessive is never resolved into the pronominal form. In the third person, however, it is otherwise, for we may use *il padre di lui, il padre di lei, il padre di loro,* instead of *suo padre, loro padre.*

46. The possessive supposes two substantives, the substantive possessing, and the substantive denoting the thing possessed. In Italian, the possessive adjective agrees with the thing possessed, in gender, number, and case. If the noun possessing, is of the third person plural, the possessive agrees with it, but in this case it must be called rather a pronoun, than an adjective, since the expression *il loro libro,* their book, is the expression of a pronoun, and is a true genitive, in which the *segnacaso* is understood.

47. In Italian, the possessive is used with the definite article, except in a few cases which we will specify. It is used without the article, when it is referred to the most intimate relations of the possessor. In this case, it is only natural that the article should be omitted. For the use of the article is to individualise the object, and distinguish it

among others of the same species or genus. It is therefore not necessary to prefix the article to substantives, which are individualised in their very nature. If the relationship is distant, the article is used or not, according to the necessity which may or may not exist, for defining individuality more clearly. Thus, if I have a cousin staying with me, I might say, if I were to enquire for him, *E' tornato mio cugino,* has my cousin returned? But if I speak of him, when I am away from home, in that case the individuality is not so clear, and I should therefore make use of his personal name. Thus we say, *mio fratello,* my brother; *mia zia,* my uncle; *mia sorella,* my sister, &c., when one is only mentioned, and there is no danger of confusing him with others. On the contrary, if we speak of one in particular, and we wish to avoid all uncertainty regarding his individuality, in this case we should say, *mio fratello Giovanni,* my brother John; *mia sorella Annetta,* my sister Annette; *mio zio Egidio,* my uncle Egidius.

EXAMPLES.

Vuoi tu, ch' io chiami quì tua sorella?
Do you wish that I call here your sister?
Sua madre era donna savissima ed onestissima.
His mother was a very wise and honourable lady.
Nostro padre ci educa con severità non disgiunta da amore.
Our father brings us up with severity, combined with affection.
Suo zio gli lasciò ogni suo avere.
His uncle left him all his property.

48. When, however, these nouns of relationship are accompanied by an adjective, the article is, under these circumstances, prefixed to the possessive. This happens because the adjective modifies the noun in such a manner as to take away the idea of singular individuality from the words *padre, madre,* and substitutes a certain generical individuality. Thus *il buon padre,* the good father, is not considered in his own absolute individuality; but in an individuality deduced

from the genus of good fathers, to indicate which, the article *il* is used. There is also another manner of using the article in such sentences as these:—*Scrivo al padre tuo*, I write to your father; *parlo alla madre mia*, I speak to my mother, &c. The article is here inserted, because in these phrases the possessive adjective *mio* includes the idea of *caro*, dear; *buono*, good: *meritevole*, deserving, &c.

49. The possessive pronouns used in such words, as *Monsignore, Messere, Madonna, Sua Eccellenza*, &c., are used without the article, and are to a certain extent titular; as, for instance, *Monsignore* is equal to *mio signore*, and so on.

If these names of titles, however, have the possessive after them, the article is then prefixed. But in this case a meaning of emphasis or increased interest is given by the definite article, which renders the noun more conspicuous, and the possessive adjective more forcible. Thus, *la Signoria tua*, or *l' Eccellenza vostra, non vorranno che un umile tuo*, or *vostro*, or *loro, devoto sia condotto a così lagrimevole fine come quello di cui è minacciato da suoi nemici.*

50. *Casa*, house, is often followed by the possessive, and is used without the article, as:—*Casa mia è sempre aperta a voi ed ai vostri*, my house is always open to you and yours. This is owing to the fact, that the idea of *casa*, a house, has a certain exclusiveness, which makes it similar to a proper name, and becomes yet more defined by the addition of *mia.*

51. In Italian the possessive is not used with nouns which clearly indicate individual possession, although in French and English the opposite custom is always adopted. Thus, we say: *Ho camminato tanto oggi, che ne ho tutte le gambe rotte*, I have walked so much to-day that my legs are all broken; *Ho il cervello pieno di pensieri*, I have my brain full of thoughts; *Gli occhi mi servono bene, abbenchè mi sia carico d' anni*, My eyes serve me well, although I am loaded with years. Throughout these examples the English possessive is used. Again, *Mi levai il cappello*, I raised my hat; *Ei*

le si gettò a' piedi, He threw himself at her feet; *Mi era cavato il giubbettino,* I had taken off my waistcoat. In these sentences the personal pronouns serve evidently to denote the persons which have the possession; and the possessive adjective itself is always left out. We have, likewise, *mi restituì la borsa,* he restored me my purse. To say, *Restituiscimi il mio danaro* would be quite proper, because the expression would acquire energy from the introduction of *mio.*

52. It occurs sometimes that the possessive of the third person expresses its meaning so inefficiently, that the noun indicating possession can scarcely be distinguished amongst other nouns. In this case the difficulty is met by introducing the genitive case of the personal pronoun of the third person. If we were to say, for example, *Mio padre scrisse alla sorella sua, dicendole che tutti i suoi beni furono devastati dalla tempesta,* My father wrote to his sister, and informed her that all his or her property had been laid waste by the tempest. *I suoi* does not state clearly, whether it is spoken of *his* or his sister's property had been laid waste by the tempest. We should say in the former case, *i beni di lui,* and in the latter, *i beni di lei*; and by substituting the personal pronoun for the possessive, this uncertainty is avoided.

53. We have also a more idiomatic method of determining the property or peculiar possession of others. The possessive alone is placed without the substantive. Thus we might say, *Egli ha consumato tutto il suo al gioco,*—This signifies, He squandered everything which belonged to him in play. The same thing may be done with regard to the plural, as *Tutti i nostri sono andati in campagna,* All our people have gone to the country; that is to say, all the individuals of our family. By analogy, also, we may say, *I nostri furono sconfitti,* All of ours (or our men) were put to the rout; this expression being understood to apply to the army of our nation or country.

54. We will conclude this Section by remarking, that the

possessive is placed, as may be seen from the examples given, most frequently before the noun. But, notwithstanding this, it may occasionally be placed afterwards. We have noticed some instances, from which we may deduce the fact, that it may be placed after the noun in a conspicuous, energetic, and determined sense. We will, however, make this still more evident, by adducing examples of the possessive after the noun, when those who are dear to us are alluded to, and under circumstances, when we desire to display tokens of affection, especially during any solemn event of life, in which communion of soul is defined in the most lively manner.

EXAMPLES.

"Italia mia, benchè il parlar sia indarno
Alle piaghe mortali
Che nel bel corpo tuo sì spesse veggio."
—*Pet. Canz.* 261.

My Italy, although to speak is bootless, for curing the mortal wounds so many of which I see on thy beautiful body.

"Pandolfo mio, quest' opere son frali
A lungo andar, ma il nostro studio è quello
Che fa per fama gli uomini immortali."—*Petr.*

O my Pandolph, we find these works finish in the course of time, but our endeavour is to do that which makes men immortal through fame.

SECTION VI.

The Relative Pronoun.

The Relative Pronoun is declined as follows:—

SINGULAR.

Nom. *Che, il quale, la quale,* who, which.
Gen. *Di che, di cui, cui del quale, della quale,* of whom, of which.
Dat. *A che, a cui, cui, al quale, alla quale,* to whom, to which.
Acc. *Che, cui, il quale, la quale,* whom, which.
Abl. *Da che, da cui, dal quale, dalla quale,* from or by whom or which.

PLURAL.

Nom. *Che, i quali, le quali,* who which.
Gen. *Di che, di cui, cui, de' quali, delle quali,* of whom, of which.
Dat. *A che, a cui, cui, a' quali, alle quali,* to whom; to which.
Acc. *Che, cui, i quali, le quali,* whom, which.
Abl. *Da che, da cui, da' quali, dalle quali,* from or by whom or which.

55. The relative pronoun is a pronominal word, which causes the mind to pause on a circumstance belonging to a substantive which immediately precedes it. It always includes a new proposition, which must be exhausted before the previous proposition can be proceeded with. The grammarians rightly call the proposition which belongs to the relative incidental; and if this were taken away altogether, the sense of the proposition, interrupted by it, would remain entire. It thus results that the relative, belonging as it does to a proposition different from the preceding, may be subject to different grammatical conditions of case. The rule is, therefore, that the relative agrees with its antecedent noun in gender and number, but not necessarily in case.

56. The relative has also the forms *il quale, la quale,* which is subject to the usual accidents of gender, number, and case. It requires the article before it, and makes the plural in *i*.

57. The relative by *che* usually assumes a more general form, in which the accidents of gender and number are not expressed; and that of case is indicated by the *segnacasi di, a, da,* which are placed before the relative itself.

58. *Che* may be changed into *cui* in the oblique cases, but never in the nominative.

59. *Cui* is sometimes necessary, when there would otherwise be a doubt as to the subject of the proposition.

60. If the genitive of the relative pronoun is genuine, it ought to have a noun to which it belongs. This phrase, *La donna di cui vi ho parlato,* the lady of whom I have spoken to you, would only be an apparent genitive. But when

it is a genitive of the substantive, it is usual to place the article of the substantive first, then the relative *cui*, preceded sometimes by the *seguacaso di* (which however is better omitted); and after *cui* is placed the substantive to which the article belongs. Thus, *il guerriero, la cui fama è immortale, mancò ai vivi*, The warrior, whose fame is immortal, departed from the living. Here the article of *fama* goes first, then *cui*, and last of all *fama*. This is the preferable construction, although it is allowable to use the *segnacaso* before *cui*.

61. Among the various forms of pronouns it is well to know under what circumstances *il quale* or *la quale* should be used. It sometimes happens that one proposition is mixed up with another in which *che* is used repeatedly; and in that case, in order to give a little diversity to the sentence, *il quale* or *la quale* are introduced. It also occurs occasionally, that two nouns, which occupy the place of antecedents, are so placed at the same time, that it becomes necessary to make it known to which of these the relative belongs. For this reason the relative has the full form, in order to show clearly to which of the two nouns it belongs, since they frequently differ in number and case.

EXAMPLE.

I beni di questa vita, che l' uomo tanto desidera, sono fugaci e vani.

The goods of this life, which man so much desires, are transitory and vain.

In this sentence, *che tanto* might be referred either to *vita* or *beni*. If the words *i quali* were used, it would be at once understood, that the relative applied to *beni*.

62. *Chi* is a relative pronoun applied to persons, and signifies the same as *quegli che*, that person who. It happens that *chi* can be used absolutely, as well as interrogatively. As an interrogative, it is necessarily used by itself, as *chi è?* who is?

Che, what, interrogative, means what thing? as *che volete*, what thing do you wish? *Che fu detto oggi nell' assemblea?* What was said to day in the assembly? In these phrases, *chi* and *che* are naturally at the beginning of the sentence. If the sense is not interrogative, and *chi* is used, it then signifies *quegli che*, being understood of a person, as *chi è saggio è amato*, he who is wise is loved. If the antecedent is given, *chi* must be changed into *che*, as *quegli che*, or *l' uomo che è saggio è amato*. Thus, *chi* is never found, except when it stands by itself.

With these remarks we conclude our treatise on the pronouns.

Exercises on Pronouns.

1. Now I tell you clearly I can no longer put up with it. I have endured too much of it.

Clearly, *bene;* (that) I can; longer, *più;* put up with it, *soffrire* (it). I of it (of them), *ne;* have; to endure, *comportare;* too much, (many), *troppe*.

2. We (2) are (1) more ready to complain of misfortunes than to be satisfied with success.

Ready, *labile;* to complain, *a rammaricarsi;* misfortune, *sciagura;* to be satisfied, *lodarsi;* with (of the); *ventura*.

3. One more easily remedies a great flood, by giving it its course, than by offering any obstacle to it.

(To) a great; flood, *piena;* one, *si;* to remedy, *riparare;* more easily; by (to); giving (to) it; its, *il suo;* by (to) offering it, *fare* (to it); obstacle, *ritegno*.

4. When any one who is in prosperity is loved, it* is an* uncertain thing whether his* good fortune or his* person is the object of affection.

Who is, *posto;* is, *viene;* loved; uncertain thing is: (the) good fortune, *prosperità;* or his . . . of affection, *o se àmisi la persona*.

5. He wished, however, to give him two very beautiful bowls of silver.

He wished (to) him, *volevagli;* however, *pur;* *donare;* bowl, *nappo*.

6. Look at* that* brute of a* man, who dares, wherever I may be, to speak before (of) me.—*Bocc.*

To look, *vedere;* brute, *bestia;* dares, *ardisce;* wherever I, *dov' io.*

7. Whenever I scold her about it, she makes excuses which are not to the purpose, and makes faces at me.—*Fir.*

Quando io; her; to scold, *sgridare;* she makes, *ella truova;* which; are . . . purpose, *non v' entrano;* and . . . at me; *e fammi ceffo.*

8. Look at* him, how he* stands overcome by passion and full of spite.

Look, *vedi;* to stand, *stare;* overcome by passion, *tutto ingrognato;* full of spite, *dispettoso.*

9. You, ladies, when you think too much about any* thing (pl.), on account of your* little power* of* reasoning you confuse yourselves about it.

About (to the); on account of, *per lo;* reasoning, *discorso;* your (which you have); you; yourselves; to confuse, *avvilluppare;* about it, *dentro.*

10. Having seen (2) him (1) so determined, I did not say another* word to him.

Having; not to him; did say, *dissi;* another (more) word.

11. The continual possession of anything produces a kind of* satiety, which it* is necessary to avoid by depriving oneself of it for a time; which short privation makes afterwards the sweeter the new possession.

Of anything, *delle cose;* to produce, *generare;* a kind, *una certa;* which, *la quale;* it is necessary, *bisogna;* to avoid, *schifare;* by (with the); for a time, *per qualche spazio;* which short; *privamento;* makes, *fa;* afterwards, *poi.*

12. The beauties of this world come from Him who is the dispenser and master of them and of everything, the which He sends to us in the form of messengers inviting us to love Him.

Come, *vengono;* (arrange) who is of them and of every (other) thing the dispenser and master; the which, *le quali;* to send, *mandare;* in the form, *a guisa;* of messengers; inviting us, *invitantici;* to.

13. There is this considerable (2) difference (1) between the man who paints on canvass, and the man who casts in bronze; he* who paints can easily correct an error which* he* has* made, whereas he* who casts cannot.

There is, *v' ha;* between the man who, *fra chi;* on canvass, *in tela;* to cast, *fondere*; (that) an (the) error; made, *fatto;* whereas, *là dove;* cannot, *non può;* (correct it).

14. He* who is envious is more miserable than the person whom he envies.

Who is envious, *chi porta invidia; misero*; the person, *colui;* (to) whom, *a cui;* he envies, *egli la porta.*

15. He became, in consequence of it, the most jealous man in the world.

He; in consequence; of it, (translate) *ne.*

16. I most clearly perceive that in your (2) heart (1) you begin somewhat to laugh at me.

I perceive, *mi accorgo;* clearly, *benissimo;* that in heart your; somewhat, *alquanto*; at me (*of* me).

Readings on Poetry.

1. Però ch' io sono a tal punto condotto,
Ch' io non conosco quasi ov' io mi sia,
E vado per la via
Com' uom, ch' è tutto fuor d' intendimento.
—*Fazio degli Uberti.*

Therefore I am brought to such a point, that I do not know, as it were, where I am, and go along the road like a man who is quite out of his mind.

2. Principe invitto, disse, il cui gran nome
Sen vola adorno di sì chiari segni,
Che l' esser da te vinte, e 'n guerra dome
Recansi a gloria le provincie, e i regni.—*Tasso.*

O invincible Prince, he said, whose great name flies abroad, adorned with such noble signs, that provinces and kingdoms consider it a glory to be conquered by you, and subdued in battle.

3. Vassene il tempo e l' uom non se n' avvede.—*Dante.*

Time passes away, and man takes no notice of it.

4. Che quando ancor io 'l celi a tutto il mondo,
Celar nol posso alla mia coscienza:
L' alma che sente il suo peccato immondo,
Pate dentro di sè tal penitenza,
Ch' avanza ogn' altro corporal martire,
Che dar mi possa alcun del mio fallire.—*Ariosto.*

Which although I may conceal it from all the world, I cannot conceal from my own conscience: the soul which feels its own wicked sin, feels within itself a punishment which exceeds all other bodily suffering which any of my faults could occasion me.

5. Figlia mia, io t' ho affogata,
So, ch' io t' ho mal maritata.—*Lor. Med.*

My daughter, I have ruined you, I know, because I have married you badly.

6. A ciascuno il suo giorno ultimo è scritto.

To every one his last day is appointed.

7. Chi mi darà la voce e le parole
Convenienti a sì nobil soggetto ?—*Arios.*

Who will give me the voice and the words appropriate to so noble a subject.

8. Sono come il coltel, che se tu 'l prendi
Da quella parte, ove per uso umano
La man s' adatta, a chi l' adopra è buono;
Ma a chi 'l prende ove fere, è spesso morte.—*Guar.*

I am like a knife, which, if you hold it by that part where the hand fits itself to it for the service of man, is good for whoever makes uses of it; but to him who seizes it by the part where it cuts, it is often death.

9. Ella, postosi innanzi il suo ventaglio,
Con la coda dell' occhio il rimirava.—*Triss.*

She, holding her fan before her, with the corner of her eye regarded him.

10. E fo' come augellin, che s' affatica
Per uscir della rete, ov' egli è colto,
Ma quanto più si scuote e' più s' intrica.—*Bembo.*

And I act like a bird, which wearies itself to escape from the net in which it is caught; but the more it beats against it, the more it entangles itself.

11. Lodata passa e vagheggiata Armida
Tra le cupide turbe, e se n' avvede:
Nè 'l mostra già, benchè in suo cuor sen rida,
E ne disegna alte vittorie e prede.—*Tasso.*

Praised and gazed after, Armida passes on amongst the eager multitude, and she is aware of it; nor does she however show it, although she smiles at it in her heart, and designs from it great victories and spoils.

12. Si vede per gli esempj, di che piene
Sono le antiche e le moderne istorie,
Che 'l ben va dietro al male, e 'l male al bene,

E fin son l' un dell' altro e biasmi e glorie,
E che fidarsi all' uom non si conviene
In suo tesor, suo regno e sue vittorie;
Nè disperarsi per fortuna avversa,
Che sempre la sua rota in giro versa.—*Arios.*

One sees by the examples of which ancient and modern histories are full, that success follows close upon failure, and failure upon success, and that the end of one and the other are blame and glory; and that it is not good for man to put trust in his treasure, in his kingdom, and his victories, nor to despair on account of adverse Fortune, who always is turning round her wheel.

CHAPTER XI.

The Regular Verbs.

Section I.—The Verbal Forms.

We shall discuss the verbs in a somewhat brief manner, as the student, by the means of the Exercises, has already gained considerable information concerning them.

1. In Italian we possess three conjugations, which are distinguished, as in Latin, by the termination of the infinitive mood. The first conjugation has its infinitive ending in *are*, the second in *ere*, and the third in *ire*. Every Italian verb falls under one of these three conjugations, according to the termination of the infinitive mood.

2. The part of the verb which is subject to change is the characteristic termination of the infinitive mood; the preceding letters are immutable. Thus *are, ere, ire*, are the parts which suffer change; and these according to the conjugations of these verbs.

3. Throughout every tense and mood of these conjugations the second person singular ends in *i*, the first person plural in *mo*, and the second person plural in *te*. The third person plural of all tenses, except the future, the conditional, and

the imperfect subjunctive, end in *no* preceded by a short syllable. The future assumes *nn* in the third person plural, and the conditional and the imperfect of the subjunctive make this person in *ro*. The two last syllables are short.

4. We will now mention the tenses in succession, and give some general rules. All three conjugations change their respective terminations, *are*, *ere*, *ire*, into *o* in the first person singular of the present, and *i* in the second. In the third person the present of the first conjugation ends in *a*, and those of the second and third have their termination in *e*. The first person plural ends in *iamo*: the second in *ate*, *ete*, and *ite*. In the first conjugation the third person plural ends in *ano*; and in the second and third it ends in *ono*, the vowel of the penultimate being short in both cases.

5. The imperfect is formed by changing the *re* of the three conjugations into *va*, *vi*, *va*, *vamo*, *vate*, *vano*. The letter *v*, therefore, is the characteristic of the imperfect tense. Before *v* it takes *a*, *e*, or *i*, according to the conjugation. All verbs form this tense in the same manner, except the verb *essere*, the imperfect of which is *era*.

6. The preterite changes *are*, *ere*, *ire* into *ai*, *ei*, *ii*. The second person singular always ends in *sti*, into which the termination in *i* of the first person is changed, and is thus increased by a syllable. The third person ends in *ò*, *è*, *ì* accented, according to the conjugation. The first person plural ends in *mmo*, the second in *ste*, by changing the final *i* of the second person singular into *e*. The third person ends in *rono*.

7. The future tense always adopts *r* for its characteristic, and ends in *rò*, *rai*, *rà*, *remo*, *rete*, *ranno*. In the first conjugation *e* takes the place of *a* before the *r*. This is done for the sake of euphony. We must observe that the first person of the future ends in *rò*, and the third in *rà*, both of which terminations are accented, that its first person plural differs solely from that of the conditional in having one *m*

instead of two, and that the third person plural ends always in *nno.*

8. The conditional, on account of its affinity with the future, has the same characteristic *r*, and ends in *rei, resti, rebbe, remmo, reste, rebbero.* It follows the example of the future also, in changing the *a*, which would naturally precede the characteristic *r* into *e.* The conditional always makes the third persons singular and plural in *rebbe* and *rebbero,*—which in an elegant style may be changed into *rebbono,*—and a double *m (mm)* is introduced into the first person plural.

9. The only thing we have to observe with regard to the imperative mood, which is rather capricious in its formation, is this—that the third persons singular and plural are always the same as those of the present subjunctive. The second person singular of the imperative, when used negatively is expressed always by using the infinitive mood with *non* prefixed, as *non parlare,* do not speak; *non leggere,* do not read.

10. The present of the subjunctive reverses the original vowels of the infinitive mood. Thus in *are* the *a* is changed into *i;* in *ere* and *ire* the *e* and *i* are changed into *a.*

11. The imperfect of the subjunctive is formed by placing *ss* after the *a, e,* and *i* of the terminations *are, ere,* and *ire.* It preserves always the same characteristic of *ss.* The gerund of the first conjugation ends in *ando,* that of the second and third in *endo,* never in *indo.* Finally, the past participle ends generally in *to,* although many verbs make it in *so.*

Section II.

Observations on "Essere" (to be) and its Latin affinities.

(*a*) The present tense of *essere* has a direct Latin derivation in the forms *sono, siamo,* and *sono* (plur.), which are derived from the Latin *sum, sumus,* and *sunt.*

The imperfect is also directly derived from the Latin imperfect *eram*, *eras*, *erat*, etc., and also resembles the Latin in this respect. In Italian the imperfect of this verb is deficient in the characteristic *v* (except the first and second persons plural), just as the Latin equivalent *eram*, &c., refuses to adopt the usual characteristic *b*, which is used in the imperfect tense of the regular Latin verb.

(*b*) The preterite is throughout of pure Latin derivation :—*fui*, *fosti*, *fu*, &c., being clearly derived from the Latin *fui*, *fuisti*, *fuit*, &c.

(*c*) The subjunctive present is derived from the Latin subjunctive. Thus, from the Latin *sim*, *sis*, *sit*, &c., we have *sia*, &c.

The past participle of *esse* is wanting in Latin ; and *esserè* has the same defect, but the Italians have supplied the deficiency by adopting in its place *stato*, the past participle of *stare*, which is used in some of the past tenses of the passive voice.

There is no occasion to trace the affinities of the verb *avere*, to have, with the Latin : for they are few and of little importance, with the exception of its similarity in the infinitive mood. In Latin the verb *habere*, to have, is regular ; but the Italian *avere* is an irregular verb.

12. The special office of the verbs *essere* and *avere* may be thus defined :—

The verb *avere* is combined with the past participle of the verb that is to be conjugated ; and in this manner the compound tenses are formed, as :—*Ho amato*, I have loved ; *aveva amato*, I had loved ; *avrò amato*, &c., I shall have loved, &c.

The verb *essere*, when used in an auxiliary sense, is employed in forming the tenses of the passive verbs, which are all compound, as :—*Io sono amato*, I am loved ; *Io era amato*, I was loved ; *Io sono stato amato*, I have been loved.

13. The neuter verbs which are conjugated with *essere* do not suffer the participle *stato* to be placed between the auxiliary verb and the past participle. A great number of these neuters may also use the verb *avere* as an auxiliary, as in these instances :—*Io sono vissuto*, and *Io ho vissuto*, I

have lived; *Io sono arricchito,* and *Io ho arricchito,* I have become rich; *Io sono deciso,* and *Io ho deciso,* I have decided. Some take the verb *avere* as their sole auxiliary, as:—*Io ho scritto,* I have written; *Io ho letto,* I have read; and others are never found except with the verb *essere,* as:—*Io sono nato,* I am born.

14. Verbs, which have a pronoun affixed, assume the verb *essere,* with more correctness than *avere.* In using the verb *decidersi,* to decide with oneself, it would be better to say, *Io mi sono deciso,* I have decided with myself, than *Io mi ho deciso;* also *mi sono afflitto,* I am afflicted, would be a more correct phrase than *mi ho afflitto.*

We have to notice, lastly, a speciality of the verb *to be,* that in Italian it is auxiliary to itself. Every time that the verb *essere* is found in a compound tense, *essere* is used in place of the usual auxiliary, *avere.*

Section III.

General Affinities of the Latin and Italian Verbs.

We will now proceed to notice the affinities between the Latin and Italian verbs.

(*d*) In Italian, the primary verbal expression, which is naturally the infinitive, has the Latin forms, *are, ere, ire.*

(*e*) The Latin vowel terminations are used in Italian when the tenses are not compound. Thus *o,* the termination of the first person singular of the present tense, is common to the two languages. The same may be said with regard to the *e* of the infinitives, and the *i* of the first person of the preterite.

(*f*) The affix *is* of the Latin second person singular loses the final consonant *s* and becomes *i.*

The Latin ending *mus,* which is used for the first person plural, loses its *s,* and is changed into *mo.* In the second person plural *tis* is changed into *te,* and in the third person of the same number *nt* is changed into *no.*

(*g*) The imperfect tense changes *b* into *v*, and is then conjugated in the regular manner, as, *amava, credeva, sentiva; amavi, credevi, sentivi;* from *amabam, credebam, sentiebam*. In the latter case, *ie* is changed into *i*.

The preterite has *i* in the first person and *sti* in the second, and has frequently a Latin derivation with some accidental changes of letters. It always loses the Latin characteristic *v*, as: *amai, udii,* for *amavi, audivi,*—and changes *x*, which is never used in Italian, into *ss*, as : *dissi*, from *dixi*.

(*h*.) We were disposed to imagine that *r*, the Italian characteristic of the future and conditional, derived its origin from *ero*, the future of *sum*, the second future *ero*, and the future participle in *rus, ra, rum*. There is another theory, however, which is entitled to great respect on account of the great authors who have given their sanction to it. This may be given in the following terms:—

The Italian future is formed by adding the present tense of *avere* to the infinitive of the verb, and then connecting the two together. Thus the original form of *parlerò*, would be *parlare-ho*, I have to speak, I will speak ; *parlerai* would be *parlare-hai ; parlerà*, would be *parlare-ha*. The *emo* and *ete* in *parleremo* and *parlerete*, are contractions of *avemo, avete*, and *parleranno* is formed from *parlare-hanno*.

The same peculiarity is traced in all languages derived from the Latin, as in French—*aimer-ai, aimer-as, aimer-a*, &c. The conditional is the infinitive with the preterite of *avere*. *Parlare* joined to *hei* (an antiquated form of *ebbi*) forms *parlerei*, &c.

(*i*) The present of the Italian subjunctive has a certain affinity with its Latin equivalent in the reversal of the vowels of the infinitive. In the first conjugation (*are*), the subjunctive present is formed with *i*. In the second and third conjugations (*ere* and *ire*), it is formed with *a*. A similar transmutation of vowels takes place in Latin, in which language *are* is changed into *e*, *ere* long into *ea*, *ere* short into *a*, and *ire* into *ia*. From the Latin *amem, videam, legam*, and *audiam*, we have, therefore, the Italian *ami, veda, legga*, and *oda*.

Considering that the characteristic of the imperfect of the subjunctive is *ss*—*assi, essi, issi*—we are induced to derive it from the

Latin pluperfect tense of the subjunctive. This is undoubtedly the case, although we must allow there is a remarkable deviation in the sense itself, since we cannot derive the Italian characteristic of the imperfect subjunctive from any other source; and, as a kind of corrective for assuming the form of the Latin pluperfect, we find that the imperfect loses the radical characteristic of the perfect, *x*, or *v*, or any other, and assumes the radical letters of the infinitive: as, from the Latin *dixissem*, pluperfect, is made the imperfect *dicessi*—from the Latin *amavissem*, *amassi*, and from *rexissem*, *reggessi*, and so on.

(*k*) The past participle ending in *to* is derived from the Latin in *tus*, and that in *so* from the Latin in *sus;* as, from *amatus*, *amato*; from *affixus*, *affisso*, &c. This is another mode of discovering reasons for the verbal irregularities of Italian, as we shall perceive farther on.

(*l*) The participle present follows the rule which we have previously laid down with regard to nouns. Thus, in Italian, it is formed from *ante* and *ente*, the Latin singular terminations of the ablative case. *Amans*, *amantis*, makes *amante* in the ablative case, which also serves to express the Italian equivalent. From *videns*, *videntis*, we have the ablative *vidente* and the Italian *vedente*.

Of the gerunds in *ando* and *endo* we will say nothing, in spite of their apparent derivation from the Latin; inasmuch as the Italian signification, which is that of the participle present, is so different from the Latin gerunds.

(*m*) The affinities between the tenses, which are derived from the Latin perfect and their Italian equivalent, cannot be considered great or important, as in our language these tenses are formed by the help of an auxiliary verb united to the participle past.

Section IV.

Affinities of the Latin and Italian Moods.

(*n*) In the infinitive mood the Italian verbs bear a great resemblance to the Latin. It may, however, be of use to make some observations, in order to establish some regular principle, and define properly the nature of the deviations.

(*o*) Verbs, which are derived from the first conjugation, preserve the Latin infinitive without making any change. The chief difference between the Latin and Italian languages consists in this—that those verbs which in Latin have no regular form for the perfect, in Italian assume the regular form. The two irregular verbs—*stare*, to stand; *dare*, to give—must be excepted.

(*p*) Verbs of the second Italian conjugation are derived from the Latin second and third, which are in our language assimilated and reduced to one form. This assimilation is founded on the following reasons :—

Very few of the Italian verbs, which are derived from the Latin second conjugation, preserve the original quantity of *ere* long. Those that do preserve it are the following: *vedere*, to see; *tenere*, to hold; *piacere*, to please; *parere*, to appear; *dolere*, to grieve; *dovere*, to be necessary; *valere*, to be worthy of; *giacere*, to lie down; *calere*, to care for; *rimanere*, to remain; *solere*, to be accustomed; *tacere*, to be silent; *godere*, to enjoy; *temere*, to fear; *possedere*, to possess; *sedere*, to sit down, with their compounds.

We may also add *potere* and *volere*, the forms of which by no means correspond with the Latin *posse* and *velle*.

(*q*) Many, as we have previously remarked, change *ère* long into *ere* short, as *ardere*, to burn; *ridere*, to laugh; *muovere*, to remove; *splendere*, to glitter; *rifulgere*, to shine (from the Latin *fulgeo*); and others. *Cadere*, to fall; *sapere*, to know, pass from the third Latin into the second Italian conjugation, being in Italian *cadère*, *sapère*.

But this very rarely occurs, since in these instances the Italian language prefers usually that these verbs, if any change is made, should adopt *are* as the form of the first conjugation: as from *deserere* is formed the Italian *disertare;* from *despernere*, to despise greatly, we have the Italian *disprezzare;* and from *diffidere*, to distrust, the Italian *diffidare*.

(*r*) We ought also to remark that the Italians change the infinitive of Latin verbs of the third conjugation which have an inceptive meaning into *ire*, and occasionally into *are;* and moreover some verbs also, of the second Latin conjugation, change their infinitive into *ire*, and in some very rare cases into *are*. We will hereafter notice the first class we have mentioned; of the second we will now give a few examples:—*Callere* (in the sense of to be hardened;) *monere*, to advise; *pallere*, to be pale; *favere*, to favour; *augere*, to increase; *vovere*, to vow, etc.; make *incallire*, *ammonire*, *impallidire*, *favorire*, *aumentare*, *votare*, etc.

(*s*) All these changes which we have enumerated, and the consequent paucity of Italian verbs ending in *ere* long, justify the Italian plan of uniting the two Latin conjugations into one. The alteration is also sanctioned by the circumstance, that the past tense of the regular verbs always assumes the same termination. It makes no difference whether the *ere* of the Latin infinitive be long or short. Thus, from *credere* we have *credei;* from *possedere*, *possedei*, &c.

SECTION V.

The Moods.

15. The indicative mood has an absolute character, as in other languages, and is for that reason not subject to any special grammatical modifications which require explanation.

16. The subjunctive has in Italian the same meaning as in English. It varies in its form only so far as it requires a certain degree of accuracy in fixing the conjunction of dependence, *che*, that, which in the English language would be often considered needless.

17. The subjunctive is a verb depending on another verb. Its true meaning is this—that a condition of existence or of action is effected in dependence on another condition of existence or action. Thence it follows, that the condition which it indicates must always be hypothetical, since it is dependent on some other action.

18. The antecedent of the subjunctive must have an undecided signification; since if this were not the case, it would not admit any condition of dependency to follow it, and for that reason would not admit the subjunctive.

Credo che sia partito, I believe that he has set out; *Spero che guarisca presto,* I hope that he will soon be well; *Desiderava molto ch' egli si risolvesse ad un partito,* I desired much that he would make up his mind. In these examples the hypothetical character of the subjunctive is evident.

19. It occasionally happens that the subjunctive mood follows verbs of positive signification; but the dependent verb is still indeterminate, and preserves entirely its hypothetical signification. In such a case the hypothetical condition of the subjunctive verb is expressed by a conjunction, which unites the dependent verb with the principal. Thus we say: *Gli scrivo, affinchè egli non creda che l' abbia dimenticato,* I write him, in order that he should not think that I have forgotten him; *Ordino e comando che sia scacciato dalla società nostra,* I order and command that he should be turned out of our society; *Gli parlai fermo, perchè si penta del suo errore,* I spoke to him firmly, in order that he might repent of his error.

20. There are some conjunctions which have in themselves an indecisive meaning. These require the subjunctive, on account of their own indecisive meaning. *Purchè, ancorchè, tuttochè, benchè, avvegnachè,* &c., which are conditional conjunctions, are followed by the subjunctive, because they possess a hypothetical meaning.

21. These are the general directions for the Italian subjunctive. We have, however, one observation to make, although we know not whether it has occurred to other grammarians. In order to place the dependent verb in the subjunctive, it is necessary that the subject of the dependent verb should not be the same as the subject of the antecedent. If the two subjects are the same, the dependent verb is then found in the infinitive mood, since one meaning alone exists which is completed by the infinitive; and the two verbal conditions united under the same subject, constitute one idea alone. This, of course, cannot be the case when the subjects of the

two verbs are different, since it is not possible that two agents, both of which have an operating force, should constitute a simple action.

Thus we say: *Credo di conoscerlo,* I think that I know him. It would be improper to substitute, *credo che lo conosco,* since *credere* and *conoscere* being applied to the same subject, cannot even in imagination be disjoined, as would necessarily be the case if we said, *credo che tu lo conosca.* Again, we say, *Desidero di sapere tutto l' affare,* I desire to know all the business; because *desiderare* and *sapere* have the same agent. Under other circumstances we should use the subjunctive, as: *Desidero che tu sappia tutto l' affare,* I desire that you should know all about this.

The same observations may be made with regard to interjectional phrases which render the sense optative, as: *Dio volesse!* God grant! which is used in the subjunctive, because the sense is hypothetical.

22. When a dependent verb is found in the infinitive, on account of its having the same subject as the principal verb, the prepositions *di* and *a,* and sometimes also *per,* are placed as a kind of link between the two verbs. In fact, if we observe closely we shall find that *di, a,* or *per* supply the place of the regular construction of the dependent verb. The preposition *di* is used when the connexion between the two verbs is of a close and direct nature. *A* or *per* are used to indicate that the action of the dependent verb is the scope of the action expressed by the antecedent, or indicates the tendency of the action itself:—*Lo chiama per dargli un ammonizione,* He calls him to give him an admonition. This is equivalent to, *Egli lo chiama perchè* (or *affinchè*) *egli stesso gli dia una buona ammonizione.*

23. There is a peculiar class of verbs possessing a kind of inchoative signification of volition or energy. These have in themselves no complement of action, but receive it from another verb, which being added to the former makes up the true verbal sense.

These verbs are:—*Dovere,* to be obliged; *potere,* to be able; *volere,* to will; *bisognare,* to be necessary; *sapere,* to be able; *lasciare,* to permit; and also *fare,* when equivalent to the English verb *to cause.* The verbs which follow these, and which we term their complements, are added without a preposition. The two seem to be considered as constituting one definite meaning alone, and so as not needing the interposition of any other word.

EXAMPLES.

Le preterite cose malfatte si possono più agevolmente biasimare, che emendare.—*Bocc.*

Past things badly done may more easily be blamed than amended.

"Conviene ivi lasciar l' usato corso."

It is better here to leave the accustomed course.

Se medesimo esaltava con parole da fare per istomacaggine le pietre saltar fuori del muro e fuggirsi.—*Bocc.*

The same person used such boasting words, that he made the stones through disgust jump out of the walls and fly away.

"Dee l' uom d' intorno e dentro, e lungi e presso,
Guardar, e ornar, e pulir l' alma spesso.—*Vitt. Colon.*

Man ought to look around, and within, afar off and near, to adorn and polish the mind frequently.

24. When the sense indicated by the principal verb admits no idea of uncertainty, or rather of hypothesis, but on the contrary has a fully defined meaning,—in such a case the dependent verb adopts the indicative mood. Thus we say: *Conosco che tu hai ragione,* I know that you are right. In this phrase there is nothing that is hypothetical, and the tense is entirely definite. The same thing may be noticed in the following sentences:—*Vedi che la maggiore parte degli uomini agiscono per interesse,* You see that the greater portion of the human race act through motives of interest; *Comprendo che non vi è mezzo di persuaderlo,* I understand that there is no means of persuading him; *Son certo che egli vive nella miseria,* I am certain that he lives in misery.

35. We must observe that in all cases when the dependent verb is found in the future, the usual rules lose their efficacy, since the subjunctive has no future of its own, and must consequently adopt that of the indicative. Thus we have, *Credo che verrà entro un mese dall' Italia,* I believe that he will come from Italy within a month; *Spero che si risolverà perdonargli,* I hope that he will resolve to pardon him; *Conosco ch' egli farà bella carriera,* I know that he will make a good career; that is to say, I know that he will get on well.

36. Dependent verbs of the perfect tense cannot be found in the subjunctive mood, because the nature of this tense is decisive, and therefore cannot be hypothetical. The subjunctive mood, indeed, by reason of its very nature has no such tense. Take as an example: *Mi dissero che egli già venne a Parigi,* They told me that he has already arrived at Paris. If, on the contrary, we say, *Mi dissero ch' egli sia già arrivato a Parigi,* They told me that he has already arrived at Paris, it is manifestly uncertain whether the person alluded to has arrived; and if he has done so, *arrivato* is the participle referring to what may be past.

Section VI.

The Tenses.

37. The present tense has in all languages an effective and actual force. We do not wish to enter into any subtle discussions with regard to this tense. We prefer taking it in its most obvious signification, when it indicates a state or action progressing towards completion, but not actually completed. A more precise distinction has to be made with regard to the past present, and past perfect.

38. The past present indicates a past condition, which is considered in the past as if in the act of completing itself: the preterite, a condition quite completed in the past. The

past present may often be expressed in English by adding *was*, &c., to the participle present, as: *Io scriveva,* I was writing. This solution is not, however, always possible.

In a rational sense the past present indicates a past condition; but we conceive it as if the action were prolonged in the space of time which is really past, although it revert to the action which actually is completing itself in the past, including the idea of repetition, or habit, or continuation.

This is, therefore, a tense which is much used in descriptions and in poetic readings, in order to revive the past in colours designating a past actuality. It may, therefore, be termed, to a certain extent, the artistic tense, since it gives a faithful representation of the past; but in a condition of actual realization in the province, however, of the past, and referred to at that time, though yet not completed. If persons or things are described by poets or writers of romance, this tense is one they frequently use.

(*t*) The Italian language has this tense in common with the Latin, but its importance is of a very different nature. What comparison can be made between a tongue which is full of actualities, past or present, and a dead language in which the mind has to transport itself to times and customs long obsolete, and which belong only to the province of history, and to imagine for itself actualities from which it is separated by the lapse of so many centuries?

39. The tense which indicates a long-past condition is the complete past, and this we may call an historical tense; since, by the means of it, the mind is not directed to one action or condition, as if in the act of completion in the past, but one which had already been effected in the time referred to, and of which we intend to give an instantaneous and sudden notion, presently to give place in a successive order to other representations of past actions. This we call the *historical tense,* inasmuch as it is always used to represent that which has passed, and to arouse instantaneously a full

idea of it in the mind. Historians make as much use of this tense as romancers do of the past present, since the former regard things as having been completed, whilst the latter consider them in a descriptive, but not an historical sense, as being in process of completion.

We have spent some time in drawing this distinction between the two tenses, because it is rather difficult for natives of England to enter into this matter thoroughly, as the past present is not found in their language.

40. The past indefinite indicates a past condition, which is neither so remote nor so absolute as to exclude the idea of actuality; although it does not, like the imperfect, indicate an action in process of completion.

Thus if I say, *Io ho scritto,* I have written; *voi avete parlato,* you have spoken; the effect of *h*o and *avete* is to indicate a condition of existence, which has not yet, it is true, fully trespassed the boundaries of the past, but has still some connection with an actual present existence, and therefore has not as it were, entered the domain of history. The action, however, is past and already completed in the past; and thence it arises that this tense is often confounded with the preterite.

41. Many verbs of the third conjugation in *ire* form the present tense in a peculiar manner. A great number of these verbs are used to indicate an incipient action; and this inceptive meaning is in Italian expressed by using the termination *isco* in the present. Verbs of this kind, therefore, which indicate an inceptive and progressive condition of the substantive, change the *ire* of the infinitive into *isco, isci,* and *isce* in the present, and into *isca,* &c., in the subjunctive moods, and in the corresponding manner in the imperative.

Some of these verbs are as follows: *aggrandire,* to grow tall; *affievolire,* to become weak: *ammutolire,* to grow dumb; *arricchire,* to grow rich; *avvizzire,* to become withered; *impallidire,* to grow pale; *impoverire,* to become poor, and others.

A termination of this kind is only used in the present tense. The present alone can give the idea of a change actually in progress; for if the change is completed, the verb must necessarily be in one of the past tenses, and all inceptive idea is lost.

(*u*) Their origin is evidently Latin, which has a class of inceptive verbs which make the infinitive in *scere*, which termination is in Italian changed into *ire*. We will take as examples: *clarescere*, which becomes in Italian *chiarire*; *florescere*, *fiorire*; *erubescere*, *arrossire*; *evanescere*, *svanire*; *exhorrescere*, *innorridire*; and many others. We can, therefore, trace the origin of the Italian inceptive termination to the Latin form ending in *scere*.

(*v*) Verbs ending in *ire*, which are derived from the Latin form in *ire*, are not inceptive, and therefore do not form the present in *isco*. *Audire*, to hear, makes in the present tense *odo*; *nutrire*, to nourish, *nutro*; *servire*, to serve, *servo*; *mentire*, to lie, *mento*; *vestire*, to clothe, *vesto*. All these verbs are derived from the Latin fourth conjugation.

(*w*) Many verbs, which belong to the Italian conjugation in *ire*, are derived from other Latin conjugations. They have no inceptive sense; and although they have passed into the Italian third conjugation, do not adopt *isco*. We may take as instances, *seguire*, to follow; *fuggire*, to fly; *convertire*, to convert.

42. Some other verbs in *ire* may either assume *isco* or dispense with it. In strictness, however, these have no inceptive signification, as: *abborrire*, to execrate or to abhor; *inghiottire*, to swallow up; *languire*, to languish; *mentire*, to lie: *nutrire*, to nourish.

43. There is also a large class of verbs which make the present tense in *isco*, and are yet perfectly free from any inceptive meaning. We will take a few examples: *abolire*, to abolish; *aderire*, to consent; *aggradire*, to be pleased with: *allestire*, to prepare; *ammanire*, to prepare; *ammollire*, to soften; *ammonire*, to admonish; *atterrire*, to terrify; *attribuire*, to attribute, &c. &c.

It may be observed, however, that the greater part of the

verbs which end in *isco*, and are not inceptive, bear a transitive signification. The inceptive verbs are neuter, and in this way a distinction may be easily established. To put it in other words—the inceptive verbs are subjective: that is to say, their action is confined to the agent; while the others having the present in *isco*, are objective: that is to say, they do not exercise their energy on the agent, but on another object. From this principle it also follows that the inceptive verbs being neuter, take the verb *essere* as an auxiliary. On the contrary, the transitive verbs always make use of *avere*.

44. Some few Italian verbs convey an idea of reiteration, augmenting by a syllable the internal form of the verb itself, and occasionally making use of some peculiar sound. We will mention a few of these: *spumeggiare*, to keep on foaming; *spesseggiare*, to thicken; *albeggiare*, to dawn by degrees; *dormicchiare*, to sleep softly, or interruptedly; *scarabocchiare*, to scribble; *rimbambolire*, to grow childish, &c.

(*x*) The Latin language forms these verbs by a more regular process. It introduces usually another syllable into the verb, as: *factitare*, *dormitare*, *fructicescere*, *imperitare*, *cantitare*, which possess considerable affinity with the inceptive verbs.

45. Throughout the whole of our book we have frequently alluded to the regular verbs, and have also illustrated them in many of our exercises, so we shall not enlarge upon them any further. Before proceeding to the irregular verbs, we will, however, note the difference between the participle present and the gerund—between which in English no distinction is made in form.

46. The gerund is a form which is used when the participle has a verbal signification. This occurs when it is not taken with a substantive. When the contrary happens, it partakes of the nature of the adjective more than of that of the verb, and the participle present is substituted; but this occurs very rarely in Italian.

Exercises on the Regular Verbs.

1. But as abundance of things produce disgust, so things* wished for,* being denied, increase the appetite.

But (so) as; *copia*; to produce, *generare*; disgust, *fastidio*; (the) being; (the) wished; denied; *moltiplicare.*

2. Numa Pompilius devoted the right hand* to the observance of promises; with the right hand* they honored each other; by the right hand* they swore, as being* the* seat of faith and the* instrument of valour.

To devote, *consacrare;* observance of promises, *fede;* with (for); each other, *si;* by, *per;* intrument, *ministra.*

3. We will give you riches and commands over many nations, and we will defend your fame, and advance your name and make it glorious.

Commands, *signorie;* over (*di*); nations, *genti.*

4. With much courtesy you overcome my bad fortune, accepting everything that* was* done by me with a good grace.

With (the); to overcome, *vincere;* bad, *mala;* accepting, *pigliando;* by me done; with . . . grace, *in buon grado.*

5. The richest soil would become bad, if the Nera were to be divided, as was designed, into many streams.

Grass soil, *grasso terren;* to become bad, *andar male;* were to be divided, *se si spartisse;* as was, &c., *come si, &c.*

6. This horrid commencement let be to you no other than to travellers is* a rugged and steep mountain.

No other, *non altrimenti;* traveller, *camminante;* a mountain; rugged, *aspra*; steep, *erta;*

7. O valley! whose beautiful bosom the rivulet streaking through* with a gentle course, renders so lovely and delightful to those who look upon it.

Bosom, *seno;* (turn—with a gentle course streaking a rivulet); with a gentle, *con lento;* streak, *rigare;* a rivulet, *un fiumicello;* so, *assai*; lovely, *bella;* to those, &c. (turn the all into the participle present plural of *riguardare*).

8. He groans all the night, and renews his lamentations, mingled with complaints.

Renew, *rinovellare; lamento; commisto;* with (of); complaint, *querela.*

9. The dear little dog was well formed, and covered with fine white hair all in ringlets, and with so much regularity that it* appeared that nature had (sog.) used art in curling (inf.) them (it). The ears in the form of two branches of palm trees bent to the ground. She* had a little face severed under the head, which was a proof of* her noble breed; and you saw in her mouth a beautiful row of teeth, small, sharp, white, and equal. It gave a wonderful increase to her charm, her* running at one time about the house with a lively impetuosity and a pleasing boldness; at another time playing on the lap of her mistress, or lying at her feet rolled in a circle; that (which), moreover, rendered her more precious than pearls and rubies was the fidelity and vigilance which the pretty creature shewed in the* room, because there, as if in her own* territory, at every opening (inf.) of the* door, at every movement of a foot, or at any* other trifling noise, all full of pride she* advanced to the attack with sharp and incessant barking. Nor did she ever fail, whenever any strange person approached her, in her language, to utter to him many pretty impertinencies; nor was the rage extinguished in her, before she had roused it in her mistress, to whose threats and scoldings she would (2) still (1) answer with certain mutterings and growlings, full of resentment. And when her mistress went out of the house, nothing was heard but pitiful and painful barkings; as also at her return she was quite overpowered with joy, at one time lying down, then rolling herself on the ground; at times erecting herself on her feet, then jumping without ceasing until she leaped into her* arms, and a* hundred times, with her presumptuous tongue, she licked her* lips, and approaching to her ear, recounted everything that she had (subj.) suffered, and seen in her absence.

Was; the dear little dog, *la cagnina;* covered, *vestita;* with (of); white; fine, *sottil;* hair, *pelo;* in ringlets, *inanellato;* regularity, *maestria;* to curl, *crespare;* in the form, *a guisa;* to bend, *chinarsi; terra;* a little face, *un piccol muso;* severed, *spezzato;* head, *fronte;* to be a proof, *testificare;* noble, *generoso;* breed, *stirpe; grazioso;* row, *ordine; candido;* charm, *vaghezza;* at one time, *ora;* (the) running (inf.); about the, *per;* impetuosity, *prestezza;* boldness, *ardire;* and; at another time, *ora; scherzare* (ger.); on the (in); of (to); *giacere* (ger.); (to her); (to the) feet; (all) rolled, *rivolta;* moreover, *poi;* precious, *grata;* more than; the pretty creature *la vezzosetta;*

there, *quivi;* as if, *come;* territory, *regno;* every, *un;* door, *uscio; muover;* of a foot (of step); trifling noise, *piccolo strepito; superbia;* advanced to the attack, *dava all' arme;* incessant, *implacabile;* barking, *latrato* (plu.); nor did . . . approached her, *nè bisognava che persona sconosciuta le si appressasse;* (that) in her language; *le diceva; soavi villanie;* turn—nor did fail to utter to him; before itself extinguished in her; (than); she had . . . mistress, *che non s' accendesse nella padrona;* scoldings, *riprensione;* still, *ancora;* would, *voleva;* muttering *mormorio;* growling, *rimbrotta;* nothing was heard, *non si udivano;* but . . . barkings; *se non abbajamenti di dolore;* she . . . joy, *si struggeva tutta in festa;* at one time, *ora;* lie down; *coricarsi* (ger.); to roll, *rivolgersi* (ger.); on the, *per; drizzarsi* (ger.); on her, *in;* then, *ora;* to jump, *saltellare;* without ceasing, *senza mai ristare;* until, *finchè;* not (to her), *non le;* to leap, *salire;* (to her) licked, *rasciugava;* and with approaching (ger.) to her; (not to her); *raccontare* (imperf. subj.); *tutto ciò; patito.*

Readings in Poetry.

1. Scintillava negli occhi orribimente,
Fremea qual mugghia il toro, allorchè irato
Si prepara a battaglia, e l' ira in cima
Si reca delle corna, indi le arruota
A qualche tronco; e' l tronco e l' aure in prima
Ferendo, alto co' piè sparge l' arena,
E del futuro assalto i colpi impara.—*Vir. Enei. lib. 2.*

He sparkled in his eyes horribly. He roared as the bull bellows, when raging he prepares himself for battle, and his rage is reflected on the top of his horns—then he sharpens them against some trunk of a tree; and first striking the trunk and the air, scatters the sand on high with his foot, and prepares the blows of the coming attack.

2. Fanciulli, o voi, ch' ite cogliendo i fiori,
E le nascenti al suol tenere fraghe,
Fuggite, che nell' erba è ascoso l' angue.—*Virg. egl. 5.*

Children; O you who go collecting the flowers, and the tender strawberries growing on the ground: fly, since the serpent is hidden in the grass.

3. Come la tigre poichè in van discende
Nel voto albergo, e per tutto s' aggira,
E i cari figli all' ultimo comprende
Esserle tolti, avvampa di tant' ira,
Che nè a monte, nè a rio, nè a notte mira,
Nè lunga via, nè grandine raffrena
L' odio, che dietro il predator la mena.—*Arios.*

As the tigress when she descends in vain into her empty den, and looks around everywhere, and at last discovers that her dear offspring have been taken away, burns with such anger, that she neither looks at mountain nor river, nor night; nor does the length of the way, nor the hail restrain her hatred, which urges her on the traces of the ravisher.

4. Veniano sospirando, e gli occhi bassi
   Parean tener, d' ogni baldanza privi.—*Arios.*

They came sighing, and appeared for keep their eyes cast down, free from all boldness.

5. E la faretra e l' arco avean spezzato
   A quel protervo, e spennacchiate l' ali.—*Petr.*

Both the quiver and the bow they had broken of that perverse boy, and had plucked the feathers out of his wings.

6. Qual fiero toro, a cui di funi ignote
   Cinto fu il corno, e 'l piè da cauta mano;
   Muggisce e sbuffa, si scontorce e scuote,
   Urta, si lancia, e si dibatte in vano,
   E quando alfin de' lacci uscir non puote,
   Cader si lascia afflitto e stanco al piano;
   Tal l' indomito Re, poichè comprese
   Di affaticarsi indarno, alfin si rese.
   —*Tassoni, la Secchia Rapita.*

As a fierce bull, whose horn and foot have been bound by ropes till then unknown to him by a cautious hand, bellows and chafes, throws himself about, and starts, butts, thrusts himself forward, and contends in vain, and when at last he is not able to escape from the snares, lets himself fall distressed and exhausted on the plain. So the indomitable king, when he perceived that he was exerting himself to no purpose, ended by giving himself.

7. Apri le luci omai, volgi l' ingegno
   A più onorate imprese e miglior uso.—*Ber. Tasso.*

Henceforth open the eyes, turn the mind to more honourable undertakings and better use.

8. Indi d' uno in nn altro luogo errando,
   Si ritrovaro alfin sopra un bel fiume,
   Che con silenzio al mar va declinando,
   E se vada o se stia mal si presume.
   Limpido e chiaro è sì, che 'n lui mirando
   Senza contesa al fondo porta il lume.—*Arios.*

Then from one place to another wandering, they found themselves at last on a beautiful river, which in silence slopes to the sea, and whether it flows or stops can be scarcely told. So limpid and clear it is, that in beholding it, it carries the power of sight to the bottom without difficulty.

CHAPTER XII.

SECTION I.

The Irregular Verbs.

1. We will now give some general directions, which will serve to point out the nature of the irregularities which are found in many of the Italian verbs.

Many of the Italian verbs are distinguished by special irregularity in the present tense. This happens very naturally, as the vulgar are always inclined to modify the most common verbs, in order to pronounce them more easily and expeditiously. Persons of this kind also are much occupied with the actualities of life, and naturally make very great use of the present tense, and it thence happens that this tense is the most irregular in verbs which are frequently used.

2. Some of these verbs are, *fare*, to do; *stare*, to stand; *dare*, to give; *andare*, to walk; and the two auxiliary verbs *essere* and *avere*. We may also add the verbs *potere*, to be able; *vedere*, to see; *volere*, to wish; *morire*, to die; *udire*, to hear, &c.

3. Many of these common verbs are also irregular in the past perfect. Thus we have, *diedi*, *feci*, *fui*, *ebbi*, *volli*, *dissi*, &c.

(*a*) The reason of this irregularity of the perfect is—that these and other similar verbs are frequently used in common life, and for this reason it was not convenient to alter materially the primitive Latin form. The preterite, therefore, is always retained in a form which is either identical with, or has a strong approximation to the Latin form. Those verbs which we have just mentioned, derive their preterite from the Latin, *dedi*, *feci*, *fui*, *habui*, *volui*, *dixi*, &c.

4. In the list of the irregular Italian verbs, which we intend to give, we shall set down the irregularities of the present tense, and the anomalies in which they consist. We have to observe, moreover, that many of these irregularities arise from a verb possessing two infinitives. In such a case one person of the present tense is derived from one form of the infinitive, and another person from the second form, and sometimes one person has a double form from either infinitive, while all the present tense is occasionally conjugated from one form alone of the two said infinitives, and it happens in the following manner:

Verbs of the infinitive mood have frequently an antiquated termination, which has fallen into disuse, for which they have substituted a contracted form. Thus to commence with the most common verbs, we have from *facere, fare;* from *inducere, indurre;* from *ponere, porre*; from *sciogliere, sciorre*; and many similar instances.

In verbs of this kind the persons of the present tense are sometimes formed from the old infinitive; in other cases the old and new forms are mingled. All verbs, for instance, which have the infinitive in the contracted form *rre,* throughout the whole of the present tense, form the persons from the old form in *ere.* We have from *condurre, conducere,* the forms *conduco, conduci,* &c.*;* from *addurre, adducere,* we have *adduco, adduci,* &c.

5. Other verbs again, which do not possess the infinitive in *rre,* have the persons of the present formed sometimes from the old infinitive, and sometimes from the contracted form. The forms of the present tense may, therefore, be derived from either form of the infinitive.

The verb *fare,* for example, possess also the old form *facere.* In the present tense we have *Io faccio* or *fo, tu fai,* and in poetry *faci, egli fa,* and in ancient poetry *face; noi facciamo, voi fate, eglino fanno,* and *facciono,* which last is out of use. In like manner the verb *dire,* which has the old form *dicere* has *dico, dici* or *dì, diciamo, dite* or *dicete* (which last is out of use), and *dicono.*

(*b*) This double form of the infinitive mood is caused by the Latin derivation. From *facere* we have *fare;* from *dicere, dire;* from *ponere, porre;* from *inducere, indurre,* &c.

6. The other irregularities of the present tense cannot be traced to an etymological origin, but are solely euphonic or capricious, and even at times idiomatic: as from *valere,* we have in the present tense *valgo, vali, vale, vagliamo, valete, valgono;* and from *vedere, vedo* or *veggio, vedi, vede, veggiamo* or *vediamo, vedete, vedono,* and *veggono* or *veggiono. Vedo, vediamo,* and *vedono* are formed regularly, but *veggio, veggiamo,* and *veggono* and *veggiono* are capricious, and may also be considered to a certain extent euphonic. In *volere, voglio,* I wish, may be considered euphonic; while, on the other hand, *vo'* may be taken as idiomatic. This *voglio* or *vo'* makes the second and third persons *vuoi* and *vuole.*

7. A general notion having been already given of the irregularities of the present tense, the irregular present forms can now with advantage be studied more minutely. This tense, as we have already mentioned, is used most frequently in common life. It must be understood that, when we speak of the present, we mean to include the present subjunctive, and also the imperative, which has no other tense.

8. Another tense, which is often irregular, is the past perfect. Of this tense we will say that its irregular forms are found chiefly in verbs whose signification excludes them from vulgar use, and that its singularities are usually of a euphonic nature. From *assidersi* we have *mi assisi* (a chosen form of *mi sedei* from *sedersi*); from *frangere, fransi;* from *torcere, torsi,* which words sound better than *assidei, frangei, torcei.*

Some verbs, as it was explained, although in common use, are irregular in the present and the preterite as well. These, however, are very few, as the majority of the verbs which are irregular in the preterite are regular in the present.

(*c*) The irregularities of the preterite are to a great extent derived from the Latin language. Some rules may be given on this subject. When *x* is placed in Latin between two vowels, it changes into *ss*—as from *dixi*, *dissi;* from *produxi*, *produssi;* when *x* is preceded by a consonant, it turns into *s*—as, from *cinxi* we have *cinsi;* from *finxi*, *finsi*, &c. Some verbs retain fully the original Latin preterite—as, *vidi*, *feci*, *risi:*—and others, which in Latin do not change the consonant of the past tense, change it in Italian, in order that the present may not be confounded with the past. Thus we have in Italian *risponde* and *rispose*, which in Latin are both represented by *respondit;* *legge* and *lesse* in Italian, which in Latin are both represented by *legit*, &c.

9. We have here to make one very important observation, which will greatly facilitate the study of the irregular preterite; and which, as far as we know, has not been generally noticed. The irregularity of the preterite, which is announced in the first person, is followed solely by the two third persons. The second person singular and the first and second persons plural always follow the infinitive mood, and are formed in the regular manner. Thus from *rispondere*, *risposi*, we have *rispose* and *risposero;* but the second person singular is *rispondesti;* and the first and second persons plural are *rispondemmo* and *rispondeste*, which are formed from the infinitive *rispondere*. When a verb has two forms of the infinitive, the second person singular and the first and second persons plural are taken from the old form of the infinitive: as, *dissi*, *dicesti*, *disse*, *dicemmo*, *diceste*, *dissero*. Of this tense the second person singular and the first and second persons plural belong to the old infinitive *dicere*, since from which infinitive these persons are always taken. Thus it will be therefore easy to discover the reason which has induced us to insert in our list of the irregular verbs only, the first person of the irregular preterite. The two third persons are derived from the first,

and the other persons are formed from the infinitive, and require no particular mention.

10. The participle when its formation is irregular, has its termination in *so*, instead of *to*. Of these notice has been taken in the list of irreguar verbs.

(*d*) Many of these participles ending in *so*, follow the Latin *sus, sa, sum*. Thus *suffuso* is derived from *suffusus, a, um*; *roso* from *rosus, a, um*.

(*e*) Before proceeding further, we ask the student to notice that almost all of the irregular verbs are taken from the Latin, and this is in most cases evident without much consideration.

11. These are the irregularities of Italian verbs. We will now conclude our treatise by making some remarks on the imperfect and the future.

The imperfects of the indicative and the subjunctive are eminently regular. With the exception of the verb *essere*, which makes *era* in the imperfect indicative, there is not a single Italian verb which can be said to be irregular in either imperfect.

12. One important peculiarity of the imperfects is—that when a verb has two infinitives, the one an antiquated, and the other a contracted form, the imperfect tense are invariably formed from the antiquated form. Thus from *dire, dicere*, we have *diceva*, &c.; from *fare, facere, faceva*; from *indurre, inducere, induceva*, &c.

13. On the other hand, we have another, and a very important law, by which the future tense is always formed from the contracted form, and never from the more ancient. Thus from *ponere* we have *porre, porrò*; from *facere, fare, farò*; from *dicere, dire, dirò*; from *contraere, contrarre, contrarrò*, &c.

14. While speaking of the regular verbs, we observed that the conditional has always the same characteristic of the future. The same thing occurs in the contracted verbs, which make in the conditional *farei, direi, condurrei, trarrei*, &c.

15. The future tense has so strong a tendency to use the contracted form, that it adopts a contraction in many cases where the verb has no contracted infinitive. Sometimes, however, for the sake of variety, this contracted future is not employed. Thus from *vedere,* we have *vedrò,* and also, but more rarely, *vederò;* from *potere,* we have *potrò,* and occasionally in ancient writers, *poterò;* this is perhaps now quite gone out of use.

In the same manner, from *sapere,* we have *saprò,* and the old form *saperò* now obsolete. From *volere,* we have *vorrò,* &c. The conditional follows the usual rule, and we have *vedrei* and *vederei; potrei* and *poterei,* &c.

16. We have endeavoured in the preceding pages to simplify, as far as possible, the irregular verbs. Having done this, to the best of our ability, we proceed to give a list of such among them as may be regarded as "fundamental irregular verbs," inasmuch as all the remaining ones (which we shall give in a second list) are conjugated like one or other of this number.

List of the Fundamental Irregular Verbs.

Irregular Verbs in "are."

Andare, *to go; pres.* io vado *or* vo, vai, va, andiamo, andate, vanno; *fut.* io andrò, &c.; *imper.* va tu, vada egli, andiamo, andate, vadano; *pres. subj.* che io vada, che tu vada, ch' egli vada, che andiamo, che andiate, che vadano.

Dare, *to give; pres.* do, dai, dà, diamo, date, danno; *pret.* diedi *or* detti, desti, diede *or* dette *or* diè, demmo, deste, diedero *or* dierono *or* dettero; *imper.* dà tu, dia egli, diamo, date, diano; *pres. subj.* che io dia, &c., *and* che eglino dieno; *imp. subj.* che io dessi, &c.

Ridare, to give again, is conjugated in the same way, but *circondare,* to surround; *ricordare,* to remember, &c., are regular.

Fare, facere, *to do; pres.* fo *or* faccio, fai, fa, facciamo, fate, fanno; *pret.* io feci; *imper.* fa tu, faccia egli, facciamo, fate, facciano; *pres. subj.* che io faccia, che noi facciamo; *part. past,* fatto.

The derivatives are conjugated in the same way.

Stare, *to remain*; *pres.* sto, stai, sta, stiamo, state, stanno; *pret.* io stetti, tu stesti, egli stette, &c.; *past indefinite*, io sono stato, noi siamo stati; *imper.* sta tu, stia egli, &c.; *pres. subj.* che io stia, che noi stiamo; *imperf. subj.* che io stessi; *part. past*, stato.

Contrastare, to oppose; *soprastare*, to rule; and other derivatives, are regular; but *ristare*, to stop; *distare*, to be distant; *soprastare*, to temporise; are conjugated like *stare*.

The verbs in *care* and *gare* take *h* before *i* and *e*, as from *mancare*, to fail, *manchi*, &c., thou failest, &c.; and from *pregare*, to pray, *preghi*, thou prayest, &c.

Irregular Verbs in "ere" short.

Accendere, *to kindle*; accesi, acceso.

Accorgersi, *to perceive*; *pret.* mi accorsi, accortosi.

Addurre, *or* adducere, *to bring forth, to allege*; *pres.* adduco; addotto, *pret.* adussi, *p. p.*

Affligere, *to afflict*; afflissi, afflitto.

Appendere, *to hang up*; appesi, appeso.

Ardere, *to burn*; arsi, arso.

Ascondere, *to hide*; ascosi, ascosto, *or* ascoso.

Assidersi, *to sit down*; Io mi assisi, assiso.

Assistere, *to assist*; assistito.

Assolvere, *to absolve*; *pret.* assolvei *or* assolsi, assoluto *or* assolto.

Assorbere, *to absorb*; assorto.

Assumere, *to undertake*; assunsi, assunto.

Chiedere, *to ask*; *pres.* chiedo *and* chieggo *or* chieggio, chiesi, chiesto.

Chiudere, *to shut*; chiusi, chiuso.

Cingere *or* cignere, *to gird*; cinsi, cinto.

Cogliere *or* corre, *to gather*; colgo, colgono; *subj.* colga, &c., *pret.* colsi, colto. The other words are regular; the *future*, as usual, is made upon *corre.*

Connettere, *to connect*; connessi, connesso.

Conoscere, *to know*; conobbi, conosciuto.

Correre, *to run*; corsi, corso.

Crescere, *to grow*; crebbi, cresciuto.

Crocifiggere, *to crucify*; crocifissi, crocifisso.

Cuocere, *to cook*; cossi, cotto.

Deludere, *to delude*; delusi, deluso.

Difendere, *to defend*; difesi, difeso.

Discutere, *to discuss*; discussi, discusso.

Dispergere, *to disperse*; dispersi, disperso.

Ergere, *to erect*; ersi, erto.

Erigere, *to raise*; eressi, eretto.

Esigere, *to exact*; esatto.

Espellere, *to expel*; espulsi, espulso.

Estinguere, *to extinguish*; estinsi, estinto.

Fendere, *to split*; fenduto *or* fesso.

Fondere, *to melt*; fusi, fuso.

Frangere, *to break*; fransi, franto.

Genuflettere, *to kneel*; genuflessi, genuflesso.

Giungere *or* giugnere, *to join or arrive*; giunsi, giunto.

Intrudere, *to intrude*; intrusi, intruso.

Ledere, *to wrong;* lesi, leso.
Leggere, *to read;* lessi, letto.
Mergere, *to plunge;* mersi, merso.
Mettere, *to put;* misi, messo.
Mordere, *to bite;* morsi, morso.
Muovere *or* movere, *to move;* mossi, mosso.
Mungere *or* mugnere, *to milk;* munsi, munto.
Nascere, *to be born;* nacqui, nato.
Negligere, *to neglect;* neglessi, negletto.
Nuocere *or* nocere, *to hurt;* nocqui, nociuto.
Offendere, *to offend;* offesi, offeso.
Opprimere, *to oppress;* oppressi, oppresso.
Percuotere, *to strike;* percossi, percosso.
Perdere, *to lose; pret.* perdei *or* persi: *part.* perduto *or* perso.
Pingere *or* pignere, *to paint;* pinsi, pinto.
Porgere, *to present;* porsi, porto.
Porre *or* ponere, *to put, to place,* &c.; pongo, poni, pone, ponghiamo *or* poniamo, ponete, pongono; *pret;* posi; *impera.* poni, ponga, ponghiamo *or* poniamo, ponete, pongano; *pres. subj.;* che ponga, &c., ponghiamo *or* poniamo, ponghiate *or* poniate, pongano; *part. past.* posto.
Prefiggere, *to prefix,* prefissi, prefisso.
Prendere, *to take;* presi, preso.
Proteggere, *to protect;* protessi, protetto.
Pungere *or* pugnere, *to sting; pret.* punsi, punto.
Radere, *to shave,* &c.; rasi, raso.
Recidere, *to cut;* recisi, reciso.
Redimere, *to redeem;* redensi, redento.
Reggere, *to rule;* ressi, retto.
Rendere, *to render, restore;* resi, reso. *This verb is also regular.*
Reprimere, *to repress;* repressi, represso.
Ridere, *to laugh;* risi, riso.
Rilucere, *to shine;* rilussi; *no participle.*
Rincrescere, *to be sorry; impers. pres.* mi rincresce, ti rincresce, &c.; *pret.* mi rincrebbe, &c.; *pres. sub.* che mi rincresca, &c.; *part. past.* rincresciuto.
Rispondere, *to answer;* risposi, risposto.
Rodere, *to gnaw;* rosi, roso.
Rompere, *to break;* ruppi, rotto.
Scegliere *or* scerre, *to choose; pres.* scelgo, scegli, sceglie, scegliamo, scegliete, scelgono; *pret.* scelsi, *impera.* scegli, scelga; *pres. subj.* che io scelga, &c.; *part.* scelto.
Scendere, *to descend;* scesi, sceso.
Sciogliere *or* sciorre, *to untie or loosen; pres.* sciolgo, sciogli, sciolgono; *pret.* sciolsi; *fut.* scioglierò *or* sciorrò; *pres. subj.* che io sciolga, &c.; *part.* sciolto.
Scrivere, *to write;* scrissi, scritto.
Scuotere; scossi, scosso.
Sorgere, *to rise;* sorsi, sorto.
Sospendere, *to suspend;* sospesi, sospeso.
Spargere, *to spread;* sparsi, sparso.
Spegnere *or* spengere, *to extinguish;* spensi, spento.
Spendere, *to spend;* spesi, speso.
Spergere, *to disperse;* spersi, sperso.
Spingere *or* spignere, *to push;* spinsi, spinto.

Stringere *or* **strignere,** *to squeeze, to press; pret.* strinsi, stretto.
Struggere, *to melt, to dissolve;* strussi, strutto.
Svellere *or* **sverre,** *to pluck up;* svelsi; *fut.* svellerò *or* sverrò; *past. part.* svelto.
Tendere, *to tend;* tesi, teso.
Tergere, *to wipe, to clean;* tersi, terso.
Togliere or torre, *to take away;* tolgo, tolgono; pret. tolsi; tolga, &c. tolto.
Torcere, *to bend, to twist;* torsi, torto.
Trarre *or* traere, *to draw; pres.* traggo, traggi *or* trai, trae, tragghiamo *or* trajamo, traete, traggono; *imp.* traeva, &c.; *pret.* trassi; *fut.* trarrò, &c.; *imper.* traggi, tragga, trajamo, traete, traggano; *pr. sub.* che io tragga; *gen.* traendo: *part.* tratto.
Vincere, *to vanquish;* vinsi, vinto.
Vivere, *to live;* vissi; *fut.* vivrò;
Volgere, *to turn;* volsi, volto.

Irregular Verbs in "ere" long.

Bere, bevere, *to drink; pre.* bevo, bevi &c.; *or* beo, bei, bee, beiamo, beete, beono; *imp.* beveva, &c., *or* beeva, &c.; *pret.* bevvi *or* bebbi *or* bevei; bebbe *or* bevve *or* bevette, *or* bevè; bèbbero, *or* bevvero, *or* beverono, *or* bevettero; *impera.* bevi *or* bei, &c.; *subj. pr.* che io beva *or* bea, &c.

It is seen that bevere *is regular, and* bere *irreg.*

Cadere, *to fall, reg., and also* caggio, caggiamo, *and* caggiono; *pret.* caddi; *subj.* caggia, &c., *especially in poetry.*

Dolere *and* dolersi, *to complain; pres.* mi dolgo *or* doglio, ti duoli, si duole, ci dogliamo, vi dolete, si dolgono; *pret.* mi dolsi; *fut.* mi dorrò, &c.; *impera.* duoliti, dolgasi, dogliamoci, doletevi, dolgansi; *pres. subj.* che mi dolga, ci dogliamo, vi dogliate, si dolgano.

Dovere, *to owe;* devo, devi *or* dei, deve *or* dee, devono, *and* debbo *or* deggio, debbe, dobbiamo, dovete, debbono, deggiono *or* deono; *pres. subj.* che io debba *or* deggia, &c.; dobbiamo, dobbiate, debbano *or* deggiano.

Parere, *to appear; pres* pajo, pari, pare, pajamo, parete, pajono; *pret.* parvi *or* parsi; *f.* parrò *or* parerò, &c.; paruto; *or* parso.

Persuadere, *to persuade;* persuasi, persuaso.

Potere, *to be able; pres.* posso, puoi, può *or* puote, possiamo, potete, possono; *no imperat.; subj.* che io possa, &c.

Rimanere, *to remain; pres.* rimango, rimani, rimangono; *pret.* rimasi; *fut.* rimarrò; *imper.* rimanti, rimanga, rimaniamo, rimanete, rimangano; *pres. subj.* che io rimanga, rimaniamo, rimaniate, rimangano; rimasto *or* rimaso.

Sapere, *to know; pres.* so, sai, sa, sappiamo, sapete, sanno; *pret.* seppi; *imper.* sappi, sappia, &c.; *pres. subj.* che io sappia, &c.

Sedere, *to sit down; pres.* siedo *or*

seggo, siedi, siede, sediamo, sedete, siedono *or* seggono; *impera.* siedi, segga, seggano; *pres. subj.* che io segga, &c.; seggano; *part. past*, seduto.

Solere, *to be accustomed; pres.* soglio, suoli, suole, sogliamo, solete, sogliono; *sub.* che io soglia, soglia, soglia, sogliamo, sogliate, sogliano; *pret.* io sono solito, &c.; *part. past*, solito.

Tacere, *to be silent; pres.* taccio, taci, tace, tacciamo, tacete, tacciono; *pret.* tacqui, tacesti, &c.; *impera.* taci, taccia, tacciamo, tacete, tacciano; *pres. subj.* che taccia, &c.

Tenere, *to hold; pres.* tengo, tieni, tengono; *pret.* tenni; *fut.* terrò, &c.; *impera.* tieni, tenga, tengano; *pres. subj.* che io tenga, &c.; tengano.

Valere, *to be worth; pres.* vaglio *or* valgo, vali, vale, vagliamo, valete, vagliono *or* valgono; *pret.* valsi; *fut.* varrò, &c.; *pres. subj.* che io valga *or* vaglia, &c.

Vedere, *to see; pres.* vedo, veggo *or* veggio, vedi, vede, vediamo *or* veggiamo, vedete, vedono *or* veggono; *pret.* vidi; *impera.* vedi, veda *or* vegga, vediamo *or* veggiamo, vedete, vedano *or* veggano; *pres. subjunct.* che io veda *or* vegga, &c.

Volere, *to be willing; pres.* voglio *or* vo, vuoi, vuole, vogliamo, volete, vogliono; *pret.* volli; *fut.* vorrò, &c.; *no imperative; pres. subj.* che io voglia, &c.

Irregular Verbs in "ire."

Apparire, *to appear;* apparii *or* apparvi, apparito *or* apparso.

Aprire, *to open; pret.* aprii *or* apersi; *part. past*, aperto.

Cucire, *to sew; pres.* cucio, cuci, &c.; *imp.* cuci, cucia; *pres.* sub. che io cucia, &c.

Dire *and* dicere, *to tell, to say; pres.* dico, dici *or* dì, dice, diciamo, dite, dicono; *pret.* dissi; *imper.* dì, dica, diciamo, dite, dicano; *pres. subj.* che io dica, &c.; *part. past*, detto.

Empire, *to fill; pres.* empio, &c.; *impera.* empi, empia, &c.; *pres. subj.* che io empia, &c.

Instruire, *to instruct;* instrussi or instruii, instruito *or* instrutto.

Morire, *to die; pres.* muojo *or* moro, muori, muore *or* more, muojamo *or* moriamo, morite, muojono; *fut.* morirò *or* morrò, &c.; *imper.* muori *or* mori, muoja *or* mora, muojamo *or* moriamo, morite, muojano *or* morano; *pres. subj.* che io muoja, muojamo *or* moriamo, moriate, muojano *or* muorano; *part.* morto.

Salire, *to ascend; pres.* salgo *or* salisco, saliamo *or* sagliamo, salite, salgono; *imper.* sali, salga, &c.; *pres. subj.* che io salga, saliamo *or* sagliamo. salgano, &c.

Seguire, *to follow; pres.* sieguo, *or* seguo; *impera.* siegui; *pres. subj.* che io siegua *or* segua, &c.

Soffrire, *to suffer*; *pret.* soffrii *or* soffersi; *part. past.* sofferto.

Udire, *to hear*; *pres.* odo, odi, ode, udiamo, udite, odono; *imperat.* odi, &c.; *pres. subj.* che io oda, &c.

Venire, *to come*; *pres.* vengo, vieni, &c.; *preterit*, venni; *fut.* verrò; *pres. subj.* che io venga, &c.

Venire sometimes is used for the auxiliar *essere.*

Uscire *or* escire, *to go out*; *pres.* esco, esci, esce, usciamo, uscite, escono; *imperat.* esci, esca, usciamo, &c.; *pres. subj.* che io esca, &c.

The following Verbs are conjugated after the forms of the preceding Irregular Verbs.

Verbs in "ere" short.

Accingersi, *v.* cingere.
Accogliere, *v.* cogliere.
Accorrere, *v.* correre.
Accrescere, *v.* crescere.
Alludere, *v.* deludere.
Ammettere, *v.* mettere.
Ancidere *v.* recidere.
Anteporre, *v.* porre.
Apporre, *v.* id.
Apprendere, *v.* prendere.
Arrendersi, *v.* rendere.
Ascendere, *v.* scendere.
Ascrivere, *v.* scrivere.
Aspergere, *v.* spergere.
Astergere, *v.* tergere.
Astrarre, *v.* trarre.
Astringere, *v.* stringere.
Attendere, *v.* tendere.
Attingere, *v.* tingere, (p. 215.)
Attorcere, *v.* torcere.
Attrarre, *v.* trarre.
Avvincere, *v.* vincere.
Avvolgere, *v.* volgere.
Commettere, *v.* mettere.
Commovere, *v.* movere.
Compiangere, *v.* piangere, (p. 213.)
Comporre, *v.* porre.
Comprendere, *v.* prendere.
Comprimere, *v.* opprimere.
Compromettere, *v.* mettere.
Compungere, *v.* pungere.
Conchiudere, *v.* chiudere.
Concludere, *v.* deludere.
Concorrere, *v.* correre.
Concuocere, *v.* cuocere.
Condescendere, *v.* scendere.
Condurre, *v.* addurre.
Configgere, *v.* affliggere.
Confondere, *v.* fondere.
Congiungere, *v.* giungere.
Consistere, *v.* assistere.
Cospergere, *v.* spergere.
Contendere, *v.* tendere.
Contorcere, *v.* torcere.
Contraporre, *v.* porre.
Contrarre, *v.* trarre.
Convincere, *v.* vincere.
Corre, *v.* cogliere.
Correggere, *v.* reggere.
Corrispondere, *v.* rispondere.
Corrodere, *v.* rodere.
Corrompere, *v.* rompere.
Cospargere, *v.* spargere.
Cospergere, *v.* spergere.
Costringere, *v.* stringere.
Decidere, *v.* recidere.
Decrescere, *v.* crescere.
Dedurre, *v.* addurre.
Deporre, *v.* porre.
Deprimere, *v.* opprimere.

Deridere, *v.* ridere.
Descrivere, *v.* scrivere.
Desistere, *v.* assistere.
Detrarre, *v.* trarre.
Diffondere, *v.* fondere.
Dimettere, *v.* mettere.
Dipingere, *v.* pingere.
Dirigere, *v.* erigere.
Disapprendere, *v.* prendere.
Discendere, *v.* scendere.
Disciorre, *v.* sciogliere.
Disgiungere, *v.* giungere.
Dismettere, *v.* mettere.
Dismuovere, *v.* muovere.
Disperdere, *v.* perdere.
Disporre, *v.* porre.
Distendere, *v.* tendere.
Distinguere, *v* estinguere.
Distogliere, *v.* togliere.
Distrarre, *v.* trarre.
Distruggere, *v.* struggere.
Disvellere, *v.* svellere.
Dividere, *v.* recidere.
Eleggere, *v.* leggere.
Elidere, *v.* recidere.
Eludere, *v.* deludere.
Escludere, *v.* deludere.
Esistere, *v.* assistere.
Esporre, *v.* porre.
Esprimere, *v.* opprimere.
Estendere, *v.* tendere.
Estrarre, *v.* trarre.
Figgere, *v.* affliggere.
Fingere, *v.* pingere.
Frammettere, *v.* mettere.
Frapporre, *v.* porre.
Friggere, *v.* affliggere.
Illudere, *v.* deludere.
Immergere, *v.* mergere.
Impellere, *v.* espellere.
Imporre, *v.* porre.
Imprimere, *v.* opprimere.
Inchiudere, *v.* chiudere.
Incidere, *v.* recidere.
Includere, *v.* deludere.
Incorrere, *v.* correre.
Increscere, *v.* crescere.
Indurre, *v.* addurre.
Infingere, *v.* fingere, (this page.)
Infondere, *v.* fondere.
Infrangere, *v.* frangere.
Inframettere, or Intramettere, *v.* mettere.
Ingiungere, *v.* giungere.
Inscrivere, *v.* scrivere.
Insistere, *v.* assistere.
Insorgere, *v.* sorgere.
Intendere, *v.* tendere.
Intermettere, *v.* mettere.
Interporre, *v.* porre.
Interrompere, *v.* rompere.
Intingere, *v.* tingere, (p. 215.)
Intraprendere, *v.* prendere.
Intridere, *v.* recidere.
Introdurre, *v.* addurre.
Intromettere, *v.* mettere.
Manomettere, id.
Ommettere, idem.
Opporre, *v.* porre
Percorrere, *v.* correre.
Permettere, *v.* mettere.
Persistere, *v.* assistere.
Piangere, *v.* frangere.
Posporre, *v.* porre.
Percorrere, *v.* correre.
Premettere, *v.* mettere.
Proporre, *v.* porre.
Prescegliere, *v.* scegliere.
Prescrivere, *v.* scrivere.
Prostendersi, *v.* tendere.
Protrarre, *v.* trarre.
Rabbattere, *v.* battere.
Raccendere, *v.* accendere.
Racchiudere, *v.* chiudere.

Raccogliere, *v.* cogliere.
Raggiungere, *v.* giungere.
Ravvolgere, *v.* volgere.
Riassumere, *v.* assumere.
Rescrivere, *v.* scrivere.
Resistere, *v.* assistere.
Restringere, *v.* stringere.
Riaccendere, *v.* accendere.
Riardere, *v.* ardere.
Richiedere, *v.* chiedere.
Richiudere, *v.* chiudere.
Ricingere, *v.* cingere.
Riccogliere, *v.* cogliere.
Ricomporre, *v.* porre.
Ricondurre, *v.* condurre, (p. 212.)
Ricongiungere, *v.* giungere.
Riconoscere, *v.* conoscere.
Ricorrere, *v.* correre.
Ricorreggere, *v.* correggere, (p. 212.)
Ricuocere, *v.* cuocere.
Ridurre, *v.* addurre.
Rifondere, *v.* fondere.
Rifrangere, *v.* frangere.
Rifriggere, *v.* affliggere.
Rileggere, *v.* leggere.
Rimettere, *v.* mettere.
Rimordere, *v.* mordere.
Rimuovere, *v.* muovere.
Rinascere, *v.* nascere.
Rinchiudere, *v.* chiudere.
Rinvolgere, *v.* volgere.
Ripercuotere, *v.* percuotere.
Riporre, *v.* porre.
Riprendere, *v.* prendere.
Riprodurre, *v.* addurre.
Ripromettere, *v.* mettere.
Riscrivere, *v.* scrivere.
Riscuotere, *v.* scuotere.
Risolvere, *v.* assolvere.
Risorgere, *v.* sorgere.
Risospingere, *v.* spingere.
Rispingere, *v.* idem.
Ristringere, *v.* stringere.
Ritingere, *v.* tingere, (p. 215.)
Ritogliere, *v.* togliere.
Ritorcere, *v.* torcere.
Ritrarre, *v.* trarre.
Rivivere, *v.* vivere.
Rivolgere, *v.* volgere.
Schiudere, *v.* chiudere.
Scommettere, *v.* mettere.
Scomporre, *v.* porre.
Sconfiggere, *v.* affliggere.
Scontorcere, *v.* torcere.
Sconvolgere, *v.* volgere.
Scorgere, *v.* accorgere.
Scorrere, *v.* correre.
Scuotere, *v.* percuotere.
Sedurre, *v.* addurre.
Smungere, *v.* mungere.
Smuovere, *v.* muovere.
Socchiudere, *v.* chiudere.
Soccorrere, *v.* correre.
Soggiungere, *v.* giungere.
Sommergere, *v.* mergere.
Sommettere, *v.* mettere.
Sopporre, *v.* porre.
Sopraggiungere, *v.* giungere.
Sopraporre, *v.* porre.
Soprascrivere, *v.* scrivere.
Sopravvivere, *v.* vivere.
Sopprimere, *v.* opprimere.
Sorprendere, *v.* prendere.
Sorreggere, *v.* reggere.
Sorridere, *v.* ridere.
Soscrivere, *v.* scrivere.
Sospingere, *v.* spingere.
Sottintendere, *v.* tendere.
Sottomettere, *v.* mettere.
Sottoporre, *v.* porre.
Sottoscrivere, *v.* scrivere.
Sottrarre, *v.* trarre.
Sopraggiungere, *v.* giungere.
Sporgere, *v.* porgere.

Stendere, *v.* tendere.
Storcere, *v.* torcere.
Stravolgere, *v.* volgere.
Subdividere, *v.* dividere, (p. 213.)
Svolgere, *v.* volgere.
Supporre, *v.* porre.
Sussistere, *v.* assistere.
Tingere, *v.* pingere.
Togliere, *v.* cogliere.
Tradurre, *v.* addurre.
Trafiggere, *v.* affliggere.
Trascegliere, *v.* sciegliere.
Trascendere, *v.* scendere.
Trascorrere, *v.* correre.
Trascrivere, *v.* scrivere.
Trasfondere, *v.* fondere.
Trasmettere, *v.* mettere.
Trasporre, *v.* porre.
Travolgere, *v.* volgere.
Uccidere, *v.* recidere.
Ungere, *v.* pungere.
Vilipendere, *v.* sospendere.

In "ere" long.

Antivedere, *v* vedere.
Astenersi, *v.* tenere.
Avvedersi, *v.* vedere.
Compiacere, *v.* piacere, (this page.)
Condolersi, *v.* dolere.
Contenere, *v.* tenere.
Decadere, *v.* cadere.
Detenere, v. tenere.
Dispiacere, *v.* piacere.
Dissuadere, *v.* persuadere.
Equivalere, *v.* valere.
Giacere, *v.* tacere.
Intertenere, *v.* tenere.
Mantenere, idem.
Ottenere, idem.
Piacere, *v.* tacere.
Possedere, *v.* sedere.
Presedere, idem.
Prevalere, *v.* valere.
Provvedere, *v.* vedere.
Rattenere, *v.* tenere.
Ravvedersi, *v.* vedere.
Riavere, *v.* avere.
Ricadere, *v.* cadere.
Risapere, *v.* sapere.
Risedere, *v.* sedere.
Ritenere, *v.* tenere.
Rivedere, *v.* vedere.
Rivolere, *v.* volere.
Soggiacere, *v.* giacere, (this page.)
Soprassedere, *v.* sedere.
Sostenere, *v.* tenere.
Spiacere, *v.* piacere, (this page.)
Sprovvedere, *v.* vedere.
Trattenere, *v.* tenere.
Travedere, *v.* vedere.

In "ire."

Assalire, *v.* salire.
Avvenire, *v.* venire.
Benedire, *v.* dire.
Circonvenire, *v.* venire.
Comparire, *v.* apparire.
Construire, *v.* instruire.
Contraddire, *v.* dire.
Contravvenire, *v.* venire.
Convenire, *v.* venire.
Coprire, *v.* aprire.
Discoprire, idem.
Disconvenire, *v.* venire.
Discucire, *v.* cucire.
Disdire, *v.* dire.
Divenire, *v.* venire.
Escire, *v.* uscire.

Maledire, *v.* dire.
Offrire, *v.* aprire.
Predire, *v.* dire.
Prevenire, *v.* venire.
Riapparire, *v.* apparire.
Riaprire, *v.* aprire.
Ribenedire, *v.* dire.
Ricoprire, *v.* aprire.
Ridire, *v.* dire.
Riescire, *v.* escire.
Rinvenire, *v.* venire.
Risalire, *v.* salire.
Riconvenire, *v.* venire.
Riuscire *or* riescire, *v.* uscire.
Scomparire, *v.* comparire, (p. 215.)
Sconvenire, *v.* venire.
Scoprire, *v.* coprire.
Scucire, *v.* cucire.
Sdrucire, idem.
Sovvenire, *v.* venire.
Svenire, *v.* venire.

SECTION II.

The Defective Verbs.

Angere, to afflict; only *ange*, he afflicts.

Algere, to freeze; only the pret. *alsi*, &c.

Arrogere, to add; now only used, but seldom, in the second and third pers. pre. ind. sing. *arrogi* and *arroge*.

Assidersi, to sit down; only the pret. *mi assisi*, &c.; and very seldom the present *assido*, &c. The p. p. *assiso* is an elegant word.

Calere, to care; impersonal with the dative affix.; pres. *mi cale*, &c., no plural; imperf. *caleva* and *calevano;* pret. *calse* and *calsero;* subj. pre. *caglia* and *cagliano;* imperf. *calesse* and *calessero;* ger. *calendo;* p. p. *caluto;* the compound tenses with the auxiliar *essere*.

Colere, to worship, or revere; only *colo* and *cole*.

Estollere, to exalt; has only *estollo*.

Fiedere, to wound; has *fiedo, fiedi, fiede, fiedono; fiedeva*, &c.; *fiedei*, &c.; *fieda*, &c.; *fiedessi*, &c.; and *fiedendo*.

Gire, to go, possesses only the following forms:-- *gite, giva* or *gia*, &c.; pret. *gii, gisti, gì* or *gìo*, &c.; *girò*, &c.; *girsi*, &c.; the impera. *giamo, gite;* and subj. pres. *giamo* and *gite; gissi*, &c.; *gito*, and all the compound tenses *sono, sarò*, &c.; *gito*.

Ire, to go; the only forms, *ite, iva*, &c.; *irò*, &c.; and the compound tenses with *essere* and *ito*.

Licere and *lecere*, (not used) to be lawful, we have *lice* or *lece*, and the impersonal *esser lecito*, &c., is used instead.

Molcere, to sooth; only *molci, molce, molceva*, &c.; *molcessi*, &c.; *molcendo*.

Olire, to be fragrant; only *oliva* and *olivano*.

Riedire, to return; only *riedo, riedi, riede, riedono, ch' egli rieda, che riedano*.

Urgere, to urge; only *urge; urgeva; urgevano; urgesse, urgessero*, and *urgendo*.

Exercises on the Irregular Verbs.

1. Here stand steady; do not allow thyself to be turned; and go straight forward.

Here, *quivi;* stand (2nd per. sing.); steady, *forte;* to allow oneself, *lasciarsi* (2nd per. sing. impera.) to turn, *svolgere;* straight forward, *diritto.*

2. O* my (2) Lord (1), I am but groping my way, as not knowing of the things of the world more than this, that I know that*, with these speculations of mine, I may easily make mistakes, and recite some nonsense.—*Ber. Tas.*

I am but groping my way, *io vo' a tentone;* as, *perchè;* this, *ciò;* (myself) know (pres. subj.); I may (I can); make mistakes, *errare;* nonsense, *simplicità.*

3. Having* repented himself of his fault, he did penance.

To repent (himself), *ravvedersi* (par. past); fault, *scapputa;* to do *fare.*

4. I am rather induced by regard for your honor, and by the love I bear you, to perform this office of reprimand.

I am (say), I come, the verb *venire* being for the auxil. *essere;* to induce, *tirare;* regard, *desiderio;* perform, *fare; riprensione.*

5. His countenance is covered with and full of wrinkles.

Volto; covered, *ingombro* (for *ingombrato*); wrinkle, *ruga.*

6. The (2) dark (1) tempter (3) came in the* form of a* good angel.—*Caval.*

The *lo; tenebroso;* form, *ispezie.*

7. The mistakes which are made in other things one may sometimes correct; but those which are committed in war, the penalty of them suddenly following, one cannot amend.

—*Macch.* "*Arte della Guerra.*"

Errore; si; fare (third per. plu. pre.); *si; potere* (third per. plu. pre.); *si;* commit, *fare* (third per. plu. pre.); to follow, *sopravvenire* (ger.); suddenly, *subito; pena;* not; *si;* &c.

Readings on Poetry.

1. M' avvien, come a chi il Sol, fulgente e puro,
Mirar vuole, e non può, che offende il viso,
E ciò che vede poi gli pare oscuro.

It happens to me as to one who wishes to look upon the sun shining and clear, and cannot, for it blinds his sight, and what he sees appears to him obscure.

2. Ride Armida a quel dir, ma non che cesse
Dal vagheggiarsi, e da suoi bei lavori.
Poichè intrecciò le chiome, e che ripresse
Con ordin vago i lor lascivi errori,
Torse in anella i crin minuti, e in esse
Quasi smalto sull' or, cosparse i fiori,
E nel bel sen le peregrine rose
Giunse a nativi gigli, e 'l vel compose.—*Tasso.*

Armida smiles at those words; but not so that she ceased from complacently adorning herself, and from her beautiful labours. Having plaited her hair, she restrained in elegant disposition their wanton vagaries, twisted in curls the delicate hairs, and over them, as enamel on gold, scattered flowers; and on her beautiful bosom joined the rare roses to the native lilies, and arranged her veil.

3. Il Conte, che seguiva il suo costume,
Rispose "buona notte," e spense il lume.—*Tassoni.*

The Count, who followed his own custom, answered "good night," and put out the light.

4. I' son colui, che tenni ambo le chiavi
Del cor di Federico, e che le volsi,
Serrando e disserrando sì soavi.—*Dante.*

I am he who held both the keys of the heart of Frederick, and who turned them, locking and unlocking them so softly.

CHAPTER XIII.

The Indeclinable Parts of Speech.

SECTION I.

The Prepositions.

1. Having now arrived at the indeclinable parts of speech, we do not intend to be in any way diffuse with regard to their different uses and idioms. It would be especially useless to enter into very minute investigations concerning the prepositions, as their primitive sense is very easily learnt; and it is not within the province of a

grammar to give all the gradations and deviations of their meaning, when they are used in a figurative sense.

In accordance with this principle, we shall not take more notice either of the prepositions, or of the conjunctions and adverbs, than is required by strict grammatical necessity.

2. To begin, therefore, with the prepositions, we will say that the only thing concerning them which can be considered to be of a very important nature, is that they possess two meanings, one of which is primitive, and the other exceptional or additional.

If the primitive and natural sense of every preposition were only to be used, we say that the only simple method would then be to translate them at once from the native language of the student into that which he is learning, which is of course in the present instance Italian—we cannot then go very far wrong.

3. We will commence with some of the most simple of the monosyllabic prepositions—*di*, of; *a*, to; *da*, from—taken in the sense in which they are used, as *segnacasi* (case-signs), and we shall find no diversity in the two languages. Likewise *in*, when it expresses a certain relation to a place; *con*, when it used to indicate an accompaniment; *su*, when is used to indicate position;—have the same signification in Italian and English. *Per* cannot be defined with so much precision since its signification is indeterminate. But *sotto*, under; *sopra*, above; *intorno*, around; *davanti*, before; *dopo*, after; *indietro*, after; *dirimpetto*, in front of: *discosto*, distant from; *fuori*, out; *presso*, near; *perentro*, within; *senza*, without, are prepositions which indicate a determinate relation of place or position, and do not vary in meaning, when they are transferred from one language to the other, as from English to Italian, and *vice versâ*.

4. We must observe here that in the Italian language, many prepositions are used, which are by no means primitive monosyllables, but on the contrary, are often accompanied by

di and *a*, and may also be taken with the accusative case. Thus we can say, *dentro della casa, dentro alla casa, dentro la casa* according to pleasure—*di sopra del tetto, al tetto*, or *il tetto* without altering the sense. It would require a long treatise to explain the reason for so great a difference in construction. But, although it would require some toil to define this matter clearly, even if it were possible, the profit gained would not be equally certain. It is better to fix, simply without any further investigations, what are the prepositions which may be taken with the genitive and dative, what those with the genitive alone, and what with the genitive, dative, and accusative; and lastly, what with the ablative. When this is determined, the *segnacasi* are placed between the preposition and the substantive, and so they fix what cases these prepositions respectively govern: and by this means, therefore, we consider *di, a, da*, as simple signs of the cases which are governed by prepositions.

(*a*) This method of treating the prepositions is authorised by the Latin language, in which the prepositions govern the accusative or the ablative, or one or other of these cases according to the meaning. We make them govern the genitive, perhaps, because it is simply a mere chance whether a preposition governs one case rather than another; so the genitive in Italian is used often when in Latin *de* would be used with the ablative case, merely because *de* and *di* give a similar sound. Thus *egli parla di te* is equivalent to *de te loquitur*. Likewise *a* is often substituted for the Latin *ad*, on account of the resemblance of sound, although they govern a different case. When *di, a, da*, or the accusative case are used in this manner, they are only imitations of, or derivations from, the Latin cases, which are expressed in Latin by a variation in the terminations, and in Italian by the *segnacasi*, these being in themselves unmeaning, and mere links of words. In Italian, there is no fixed rule when each particular case should be used with a preposition; and the slight diversity which exists cannot be explained without referring it to individual taste. In Latin, on the contrary, rules are laid down which determine when a preposition must be taken with one case, and when with another.

5. Here we give a list of the Prepositions, with the cases by which they may be followed :—

Accanto, dat.	Near, just by.
Allatto, gen. dat.	Aside, by the side of.
Attorno, gen. dat.	Around.
Appresso, gen. dat.	Near, hard by.
Avanti, dat. acc.	Before.
A seconda, gen.	According to.
Circa, dat. acc.	Concerning.
Contro, gen. dat. acc.	Against.
Davanti, dat. acc.	Before, opposite to.
Dentro, gen. dat. acc.	Within.
Dinanzi, dat. acc.	Before, in presence of.
Dopo, gen. dat. acc.	After, since, behind.
Di quà, abl.	Here, on this side.
Di là, abl.	Beyond, on that side.
Dietro, dat. acc.	Behind, after.
Di sotto, gen. dat. acc.	Beneath, under.
Di sopra, gen. dat. acc.	Above, upon.
Dirimpetto, dat.	In front of, facing.
Discosto, abl.	Distant, far from.
Entro, gen. dat. acc.	Within.
Eccetto, *eccettuato*, acc.	Excepted.
Fuori, gen.	Out, without.
Fra, gen. acc.	Between, among.
Fino, dat.	Even to, as far as.
Giusto, dat. acc.	According to.
Incontro, gen. dat.	Against.
In mezzo, gen. dat.	In the middle.
In faccia, dat.	In front of, opposite.
Innanzi, dat. acc.	Before, in presence of.
Incirca, dat. acc.	About, near.
Insino, *infino*, dat.	Till, as far as.
Intorno, gen. dat.	About, near.
In rispetto, dat.	In comparison of.
Lontano, *lungi*, abl.	Distant, far from.
Lungo, *acc.*	Along, near.
Oltre, dat. acc.	Besides, beyond.
Presso, gen. dat. acc.	Near, nigh, among.
Perentro, gen. dat. acc.	Within.
Prima, gen.	Before, in time.

Per rispetto, dat.	For the sake of.
Rispetto, dat.	With regard to.
Senza, gen. acc.	Without.
Secondo, acc.	As, according to.
Sotto, gen. dat. acc.	Under with.
Sopra. gen. dat. acc.	Over, upon, on.
Vicino, gen. dat.	About, near.
Verso, gen. acc.	Towards.

6. Before we dismiss the subject of the prepositions, we have to mention a very great difficulty which is encountered in their use, to be only overcome through a thorough knowledge of the Italian language. No regular rule can be laid down which will determine under what circumstances a preposition is used in a secondary signification. This is the origin of the variety and the difference of meanings, which prepositions bear in different languages.

If I say, *Io partii di Parigi*, I set out from Paris, *di* occupies the place of *da;* but the English equivalent of *di* (of) is not uséd in this exceptional sense, and the proper word *from* is required.

In this expression, *La fanciulla dai capelli biondi*, the girl with fair hair, *dai* is a substitute for *coi*. In English, on the contrary, *dai*, from the or by the, as an equivalent of *coi*, cannot be used; the preposition *with* is necessary, in order to give the proper form. The English say, *The fleet is at sea*, and use it instead of the preposition *in*, which is requisite for the Italian form *in mare*. If we say, *Io dissi fra me: fra*, among, is substituted for *dentro*, within. In English, however, the proper word must be used: within myself, *dentro di me*.

7. The real difficulty, therefore, in the use of prepositions lies in the fact, that they are so often used in a sense which is totally different from that of the primitive. To treat this subject at length is not compatible with the true purpose of a Grammar, as it would be necessary to give innumerable examples of these exceptions. The study of the Italian classical authors will by degrees give the requisite knowledge.

Section II.

The Adverbs.

8. We have no reason for dwelling much on the adverbs, as they possess in themselves a positive qualificative meaning applied to verbs, and are by nature indeclinable. The few remarks which we consider necessary bear reference to their analogies with adjectives in the comparative and superlative degrees, and also with their augmentative and diminutive forms. These we have already made in the chapters which are devoted to the consideration of these forms. The student has also already been informed that their usual termination is in *mente;* and this knowledge has been impressed on his mind through the medium of the Exercises.

9. It may also be observed that adverbs are frequently developed into phrases. This property is, however, common to all languages, and under these circumstances they become adverbial expressions rather than adverbs, and are subject to the ordinary rules of syntax belonging to sentences. We have not considered it necessary to give a catalogue of adverbs, as their sense is defined in dictionaries with sufficient minuteness. These observations will, we think, be found sufficient; but we shall give in the Exercises some instances of the use of adverbs, which will increase the student's knowledge on this point.

Section III.

The Conjunctions.

10. The conjunctions also may be passed over without entering into any minute investigation concerning their various offices, a knowledge of which can only be acquired through practice. The conjunction, moreover, being an indeclinable part of speech, can usually be translated with little difficulty.

It is nevertheless necessary to give the different meanings of many conjunctions, taking them one by one; and in doing this we must avail ourselves of the same principle to which we appealed while treating of the prepositions. The primary meaning of a conjunction is direct, obvious, and common to all languages, and a direct translation is all that is required: as in these examples: *perchè,* because; *acciocchè* and *affinchè,* in order that; *ancora,* still; *altracciò,* besides; *pure,* however, &c.

11. There are, however, significations of a more complicated nature, and these cannot be used in the same manner in all languages. For instance, the primitive meaning of the English word *since,* would be expressed in Italian by *dacchè,* as—*Dacchè egli è partito, non trovo pace.* Since he has left, I find no peace. When, however, *since* is rendered by *giacchè* and *poichè,* it then becomes doubtful whether there is any community of usage in the two languages. *Since* is then used as it were in a lateral sense, as—*Giacchè* or *poichè volete così devo piegarmi.* Since you will have it so, I must beg. In this phrase, however, *poichè* might be substituted, but with less propriety. But in this example, *non lasciavam l' andar perchè ei dicesse,* we did not cease going on, although he spoke, *although* ought strictly speaking to be translated by *benchè.* How could we give any rule which would inform the student, that here *perchè,* because, has the meaning of although?

12. There is also another species of conjunctions, a knowledge of which can only be acquired by practice. These have an indefinite and special meaning which indeed will not bear translation. We will give a few examples—*Pure; dite pure,* you may well say, (here its meaning is quite indefinite.) *Anzi;—Io poco l' amo, anzi la odio,* I love her little, nay I hate her. *Anzi* may be in some way expressed by nay, although it has an inexplicable meaning of its own. *Eppure si muove,* it moves, however. *Eppure* is here used to express *in spite of it.* Others of the same description may be found which we do not mention here, but rather permit the student to become acquainted with through practice.

13. Some conjunctions have correlatives either expressed or understood. *Come* is taken in this manner with *così*. *Come egli è deciso di partire così io gli dò il mio consenso,* as he has decided to depart I give him my consent. *Come* and *così* might here be translated by *as* and *so*. They are used sometimes to express the comparison of equality, as: *Egli è così bello come buono,* he is as fair as he is good. In this phrase *come* might be omitted, and is here represented by *as*. The conjunction *o* takes a second *o* as a correlative. These are in English represented by *either—or;* and *oppure—o* also has a similar meaning as well as *ovvero.* For *neither—nor* we use *nè—nè.*

14. We have also some conjunctions which are compounds of *che* and some other word, as: *affinchè,* in order to, for *affine che; comechè,* although, for *come che; ancorchè,* for *ancora che: benchè,* however, for *bene che;* and others.

15. We will finally observe that some conjunctions have so hypothetical a meaning, that they cannot be used except with the subjunctive mood. Others again, on account of their positive and definite signification always require the indicative. The same thing occurs very frequently in the English language.

The conjunctions which govern the subjunctive mood are as follows: *affinchè, dato che* (in the event that), *se, se mai, quantunque,* and some others. Those which govern the indicative are, *dunque, pertanto, perciò, onde, laonde, anche, ancora, fuorchè, non, nè,* and others, which do not admit any hypothetical idea.

Thus we say: *Io sono venuto, affinchè mi diate un consiglio,* I have come, in order that you may give me advice; *Ancorchè non mi siate amico, vi voglio favorire,* although you are not friendly, I wish to favour you; *Dato che la cosa sia così io non intendo impacciarmi,* if the matter is so, I do not intend to meddle with it; *Se mai vi decidiate, fatemelo sapere,* if you ever decide let me know; *Quantunque abbia delle pecche, egli è un caro uomo,* whatever faults he may have, he is a dear man.

16. With the indicative we have, *Dunque egli prese il suo partito,* he then decided on his course; *Pertanto si vedevano ogni giorno,* they therefore saw each other every day; *Perciò egli viene assolto da ogni responsabilità,* he therefore becomes absolved from all responsibility.

Section IV.

The Interjections.

17. In order to complete our Grammar it is necesary to notice the interjections. What, however, can we say concerning these expressions which are subject to no rule and have no form? They may be said to have no form—or if they have, it is subject to caprice—since they do not derive their origin from language but from nature itself, and are not grammatical, but onomatopœic. Only under certain circumstances do interjections assume an artificial form, and these cases are by no means uncommon.

18. For this very reason we may perhaps venture to divide them into two classes—the primitive, which is found in all languages; and the additional, which is probably of later origin, and bears a different character, according to the structure and genius of the various idioms. It may be noticed that there is a greater or less variety of interjections in proportion to the copiousness of the language, and the vivacity of the nation which speaks it. We will now conclude by giving a list of the most important Italian and English interjections, primitive and otherwise, taken partially from Mariotti.

Principal Interjections.

The following interjections are frequently used :—

oh! *che mai dici?*	*oh!* what sayest thou?
ohimè! *i fratelli!*	*alas!* my brothers!

ehi! *chi è di là?*	*eh!* who is there? who is in waiting?
via, *non lo sgridate!*	*come,* do not scold him.
via, via! *che importa?*	*come, come,* what matters it?
eh via, *scsocchezze!*	*oh come!* nonsense!
su, su, *fedeli miei,* su via, *prendente le fiamme e il ferro, urdete ed uccidete.*	*up, up,* my faithful ones, *come!* take fire and sword, burn and slay!
deh! *perdonategli,*	*oh!* pray *do* forgive him.
dì su! *che vuoi?*	*speak out, say freely,* what wouldst thou?
orsù! *parliam d' altro,*	*now come,* let us talk of something else.
e così, *come va la salute?*	*well then!* how is your health?
guai a voi, *anime prave!*	woe to you, ye depraved souls!
che peccato! *così giovane dover morire,*	what a pity, to have to die so young!
peccato *che non abbia danaro,*	*pity* he has no money!
ah, pur troppo!	*ah, too truly!*
oh! questa è bella!	*oh, this is fine!*
oh! questa sì che è bella!	*oh, this is indeed fine!*
oh bella! *che ci ho da fare?*	*very nice indeed!* what have I to do with it?
oh curiosa! *che colpa ci ho io?*	*how very odd!* how am I to blame for it?
se ci coglie stiam freschi!	if he catches us, *we are in a fine mess.*
sta fresco *anch' egli, poveretto,*	he also *is in a nice predicament,* poor fellow!
evviva! evviva!	*hurrah! hurrah!*
viva *l' Italia!*	*God bless* Italy! hurrah for Italy.
evvivano *i galantuomini,*	*long life* to honest men. *Success* to honest men!
che seccatura!	*what a bore!*
me lassa!	*woe is me!*
ahi, miseri!	*alas! the unhappy ones!*
pietà, Signore!	*have mercy, Lord!*
animo!	*courage!*
bagatella!	*a trifle; a little trifle!*
eh giusto! per l' appunto!	*just so; exactly so!*
ma bravo! ma bene!	*bravo; well done!*
tutti gridavano dalli! dalli!	all cried out, *have at him; give it him!*
zitto, zitto, piano, piano!	*hush, hush! gently, gently!*

zitta, *ragazza mia!*	*hush*, my dear girl!
zitte, *ragazze mie!*	*hush*, my good girls!
ohibò! *che discorsi son questi,*	*O fie!* how you do talk!
vergogna! *m' avevute promesso di non farla più,*	*for shame!* you had promised not to do that again.
non tradirmi per pietà!	do not betray me, *for pity's sake!*
fate piano, per carità!	go gently, *for charity's sake!*
aiutatelo, per amor di Dio!	help him, *for God's sake!*
grazie, *signore, non v' incomodate,*	*thanks*, sir, do not trouble yourself.
tante grazie *del buon consiglio,*	*many thanks* for your good advice.
mille grazie *della finezza,*	*a thousand thanks* for your kindness.
che bella cosa *poter dire: comando io!*	*what a nice thing* to say: I am the master.
mala cosa *nascer povero!*	*it is a bad thing* to be born poor!
misecordia! che spettacolo!	*mercy, what a sight!*

Exercises on Prepositions, Adverbs, Conjunctions, and Interjections.

1. What is the meaning of *apporre?* To maintain that one has said and done a thing which he has (subj.) neither done or said.

What is the meaning, *che vuol dire;* to maintain, *dire.*

2. As the foam (plu.) of the sea, tossed by the wind and waves, now comes (2) forward (1) and then returns (2) back (1).

As, *quali;* foam, *schiuma;* of the sea, *marino;* to toss, *sospingere;* turn—by the wind, by the waves tossed: then, *quando.*

3. Waiting (ger.) place and time for* (to the) their wicked purpose.

Wicked, *malvagio; proponimento.*

4. Men in general do not esteem (the) things according to their value or their merit, but according to* (the) success.

In general, *per lo più;* according, *secondo;* turn, (the) value and merits theirs.

5. Both* (and) day and night, both* (and) morning and evening, both* now and for* ever, with* a* (to) very loud voice, I offer to you the* warmest prayers.

To offer, *porgere; prego.*

6. Wherever I am, there* are sighs both day and night.

Dovunque; are sighs, &c., *turn,* day and night one sighs.

7. After the manner of rivers, the which deriving their origin from one and the same source, sometimes separate, and the one takes its course on this side, the other on that.

After the manner, *a guisa;* deriving . . . source, *nascendo da una medesima scaturigine;* to separate, *diramarsi;* and the one, &c.; *turn*, and the one of here, (*di quà*) and the other of there, (*di là*) takes its; course, *cammino.*

8. That which neither the* chastisements of a* master nor the* threat (plu.) of a* father, nor flattery (plu.), nor rewards, nor skill, or labour or talent, or any instruction, fail to obtain, is oftentimes done by love, agreeably and delightfully.

Chastisement, *battitura;* reward, *guiderdone;* flattery, *lusinga;* skill, *arte;* labour, *fatica;* talent, *ingegno; ammaestramento;* fail to obtain, *non può fare;* is done, &c.; *turn*, does it love oftentimes, &c., *agevolmente e dilettevolmente.*

9. Rinaldo (2) said (1), I am suffocated with* (of) thirst.

To be suffocated, *affogare.*

10. I find myself now, according to my opinion, quite cured.

According, &c., *a mio credere;* quite healthy.

11. I bit both my* hands through grief.

Both, *ambo;* (the) hands; through, *per;* to bite, *mordersi.*

12. He* has already one foot within the ditch.

Within, *dentro;* ditch, *fossa.*

13. Although love frequents more willingly joyful palaces and luxurious rooms, it (3) is (2) not, (1) however, but* that he* sometimes causes his power to be felt among the thick woods, and among the frigid Alps.

Joyful, *lieto; palagio;* luxurious, *morbido;* rooms; more willingly; to frequent, *abitare;* however, *però; alcuna volta;* causes, etc., *turn*, among; it, *egli; fra*, the; thick, *folti;* woods; and among the; frigid, *rigide;* Alps; (not); to cause; *fare;* his; power, *forza;* to be felt, *sentire.*

14. In order that I may no longer (3) detain (2) you (1) (thee) in discourse.

Longer, *più;* discourse, *parole.*

15. We will ourselves mount up there, not only to avoid the bites, but also the barkings of that beast of a dog.

We will . . . there, *ce n' andremo lassuso;* to; avoid, *fuggire;* not only; dog, *cane;* beast of a, *accio;* (end *cane*, in *accio.*)

16. If the advice succeeds, the praise is attributed* alone to him

who is advised; if it does not succeed, the blame is always of him who gives it.

To succeed, *riescire;* to him who is advised, translate *del consigliato;* of him, etc., translate *del consigliere.*

17. Although anger oftentimes takes possession of men, and more so* of one than of another, nevertheless, it is attended with more mischief in women. Nor is there* any thing wonderful in that, because if we would examine well*, we shall see that the fire of its nature is* more readily kindled in light and yielding things, than in those* which* are* (the) more hard and heavy.

Although, *comechè; sdegno; sovente;* takes, etc., *turn,* in the men may happen; of one, *in uno;* it is attended, etc., *turn,* already, *già;* with greater; mischief, *danno;* it is, *si è;* in (the) women seen; nor is . . . in that, *nè è di ciò maraviglia;* to examine, *riguardar;* would, *vorremo;* more readily, *piuttosto;* yielding, *morbide;* things; is kindled, *si apprende;* heavy, *gravoso.*

18. O always sad and lamentable day.

Sad, *acerbo;* lamentable, *lagrimevole.*

19. Alas! love carries me away, where I would not wish to be.

To carry away, *trasportare;* where, *ove;* I; would not wish to be, *non voglio.*

20. Oh! pitiless death! Ah! cruel life!

Pitiless, *dispietata!*

21. Up drums and trumpets, play away with us.

Up, *su;* drums, etc., *tamburi;* play away with us, *datevi dentro.*

22. Oh! do not allow, O Lord, that my soul should be inveigled. But be thou her guide, her escort, and her light.

Oh! *Deh;* to allow, *lasciar;* should be inveigled, *sia colta;* (thou) escort, *tu scorta.*

Readings in Poetry.

1. Di voce in voce e d' una in altra orecchia
   Il grido, e 'l bando per la terra corse.—*Arios.*

From voice to voice, and from one ear to another, the cry and the proclamation ran through the earth.

2. Vincasi per fortuna o per ingegno,
   Fu il vincer sempremai laudabil cosa.—*Arios.*

Whether one conquers by fortune or by talent, to conquer has always been a laudable thing.

3. Che contra il ciel non v' ha difesa umana.—*Petr.*
Since against heaven there is no human defence.

4. Più giorni me n' andai, mattina e sera,
Per balze, per pendici orride e strane,
Dove non via, dove sentier non era.—*Arios.*
Many days I wandered, morning and evening, over cliffs, over horrid and strange precipices, where there was no way, where there was no path.

5. " Ma 'l trovo peso non dalle mie braccia."
But I find it no weight for my arms.

6. Di quà, di là, di su, di giù gli mena.—*Dante.*
On this side, on that side, above, below, he leads him.

7. La spada di lassù non taglia in fretta.—*Arios.*
The sword does not fall quickly from above.

8. Non sa come amor sana e come ancide,
Chi non sa come dolce ella sospira,
E come dolce parla e dolce ride.—*Petr.*
He does not know how love cures and how it kills, who does not know how sweetly she sighs, and how sweetly she speaks, and sweetly smiles.

9. "Come e' fu sulla porta, i gabellieri,
Gli furono in un tempo tutti adosso."
When he was at the gate, the Custom house officers were in a moment upon him.

10. Come pari d' ardir, con forza pari,
Quinci austro in guerra vien, quindi aquilone.—*Tasso.*
As equal in courage, with equal force, on one side the south wind engages in the strife, on the other the north.

11. Or rime, or versi, or colgo erbette e fiori.—*Petr.*
At one time I collect rhymes, at another verses, and at another delicate herbs and flowers.

12. Pommi ove il sole uccide i fiori e l' erba,
O dove vince lui 'l ghiaccio e la neve etc.—*Petr.*
Place me, where the sun kills flowers and grass, or where the ice and snow overcome him.

13. E giungo ad un torrente, e riserrato
Quindi da ladri son, quindi dal rio.—*Tasso.*
I arrive at a torrent, and am shut in on the one side by the robbers, and on one side by the river.

14. Pazzo chi al suo Signor contraddir vuole,
Se ben dicesse che ha veduto il giorno
Pieno di stelle e a mezzanotte il sole.—*Arios.*

He is a fool who wishes to contradict his Master, even although he should say that he had seen the day full of stars, and the sun at midnight.

15. Deh, se riposi mai vostra semenza.—*Dante.*

Oh! if ever your race should be at rest.

16. "Deh scocca morte omai l' ultimo strale."

O sad death, throw now your last dart.

17. Spesso l' ombra materna a me s' offria,
Pallida imago, e dolorosa in atto:
Quanto diversa, ohimè, da quel che pria,
Visto altrove il suo volto avea ritratto!—*Tasso.*

Often the shade of my mother presents itself to me, a pale image, and actually full of grief: how different, alas! from that which formerly her countenance seen at other times had pictured to me.

CPSIA information can be obtained
at www.ICGtesting.com
Printed in the USA
LVHW040426110522
718423LV00002B/438

9 783375 007942